WALTZ IN SWING TIME

JILL CAUGHERTY

Black Rose Writing | Texas

This is a work of fiction. Names, characters, businesses, places, events, and incidents are either the products of the author's imagination or used in a fictitious manner. Any resemblance to actual persons, living or dead, or actual events is purely coincidental.

ISBN: 978-1-68433-478-0
PUBLISHED BY BLACK ROSE WRITING
www.blackrosewriting.com

Printed in the United States of America
Suggested Retail Price (SRP) $20.95

Waltz in Swing Time is printed in Sabon

*As a planet-friendly publisher, Black Rose Writing does its best to eliminate unnecessary waste to reduce paper usage and energy costs, while never compromising the reading experience. As a result, the final word count vs. page count may not meet common expectations.

Praise for
WALTZ IN SWING TIME

"*Waltz in Swing Time* is a moving account of a life long-lived, the extraordinary stories behind a seemingly ordinary woman. Shifting masterfully between the past and present, Caugherty renders the indignities of old age and the early history of Irene's life with equal richness. A lovely debut novel from a deft and insightful writer." –Rae Meadows, bestselling author of *I Will Send Rain* and *Mercy Train*

"This gripping, vivid novel, set against Depression-era Utah and a modern-day, upscale retirement home, is at once a portrait of the complicated bond between mothers and daughters, a thrilling love story, and a powerful meditation on the meaning of freedom. Born into a devout Mormon family, Irene Larsen must cut ties with both family and church to pursue her dream of performing on stage. Fierce - and fiercely talented - Caugherty's heroine will imprint herself on readers, and they will be glad she did. This is a beautiful debut by a gifted author." –Abigail DeWitt, author of *News of Our Loved Ones* and *Dogs*

"In this poignant debut novel, which sparkles with a love of music, the character of Irene Larsen overcomes myriad obstacles to blaze her own path. Deftly moving between 2006 and the Depression-era 1930s, Jill Caugherty paints a vivid portrait of a woman transformed by both circumstance and her own decisions." –Heather Bell Adams, author of *Maranatha Road* and *The Good Luck Stone*

"*Waltz in Swing Time* is a powerful testament to music's timeless ability to inspire our passions and even define our fates. With a narrative that jumps effortlessly between the protagonist's formative years during the Great Depression and her latter years in 2006, Jill Caugherty's debut novel brings to life an era that is falling further and further into the reaches of history, as well as the struggles that those who lived through it endured." – Daniel Maunz, author of *Questions of Perspective*

"On its surface, *Waltz in Swing Time* is the story of Irene Larsen and how she meets the love of her life. There is more, though. We're in the mind of Irene at 89 years old as she looks back on her life. We see her inner struggles as she faces deteriorating health and memory, the present replaced with visions of the past. At times poignant and always engaging, Jill Caugherty's debut novel is awash with word salads and a narrative that calls to mind *Goodbye Mr. Chips*. A moving story of love, growing old, and remembrance." – Caleb Rocke, author of *As Seen in a Mirror: Beginning of the End*

WALTZ

IN SWING TIME

CHAPTER ONE

March 2006.

At any moment, one of the women who spoon-feeds me my pills will stop by my unit and find I'm gone. If I'm lucky, she won't intercept me as I amble to the cafeteria. But if she catches me, she'll approach gently, all smiles, nonetheless determined to guide me back to my quarters and complete her mission.

Quick with one-liners, Harold might have called this place a way station for the frail, or else a preschool for grownups.

Clutching my oversized pocketbook, I make my way down the corridor. As promised in the Golden Manor brochures, the carpet is new; the cathedral-style windows sparkle in the spring sunshine. Potted plants sit at the corners of the hallways. Spaced every twelve feet, the freshly painted doors of each identical one-bed/one-bath apartment display the unit number in bright gold stenciling, along with the resident's name. Several of these doors are propped wide open. Inside #3245, my friend Marcie reclines on a lazy boy facing the corridor, as though she were swinging on a porch rocker overlooking a neighborhood street.

"Yoo-hoo, Irene!" she calls. As if I could have missed her.

Marcie has a plump, pink face, surprisingly unlined, and favors University of Washington sweatshirts that a relative evidently sends to keep her in endless supply. In a stage whisper, she gives me the latest about an eighty-year-old acquaintance who fell and broke both hips last week.

"They're sending her off to the nursing wing," she clucks.

We both know what this means: graduation to round-the-clock medical supervision and a final slog of indeterminate length.

"What a shame."

"No nearby relatives, either. Just a son somewhere in New Jersey."

"You think he'll come, now that she's in serious trouble?"

Marcie shrugs. "That's anyone's guess. I don't believe she's had any visitors since she got here."

"That's not only sad, it's wrong."

At the Manor we're tucked out of the way, so our kin can persuade themselves we're living our last years in an adult amusement park with nourishing meals, daily entertainment, and nurses who might otherwise be mistaken for well-heeled wait staff. A parody of a fairytale in which no one acknowledges the dragon at the end.

"Come with me to the cafeteria," I say. "I want to go to the courtyard afterward, before the madding crowd arrives."

Marcie nods, depresses the button of her recliner, and swings her feet onto the plush floor. Gripping the arm of the chair, she rises slowly, fighting to steady herself.

Just ahead, a nurse wheels a hunched-over gentleman up the carpeted ramp. Although the woman is no lightweight and could probably coax the chair into a swift roll if given the chance, they advance at a snail's pace, because the man fidgets and makes soft, dog-like whines. As Marcie and I overtake them, the man wheezes, and the nurse fishes a Kleenex from her pocket, which she uses to dab his mouth. Undoubtedly they're from the nursing wing.

Here in the assisted living quarters, you're more likely to see widowed ladies teetering down the halls, waving at other residents. We wear our hair in stiff bouffants, courtesy of the Golden Manor stylist, and pretend amusement at someone's bad joke or a brainless flick in the community room. Collectively, we suffer from a host of ailments: arthritic joints, hearing loss, macular degeneration, heart disease, osteoporosis, nephritis.

Marcie and I enter the cavernous ballroom with its round tables, adorned with white linen cloths, floral centerpieces, and polished silverware. Bland, electronic renderings of familiar melodies faintly thrum through the loudspeakers.

Often at mealtimes, two or three ladies flag me down from across the room, hoping I'll join their table for the entrée du jour the staff has prepared for lunch or dinner, usually served with a dessert of jello or tapioca to soothe our weak stomachs.

They're as charmed by my stale stories as if I had doled out chocolate-frosted cupcakes. Bea chuckles so hard she almost chokes on her false teeth, and occasionally, Candy spits out a mouthful of peas. But today, since it's barely eleven, our little gang has not yet assembled, so Marcie and I find a table by a window overlooking the courtyard. Even the piano sits empty in the corner.

One of the wait staff approaches, flourishing a heavy dinner cloth over his forearm, and bearing a pitcher of iced tea, which he pours into two glasses.

The nurse attending the man in the wheelchair arrives, huffing slightly, and scoots her charge to the table opposite us. Straightening, she turns and notices us.

"Do you mind?" she begins. "He might like a little company."

I am nodding before she has finished speaking, shoving aside one of the chairs at our table so she can wheel him over.

She flashes me a grateful smile, then bends to the man's ear. "Aren't you the lucky gentleman today? Two ladies to talk with at lunch."

He squints at us from beneath a pair of thick spectacles and makes a chortle that could be confused with a baby's gurgle.

"This is Samuel," the nurse says.

As Marcie and I offer our names, Samuel gazes at us without interest, then turns toward the baby grand piano, clasping his hands and moving his lips, though I cannot make out what he says.

The nurse sighs and touches Samuel's shoulder. "He enjoys listening to music. Does him some good. But I don't think the pianist will be here till noon."

Samuel's mottled hands tremble, and his lips bare back, exposing a row of crooked teeth and a gold crown.

"I used to play piano," I hear myself saying. "A lifetime ago. I'd be glad to play for him."

Marcie raises her eyebrows and leans toward me. "You're a pianist, Irene? I had no idea."

Sliding onto the bench, I arrange my fingers onto the keys and consider what to play. It's been years since I touched a keyboard. A quiver dances through me. Not stage jitters, but an unbidden memory of myself as a girl on our farm, drifting my hands into minuets, waltzes, love melodies, as my mind whisked me on journeys elsewhere. At first I hesitate, afraid of the phantoms I might awaken, but out of habit, my fingers spring into motion.

From the piano's core, a deep, mellow sound crashes into the dining room and ricochets off the walls, interrupting the din of Muzak, clinking utensils and conversation. At first it startles, a bold presence that demands attention, but I navigate my way into it, securing myself to its rhythmic groove. The notes swell and dip, butterflying into a dizzying array of colors.

It's funny how age doesn't matter with music. All other physical acts may falter or fail at eighty-nine, but not this. Retracing familiar pathways, my fingers fly up and down octaves almost as effortlessly as they did half a century ago. Swaying on the bench, I run through a number of songs from the thirties: "Smoke Gets In Your Eyes," "It Don't Mean a Thing If It Ain't Got That Swing," and "You Must Have Been a Beautiful Baby."

A pleasantly full sensation in my belly lulls me into that other state, where nothing from the outside can reach me. All the same, I'm dimly aware of a small crowd gathering.

When at last I drop my hands into my lap and swivel around, Marcie stands a foot away, joined by Bea and Candy, who have apparently just arrived. They clap and cheer.

"What else have you been hiding from us, Irene?" Candy calls.

I start to answer in kind, but my eyes lock on Samuel in his wheelchair, at the periphery of my circle of friends. His mouth gapes open, as if he has attempted to muster his voice, and all that has escaped from his lips is a croak. But despite his sunken cheeks, shrunken spine, and the waxy, cadaverous color of his skin, his eyes are wide, shining beneath his spectacles. The music, I sense, is his last connection with the person he used to be. At some level, all of us here are lost from our former selves, the ones whose actions in the world had startling ripple effects on others.

After lunch, while my friends enter the community room for a game of cards, I head for the double doors that lead into the courtyard and its crisscross of flagstone paths that converge in a circle of concrete, covered by a green awning.

The staff have planted spruce trees, beds of geraniums, daisies, petunias, and rose bushes. On the far left, facing north, they plunked down a bench so that those of us meandering outside can have a "nice quiet place to chat," as one of the staff members explained.

Unloading my pocketbook onto the seat, I step beneath a Pacific Northwest spruce and lift my face toward the sun.

From one of the third floor windows overlooking the courtyard, a pale shape appears. It hovers at the glass, as if pining for the scene below. Then, just as suddenly, it vanishes. Perhaps a nurse entered the unit, and the poor soul felt obliged to make a hasty retreat.

A little chill passes through me. As a girl, you learn not to make waves. And where does it get you? You're rewarded with entry to a place like this, where you're declared too old and unwell to do the things you enjoy. So you're resigned to following more rules.

A fellow with a cane, accompanied by a younger woman who could be his daughter, stroll into the garden, heads bent together. Soon enough I decide the woman isn't his daughter, after all, because they seem to be patting each other's cheeks, standing inches apart as they confer.

Deirdre will be sorely disappointed if she thinks I'll meet a gentleman at the Manor. Slumping onto the bench, I picture Harold shaking his head in mock dismay.

"So this is what it's come to, Irene. A cell at the Golden Manacles. Rubbing shoulders with these bony bags who've got one foot in the grave and the other in a walker. Why are these hens dolling up like they're trying to get a date to the school dance? They can't even see well enough to pencil in their eyebrows in the right places."

That's how Harold coped with unpleasant situations: by cracking jokes.

My two sons, Rod and Jack, are scattered around the country, but since Deirdre and I live in the same town, she has assumed responsibility for me, the way you might grab the hand of a wayward toddler you happen to see wandering by herself in a mall.

Several days after my triple bypass surgery, she telephoned the Golden Manor, evaluated the costs and my savings, and put me here straightaway.

"It's best, Mom. They've got nurses on call to make sure nothing happens."

"I'm staying put in my own home. I may be down, but I'm not an invalid."

Deirdre had done her best to stay calm. "Dr. Shah said that for now you're not to move around much."

"I can manage. I know enough not to do something stupid."

"You say you'll take it easy, but then you're liable to do more than you should. One little slip, and we'd be back to the hospital and square one."

"Why don't you put me up in your house, in that case?"

Deirdre hadn't looked me in the eye. "You know that wouldn't work, either. For one, I'm not a nurse. And for another, you don't listen to me."

"I'm your mother. *You're* supposed to listen to *me*. If it's too much to ask, then say so." My voice had grown shrill.

A sigh. "That's not it at all. The problem's that it's not practical. At Golden Manor you'll have all your meals cooked for you; you'll have fun things to do every day like crafts and bridge; and you'll be around other people your age."

"Don't you dare. I won't go." Venom had spilled from my lips, surprising me.

Slowly I withdraw my old-fashioned, battery-operated tape recorder and microphone, which together barely fit inside this pocketbook. Both must be nearly thirty years old, a gift from Deirdre when she, her husband and their kids lived miles away, and she sent me recordings of Amy and Tom Junior reciting poems and singing.

Here we rarely discuss the details of who we once were, back when we figured centrally in others' lives. Our old selves go unacknowledged, and isn't that as good as letting them slip away unclaimed, as though they never happened? Because of this, and the specter of invalids like Samuel whose voices have deserted them, it's time I lay down the facts of my life and make sense of what they amounted to, added together.

My story could easily have taken a different turn. That girl from seventy odd years ago is a radically foreign version of the woman she became. Certainly there were expected, more traditional paths I could have chosen. But I did not.

All the same, it wasn't a decision that charted my course, not at first, but a ripple of unforeseen events, which swept my family and our neighbors to the brink of ruin. It began innocently, a gentle current. Swiftly, though, it gathered momentum until, like foaming rapids snaking beneath a swimmer, it dragged us down. We struggled to resurface, but by then it was too late. We had been carried too wildly astray.

All I need are my simple implements, no computer or fancy electronic gadget. If she knew, Deirdre would arch her eyebrows and dissuade me from remembering things that might make me sad. But maybe someday a relative will listen to the tape and catch a glimpse of the world from my miniscule corner in history.

I turn on the mic and start to speak - haltingly at first, then more surely as memories spring to mind. It hasn't been more than a minute or two when I spy Doris, one of the ladies who administers my pills, striding toward me from the other side of the courtyard. As petulant as a little girl about to be dragged from the playground, I switch off the mic.

Doris calls out with a jovial, "There you are, Irene! It's way past time for your medicine, sweetie."

I raise my head and salute her, and she blinks, caught off guard. Sliding the tape recorder into my pocketbook, I chuckle and say, "I surrender, ma'am. Lead me back to the enemy camp."

CHAPTER TWO

May 1932.

Once in a while, a niggling feeling might settle upon you, a faint alarm that something's not right, though you may thrust it aside and chalk it up to nerves. Much later, after our fortunes turned upside down and we plunged headlong into a crisis, I recalled how I'd glimpsed a sliver of trouble that day and spun away. It had been like floating down a placid river and spying frothing water cresting over a boulder. I didn't register the danger until the brook thundered suddenly into a violent torrent, threatening to seize us in its wake.

Everything about that Saturday started out familiar: feeding the chickens and gathering eggs in the hen house, filling the wood box, tending the vegetable garden, sweeping the kitchen and wiping the counters. Our nearest neighbors, the Petersens, and three of their five children were to join us for supper that evening, which made the chores more tolerable. It meant we would get to play cards, entertain each other with a little music, and listen to a Saturday evening program on the radio.

Still, when I knew Mother wasn't looking, I swept the same spot on the kitchen floor and gazed out the window at the thick patch of cottonwoods, and beyond it the peach and apple orchard. Out there, if you were a boy or a lucky girl, you could run and play tag and skip stones by the river. I was too old for that now, but as I did while playing piano, I allowed my mind to float into another world: Indians galloping across a wide plain as wind whipped down their backs and swallowed their shouts, tomahawks shaking, mountains rising like stone giants behind them.

Our wheat farm in the community of Paradise, Utah, on the outskirts of the town of Hyrum in Cache Country, spanned one hundred acres. The snowy peaks of the Bear River Mountains in the Wasatch Range climbed to the east in the distance. The river ran on the south side, abutted by a rocky ridge. Our house, a low gabled Craftsman bungalow with a wide front porch, faced the west and was surrounded by a cedar post fence that Dad and the boys had built several summers ago. In the fall, Lombardy poplars and maples burst into scarlet billows. Dad liked to joke that you couldn't find a finer farm in all of Paradise.

Inside my imagined world, coyote pups trotted on the plains, and canyons glowed fiery red at sundown. Covered wagons, much like those our Mormon ancestors rode on their journey west, rumbled in a train across the prairie, kicking up clouds of dust.

My fingers loosened their grip, and the broom handle clattered to the floor.

From the dining room where she was darning socks, Mother snapped, "Idle hands are the Devil's playthings."

Her voice snatched me back to the farmhouse. As she marched into the kitchen, shaking her head, I picked up the broom. She was a tall, large-boned woman of Norwegian ancestry, almost Dad's height, with high cheekbones, clear blue eyes, and coils of pale hair that she twisted away from her scalp into a severe bun. At just over five feet tall, I was still a little child, as far as she was concerned. Now that I was a freshman in high school, I thought it time she stopped scolding me.

"I'll sweep the parlor," I offered, hoping that when I finished, I could draw up to the old upright Kimball piano, which Dad had purchased years ago at a farm auction, on Mother's urging.

Gripping my shoulder, Mother steered me to the sink. "I need your help with supper."

Without releasing her hand, she pointed to a bowl of peas in the sink. Bristling, though I was careful not to show it, I rolled up my dress sleeves and began snapping the green stalks.

In our narrow attic bedroom, where our conversations were rarely overheard, my younger sister Minnie and I often grumbled that Mother allowed the boys the most freedom and fun. After school and chores, they hunted rabbits, kicked balls, shot marbles, climbed trees. In summer, they swam in the river bottom. Minnie and I, on the other hand, were expected to sew, cook, clean, and remain sedately restrained, however much we might want to bound after the boys.

A little before six o'clock, Mr. and Mrs. Petersen arrived with Mae, a year older than I, and two younger children, close in age to my brothers Luke and Jeremiah.

Mae, who had a beautiful soprano voice, took the lead in most of the high school musicals. Mother and Dad often compared her to the "Original Radio Girl," Vaughn De Leath. Now Mother complimented her on her new linen dress, the same shiny hue as Mae's own chestnut hair. In response, Mae boasted she had finished sewing the gown that afternoon. If given the choice, I reckoned, Mother would gladly have traded me for a daughter like Mae.

Crammed together at the long table in the dining room, we ate platters of baked chicken, peas, corn, and buttered rolls for supper. My oldest three brothers, Jacob, Wylie and Hiram, sat shoulder to shoulder on one side of the table, their long limbs folded beneath their chairs. Minnie helped me clear the dishes and serve peach pie for dessert.

"You suppose we'll get to hear a program?" she whispered when we were alone in the kitchen.

"If we're lucky. But all bets are off if Mae gets to singing."

She shot me a look. "Reenie, you're wicked."

We squeezed our sides to smother our giggles.

Dad moved a few extra chairs into the parlor and lit the kerosene lamp. While Mother and Mrs. Petersen chatted together on the sofa,

Jeremiah and the Petersens' six-year-old daughter squatted on the floor nearby with wooden spoons and tin cups that they banged and arranged into pretend people and animals.

If we didn't have company, Dad might have read scriptures aloud. But tonight my brother Wylie brought out his saxophone, bought secondhand from a man in town, and played "Red River Valley," "You're A Grand Old Flag," and "My Gal Sal."

My instrument was the piano. When I was seven, Mother had persuaded a lady from the ward to give me lessons in exchange for eggs that I cleaned and packed, and I had been inseparable from the Kimball ever since. Although my teacher taught the classics, I learned to pick out popular tunes by ear. My favorites were the rags, which stirred a hidden soul within the piano to life and transported me to a colorful dance hall of swirling skirts and an orchestra that swelled to a roar.

When Wylie finished, and the adults had clapped, Minnie and I crowded near the radio at the foot of Dad's chair, hoping for a program.

As Dad reached for the knob, my brother Hiram winked at Mae and called, "Aw, let's not waste batteries listening to a scratchy voice. Besides, Mae can sing for us, and she sounds just as good as any radio queen."

Dad swiveled in his chair. "Go ahead, Mae. Choose whatever you'd like to sing."

Minnie gave me a knowing look, and I pursed my lips.

As she often did when asked to sing, Mae shook her head coyly and pretended to refuse, her cheeks glowing pink, likely with the drama and delight of being fawned over. It was a little play I had watched many times before. At last, Dad, joined by Mother, Jacob and Hiram, succeeded in cajoling her.

"Oh, but we'd love it if you would. It's such a treat to listen to you, just like having a grand opera singer perform in our own little parlor."

Giggling, Mae rose and moved near the kerosene lamp. "Only if Irene will accompany me." At the sound of my name, I also rose and sat at the piano bench, not wanting to partake in her little act but resigned to do it, anyway.

Hands clasped at her bosom, she lifted her chin and sang a few old-time songs the adults enjoyed, including "Oh You Beautiful Doll" and "Let Me Call You Sweetheart."

There it was again, the hot stab of envy, akin to hatred, every time she trilled her voice. I managed to stifle it down by arranging my features in what I hoped was an impassive expression, and forcing my back to stay straight and rigid. My secret, uncharitable wish was that someday I would outshine her entirely as a dazzling pianist performing before a large audience.

We ran through half a dozen songs, until Mae declared she was worn out, and would sing but one more.

Eyelids half closed, lashes fluttering, face lifted demurely, she ended with Hiram's request:

"Stars shining bright above you

Night breezes seem to whisper 'I love you'

Birds singing in the sycamore trees

Dream a little dream of me.

Say nighty-night and kiss me

Just hold me tight and tell me you'll miss me

While I'm alone and blue as can be

Dream a little dream of me.

Stars fading but I linger on, dear

Still craving your kiss

I'm longing to linger till dawn, dear

Just saying this.."

When she had finished and curtsied with a blush, Hiram clapped the loudest of anyone.

"My stars," Mother said to Mrs. Petersen beside her, speaking loudly enough for all of us to hear. "Doesn't Mae have the most gorgeous voice you ever heard?"

I slipped off the bench and slid back onto the floor, next to Minnie. Mother did not mention my prowess at the piano, but of course, I was only the sidekick in the show. Mae stole a glance at Hiram, who beamed at her, and she settled beside him on the floor, tucking her feet beneath her dress.

Minnie elbowed me, and I concealed the giggle that threatened to rise from my throat, as surely as if she had whispered, "Hiram's sweet on Mae."

As Mother and Mrs. Petersen continued chatting about Mae's vocal talents, my eyes locked on Jeremiah, who steered a make-believe truck and hollered, "Beep beep! Move back!" He must have caught me watching him, because he grinned at me, then wandered away from the other children and climbed into my lap.

I threaded my fingers through his hair. "We've got to give you your bath tonight, Little Man. You're as filthy as a great big sow."

"Oink."

I pretended to twist his nose, and he laughed out loud.

"Reenie, when you give me my bath, let's pretend we're in Snowchootaney. In the palace."

I tousled his hair and nodded. We talked about this magical invention of ours so often that in our minds it had become a place we could point to on a map – just there, on the other side of the Wasatch Mountain Range, within our reach if we decided to strike out by foot someday.

"Dad, may we please hear a program?" Minnie winked at me, and I immediately straightened and waited for his response.

"At least a few minutes of the news," Jacob added.

Dad conceded, "We'll keep it short." He turned the knob to KDYL, the station out of Salt Lake City, and the sound of an orchestra, distant and scratchy, blared through the tube.

"What time is it?" Dad asked Jacob.

"Five till eight. News is at the top of hour."

I had no interest in the news. It was the music and shows I yearned to hear, but I kept quiet, hoping Dad would forget about wasting batteries after he'd heard the headlines.

Jeremiah laid his head against my shoulder and hummed, as I strained to hear the song the orchestra was playing, "Blue Skies." The instruments crescendoed to conclusion and fell silent, and the announcer's deep, throaty voice cut in, with a report of the continued plummeting stock prices on Wall Street, including U.S. Steel, General Motors, RCA, and Blue Ridge. That news, at least, was no surprise.

In Salt Lake City, he assured us, over one thousand Boy Scouts had collected clothing and bottled fruit for the unemployed. He said a few other things about the trouble in our little corner of Utah, but his words had become background noise I didn't bother to follow.

Dad's face had paled, for some reason, and he harrumphed and flicked off the radio. Mr. Petersen drummed his fingers against his knees. Mother and Mrs. Petersen had looked up from their conversation to digest what was said, but they bent their heads together again, discussing recipes and children.

"You'd think no one cares about anything but New York," Jacob said, breaking the men's silence. "That's all they report anymore."

Mr. Petersen nodded, still tapping his knees. "Those fool brokers and bankers started this mess, trading air. Fact, when it comes to solid things, they're just as helpless. Can't tell a carrot from a turnip, let alone feed a family with good soil and their own hands."

Dad cocked his head and addressed Wylie, who sat perched on the piano bench. "That's what happens to greedy folks. The bankers worshiped a false god, and now they've good as landed in the poorhouse. Nothing left but shame."

"Amen to that," Mr. Petersen said.

Wylie cleared his throat. "It's not just them. If so many folks hadn't got knee-deep in debt, there'd be more money to go around."

He had once told me confidentially that when he grew up, he would leave the farm and take an office job in a city where he could do what he excelled at – calculations. He thought it would be considerably more manageable and profitable than farm work.

Dad shot him a scalding look, as though suspecting he harbored this secret desire, and Wylie cast his eyes away.

Mr. Petersen said, "No time to lie down or panic. I aim to get a row crop tractor. That'll increase my production at least twofold, I reckon."

"You can get a loan?" Dad raised his eyebrows.

"Might. I've already got a few lines of credit. I might could use this year's crop as collateral."

"You'll be awful lucky, then. I hear they're turning folks away. And then they're going after the ones who've defaulted."

"That's a chance I'll have to take."

Dad lowered his voice, unaware I was listening. "Hannah doesn't know it, but we're close to..." He stopped short, his face grim, and flattened his hand, slicing it through the air.

I didn't completely grasp what he meant, but in his voice I detected something I hadn't heard before, the tilt of fear.

Dad continued, "Went down to the bank a month ago and withdrew everything. I wasn't about to wait like a fool to see which one would fail next. Hannah was terrified we'd be burgled. So I soldered together a little metal fireproof safe and wired it down to the floor in the bedroom. Ran the chain out back behind the Apache plume. Next I'll sell some cattle."

He broke into a sputtering cough, and when he raised his head again, a gray shadow had crossed over his face, suddenly making him look haggard, older. Silently I willed him to stop coughing and follow Mr. Petersen's suggestion to be strong, to sit up straight and not give up. I don't know whether it was because I didn't want to see him this way, or because I was tired myself, but my heart skipped a beat, and I clenched both hands against my chest.

"Only way I see through this is to double up my production," Mr. Petersen repeated. "We've hit the worst. By next growing season, things will have turned around, anyway."

"Can't count on that," Wylie muttered.

"What's that?" Dad asked sharply.

Wylie shrugged and gazed at his shoes. "What I mean is, there's no guarantee that things will be better anytime soon, is all. People keep taking out loans, there's bound to be more trouble."

To my surprise, Dad leaped to his feet and towered over Wylie. "You're talking out of line." He raised a fist, as though he might sock Wylie.

The room had gone silent, and all eyes turned toward Dad.

"I'm sorry, sir," Wylie mumbled, continuing to stare at his shoes.

"Don't apologize to me. Apologize to Mr. Petersen here."

"There's no need..." Mr. Petersen broke in.

"Yes, there is," Dad said. "He spoke out of line. Getting too big for his britches."

I stared at the pair of them, Dad and Wylie, both behaving queerly – Wylie no longer shy and reserved, Dad unusually outraged, the pulse in his temples beating erratically.

Wylie uttered something faintly.

"Louder," Dad insisted, and took a step closer to him, still clenching his fist.

"I'm sorry, Mr. Petersen," Wylie said, and flushed a deep red.

Jeremiah wriggled on my lap and squirmed free. Across the room, Hiram whispered something to Mae that made her laugh. She must have sensed the awkward timing, because her hand flew to her lips, but it was too late. The men had turned in her direction. Gazing at his daughter with furrowed brow, as if she had reminded him of a pressing obligation, Mr. Petersen abruptly rose and summoned his family.

Mother and Dad made the usual protests that it was too early for them to leave. Couldn't they at least enjoy a little more pie? Listen to a little more music? Play a game of cards? Undeterred, Mr. Petersen politely refused and shuffled his crew out the door, and Mrs. Petersen uttered a hasty thank you to Mother.

After they left, I felt a wash of relief, as though they had carried away gloomy traces of the evening: the radio announcement and the discussion it had spurred, Dad's wan face and strange words, the heated exchange with Wylie.

After taking turns bathing, and before Minnie and I prepared for bed, I ventured downstairs to fetch a glass of water. Hushed, urgent voices made me freeze and clutch the banister. I glimpsed my parents huddled at the dining table in the dim kerosene light. Knowing they would be furious if they heard me, I prepared to creep back to the attic. But something about the sharp tone of their conversation, like a leather ball ricocheting back and forth, made me linger and peek at them, in an attempt to make out the words.

"You want to keep the farm?" Dad swiveled toward Mother and glared, his face dark with anger.

She recoiled, and at last gave a short nod.

"Then listen careful. Our income's down over fifty percent from last year. I won't wait for it to go up in smoke. Then there won't be any mortgage to pay, because the bank will kick us out on the road, same as those bums at the rail yard."

Mother didn't answer.

"Maybe you don't understand how dire things are, Hannah. Lines of people are looking for handouts cause they can't get work. And others have been foreclosed. You know about the Randalls. We're not so far from them. Not by a long shot. We'll have to make some hard choices and sell the things we can live without. Like the piano."

Mother flinched and hugged her chest, as if he had delivered a blow. My mind froze, and I dared not consider the implications of what he had said.

At last she declared, "We're doing our part to save. We've let down the girls' hems and patched sheets, and I've tucked away those old feed sacks to use as material. Irene helped me reline the boys' coats with a couple of old blankets. Besides, we've got what we need right here on the farm." She began ticking off her fingers, one by one, "The wheat for flour, hens for eggs, cows for milk, vegetables and fruit that we've bottled straight from the garden and orchard and stowed in the cellar."

Dad gripped his head and thundered, "That's small fry, woman."

Not waiting to hear more, I tiptoed upstairs, taking care to avoid the creaking step, third from the top.

In the attic, I said none of this to Minnie. Nestling with her beneath the down quilt, I listened as she prattled about Greta Garbo, our shared dream of taking the train into Salt Lake City, dining out, performing music before a cheering audience. The lull of her voice in the dark calmed me, returned us to before, where anything was plausible. We need only speak it out loud, spin up plans.

Wall Street and its problems and even Dad's warnings seemed as distant as a foreign land you might read about in the paper, reflect upon idly then quickly forget – nothing that held personal meaning, no place you'd ever visit.

We didn't see it coming, the trouble that lay somewhere ahead. We didn't even have a name then for what came later. But surely I felt it churning inside my chest – the beginnings of a wild river that might, at any moment, cascade into whitewater rapids.

CHAPTER THREE

April 2006.

Sometimes, upon waking in the mornings or in the haziness following an afternoon nap, I momentarily forget where I am. Occasionally, I even feel sure I'm back in my attic room in the Paradise homestead, with my dress laid neatly on the chair beside me, hairbrush and mirror arranged at the bureau. I start to call out to Minnie to rise, but then I glance down at my wrinkled old claws with their purply-blue veins, and feel the telltale sporadic quiver of my damaged thumper, and the reality of where I am slams into me at once. I catch a whiff of the Lysol bleach emanating from my handicapped-fitted bathroom, take in the metal bars surrounding the sides and foot of my bed, the adjustable head rest and mattress lever, the big red call button on my nightstand, the shabby carpet and whitewashed walls, the neat row of pills along my dresser, and the television suspended on the wall above it. My stomach sinks, as if I'm a child on whom a cruel joke has been played.

Shortly afterwards, as if on cue, Doris or Cindy or occasionally another lady enters with a brisk knock and smile, usually bearing a glass of juice and my assortment of pills. This morning it's Cindy.

"Top of the morning, Irene!" she bellows. "How you doing, sweetie? Get a good night's sleep?"

Although she doesn't expect a reply, I generally return a little platitude in kind.

"I can't complain. I could dance the shag if only I could drag these creaky old bones out of bed. It's as good as it's going to get at my age, you know."

She laughs. "That's not so bad, then, is it? If I can get through a night without waking up more than twice, I call it a good one, and I'm probably half your age. It's the hormones," she adds with a wink.

Her hair is swept back in a ponytail, and she wears pastel pants and a flowery-printed muumuu that dangles past her waist. She has strong, thick arms that serve her well in moving heavy objects about my room, and now propping me against the headboard.

As she prepares my pills, Cindy flips on the television to one of the shock-and-dismay talk shows in which surprise guests are invited onstage to reveal secrets. But since it's Cindy, I don't mind. She has a childlike innocence about her – a simple, straightforward way of seeing things, coupled with a perky sense of humor that proves she hasn't become jaded like so many of the other staff who work in assisted living homes.

"Can you believe that boy?" I mutter after a minute of peering at the screen. "Calling his own mother a whore."

Cindy hands me my blood pressure medication, which I dutifully swallow with a sip of juice.

She shakes her head. "I don't know what's gotten into most of the kids nowadays. They don't have any shame. They'll say things to an entire TV audience I wouldn't dare say in private."

Of course, I know that's not entirely true. Once Cindy used a few choice words when she learned about the night I had shivered, cold and panicky after a bout of palpitations, because the Golden Manor staff had deemed my call from the assisted living wing as lower priority.

On the TV screen, the boy continues to berate his mother, accusing her of running around with half a dozen men while he apparently had to support her and the rest of his siblings. The host claims that following the commercial break, the audience and the boy's mother will be surprised to learn how he supported his family.

I blow through my teeth. "I can't understand how these families can go on TV and say such nasty things about each other."

Cindy hands me another pill, and seems ready to smile, though her face fixes itself into a sympathetic expression. "I don't know, either, Irene. Things aren't the same as they once were, are they?"

"You can say that."

"But you know, I heard a lot of things are made up on these shows. They hire people who aren't even related to one another to pretend to have public arguments. For the ratings."

"If that's the case, go ahead and turn it off, dear."

"You're sure? I can change to another channel."

"I've seen enough for one day. And then some."

I realize belatedly that Cindy had probably wanted to watch the rest of the show, but she turns off the television, all the same.

"Remember, your daughter's coming after breakfast to take you to the doctor."

I nod, not looking forward to the ever more frequent trips to Dr. Shah's office.

In the dining room, I join Candy, Marcie, Midge, and Donna at a table in the center of the hubbub, and work through a bowl of oatmeal, fresh blueberries, toast, and juice.

After the staff has cleared our bowls and plates, we lean around the table, gripping the coffee mugs and making small talk, any excuse for lingering a little longer.

"I can remember when I used to enjoy fresh brewed coffee," Marcie says. She closes her eyes. "Just as strong as you please and fresh. It smelled so good. I used to sit on our back porch and drink it in the early mornings when the kids were getting ready for school. Woke me right up."

"Irene," Candy cuts in, "Your daughter's here."

I glance up and see Deirdre, dressed in a silky pants suit and matching heels, marching across the dining room toward our table. My daughter is tall and lithe and cuts an imposing figure. As a young woman, before having kids, she worked as a local city council member and later as a town planner, responsible for preserving historic sites. Both positions taught her excellent negotiation skills. Her blond hair sweeps into a wave that crowns her face. At sixty-four, she still has her youthful looks and gait.

Deirdre greets my friends with a smile. "Sorry to interrupt, ladies, but Mom's got a doctor's appointment in thirty minutes."

"You're not interrupting a thing," Candy says, waving her hand. "We're wasting our time as usual, dragging your mother down with us."

I wink. "I don't need any dragging down. I'm already there."

"Are you ready, Mom? It might take a little while. We have to drive across town."

I rise more creakily than I intended. Marcie throws me a sympathetic glance. The others watch in cowed silence as Deirdre leads me briskly from the dining room.

She holds open the passenger door of her silver sedan, waits while I buckle my seatbelt. As we pull out of the Manor parking lot and onto the highway leading into town, she chats about the flowery buds that have emerged in her garden, with their "little green heads."

After a few minutes, she ventures, "Dr. Shah's nurse said over the phone that he'll think about changing your medication. On account of the mood swings you've been having."

My lips open and close, but I can't seem to compose my thoughts.

At last I manage, "I don't know what you mean by mood swings."

"Well, now. I thought those blood pressure pills you've been taking have made you feel a little out of sorts lately."

I shake my head.

Deirdre continues in a rush, "One of the staff told me they often find you in the courtyard, all alone, sometimes talking to yourself. And you've lost your temper a few times with me. You're not yourself. Dr. Shah's nurse thinks it has everything to do with this medication you're on."

I brace myself against the seat. "It's no one's business if I go to the courtyard by myself. There's no point in blaming the medication when all I want is a little privacy." Despite myself, my voice rises.

Deirdre looks at me and says softly, "I know how difficult all of this has been, everything that's happened in the last year. You used to be so upbeat. Nothing got to you."

We speed past two storied suburban houses with manicured front lawns that give way to drab rows of office buildings, shopping complexes, and the usual arrangement of grocery stores, home improvement stores, and Target or Walmart adjacent to fast food chains. Deirdre drives fast. I can't see her eyes beneath her mirrored sunglasses.

"It's not the pills," I say, but it might well be I said it inside my head, because Deirdre gives no sign of having heard.

When we arrive at Dr. Shah's office, we have to thread our way through the waiting room, which is jammed with elderly patients and a handful of baby boomers. A talk show plays on the overhead TV screen. Deirdre guides me to a pair of chairs near the reception window and gestures for me to sit as she signs in.

I pick up a magazine and thumb through it. Celebrity fodder and wonder diets, beauty tips, and the latest fashion.

When at last a nurse pokes her head through the door and calls, "Mrs. Stallings?" I rise hastily and nearly trip.

Deirdre grips my elbow and waves, and the nurse opens the door for us with a mechanical smile. The room where she leads us is much like all the doctors' rooms I have visited in the past ten years: small, cold, white, equipped with a metal examining table, sink, wall disinfectant and supply cabinet. I'm relieved not to be asked to change into a paper gown.

Deirdre peeks out the mini-blinds of the small window.

"You'll let the doctor ask all his questions, won't you?" she says, without turning around to face me.

"As long as I have the chance to ask my questions, too."

Someone raps on the door, and Dr. Shah enters. He is a neat, trim man, fifty-five or sixty, with a combed shelf of graying hair and rimless spectacles.

With a peremptory greeting, he slides into a stool on wheels, and asks me to describe the problems with my medication.

"Her blood pressure pills have caused some unfortunate side effects," Deirdre says.

Dr. Shah looks at me.

Deirdre puts in swiftly, "She's had mood swings where she gets to feeling low, or else she grows angry and lashes out. Your nurse mentioned those symptoms could be side effects of the pills."

Dr. Shah hesitates. "Occasionally, but not as often with the diuretics. But to be honest, there are no blood pressure drugs out there that don't have some side effect. Mrs. Stallings, have you felt a little down lately?"

"No more than I have for the past few months."

"It's been hard for her recently with the surgery and the move to the Manor," Deirdre explains. "But even if it isn't the blood pressure medication that's causing it, perhaps you'll give her something that can level out her moods."

"No," I say, more loudly than I intended.

Dr. Shah nods. "According to my chart, Mrs. Stallings, you've been taking aldactone for four months. So I would have expected some of the more common side effects to have occurred when you first started taking it. For most people, the side effects clear up as their bodies adjust to the medication." He squints at me. "Whether the medicine's working effectively is another question. Your blood pressure was still high at the last few visits."

Deirdre presses her lips together. "That's something to consider, too. I thought we might try a different medication to see whether anything changes. She hasn't been her usual self."

"If the medication isn't working, why not take me off it? I'd just as soon not take it at all."

"We have to keep you on something, Mrs. Stallings," Dr. Shah says sternly, wagging a finger at me. "We've got to moderate your blood pressure and cholesterol on account of your cardiomyopathy. It's not going away on its own. You're one stage away from advanced heart failure."

"Please can we not talk about the gloom and doomsday scenarios," Deirdre says.

"Two nice ladies come by every day to make sure I take my pills." I hope this will put an end to the discussion and our visit.

"I'm not suggesting something as extreme as Prozac, but just a mild antidepressant," Deirdre presses.

"Absolutely not." I rise to my feet, clutching my purse.

Dr. Shah also stands and appraises me, over the top of his chart. "Okay, Mrs. Stallings, no one's going to prescribe anything against your wishes. But we'll need to re-evaluate the aldactone if it isn't lowering your blood pressure sufficiently. I'll have a nurse take a reading on your way out, and we'll discuss what, if anything, we should do at your next visit."

Giving us a cursory nod, he backs out the door and trots down the hallway, evidently running late for his next appointment.

"I was hoping you'd let the doctor give you a prescription to help you feel a little more like yourself," Deirdre says, sounding disappointed.

"I do feel like myself. Even if I'm sad, my emotions are real, not out of a bottle."

Before Deirdre can respond, a nurse enters, wheeling the blood pressure machine. Deirdre holds her elbows and paces the room while the nurse connects my arm to the machine.

"One-sixty over ninety," the nurse says, snapping the cuff off my bicep. "High. I'll let Dr. Shah know."

As we ride back to the Golden Manor, I gaze at the tulips along the highway, startling blooms of pink, gold and blue that at one time would have excited me about spring and bursts of new life. With surprise, I realize I hadn't even remembered that it's April. In fact, it seems we're about to enter the slosh and drizzle of winter again, as though there's no other season left to anticipate.

"Will you think about it?" Deirdre is saying.

"About what?"

"Changing the medication. Especially since it isn't working."

"Oh, that. I'd rather not take anything."

"You know what Dr. Shah said, Mom. And you've got to start listening to me, too. Like it or not, medication is the only answer to the problem you have. So we've got to make the best of it." Her voice is steely, brisk.

It's a forgone conclusion, of course, that I will take a new medication, probably one that manages to lift my mood while lowering my blood pressure, if such a cocktail exists. But I won't do it without offering resistance, even if that is all I have left to give.

Deirdre signs me in and escorts me back to my room, planting a soft kiss on my cheek. I squeeze her hand. Of course she means well. I have to remind myself of this sometimes.

After she leaves, I slide into the easy chair in the corner of the room and close my eyes. Lunch is another hour away. It would be tempting to fall asleep here, still dressed in my day clothes, shoes tossed aside. But then I remember the tape recorder and mic, and decide to steal a little more time in the courtyard. Out there I can clear my head of the stale Manor air and remember myself as a girl with her family, struggling against the undertow, until that past with its dark underbelly seems oddly more real than this soft, cushy present.

CHAPTER FOUR

July 1932.

Until the day of the church supper, we'd fallen into the frantic summer preparations of picking peaches and apples, threshing, haying, canning, and making preserves. But immediately after that day, our routine collapsed, like good solid earth tumbling under a tilling machine, the roots plundered from the ground in the upheaval.

It was a Saturday evening, and we had just returned from a potluck at the Paradise ward. After the meal, the adults had chatted in loose, welcoming groups, while the little ones ran outside, playing tag or jacks, and the older kids supervised.

Jeremiah had chased a squadron of his playmates outdoors, and grass, dirt and peach cobbler had wormed into his hair, stained his clothes.

Now I knelt in front of the tin tub before the kitchen stove where we held our weekly bath ritual. From the time I was eleven and he was two, I helped Jeremiah, who insisted I draw his bath for him. As the littlest and youngest, he always took his bath first, so he could go to bed directly afterwards, smelling fresh for Sunday school the next morning. I looked forward to the stories we invented about our magical land, Snowchootaney.

While Jeremiah rolled marbles on the floor, I heated water in a copper kettle over the kitchen fire and tipped it into the bucket, repeating the process until the tub held just enough water to scrub his little body clean. After sprinkling Lux flaxes into the tub, I struggled him out of his clothes.

Most weeks I allowed him a few minutes of playtime in the warm water before I bathed him, but tonight he was unusually listless, and sat slumped against the rim of the tub. He must be tired from his running and playing at the potluck, I reasoned.

"Have you seen anyone special in Snowchootaney tonight?" I prompted.

At first he didn't seem to hear me, but then he glided the grubby gray bar of lye soap over our heads. "Reenie, look at this. A big white bird is flying over Snowchootaney. It can see the whole countryside, it's so high."

"And what is it scouting for? Is it hungry for little boys?" I teased, splashing a few drops of water onto his face.

"Naw. It's going to swoop down for fish and frogs. Only if it gets hungry. But it won't."

"And why not? All living creatures have to eat."

For a moment he was silent, and I decided he hadn't heard.

"Not this bird. It's got special powers. He used to be a prince, but he decided he was too bored living in a palace, so he grew wings and flew and flew everywhere."

"Can he grant a pair of wings to anyone he likes?"

"Yes. And guess what else?" He squinted his face in concentration, looking past me. "He can make the sky change from blue to purple to silver to gold. And turn rainbows into ice cream sodas. And make trees into giant toads."

I rubbed his chest, arms and legs with the washcloth.

"Reenie? When we go there, to Snowchootaney, I'll talk to this bird. And I'll ask him to let us ride on him for a little bitty while. We'll fly all over and see everything from way up high, just like that bird can."

I smiled. "We will. What fun!"

Suddenly Jeremiah shivered and wrapped his hands around his arms. "Can't you make it warmer? It's plenty cold."

I opened the oven door to give more heat. "Give it time, honey. It'll warm up before you know it."

He continued to shiver. Impulsively, I touched the blond tresses that curled against his forehead, and withdrew my hand in surprise at the sticky heat. "Jeremiah, you're burning up!"

"No, I'm not. I'm awful cold, I already told you so."

I stopped scrubbing and peered at him. His cheeks were flushed, something I hadn't noticed earlier. "I expect you've got a little fever." Slowly I passed my hand over his cheeks and down his chin, then startled at the sight of a faint red bruise. "What's this on your neck?"

He shook his head. "Don't know. But my throat hurts."

On closer inspection, I saw that his neck was dotted with a smattering of tiny red bumps. "Have you been rubbing it?"

"Naw. It hurts *inside*."

"I see." I felt for lumps. "You've got some swollen glands. Tell you what we must do. We must finish your bath and send you off to bed."

I expected resistance, but Jeremiah was silent.

As I rinsed him with a bucket of warm water from the stove, he confided, "I sure don't feel so good."

"I know, honey. That's all right. It's a little fever that came on all of a sudden. After you've had a chance to sleep, you'll wake up feeling one hundred percent better tomorrow morning."

"You 'spose?" He looked at me uncertainly.

I lifted the towel from the top of the kitchen stove and helped him step out of the tub. "Sure." As I wrapped the towel around him, I gave him a quick kiss on the forehead. "Now let's get you bundled up as warm as can be and off to bed."

◀ ♫♪ ▶

Minnie and I woke at dawn to dress. Since it was the Sabbath, we weren't expected to do the bulk of our chores, which normally included tending the garden, cleaning the chicken coop and ironing. I went downstairs to make breakfast. To my surprise, Mother was asleep in a straight-backed chair in the kitchen, a woolen shawl wrapped around her lap and legs.

She snored softly. As I lit the kitchen stove, she stirred and jerked in her chair. "Who's there?"

"It's all right, Mother. It's only me. Irene."

She blinked and tilted her head toward me, then gathered the shawl around her shoulders. "Jeremiah's in a bad way. I've been up with him half the night."

I laid down the matches. "He had a fever last night."

"It's much worse now. He can't hardly get comfortable. He's been moaning and thrashing. Vomited up near everything I've given him, too. If he doesn't improve any after today, I'll send Jacob into town to fetch the doctor."

"But it's just a little fever. Surely it'll pass."

"He's got the rash now. I saw it myself on his neck and chest. Ach. I pray to God he doesn't have what the Hendricks boy's got."

"What's he got?" I said, heart pounding. I took a step away from the stove, and laced my fingers together.

"The whole family's quarantined. That's why they weren't at the potluck yesterday. The youngest boy, the one Luke's age, is down with a bad case of scarlet fever."

"Scarlet fever?" I had only heard about it in hushed circles. Last year, at the beginning of the school year, one of my school friends' youngest sister had died of it. "He'll be all right, Mother. It will pass." I murmured the reassurance as much for myself as for Mother.

She closed her eyes and ordered, "Go heat up some milk."

My hands trembled as I stirred the milk on the stove. Now I heard the moans from Dad's and Mother's bedroom, where Jeremiah lay on a trundle bed. The cries were low, occasionally broken by piercing yelps, like a wounded dog.

Mother seized the jug as soon as I had poured the milk into it. I followed her to the bedroom. When she noticed me at her heels, she said,

"If you're going to see him, you may as well make yourself useful. Go fetch a wet washcloth."

I did as she instructed. Apparently having kept an early morning vigil, Dad sat in the chair beside the door, drawing on his boots.

Jeremiah's little body writhed on Mother's and Dad's four post bed. I advanced toward Mother, who gripped the milk jug in both hands. It was still full.

"Jeremiah," I whispered, leaning over the bed, "It's Reenie, honey." His head turned in my direction, but his eyes were glassy, devoid of any recognition, his face flushed and swollen.

When I touched his forehead, it was raging hot, and I quickly withdrew my hand. "Let's sponge you off, little man. You'll feel better, nice and cool."

Mother took the washcloth from my hands. "Go on and fix breakfast. The boys will be waiting and hungry any minute now."

"Reenie," I thought Jeremiah murmured. I glanced behind me, but Mother had turned him away and was peeling off his clothes.

In the kitchen, Minnie stood at the stove, stirring eggs and bacon rashers. She looked at me, raising her eyebrows.

I shook my head and gathered more eggs from the icebox. We both froze as a howl burst from the bedroom.

"I can't hardly stand it," Minnie said. "What's wrong with our little man?"

I didn't want to name the illness, as if by maintaining silence I could ward off an omen, keep Satan at bay. "Down with a fever, is all. It will pass, God willing."

Minnie slit her eyes at me, suspecting I wasn't saying everything. Fishing a pin out of her apron pocket, she held it between her teeth while gathering her blond ponytail into a bun, then stabbed it into place.

As I laid out the silverware and poured milk for Dad and the boys, I listened for noises from the back room. Dad, Wylie, Hiram, and Luke finished off the eggs, bacon, muffins, cheese, and milk rapidly, without speaking. Jacob, who was a Deacon at the Church, had already gone into town for a special quorum meeting at the ward, where the Bishop's wife would serve him breakfast.

Minnie and I sat at the table, but I could only eat a few bites of my muffin before I pushed it away. When a loud piercing wail rang from the bedroom, Minnie's hand shook so hard she splashed milk from her glass onto the table. The terrified look in her eyes mirrored how I felt. I bit my lip and started to rise, but she had already begun mopping the table with her kerchief.

Dad wiped his lips and rose. "Bring him a little something," he whispered, and patted my shoulder before heading out of the house to check on the horses.

As soon as Minnie and I had washed and dried the dishes, I carried a muffin and a slice of bacon into the bedroom.

The room was still and dark as twilight. The curtains hung low, and immediately upon entering, I smelled the putrid-sweet stench of vomit. Mother bent over the bed. As I entered, she swung around, frowning at the food I had brought in.

"He can't keep a thing down. It's no good giving him anything solid. You'd best take that back. The smell of it will turn his stomach." She turned back to the little bundled figure on the bed. He must have jerked his legs, because the bedsprings shook, and Mother bobbed her head back in surprise.

"Can I try offering him water?" I asked. For a long time she was silent, until I wasn't sure she had heard me.

Then she allowed, "Maybe a few drops around the lips. He's fading in and out."

I stared at the back of her bun of blond hair threaded with gray and her white-collared, long-sleeved dress, and slipped out of the room, just as the bed shook with another convulsion.

When I returned with a glass of water, Mother had slid the corner chair to the side of the bed and was pinching Jeremiah's cheeks.

"Speak to me, son! Don't slip out. Stay with me."

I dropped to my knees beside the bed, clutching the glass. Jeremiah twisted from side to side, his eyes wide and wandering, his bright, red-spotted tongue drooping from his mouth. Occasionally his legs or arms made a sudden spasm that shook the bed, and he gave a low moan.

I dabbed my fingers in the water and rubbed his lips. Sweat beaded on his forehead and upper lip. Once, as I smoothed his temples with water, his eyes fluttered open and seemed to focus on me, then he sighed and closed them.

At half past eight, Dad, Minnie, and the boys left for church, while Mother and I remained behind with Jeremiah. We took turns sponging and fanning his face, neck, and chest, and dribbling drops of water onto his lips and mouth. As Mother had suggested, he drifted in and out of consciousness. During his lucid moments, he yelped and retched what little was left in his stomach into the tin bowl I held for him beneath his head. Apparently his stomach ached, too, because he clutched his abdomen, and his entire body seemed to tense until the vomiting spasm had passed.

I wanted nothing more than to will him back to strength, or barring that, trade places with him so he need not suffer. It was inhumane for such a small child barely six years old to endure this torture. I bowed my head and whispered a prayer.

At noon, not long before the churchgoers were due to return home, I noticed that Jeremiah had clenched his fingers against the palms of his hands. Try as I might, I couldn't pry them apart when I sought to soothe him. They were as rigid as nails. I stroked his arm and murmured what little comfort I could think of.

His face was now flushed and dark red, and I feared his temperature had risen dangerously. When I pointed this out to Mother, she agreed it was time to fetch the doctor.

I ran down the lane and met my family as they rode back from church in the Model T. Dad let Minnie and the younger boys out of the car while he and Jacob reversed, cranked the engine, and sputtered back down the dirt road toward town.

It was almost eight at night before Dr. Thomas pulled up beside our house. I stumbled outside, tears spilling down my cheeks. Jeremiah's condition had deteriorated rapidly in the last few hours. While Mother and I frantically tried to cool him down and wet his lips, his face had grown extremely hot, and his moments of consciousness had drifted farther apart. Even while unconscious, he clenched his teeth and dug his fingernails against his palms.

As Dr. Thomas, black bag in hand, entered Mother's and Dad's bedroom, Jeremiah lay unconscious, his eyes rolled back behind his head. The doctor gently led Mother aside. She did not cry often, but she wept now, silently, hiding her eyes with the back of her dress sleeve. I held onto her, while Dr. Thomas lifted his stethoscope and thermometer out of the bag. He placed the probe on Jeremiah's chest, listened, then shook his head, his eyes hooded.

"Faint pulse. Almost imperceptible."

When he inserted the thermometer into my brother's mouth, it registered 105.5 degrees. I sank to my knees and uttered a prayer.

The doctor lifted a flask of brandy from his bag and dabbed it against Jeremiah's nose and mouth. For a minute his eyes flew open, and the doctor motioned to Mother to give him a little milk. She did, and he immediately vomited onto the bed sheets.

Dr. Thomas knelt on one knee and fished in his black bag. "It's septic scarlet fever," he said. His voice seemed to catapult at once everywhere in the room, echoing off the hardwood floors, the corner chair, the curtains, the ceiling. I could barely make out the furrows in his brow and his sunken cheeks; the gas lamp cast long shadows against the wall.

Mother stared at the doctor, her face a mask. He reached over and patted her arm, then continued digging medicine bottles out of his bag. "We'll try a little chlorate potash," he said under his breath.

Dad had come to the door and hung in the frame, watching the doctor's grim procedures, and I guessed my siblings stood behind him.

Jeremiah's limbs shuddered, and the bed springs shook violently. In a hoarse shriek, he called for Mother.

"Come here, Irene," Dad said. "You've done enough. Leave him be."

I glanced at Mother, who stared steadily at Jeremiah, as if by doing so she might will him to regain consciousness, open his eyes, smile. I touched her shoulder and left the room.

My brothers and Minnie huddled around the kerosene lamp in the parlor. I crouched on the floor and twisted my fingers together. A few times Dr. Thomas called for ice or a washcloth, and Minnie or I quickly obliged. He took whatever object we brought him at the door of the bedroom, so we were unable to so much as peek into the dark cavern where Jeremiah lay, twisting and groaning.

Two or three hours later, the door to the back bedroom opened and closed, and Dr. Thomas entered the parlor, holding his hat. Dad rose and lumbered across the room, nearly tripping over Luke. The rest of us stood, too, terrified to look at Dr. Thomas.

Dr. Thomas sighed and turned the hat over in his hands, as Dad waited, mopping his face. I held my breath, a knot gathering in my throat. When the doctor spoke, he did not meet Dad's eyes but addressed his hat, like a boy in school, ashamed to be caught without his homework.

"I'm sorry. We lost him. His temperature rose to near 109 degrees. He was suffering from violent convulsions. I'm afraid there's nothing anyone could do."

Minnie, who was clutching my hand, collapsed into my arms. I am unsure of the order of what happened next. The room whirled in a terrifying blur of muted brown and gray, and my knees buckled. Suddenly all spare light winked out, and at once I plunged into utter blackness, my eyesight having failed me. Although I groped for something anchored and solid to grab, I found nothing; I might have been floating, unmoored, in space.

Dimly, as if from a quarter mile away, Luke shouted over and over again, "Not true! Don't tell that lie!" until Dad shushed him.

Someone wailed, a keen and desperate sound that penetrated not just my ears but my core, to the tips of my toes. With the sound, my vision returned, and the room slowly sharpened back into focus. I found myself lying in a heap on the floor, my dress swamped about me as though I had sunk to the bottom of a lake, fully clothed. Minnie still clutched my hand, and her body pressed against mine. Maybe we had fallen together. Luke lay on my other side, apparently having been released from Dad. I stretched an arm until I gripped his clammy hand. The wailing noise transposed into broken, dog-like sobs.

Dad began to cough. As if trapped in a nightmare, I saw the doctor move closer to him and clamp a paw upon his shoulder.

"There's something else, Eric. Utah law requires any family with scarlet fever to be quarantined for at least twenty-one days. I've got to hang the yellow flag outside your house. I'm sorry."

Dad continued coughing, until I was afraid he had begun to choke. Finally he lifted his head and met the doctor's gaze. "I expect we'll do what we have to."

Hiram swallowed, sank onto the couch, and covered his eyes. Wylie had grabbed his knees to his chest, and with bent head, rocked against the floor. Jacob stood before the window, his back to us.

I drew myself up enough to support Minnie, my right arm braced around her shoulder, her left hand grasping my waist. With my other arm I held Luke. We stayed that way for an hour or more.

None of us had the heart to approach Mother, who remained at Jeremiah's side, long after the doctor had left. Eventually Dad ventured into the bedroom, and returned shortly afterwards, gazing at his shoes, his hand touching his chest. After settling into his chair, he said a prayer and read Psalm 23 out loud.

Much later, after Wylie had helped us carry a slumbering Luke to his bed, Minnie and I knocked on Mother's door.

"Go away, now. Leave me be," came her hissed reply.

◀ ♫♪ ▶

We buried my brother one day later. Without any neighbors or friends or even the Relief Society Ladies of the ward to help us, we had to do it quickly before the body began to decompose in the summer air.

Out of the wretched blur of funeral preparations, a few stark images rose and held. The boys shoveling dirt outside the maple tree where Jeremiah loved to play. Dad, clad in overalls, boots, and hat, hammering together a short pine coffin, pausing to wipe the sweat off his brow, then standing with hand on heart. A bearded man from the ward, our only visitor, signing a burial permit. Minnie and I helping Mother wash Jeremiah's small stiff body and dress him in his Sunday outfit.

Choking back tears, even when Mother glared at me. Grasping hands by the maple in our Sunday finery while Dad said a prayer. Shadows cloaking our faces as the sun sank. Honey bees buzzing around the starched collar of my dress as we lowered my little brother into the earth. Trembling, as I thought of his sweet, trusting face the last time I had bathed him. A fistful of dirt hitting the coffin. Mother staring at the hole in the ground as if she wished to surrender herself to it. Her shaky whisper, "Son, my baby son," as she bowed her head.

For three days after his burial, Mother lay in bed, clutching Jeremiah's hand-sewn baby gown against her chest. By the time she emerged from her room, the gown was in tatters, and she sewed it into a thin scarf that she stowed in her apron pocket.

While we remained under quarantine, no company called on us with casseroles and pies or sat with Mother in the parlor. The Petersens left a few covered dishes, notes tucked inside, on the dirt road that wound to the farmhouse.

The first time one of us mentioned Jeremiah's name following his funeral, Mother's face paled, and she staggered against the kitchen stove. Jacob stepped forward quickly and caught her beneath her arms as she fell. After she lifted her head, painstakingly slowly, and steadied herself, she fixed each of us with a steely blue gaze. We knew then not to speak of Jeremiah again in her presence.

In those first gray weeks, I caught Mother sitting in the kitchen late at night, when everyone else had gone to bed, staring into the stove, a dark shawl gathered around her shoulders. After the quarantine was lifted, she might have found solace in talking with Sister Hendricks, whose son hadn't made it, either, but maybe the presence of another mother who had suffered the same devastating blow was too much for her to stomach.

Any scarlet fever survivor, we learned, would bear scars as mementoes of his battle. Although I had stayed at Jeremiah's bedside for hours, I didn't even feel a scratch in my throat. The injustice of this, that the fever had claimed a young child and left everyone else unstricken, alternately angered me and left me awash in guilt.

While preparing for bed, I whispered his name. On Saturday evenings, as I drew my bath, our magical land of Snowchootaney glided before me. Other times, the tune he loved to sing, "Tiptoe through the Tulips," played unbidden in my head, and I couldn't decide whether to smile or cry. Just as they say you never forget your first love, the same is true with first grief. Even after I suffered other personal blows, the pain of that first heartbreak remained wedged inside my chest, an anchor for all future losses. Sometimes I laid my hand over my breast and imagined it held trapped tears that wouldn't release.

If that weren't enough, our family's downward spiral had been set into motion. The surge of the rapids had begun to yank us mercilessly underwater, rushing us like driftwood along its course and careening us among the river boulders.

CHAPTER FIVE

April 2006.

As I watch elderly "retirees" being escorted through the dining hall and courtyard, or the Golden Manor staff hurrying down the corridors in their stretch pants and white sneakers to serve iced tea or set up a card game, I realize that some folks would consider a stay in this place to be the pinnacle of the golden years. In fact, this is what we're supposed to have anticipated all our lives: the chance to be waited upon and pampered, without lifting a finger for meals, drinks, or even baths, if we choose.

But when I consider it for a little while, I know if I could exchange my life now for the hardest period I ever experienced – the first few years after the crash when more than a third of the country was unemployed – I would surely do it. We were in the same boat, sharing camaraderie and the goal to make things better.

It's funny how hardship connects you with your deepest survival instincts, so you're keenly aware of everything around you. And if you give it a go and struggle through it, you gather strength, even if you've ended the day with only a dime in your pocket and an old flour sack for a dress. You realize you can persevere with your own two hands, legs, and wits. You feel fully alive, then.

Today in the cafeteria, a woman with a balding head and tremors slumps over her dish of mashed potatoes and baked chicken. Her water glass tumbles to the floor and shatters into pieces. Without a second glance, she casts her plate aside, and it, too, cracks onto the floor. Chicken and clumps of potatoes catapult beneath the table.

The Golden Manor staff hurries to help her up, eases her into a wheelchair.

The woman glares and sputters, "Get out of my way! I won't go! Leave me be, you! You're hurting me!"

One of the attendants, a twenty-something boy with greasy long hair tied behind his head and a gap between his front teeth, bends down and speaks into the woman's ear.

"Hell no!" she shouts, raising her fists to bat him back. "You can't, and I won't let you!"

My friends and I watch the struggle in dismay. Before long, another attendant arrives and wheels the woman out of the cafeteria. All the while, she shrieks, "Let me go!"

Meanwhile, the remnants of her meal are hastily cleared away, and trundled into the trash. The staff returns to sweep away the shards of glass and chipped porcelain, and wipe down the table and chair where the woman had sat until all traces of her and her ill-fated meal have vanished.

Something about this is so wrong that I want to shout at the top of my lungs. When the greasy-haired attendant asks whether I want a refill of lemonade, I bark at him, then immediately regret it, as a startled look slinks across his face, which he conceals by narrowing his eyes and looking away. He's only a kid, after all.

CHAPTER SIX

September 1932.

Nothing made sense anymore. We had lost our rhythm and routine. Days passed when Mother did not emerge from her room, where the curtains remained drawn round the clock. Long shadows stretched across the parlor by four in the afternoon, which was Minnie's and my cue to cook supper: a fried rabbit or trout one of the boys had caught, with the last of summer's tomatoes planted around it as garnish, and smidgens of dry wheat bread, dipped in water or milk to soften. We went through the motions of sweeping the kitchen, wiping down furniture, washing and stacking dishes on the off chance that a semblance of order might restore something safe and solid that had been lost. Not even ten-year old Luke played his usual games, certainly not near the little maple tree behind the house.

I had just returned from South Cache High, the three-story brick building at the edge of Main Street in Hyrum, where I was now a sophomore. As I walked up the gravel lane to our farm, I glimpsed a figure cloaked in black, sprawled in front of the house. I could just make out the bony rise of the hip, the slope of the spine. My pulse quickened. Hiram had stayed after school for football practice, and Wylie was attending a math club meeting. Minnie and Luke were likely on their way home from Lincoln School, and Dad and Jacob were at work in the fields, way beyond earshot. I was alone.

As I approached, I saw it was a woman in a long black gown, slumped face-down, knees and feet curled against her chest in a fetal position. My mind tumbled with questions about who she was and why she lay crumpled on the ground, but none of the possible explanations made sense. A finger of sunlight that slanted upon a coil of her golden hair and tapered down to the lacy collar of her dress ignited a flash of recognition.

"Mother!" I cried, and sprinted toward her.

My stomach lurched, as though someone had lassoed a rope around it and yanked. I fell to the ground beside her and touched her hand. It was limp and cold. Her eyes were closed, her lips slightly parted. A sheen of sweat glimmered on her forehead.

While feeling for a pulse in her wrist, I leaned close to her face and repeated her name loudly, urgently.

Her eyelashes fluttered, and she gazed past me with glassy blue eyes, not registering me.

"Mother? Are you all right? Please speak to me."

She grunted, turned her face away from me.

"Shall I fetch the doctor?" I peered into her face, noting how pale she looked.

She shook her head and muttered, "Run get me a glass of water and a cold cloth."

I hurried into the house, my hands shaking.

When I returned, she was sitting up, propping herself on her elbows. I noticed a little brown vial lying beside her.

She took the glass I gave her and drank the water rapidly, until all but a swallow remained. Then she wiped her lips with the back of her hand and closed her eyes. All the while I pressed the wet cloth against her forehead.

"How're you feeling?"

She swallowed, frowning, and I slid the cloth against her cheeks and throat.

"Help me up," she managed.

Catching her under the arms, I helped her to feet, as she struggled to stand. At the last minute, I reached for the brown bottle and swept it into my dress pocket.

She leaned heavily against me, and I gripped her around the waist. Together we plodded toward the house.

Her eyes remained closed as we walked. When we made it through the door, she said, "Help me to the bedroom."

"You feeling awful poorly?"

"I don't guess. Just tired out. Don't bother untucking the covers. I'll lie on top for a spell."

Gingerly I eased her onto the mattress, slipped off her shoes, and straightened her dress at the ankles. The curtains were already drawn.

I hesitated. "Do you need anything else?"

She shook her head. "Just a little rest. You best get supper started before the boys get home."

In the kitchen I sliced potatoes and threw them into a frying pan with lard, along with a little leftover chicken from the previous night's dinner. I couldn't stop worrying about Mother. That she had fainted or else fallen asleep right in front of our house was perplexing and bizarre. She might be desperately ill. As this gnawing dread shaped itself into a possibility in my head, I made myself hum a tune, anything to distract such thoughts from taking root.

When Dad, Minnie, and the boys came home, I explained that Mother was in the bedroom, resting. Because this behavior had become so commonplace over the past month, they didn't question it.

But after Minnie and I had washed the dishes, I entered the parlor, where Dad sat reading, and told him what had happened. He waited until I had finished, then nodded. He didn't look surprised. When I fished the little brown vial out of my pocket and handed it to him, he examined it in his palm.

"This is the medicine Dr. Thomas left with your mother right after..." He frowned. "Was supposed to help her sleep a little easier after the first couple of days. I suspect she's still taking it. Still grieving hard."

Dad's face sagged, and he blinked his eyes, as if to force them open. He was exhausted, I guessed, from the slough of tasks around the farm that he and my older brothers had lately tackled: repairing barn rafters, operating the combine, bagging the last of the wheat and driving it to the nearest grain elevator. To boot, as Jacob had told me, wheat prices had sunk to several dozen pennies a bushel, and were dropping still - a mere fraction of what we had received in better times, before the state had officially declared Cache County a crop failure area.

That night, after cleaning the kitchen, I slid onto the piano bench. As my fingers raced across the keyboard, my belly relaxed, while my mind wandered into the other world conjured by the music: the elegant ladies in evening gowns, the men in tuxedoes, the shimmering light of the ballroom spritzing pink and gold across the crest of their faces, the sense that something thrilling was imminent, just in the next moment.

◄ ♫♪ ►

The following Saturday, Mrs. Petersen and Mae stood at the back door, smiling. As I beckoned them inside, Mrs. Petersen thrust a covered dish of baked chicken into my hands.

"We don't wish to intrude," she said, gazing around the room, her eyes lingering on the stack of shirts and socks on the dining table that we hadn't had time to sort and the dusty floor that needed sweeping. "Seeing it's near dinner time, we won't stay long."

Mother, sitting on the couch with a basket of beans she was shelling, made no reply. Mrs. Petersen settled next to Mother and withdrew her needle, thread and cloth, apparently deciding to forgo any conversation for the time being in favor of the steady, comforting silence.

"I'm making a quilt," she announced simply, responding to the question no one had asked.

Setting the basket aside, Mother removed from her dress pocket the thin scarf made from Jeremiah's baby gown and wound it around her fingers, as though she were seeing behind the scarf the shiny new gown it had once been, and the beautiful baby who had once worn it.

Mrs. Petersen had stopped by frequently over the last few weeks, either solo or accompanied by Mae, bringing with her a casserole dish, a loaf of bread or a bit of sewing. Occasionally she recited verses of scripture that she must have believed would offer Mother solace.

Mother received the visits with resignation, saying little except when asked a question to which courtesy demanded an answer.

Mrs. Petersen raised her head. "It would sure be nice to get a little exercise in the fresh sunshine for a moment or two. Just to walk about, Hannah. I'll be glad to go with you."

Mother did not reply, but remained gazing at the scarf. She had gained ten or fifteen pounds in the last month, though no one had the heart to tell her.

Wanting to compensate Mrs. Petersen for her time in some small way, I brought a tray of lemonade from the kitchen, along with slices of warm gingerbread.

"It's a hard row to hoe," Mrs. Petersen said. She reached over to Mother and patted her knee.

Mother didn't raise her eyes from the glass.

"And I remember how it was with my sister-in-law," Mrs. Petersen continued. "After my nephew fell ill with pneumonia and passed a little over two years ago, Ruth couldn't hardly speak. Not for days. Weeks, even. She took it so hard. We all did, of course. Then, little by little, she started coming around. It's the small stuff that helps, I remember she told me. Just doing the daily chores. Keeping busy."

Still Mother said nothing.

I served the last glass of lemonade and slice of gingerbread to Mae, who sat on the piano bench, facing the women, her hands folded in her lap.

"I oughtn't." She smiled. "Thanks, Irene."

She gestured to the space beside her, and I sat.

"And that brings me to something I wanted to ask you about," Mrs. Petersen said. "The Relief Society needs more members, especially during these hard times. Would you consider joining? We need women to sew and bake food and tend gardens."

The Cache County Commission had asked residents to report empty lots to the Church Bishops, so they could be used to plant gardens for the poor. I had seen the slogan posted on bulletin boards in town and at church: "A pig and a garden for every unemployed man in the ward." In town, a charity soup kitchen had opened. Folks called it a Hoover café.

Mother must have sensed our eyes on her, waiting for her answer, because she shifted uncomfortably and bit her lip, as though preparing her thoughts.

"You don't have to decide right away, of course," Mrs. Petersen said hastily. "Take your time to think it over. But we could use your help, Hannah. You're one of the best and fastest seamstresses in the ward."

"I can hardly take care of my own family," Mother said. She waved her arms around the room. "You can see with your own eyes. Cobwebs, filthy curtains. Garden's in disarray."

"But you have two good daughters to help you. I'm sure Irene and Minnie have been doing all they can around the house to make it easier on you." Mrs. Petersen raised her eyes to me.

"And that's so. They do what they can. But they're in school."

"We all do what we can, don't we? I'm surely not going to pressure you. It's up to you to decide what's best. These are difficult times."

"I'd like to help out if I were able, Verda. You know that," Mother said wearily.

Mrs. Petersen put an arm around Mother's neck. "You think about it. You'd do us a world of wonders, and I think you'd do yourself a bit of good, too."

Mother rested her head against the sofa cushion and closed her eyes.

"It's been hard all around," Mrs. Petersen said. She glanced at Mae and me, then added in a hushed voice, "Ole had to sell some of that equipment he recently bought in order to pay back the credit he borrowed on this year's wheat crop. And he didn't even get half what he paid for it.

All the earnings went to the bank. Every single penny. And still he hasn't paid it off. That's the terrible thing. But he tells me that's not so unusual these days."

Mae crossed her legs and stared at the glass in her hands.

Mother didn't seem to know what to say, either. She placed a hand on her forehead, as though to quell a throbbing pulse.

"Let me show you something in the garden," I said to Mae. "I want you to see the big pumpkin we're growing. It must weigh over fifty pounds."

"Yes, run along, girls," Mrs. Petersen said. "I'll fetch you, Mae, when it's time to leave."

I grabbed my sweater from the peg near the screen door in the back of the house. Mae followed me outside. The wind billowed around our dresses. The leaves on the maple tree in the back had turned a flaming scarlet. I leaned down to scoop up a particularly brilliant gold and auburn poplar leaf that Jeremiah would have liked and pressed it in my dress pocket.

I led the way to the garden, down the little lane that skirted the orchards, hoping Mae would not strike up a conversation about football season or cheerleading tryouts or any of the other school topics that didn't remotely interest me. While I endured this talk at school and somehow remembered to smile, in reality I longed to sit at the piano and relinquish myself to the music, float along an undulating wave of chords. The rest of it was a stilted masquerade of scenes that belonged to another teenager.

I hadn't realized how swiftly I had been walking until Mae tripped and uttered a small cry, and I turned.

"You walk so fast, Irene," she said with a wry laugh. "I can't hardly keep up."

"I'm sorry. I'm used to walking here alone." It was true. Since Jeremiah's death and during the quarantine, I had taken to stealing away to the orchards or the garden, escaping the stifling dark rooms, letting my mind empty, feeling only my soles tracking against the worn path.

"I can see why you would. It's so pretty now with the leaves turning."

"It's also to get away." I tilted my head back toward the house.

"Your mother's having an awful hard time, isn't she?"

"Her nerves are all shattered to pieces. It hasn't even been two months, after all."

"I know, I know. It's so soon. Of course it's too soon to get over something like that."

"I don't think you ever get over it. Not really. You might forget it for a little while. But it's always there. In the back of your head. Then when you remember, you feel it all over again. It's like waking from a bad dream and realizing it's not just a bad dream. It's what you've got to live with."

"Irene, you know how horrible I feel about Jeremiah. We all do. He was almost like a brother to us, too. I can't even begin to imagine."

We had reached the entrance to the garden. Mae laid a hand on my arm. We both stood still, and I felt the warm pressure of her hand. To my horror, my eyes clotted with tears. But Mae only gripped my arm harder.

From somewhere far away, she murmured, "It's okay. It will be all right." She slipped an arm around my waist.

I couldn't explain to her that it would never be all right again, not in the same way, but so as not to be unkind, I whispered, "Thank you." As the tears continued streaming down my cheeks, my body loosened, relaxing into her, and I leaned my head against her shoulder. It had been a long time since I had been comforted and cradled this way, like a child.

We stood together for several minutes. Somehow our historic rivalry and my old envy of Mae's voice and her beauty faded until it was petty and small, and the embrace of her friendship felt solid and warm and nice.

She waited while I blotted the tears from my cheeks, then silently handed me a clean handkerchief from her pocket. Elbows linked, because neither of us wanted to pull away, we paced through the garden until we reached the giant pumpkin. Mae smiled when she saw it.

"You could win a contest with it at the County Fair," she declared, as together we peered at the enormous head with the vine curled around it.

I started to say something in response, when we heard a whistle. Hiram vaulted over the wooden fence post behind us into the garden, apparently having seen us as he crossed from the fields to the barn. He wore his flat cap and overalls.

"Hello there, Mae," he called.

Color rose in Mae's cheeks. "Hi, Hiram."

"I didn't know you were here. Did you walk up?"

"I came with Mother. She's inside with your – with Mrs. Larsen. David and my father dropped us off at the road on their way to town."

"Are you staying much longer?"

"Just until Mother fetches me. Maybe another half hour."

"I'll drive you home when you're ready. I can borrow Dad's car."

"That's kind to offer. I'll have to see what Mother wants to do."

Hiram looked away, in the direction of the house, and back at Mae, his gaze steady. "How would you like to take a walk? Just a short one up to the creek?"

Mae hesitated, glancing at me. "Irene was showing me the giant pumpkin. We were talking.."

"It's okay," I broke in. "Go ahead."

"Won't you come, too, Irene?" Mae asked, her face creased with worry.

They waited for my reply, Hiram impatiently, as I knew he preferred to be alone with Mae.

"No, go ahead. I need to do a little weeding out here."

Mae touched my arm, and Hiram led her out of the garden. Their boisterous voices grew fainter as they wandered to the river.

Once alone, I sank to my knees, not mindful of the dirt crumbling onto my dress, and stared at the pumpkin. It lay on its side in the earth, an unexpectedly bright coppery orange, perfect for carving into a jack-o-lantern at Halloween with a little child. Feverishly I dug around the pumpkin as if I were digging a gem from a mine, yanking weeds with my bare hands from the adjacent patch of celery and garlic. I was determined to pry it loose, unfurl its fiery color, free it from the worms and mold and earth. Raise it where it could shine, perfect and whole.

CHAPTER SEVEN

May 2006.

They've changed my medication, just as I knew they would. The new stuff is no better than the old. If anything, it seems to fog my mind more. Sometimes I catch myself confusing details, like the day of the week, or forgetting the simplest things, like what I had for lunch or where I put my hairbrush. The other day I made a wrong turn on my way to the dining hall. In themselves, these confusions amount to inconveniences. But when you add them up by and by, they equal something insidious, like so many wrong turns on a journey that eventually land you down such an unrecognizable, unfamiliar landscape that finding your way home becomes impossible.

So far my complaints have met deaf ears, as Dr. Shah recommended we wait for a trial period of one to two months before evaluating the side effects and impact on my blood pressure. Meanwhile, I can't help feeling that something essential is slipping away from me, ever so gradually, not unlike the eating away of a sandstone cliff in a canyon from years of harsh winds and water, until the cliff's definition collapses, and its composite gravel and clay have washed down the mountain.

Deirdre and her husband, Tom, have invited me over to their place for dinner this weekend. Amy, my granddaughter, is in town for a short visit, and we'll have a chance to catch up. I haven't seen her in little over a year, since her wedding to a fellow who manages a hotel in Florida.

"It'll be a simple dinner," Deirdre assures me. "A casserole, salad, garlic bread, and fresh fruit for dessert. How does that sound? Tom will pick you up at six."

Though we're nearing the middle of May, the evenings are still chilly in the Pacific Northwest, and on Saturday I dress in a cardigan sweater and slacks. When Tom sees me in the downstairs lobby of the Golden Manor, he crooks his arm, and I tuck my hand into the corner of his elbow. Although my legs are in perfectly fine shape, Tom insists I move slowly, to avoid any nasty falls.

"Deirdre's made three times the food that any of us can eat," he says a few minutes later, on the ride to the west side of town.

"I thought she said she would keep it simple."

He chuckles. "She always says that, doesn't she? But then she can't help herself and cooks enough to feed an army. She's got baked chicken, a casserole, a green bean dish, bread, salad, hors d'oeuvres, and I don't know what else."

"Good heavens. I scarcely have the appetite for salad."

Another chuckle. "Don't worry, Irene. By the end of the evening, she'll see that you're stuffed to the gills, like it or not."

My daughter has a strong will by nature, which she undoubtedly gets from Harold and me, and it surfaces in full force when she plays hostess.

We pass the new mega supermarket, cross through a few stoplights, and turn up the hill toward the private gated community where Deirdre and Tom live. They built their house five years ago, when Tom retired. At over four thousand square feet, it's big by most people's standards, but considering it's just the two of them, at a time in their lives when they should be whittling down the amount of stuff they own rather than accumulating more of it, the house seems obscenely large, a McMansion of disgracefully wasteful proportions.

I lean my head against the passenger cushion and close my eyes as Tom punches in the special code at the call box that, like magic, will cause the imposing iron gates to swing open.

We climb past expansive lawns with manicured hedges and veer onto a side street that ends in a cul-de-sac.

Deirdre's and Tom's house is a custom faux Tudor, with dark brown trim and a white stone façade. The house sits on over an acre of well-tended lawn, and features a gazebo and miniature pond in the back, complete with sculpted hedges, bordered by a grove of firs and elms.

Tom slides the car into the side garage, otherwise known as the "carriage house." We climb the stairs into the long tiled alley that connects with the kitchen. Deirdre's fancy name for it is the mudroom, and here I'm to sit on a bench and remove my shoes, so they don't scratch the hardwoods.

The smell of garlic and baked chicken wafts in from the kitchen. As Tom and I make our way there, I hear a low conversation – one voice and another, a sharp ping and pong, like the rhythmic volley of a tennis ball on a clay court.

Deirdre stands in front of the stove, a checkered apron tied around her waist. An uncorked wine bottle and a half full glass sit next to her on the stone countertop. Amy perches on a stool at the island, sampling grapes from a crystal platter. Her cheeks are pillowy and pink, and her blond hair cascades down her shoulders.

For some reason she looks glum, her lips turned down and her brow wrinkled, but when she sees me, she grins and rises. "Grandma!"

I move toward her, and she catches my arms and embraces me. I hold her back to peer into her eyes, vivid cerulean orbs that glisten when she laughs. Despite the chill of the evening, she is barefoot, in shorts and a tee shirt, but her skin is warm and alive.

"You're beautiful as always, honey," I say, inhaling her rose perfume. "It's been much, much too long."

"I know. I've been running around a little lately, but I wanted to come home for a visit and see how you're doing, now that you've recovered from your surgery. You look good and strong."

"One foot in the grave, but still humming."

"Grandma, I'm serious. You don't look like a woman who's nearly ninety. You look at least ten years younger."

I smile. "I don't know about that. This assisted living place where I am now is liable to do me in. They give us all kinds of food and games and even outings, but the staff's afraid we'll blow over if we so much as lift a finger on our own. Gets me stir crazy and feeling more fragile than I really am."

Deirdre frowns, but crosses over to peck my cheek. "Sit down, Mom, won't you, and let Tom pour you a little wine." She holds my arm and helps me slide into a stool beside Amy.

I shake my head. "I don't need any wine at the moment."

Tom laughs. "No one ever *needs* wine, Irene. The question is, do you want it?"

"I don't think…"

"Oh, come on, Mom," Deirdre wheedles. "A few sips won't hurt. I read somewhere that as you get older, it's a good thing to have a little red each day. Something to do with the antioxidants. It's even supposed to be good for the heart."

Tom is already pouring a glass, and reluctantly I accept it. Deirdre tips her goblet toward me in a toast.

From the wall speakers in the adjoining family room, a lovely piano waltz plays. I tilt my head in concentration. Not so long ago, I would have been able to identify the composer immediately. Now I'm not so sure. Brahms, Chopin?

Deirdre gestures at the platter of grapes and cheese. "Have a little appetizer." She's back at the stove, stirring a tomato sauce. "Dinner should be ready in fifteen minutes."

"Can I help?"

"Just sit right there and enjoy yourself," Deirdre orders.

"Tell me," I say, turning to Amy. "How have you been? How's your husband? I want to hear everything."

Deirdre stops stirring and exchanges an inscrutable look with Tom, who rises and excuses himself to read an article in his study.

It's no secret that Deirdre and Tom are not altogether happy with Amy's situation. For years, when Amy, who has a gift for public speaking, was in high school and a freshman in college, they urged her to enter law or politics. Instead, after a spring break trip to Florida, she dropped out of college to join a dance troupe in Orlando, where she's remained for over a decade. About a year ago, she married in a small, casual ceremony by the beach. Deirdre and Tom don't think much of their new son-in-law's upbringing, which apparently involved living on welfare with a handful of siblings and a single, uneducated mother. But Deirdre has confessed she's glad that Amy has settled down, and hopes that she may even produce a grandkid someday.

Without looking at me, Amy says, "Not so great. Wayne and I are divorcing."

I raise my head quickly. "That's a shame."

Deirdre remains silent, her lips set in a grim line.

"What happened?" I ask at last.

Amy shrugs. "Things didn't work out the way I hoped. He wasn't the same person I thought he was. After a while, he started questioning me about every little thing I did, from going to the grocery store to dance rehearsals. I felt stifled."

"It's too bad she didn't figure that out months ago, before she married him," Deirdre says, shaking her head.

Amy bites her lip and stares stonily at her mother.

"At least there are no children. And you're still young," I say soothingly. "You can dust yourself off and go on."

Deirdre stabs at the sauce, churning the spoon faster and faster into the pot. "If only that were the case."

I look from Deirdre to Amy.

When Amy says nothing, Deirdre declares, "She says she's two-three months pregnant." She waits for me to digest this news. "So she'll be a single mother, scraping together a living."

"Oh honey." I lean toward Amy.

"Mom makes it sound much worse than it is." Tears spring to Amy's eyes. "I thought she might be pleased to be a grandmother, but instead she and Dad are up in arms, as if I've decided to rob a bank and flee the law."

I put an arm around her shoulders. "I'm happy for you. I know you'll be an excellent mother."

Deirdre sighs. "If she were planning to stay married, then of course I'd be pleased. But not if she's a single mom by her own choice."

I search for something to say. "Can you stick it out a little while longer, at least until after the baby is born? Maybe things will get better."

Amy shakes her head. "I thought about that, but it's become unbearable. It's gotten to the point where I can hardly step outside to get a breath of fresh air on my own. I can't imagine what would come next. When I told Wayne I wanted a divorce, he got crazy. He accused me of having an affair and sneaking around on him. He claims the baby isn't even his, which is absurd. I wouldn't want the baby to grow up in that kind of home. I've moved out, and I refuse to live with him ever again."

I think of my sister-in-law and her troubles as a young bride and nod. "Then that's the right choice."

Deirdre throws up her hands. "I've told Amy that if she were so uncertain about him, she should have taken measures to avoid getting pregnant in the first place. But no one ever listens to me, least of all my kids. If I ask them to turn right, you can be sure they'll turn left."

My grandson Tom Junior, who was expected to take over his father's business, majored in art history and moved to New York. He works as a waiter in a tiny restaurant in Brooklyn and, according to Deirdre, lives in a roach-infested walk-up apartment building without AC.

"That's not fair, Mom," Amy says in a low, dangerous voice, and clenches her fists.

"Tom says that if she's intent on getting herself into this mess, she can deal with the consequences."

"You know I haven't asked you for anything. Not a cent."

"But you're not prepared for what will happen when reality hits, and you're saddled with bills and a screaming infant and a low paying job. It's as though you want to make things as hard as they can be."

I squeeze Amy's shoulder, and stroke her hair, and she turns toward me, her eyes still swimming.

It crosses my mind that my granddaughter shares more in common with Harold and me than with her parents. For one, I know where she gets her dancing talent and impulsive streak. As for her unusual choices, I speculate they might stem from a wish to escape the routine and avoid a pampered life. Maybe she realizes that struggling toward a goal can sometimes produce more meaning than the predictability of a cozy bed and square meals. But it's entirely possible I've got it wrong, and she has no plans other than to rebel against the status quo.

"Of course, I'm worried to death," Deirdre adds.

Amy swipes angrily at her eyes. "You don't have to worry. I've told you many times. I'm an adult. I can take care of myself."

"Amy has a point, you know. Once the kids have flown the coop, you have to stand back and let them live their lives."

Deirdre paces the length of the kitchen, turns off the burner and leans against the countertop. "Remember what I said earlier? There are other options, too, that you might consider before it's too late."

A chilly strand of goosebumps pops onto my arms.

Amy glowers, and her jaw tightens. "I've made up my mind about that, too. I'm going to have this baby."

"Of course you are," I whisper. "You're strong. You'll be fine."

The timer buzzes, and Deirdre removes a covered dish and rolls from the oven.

I offer to arrange the rolls in a basket, but as I rise, the floor spins beneath me. My head swimming, I can't help think it's terribly wrong that what should be joyous news has unaccountably morphed into something dismal. I grip the arm of my chair until the lightheaded feeling passes.

Amy touches my arm and studies me with concern. "Grandma, are you all right?"

"I'm fine now," I say, managing a weak smile.

"What's wrong?" Deirdre calls in alarm.

I wave my hand. "It's nothing. Just a little dizzy spell. It's passed."

Deirdre hurries over and peers at me. "How about some water?"

"I'll get it," Amy says. "Stay right there."

They fuss over me, Amy bringing the water and holding it to my lips, Deirdre wiping my brow. As I continue to insist I am fine, and try to stand to prove it, they confer and finally agree the danger has passed. As uncomfortable as I am under their scrutiny, I'm mollified it has united them, albeit temporarily.

Deirdre straightens. "Amy, let Dad know that we're about to eat. He's hiding out in his study."

While Amy goes to fetch Tom, Deirdre guides me down the long mahogany hallway that leads out of the kitchen, past the sunken family room, and to the rear of the house, where the formal dining room overlooks the pond and gazebo. "You'll feel better after you've had something to eat, Mom," she says.

She puts me at the head of the table, facing the picture window, then uncorks another bottle of wine and lights two long ivory candles in the center of the table. Tom arrives and takes the opposite chair. Deirdre leaves and returns with a silver tray bearing the casserole, chicken, and green beans.

Amy follows with the salad bowl and rolls. Dimpling, she dips her head at us. "Voila! Dinner, Ladies and Gentleman, is served."

The piano music, a haunting nocturne, pipes from the wall speakers here, too, and I want to sink into its spell. Through the picture window, I glimpse something slippery and white darting across the lawn. I narrow my eyes, but the reflection of the light in the dining room blazes back at me instead.

For a while we're silent, eating chicken and nibbling bread. When Deirdre passes around the casserole and tries to serve me a helping, I shake my head.

"I can't possibly eat all of that. I'm already stuffed."

"Come on, Mom. This won't hurt you. You need to put on a little more weight."

"No, thank you."

"Humor me, won't you, by trying just a little? You're under no obligation to finish it."

"Really, Deirdre."

But she is already shoveling a nice-sized square of the casserole, coupled with a mound of green beans, onto my plate.

The corners of my mouth crumple, as though I'm a cranky child about to throw a tantrum, but reluctantly I lift my fork and sample a corner.

"How is it?" Deirdre asks.

I wipe my lips and nod, not looking at her.

Tom reaches across the table for the wine bottle, and says quickly, "A toast. To everyone's good health and happiness."

I cover my wine glass, but it's too late. Tom lays it aside and fills it with a vintage Cabernet Sauvignon that drips like blood onto Deirdre's lace tablecloth.

Deirdre regards the spot with a flicker of a frown, and sips her wine. I pick at the green beans on my plate. Although Amy eats heartily, she chews without any evident pleasure.

"It's so quiet you can hear a spoon drop," Tom says after a while.

Deirdre shoots him a dark look. "No one's preventing you from making conversation."

He stares at her for a minute, then turns toward me. "What's new at the Golden Manor, Irene?"

"Nothing special. The usual Bingo games and ladies with dentures and wheelchairs in the courtyard." I had hoped to lighten the mood, but I realize belatedly that I've come across as sarcastic, since the Manor is still a sore point between Deirdre and me.

Tom looks in bewilderment from Deirdre to me, then helps himself to another serving of casserole.

"Mom, try more of the casserole," Deirdre persists, with a false cheerfulness.

"Everything's delicious, but I haven't even finished what's on my plate. And I already told you, I'm quite full. My appetite isn't what it used to be."

"Tom? Amy? More for you?"

My granddaughter shakes her head. "No, I'm fine."

"Then I guess all this will go to waste." Deirdre points at the sideboard. "All that effort for naught."

Tom lays his napkin on the table. "No one asked you to make all that food."

Deirdre takes another sip of her wine. "No. You're right. No one appreciates the things I do. Not a single person."

Her words have their intended effect, the slap of reproach, and we go silent. I pick at my plate, suddenly stung with remorse, as though my own mother has materialized in Deirdre's place. It was just the thing she would have said, decades ago. Amy lowers her head and continues eating, and Tom stares out the window, apparently lost in thought.

After a while Deirdre says, "I'll bring out some fruit, if everyone's finished with the main course."

I bite my tongue, and Tom merely nods. Amy slouches, looking for all the world like she'd rather be anywhere else.

After Deirdre disappears into the kitchen with an armful of dirty dishes, I decide to cheer up Tom and Amy by telling a joke about a doctor asking his patient how long she had been bedridden. The patient looked confused at first, then replied, "Why, not for about twenty years, when my husband was alive."

Amy cackles. "Grandma! I'll bet you heard that one from Grandpa, didn't you? It sounds just like him."

Deirdre places a serving bowl of strawberries, sliced bananas, cantaloupe, and blackberries in the center of the table, along with a dish of whipped cream.

"Now this should be something you'll enjoy," she says. "Refreshing and light."

I help myself to a scoop of the fruit with a dollop of cream, and try a conciliatory, "Thanks, sweetheart. This is perfect."

She looks pleased, and I regret I hadn't thought to say something a little kinder earlier in the evening.

Later, as we sit in the family room, sipping from steaming mugs of tea, I compliment Deirdre on the dinner and ask her to play a piece on the piano. She used to play well, as a girl, but as far as I know, she hasn't played much since.

"And Amy," I suggest, squeezing my granddaughter's arm, "Why don't you play something, too, honey?"

Deirdre's pale face suffuses in a rosy hue, the color of a setting sun, which could also be an effect of the wine she's drunk. "I almost never play anymore, Mom, I'm embarrassed to say. Sometimes I don't even know why I bought that baby grand. It mainly sits in the corner, untouched. No one ever took to it the way you did. You're the pianist in this family. You should play a piece for us."

"Don't sell yourself short. I used to love waking in the mornings to the sound of your practicing. Which piece was it you used to play over and over? A Beethoven Sonatina, I think. It was lovely."

"Oh, good grief. That was fifty years ago." But she sets her mug on the coffee table and slides onto the bench. "Amy, come over here. It's your turn next."

Amy grimaces but crosses to the bench. "I'll turn the pages for you, nothing more."

After a minute of shuffling through songbooks, Deirdre plays a melody by Schumann, from his album *Of Foreign Lands and People*. It's a piece I used to play, at the start of the Depression years.

Deirdre makes a few mistakes, but I don't mind. I have closed my eyes, and now, sitting in the midst of this richly furnished room, I catch a glimpse of my daughter as a young girl. She is eager to experience where her musical talent might take her, excited about meeting the world and trying new things.

The room fades. Suddenly Deirdre and Amy have blended together: golden coiffed hair, graceful arms, one turning the pages, the other playing, forging ahead, despite the trial they will bear. That pair might be Minnie, with her blond locks, slender frame and pale green dress and me, where we sat draped together over the piano in the ward for a few stolen moments, after Dad sold the Kimball.

CHAPTER EIGHT

October 1932.

Tapping his fingers on the table, Dad barked, "Listen up. We'll never become beholden to any banker, so long as I'm around. We've got a good-sized mortgage, and we're near broke. It's high time we sell what we don't need." His gaze swept the room, alighting on the piano.

I felt a thrashing beneath my ribs, like an egg whisk beating my insides. Shivering, I clamped my hands around my arms.

Jacob said to Mother, whose face had grown ashen, "Things will turn around by and by."

"But I won't take a chance on that, either," Dad said.

Mother's fingers tightened around the knife she was holding, and the corners of her mouth turned down.

"Mr. Petersen had to sell some equipment, too," Hiram ventured. "A tractor."

I looked up from my plate, recalling what Mrs. Petersen had confided at her last visit.

"The banks are sharks," Dad spat. "They don't care a fiddle for the farmer. You miss even one payment, they'll swoop down like vultures and take you for all you've got. Ole's drawn a long line of credit. I reckon he'll try to get whatever he can for it."

Catching sight of our curious faces, forks suspended as we waited to learn more, he added, "And that's why I'm trying to make this real clear."

Mother laid her napkin down and stared at him reproachfully, her eyes cold. "Can't this wait until after supper?"

Dad shook his head and drew his lips into a thin line. "No. We've put it off long enough."

Mother's nostrils flared.

He addressed us all, but I knew his words were meant for Mother. "Months ago, I told you if things didn't turn around, we'd have to make some tough choices. Sure, I hoped we'd see a little recovery. But that hasn't happened. Price of wheat's falling apart, lowest it's been in years. Can't hardly make a living on it. And when Jacob leaves for his mission next month, we'll be down hands. So we'll sell more cattle, plus the car and piano, and take in a boarder. That's for starters."

He paused, waiting for comprehension to register. "Over the winter, I'll go to work at the wool mill outside town. See if we can bring in a little extra cash that way."

Mother gazed at the floor as he spoke, clutching the frayed cloth that had been Jeremiah's baby gown. Her chest spasmed with a cough, and she lifted the cloth to her lips.

"If we have a boarder, where will he stay?" Luke asked at last.

Dad shrugged. "We'll put some bedding in the room you boys share. You can sleep on it and let the boarder take your bunk."

Luke's face crumpled. "Why my bunk?"

"Because you're youngest, and the boarder will pay. Besides, there's plenty space. After Jacob leaves, you can have his bunk, or else we can fit a second boarder in there."

"Aw, Dad."

Dad turned on him, eyes blazing. "That's enough out of you. Every one of us will have to make sacrifices. If I catch you complaining, I'll take a strap to you. That goes for all of you." He glowered at Wylie, Hiram, Minnie, and me.

"The boarders might want a little privacy," Mother suggested.

Dad had an answer for this, too. "We can turn the parlor into a spare bedroom. We could do it easy if we needed to. Heck, we could even take in three lodgers."

I shuddered. The last thing we needed, I thought, was a house full of strange men.

Mother looked past us with glassy eyes, as if she were seeing into a different world that the rest of us couldn't. She twisted the scarf around her wrist.

I wanted only to know when they would sell the piano, but I dared not ask.

As if reading my thoughts, Dad said, "First thing tomorrow, Jacob and I will head north to sell some cattle. On our way out of town, we'll stop at the post office to tack up ads for a boarder, the piano and car. Wylie and Hiram will hold down the fort."

No one spoke, and Dad snatched his hat and overcoat and vanished out the back door, into the twilight.

After Minnie and I washed the dishes, I slipped onto the piano bench. All these years, playing the Kimball had been like visiting a friend. Now that it was to abruptly end, I felt an edge of desperation. While Jacob humored Luke with a game of marbles in the corner of the parlor, I ran through a Bach Invention, mathematical in its precision. But even as my fingers fluttered along the keys, I knew it was pointless. The music struck me as airy and inappropriate, another attempted charade of being a teenager. As much as I wanted to fill myself with something substantial and calming, I was emptied to the core. After a few minutes, I shuffled my hands into my lap, where they lay white and limp, like a pair of gutted creek fish.

The next morning, while I served porridge, Dad and Jacob bent over the farm ledger, their faces grim. As the sun cracked the horizon and smeared upward, they loaded five cows into a rickety wooden trailer, which they roped to the rear of the Model T. Dad had said they would travel to farms near the Utah-Idaho border, then south toward Salt Lake City.

From the kitchen window, Mother watched them drive away. Long after the car and its cloud of dust had disappeared from view, she remained staring into the yard.

At first Mother insisted that Wylie and Hiram continue at school, but Wylie stopped after two days, realizing he couldn't keep up with chores if he attended class. He chopped wood, fed the livestock, milked the cows, repaired a loose rafter in the barn. Knowing how much he despised farm work, I offered to help, but he shook his head.

"Stay out of this while you can, Irene. No point. You can help Mother."

Without giving a second thought to skipping school, Hiram joined Wylie. Unlike Wylie, Hiram was not a natural scholar and preferred to be outdoors, where he could use his muscles, tan his arms and face, drink in the mountain air.

"I don't like this," Mother fretted, "And I won't abide it. I want all my boys to finish school."

"I'll still finish," Wylie, now a senior at South Cache High, assured her. "I'm going to graduate next summer no matter what."

At night, exhausted from the day's labor, he nonetheless sat by the kerosene lamp in the parlor and worked through problems in his calculus book.

"He takes after my brother Paul," Mother mused, sweeping the kitchen, while Minnie and I washed and dried the supper dishes. We glimpsed the golden crown of Wylie's head in the other room, bent over his book. "Handsome and smart."

Afterwards, Mother treated Wylie with small favors. After shooing the rest of us out of his way so he could concentrate on his studies, she brought him apple cider or extra helpings of bread pudding after supper. When he entertained us with his saxophone on Sunday evening, she smiled, possibly for the first time in months, tapping her feet and humming.

The next day after school, hoping my own news might also please her, I told Mother that Mr. Olsen, the drama teacher, had asked me to play accompaniment for the upcoming school musical. It would be the first time I would play piano in the South Cache High auditorium. At Lincoln School, where I had been a student through eighth grade, I had played the school's upright piano while students marched between classes.

Making no sign of having heard, Mother didn't glance up from the sink where she peeled an onion.

"Mother, it'll be a chance to perform in front of all the students and parents at the school plays," I said, more loudly.

She placed the onion onto a wooden cutting board. "That's all well and good, but no need to get a big head. Not when there are bigger things to fuss over, and I've got my hands full." She untied her apron strings and pointed at the onion. "Here. Use this to make a stew."

Without glancing at me, she left the kitchen. I stood still, wondering at her indifference. Something inside me smarted, as though I were a child whose favorite doll had been seized and locked away.

"Just for once she could pay me mind," I muttered under my breath, grinding my toes into the floorboards. I understood she was still reeling with sorrow, but she wasn't alone. After a moment, I bent down for the matches and lit the stove.

◄ ♫♪ ►

One afternoon after Dad's and Jacob's departure, Mae and her mother stopped by the house. Wrapped in a shawl, Mrs. Petersen looked tired. Her eyes were hooded and the crest of her cheeks was creased and chapped, which might have been the result of the cold. It had been a while, I realized, since their last visit. For that matter, it had been weeks since anyone had paid a visit. I welcomed them indoors with genuine warmth, setting the apple cobbler that Mae had presented onto the kitchen table.

As I helped Mrs. Petersen out of her shawl, I expected her to mention the Relief Society and express her hope that Mother would join, as she almost always did, but she must have known better than to press the issue. Now she simply embraced Mother, who had risen from the dining table, where she was darning socks. Mother accepted her hug stiffly, but I could tell she was also glad for company, because she ushered Mrs. Petersen into the parlor, and asked how she had been. Perhaps Hiram's news about Mr. Petersen's debts had piqued her curiosity, if not sympathy.

Mae hovered nearby, gripping her book satchel, and from the color in her cheeks and the way she turned her head toward the door, I knew she hoped to see Hiram.

"Hiram's out in the field," I told her. "We can go into the kitchen if you'd like."

She nodded and followed me.

At school, I rarely saw Mae, who, like Hiram, was one grade ahead of me, but I heard about her plenty. As Secretary of the Pep Club, she organized rallies and decorated the gym before games. She also starred in most of the school musicals. Recently the gossip mills had linked her name with my brother's. Of course, I knew about their special friendship long before it became school news. Hiram had found numerous excuses to help with haying and repairs at the Petersens' farm, though Minnie and I suspected his real reason.

Minnie stood at the stove, frying fish to which she had added leftover potatoes, plus turnips and carrots we had bottled from our summer garden. When Mae offered to help, we refused and asked her to sit.

"I feel strange watching you work. But truth be known, I should start my math homework. If I don't do better on the next test, Mr. Sidmore might flunk me."

She grimaced and pulled out her book. I peeled carrots and an onion, my back to the table, but when I glanced over, Mae was furiously erasing answers in her notebook, her brow furrowed.

At last she said in frustration, "I'll never get this. I'm hopeless." Pressing her palms against her forehead, she sighed.

Inspiration struck me. "I know someone who can help."

Before she could object, I grabbed my coat and ran to the barn. A few minutes later, I returned with Wylie.

"This is just the person you need. My math genius brother."

"I didn't mean for you to come away from whatever you were doing," Mae said, smiling in apology. "Irene, you needn't have dragged him here."

Wylie didn't meet Mae's eyes, even when she greeted him. He hesitated at the edge of the table, gripping his hat between his hands, then approached slowly, sliding into the chair beside her.

As I turned back to the stove, they murmured in conference. Mae pointed out the problems she had trouble solving, and Wylie explained patiently. When I glanced over, their heads were bent together, and Wylie was writing out an equation beside a detailed illustration of the problem.

When it was time for her to go home, Mae thanked him profusely. "You near saved my neck. Mother, I would surely have flunked Mr. Sidmore's homework if it hadn't been for Wylie."

Wylie reddened. "Was happy to do it."

"Wylie's in the math club," I told Mae and her mother. "He's brilliant at problem solving."

"Well then, Mae might be calling on you for help again," Mrs. Petersen said with a coquettish smile. "I'm afraid she takes after me. No head for numbers."

"It would be my pleasure," he mumbled, sneaking a glance at Mae.

◄ ♫♪ ►

At dinner, Minnie told Hiram he had just missed Mae.

His eyes brightened. "She was here?"

"Yes, with her mother. Wylie helped her with her math homework."

Hiram looked over at Wylie, who flushed, but said nothing.

Hiram continued staring at him, his eyes menacing, and growled, "Yeah? Keep your stinking hands off my girl, why don't you, and find your own."

Wylie stopped chewing, his fork suspended in midair.

"Try over at the library. That's where the old maids gather. They might be quiet as mice, but at least they'll hang onto your every word. Maybe you'll be lucky and find one who knows how to dress herself without looking like a big gray lump."

"He wasn't..." I began, as simultaneously Minnie cried, "We asked him to help."

Seeing our flustered faces, Hiram laughed suddenly. "Ha ha. No need to get all twisted around, you knuckleheads. I was just kidding."

Something fell with a clinking clatter onto the floor.

I turned as Wylie stooped to retrieve his fork. Without a word, he dumped it onto his plate, scraped his chair away with a frown, and left the table.

"That was unfair, Hiram," I said viciously. "What's gotten into you?"

Hiram shrugged. "No one around here can take a joke. You need to get off your high horses."

I narrowed my eyes at him. "Some joke."

◀ ♫♪ ▶

On Saturday, Minnie and I knelt in the garden, raking over the long rows of soil, once ripe with tomatoes and peas, that had gone fallow since summer. It had rained overnight, and the soil was damp. Clouds scudded across the sky in filthy gray streaks, like smears of mud against cheesecloth. From far away, an engine rumbled. Standing up, I shielded my eyes against the sun as the car rounded the bend of the dirt road that wound to our farm.

When I spied the familiar Model T with the rickety trailer lagging behind, I shouted to Minnie, "They're here! Look, they've come back!"

Waving, we ran to meet the car. When the Model T rolled to a stop, Dad swung open his door and stepped out. His overalls were mud-stained and tattered, his face grizzled. He withdrew the slouch hat from his head and wiped sweat from his forehead.

I ran headlong to him and flung my arms around his neck, and he swooped me into a bear hug. He smelled of dank earth and sweat and musty wool.

"It's good to be home," he said.

Jacob emerged from the passenger side and leaned against the hood. He didn't smile, not at first, and this surprised me. Instead he scowled at the wheat field, as though he couldn't chase something disturbing from his mind. He had lost weight, and several buttons were missing from his coat. Minnie rushed to his side, and only then he grinned and folded her into his arms.

Over supper, Dad told us they had driven to over thirty farms before finding someone who was willing to buy the cattle.

"Too many folks are scared of extending themselves right now. They're struggling to make ends meet, same as us. It's a long shot to buy things they don't think they'll need."

"Then you had to sell low," Mother said.

"Not as high as I would have done six or seven months ago, but we did as well as we could have. Eh, Jacob?"

Jacob nodded, and a look of understanding passed between them.

"Will you keep the cash here?" Mother asked. After Dad had withdrawn our savings from the bank in Logan, she often reminded him that hiding money at home was akin to asking to be robbed.

"It's safe here," Dad asserted, reading the doubt in her eyes. "We're not in any danger of being burgled."

Mother frowned but said nothing.

As we waited, fidgeting, he added, "Good news is I'm gonna trade the Model T for a pickup truck and a couple of hogs. Plus we've found a boarder and a buyer for the piano. In two weeks, after Jacob leaves on his mission."

He said something more, but my mind couldn't make sense of it. A little gasp escaped from my lips, and tears sprang to my eyes. The room spun. I wanted desperately to be gone from them all. Scraping back my chair, I rose unsteadily to my feet. Hiram grabbed my arm, but I shook him off and fled to the parlor. Behind me, Mother raised her voice, and Dad interrupted with a sharp retort; but I didn't care. Turning my attention to my beloved Kimball, I sank onto the bench, bereft.

"Please don't go," I whispered, knowing how nutty I sounded.

As though cast under a spell, my fingers traveled across the keyboard and crashed into an explosive arpeggio. Over and over again I played the dark chords, letting the piano ring and swell with my rage and sorrow.

CHAPTER NINE

November 1932.

When two men arrived to cart away the piano, Mother, Minnie, and I stood against the wall and watched in silence. Memories flooded me: of the melodies I had played while immersed in my distant land, the singalongs, duets we had sung, even the little dance we held one winter when Minnie and I took turns accompanying as the other sang solos, and friends from the ward danced in the parlor. The tips of my toes and fingers felt numb, and my chest throbbed. It was as though a thief had broken into the house and robbed us of the one thing I valued the most. My stomach heaving, I bolted from the room and tripped up the stairs to the attic, where I sank onto the bed and let my head plunge to my knees.

Half an hour later, as the sun began to sink, Mother hollered up the attic steps, "Irene, come help with supper."

I hugged my knees tighter.

"Did you hear me?" she called.

It was unfair of her. She had loved the Kimball, too, but she expected me to follow her footsteps by shoving it from my mind and doing my chores, as though the piano and its swift removal had never happened.

Rising angrily, my eyes brimming, I brushed down my dress and clomped into the kitchen.

Mr. Wallace, our boarder, a wiry young man in his mid-twenties, sat at the kitchen table, playing dominoes with Luke.

"I'm sorry about the piano," he said.

Unable to trust myself to speak, I nodded and drew on an apron.

Though Mr. Wallace's Christian name was Robert, I couldn't bring myself to address him by anything but Mr. Wallace. He had traveled to Utah from his family's farm in the Midwest, when he learned about a government contract to build a dam outside Hyrum. Now he was an assistant to the lead engineer on the project. In the evenings, he dined with us and wrote letters by kerosene lamp to his mother. On weekends, when he wasn't working on the dam, he would serve as an extra hand around the farm, feeding and looking after the animals, clearing the wheat fields for the spring planting, cutting timber for firewood.

Now, feeling the absence of the piano, I was glad for his company and the added distraction.

"I won!" Luke crowed.

I looked over and caught the grin on Mr. Wallace's face, and knew he had allowed my brother the victory.

"Let's try canasta," Mr. Wallace said, and plucked a deck of cards from his pocket. "First I'll teach you how to play rummy."

As I sliced a slab of salted pork and opened a bottle of carrots we had canned in the fall, Mr. Wallace patiently explained the rules to Luke.

Over supper, he told us about the shantytown in Salt Lake City where he had camped three days ago after arriving by train, a vacant lot with tents, campfires, and makeshift shelter constructed from driftwood and newspapers. As we gaped at him, he added, "The economy will start to turn around. You'll see. Roosevelt owes the election to the farmers and the little guys. He'll make things happen."

Dad gave him a skeptical look, eyebrows raised. "What makes you think so?"

"Shoot, just last year, hundreds of farmers out in the Plains burned their crops, cause it was cheaper to use it for heat or else let it go fallow 'stead of harvesting. FDR won't stand for that kind of waste. He'll pay farmers to feed people in need, and kick the bankers to the curb."

Dad shook his head. "Terrible shame to burn up corn."

Mr. Wallace took a bite of his pork, chewing thoughtfully. "My father was a corn farmer. Lost everything we had. Folks are living with my aunt and uncle in Wichita now."

I was ashamed for him, and for a minute, no one spoke.

"Meal's delicious," he said, breaking the silence. "Better days are ahead. I'm sure of it.

Normally I would have retreated to the parlor to fill myself with a Sonatina or a ragtime tune. I couldn't help notice how deathly quiet the house had become without the booming keys of the piano, so quiet you could hear other noises: the whoosh of the faucet, squeaking of floorboards, clank of dishes. That evening, long after everyone had gone to bed, my parents exchanged curt words and hissed pronouncements they tried unsuccessfully to quell.

Unable to stop myself, I crept down the stairs.

"If we land in the poorhouse, it will be no one's fault but our own," Dad bellowed.

"And I don't understand why," Mother answered, her voice also rising. "We're doing everything we can to stay afloat. You can't blame the baker for not making bread if the utility company shuts off his gas."

"We haven't done everything. Should have started a lot sooner. Take that piano. I should've sold it months ago. I knew we had to. But I listened to you. We've got other furniture we should sell, too. Say, for instance, a couple of beds along with the sofa and dining table. The longer we wait, the less we'll get."

"The children need a place to sleep and eat. You'd have us live like barn animals."

"Think, Hannah. If we don't bring in enough cash, we'll be lucky to live in a shanty at the railroad yard, let alone the floor of this house." Dad exhaled through his teeth with a rushing noise, then both my parents fell quiet.

As I prepared to slink back to the attic, the stair creaked.

"Irene Larsen, what do you think you're doing?" Mother demanded. She appeared at the foot of the stairway, glaring, arms akimbo, before I had a chance to edge away. "Are you eavesdropping?"

"No, ma'am," I faltered. "I wanted to fetch some water."

She must have read the bald-faced lie on my face, because she shook her head in disgust. "From the looks of it, sneaking is more like it. Go! Get out of here! Now!"

Receiving the weight of her fury, like one of Hiram's fast balls slamming into my stomach, I backtracked upstairs, cheeks burning. She needn't have treated me like a swindler, I thought bitterly. But then, none of us were ourselves anymore. Clearly the grownups couldn't contain this trouble; the seething river had swollen and broken its banks.

CHAPTER TEN

June 2006.

When Deirdre comes for a visit this afternoon, as she does nearly every day, she presents me with a fresh bouquet of Columbines, primroses and miniature hollyhocks, picked straight from her backyard. She arranges the long stems in an expensive crystal vase, which she places on the end table in my unit for "a little color," and I lean back to admire them.

She tells me that Amy, now back in Florida, is feeling poorly. The last month of her first trimester has been difficult, complete with severe morning sickness and bloating so pronounced it's almost impossible for her to continue her act with the dance troupe, at least for now.

As a result, Deirdre explains, Amy took a temp job as a secretary in an insurance firm. This way, she can sit most of the day in front of a computer and rest her swollen legs and feet, at least until she has the baby.

Deirdre sounds hopeful. "You never know. She might pick the insurance business for her next career. She could go far. She's got a good head on her shoulders. If she sticks with it, she could work her way up the corporate ladder. She might do that for her child."

It's not my nature to interfere in other people's business, including my family's, but I've held my tongue long enough.

"What's the harm if she continues dancing after she has the baby? She may not enjoy the insurance business. But she seems to love the troupe."

"She can't support herself by dancing. The least she could do is try something a little more ambitious for a change," Deirdre says sharply. "As if that would kill her. If she doesn't like it, fine. But why can't she for once try out a professional job? She's smart. She just doesn't apply herself."

"You're asking the wrong person. Your father and I had nothing to do with the corporate ladder and wanted nothing from it."

Deirdre frowns and strides to the window. Her profile is wrinkled in concentration, and I consider, as I have many times before, how different we are. If we were not relatives, our paths would likely never cross; we share so little in common. And yet her fierce disapproval reminds me of my own mother's.

"And ambition isn't limited to white collar professionals," I say with a brew of anger. "Dad and I worked hard our whole lives. Only we wanted to make something of ourselves on the stage, not in a corner office."

"That's different," Deirdre says softly. "Times were different then."

After she leaves, I remain in my room but switch on the recorder. It's only then I realize how low I am. Deirdre would claim it's my pills, but I know it's not. It's something deeper, more tangled. The forced jollity of the Manor sometimes makes me want to scream. I never chose to spend my final days in a Disney Land for seniors.

My situation could be far worse, I know, but somehow that thought doesn't console me. It makes me yearn all the more for those days when we shared the conviction that if we could make it through, something better would await. Here, I have no hope.

If I'm to be charitable, this place is a type of crucible, from which something new might spring if I can endure its heat. As a young girl, I didn't understand that just when you think you've been given all you can handle, something else can come along to test your strength. And at the moment when things are looking up, you can be yanked back down like a yo-yo on a child's whimsy of string, as if made to atone for the small pleasures you'd been lulled into enjoying.

CHAPTER ELEVEN

January 1933.

I zipped through the piano accompaniment for the last number of Act One of *Three Penny Opera*. It was only rehearsal, as we were a month away from opening night, but our drama teacher, Mr. Olsen, insisted each actor "play his role like this is the real deal." Standing at the foot of the stage in the South Cache High auditorium, he nodded his head in time to the music, gestured for the leads to step together before a make-believe audience.

From the corner of my eye, I watched Mae lift her head, fling out her arms, and sashay across the stage as she sang. She played the lead role of Polly Peachum, a girl who marries the rogue Mac the Knife after knowing him for just five days, despite her parents' objections. Although the kids playing the roles of Mr. and Mrs. Peachum sang with her, Mae outshone them. Her face radiated a deep pink; her voice rang like the clear clink of a spoon against the rim of a glass as she hit the high notes.

Mr. Olsen had rewritten much of the original script himself, expurgating scenes at a brothel and any unsavory references so it would meet the approval of the Principal, our parents, and any bishop or elder at the ward.

The stage was bare for rehearsal, but we had spent hours after school and on weekends preparing the set. We would use a folding cardboard table covered with an oilcloth for the banquet in the wedding scene where Polly dines with Mac and his friends, and a large wooden crate for the jail, where Mac the Knife is eventually incarcerated, awaiting his execution. For the street scenes, we settled upon a barrel and two by fours nailed together to resemble a rickety lamppost.

I loved the excitement of the plot, unlike anything else we had staged: Polly's reckless marriage to the shiftless knave, her parents' horror, Mac's arrest orchestrated by Polly's father, the unleashing of the beggars during Queen Victoria's coronation parade, the threat of the gallows as Mac struggles to raise a bribe, and at last the reversal of fortune when the Queen pardons Mac.

As we gathered our book bags after rehearsal, Mae pulled me aside. "Don't tell anyone yet, but I might have to drop out of the play."

"Whatever for?" I asked in alarm.

"I need to help Mother. We've been late on a couple of orders. Mrs. Donovan was at sixes and sevens when she didn't get hers back on time, and she only paid us half what she owed."

She didn't look at me as she spoke. I knew she was referring to the small laundry and tailoring business that Mrs. Petersen had recently set up at home. She had casually invited neighbors, friends and ward members to drop off their mending or laundry for a small fee. To wash large piles of clothes, she set a large round tub of steaming water, combined with lard and lye, on rocks beneath a box elder. One of Mae's jobs was to wring out the washed clothes by hand before pinning them to the clothesline to dry. In the evenings, when it was too dark to do laundry outdoors, she and her mother mended and tailored clothes.

"That was awful unfair of Mrs. Donovan."

I wanted to ask Mae whether it was truly necessary that she drop out of the play, but the steeliness of her mouth and her hooded eyes warned me not to press further.

I said softly, "I sure hope you won't have to drop out. I have no idea how we'd replace you. The show would be a flop."

"Don't say that. It's bad luck, and besides, it's not true. Louise is my understudy, and she would do just fine. You know, you could sing it, too, if you felt like it. You have a lovely voice."

I imagined myself in the role of Polly Peachum, singing "Pirate Jenny" and "Love Song" and even the "Jealousy Duet." A small shiver danced over my spine. Until Mae had said it, I hadn't considered singing on stage. Playing Polly, I had to concede, would be thrilling. I would deliver the role in character as a strong-willed, independent girl standing up to her parents. Where I could not sing as beautifully as Mae, I would make up in acting. It would be a chance to try on a different skin, make-believe I was someone else in utterly foreign circumstances, if only for a few hours.

"You mustn't drop out," I insisted.

Mae shrugged. "Sometimes I think I like wearing the costumes more than performing on stage."

I understood what she meant. I had started sophomore year with a dress, blouse, sweater and pair of shoes, plus a single skirt, which I had cut and resewn from an old gown of Mother's. It was an embarrassing wardrobe for a teenaged girl who wanted to stay in fashion, but Dad had warned us against spending foolishly. We knew better, anyhow. We had grown creative in reinventing new from old: a washcloth and dinner napkins from a ripped apron, penny jar from a tin can decorated with paper, pork lard instead of butter, even a dried winter squash gourd as a serving bowl.

At church we learned that Mrs. Petersen had sold her set of fine china and silverware to a newly married couple in Logan.

"It's hard to believe," Mother said later that day, as we baked a batch of bread for supper. "Verda loved that set. Cherished it, in fact. I think it was her mother's. It's probably been in the family for years. Used to be she wouldn't dream of taking in neighbors' washing, let alone part with her china. I don't rightly know what kind of trouble they've got themselves into if it's come to this."

Of course now that we had sold the piano and fine pieces of silver, nothing should have surprised Mother.

Then on Monday, Mae did the unthinkable. She not only dropped out of the musical; she dropped out of school. This we learned from Hiram.

"They're real hard up," he explained. "Mae thinks she can get a job at the movie theater in town, selling tickets. And when she's not working there, she can help her mother with the laundry and tailoring."

None of us knew what to make of this news. I wondered whether Mae would return to school in a year or two, but dared not ask. It had been a while since the Petersen brood had come to our place for supper. Not even Mrs. Petersen had visited in over a month. In retrospect, I think they felt ashamed of their troubles, or else they decided there was little need to visit, since Hiram was down at their farm so often, paying his respects to Mae and bringing news of our family. Certainly Mother, having fallen frequently into her dark spells, had not extended an invitation.

Louise took over the part of Polly Peachum in *Three Penny Opera*. Her voice was not as lilting and melodious as Mae's, nor did she put the same energy into her role. She rehearsed the songs without emotion and moved across the stage like a wooden marionette in the wedding costume that was too small for her. Although it was uncharitable of me to think it, I knew I could do better. Closing my eyes, I pictured myself sweeping into Polly Peachum's role, dropping to my knees in despair when MacHeath was arrested, spiraling into dance upon learning of his pardon.

Despite the long duration of our rehearsals, the musical had a short, single evening run for family only, not the students. Although it had been scrubbed of anything offensive, several parents complained it contained "seedy material" unworthy of a high school performance. They accused the school and drama department of promoting an immoral lesson, that dubious characters would escape judgment despite their rotten deeds. As a compromise, we were allowed our single showing, with only a handful of parents and friends in the audience. Mother and Dad did not attend.

◄ ♫♪ ►

On the first Saturday in March, we crowded around the radio in the parlor, listening to FDR's inaugural address. Mr. Wallace's enthusiasm for Roosevelt had sparked a bit of optimism in us all.

The Salt Lake City station broadcast his deep, calm voice, crackling into the parlor, as though he were sitting right there with us. He reassured us, "Practices of the unscrupulous money changers stand indicted in the court of public opinion, rejected by the hearts and minds of men…. There must be an end to a conduct in banking and in business which too often has given to a sacred trust the likeness of callous and selfish wrongdoing."

Dad cranked up the volume, and even Mother dropped her knitting and cocked an ear toward the radio.

"Farmers find no markets for their produce; the savings of many years in thousands of families are gone… Our greatest primary task is to put people to work."

FDR explained he would seek constitutional authority to take speedy action, but barring that, he would use his executive power to wage a war against the crisis, as if a foreign enemy were invading the nation.

Mr. Wallace slapped a fist against his thigh, and Wylie, sitting cross-legged on the floor, nodded and twisted his hands around his knees.

"That's what we need," Dad said. "Someone who can finally put his back into this for the little guys, not just the bankers."

Mr. Wallace smiled. "Just like I told you. He knows what this country needs."

Suddenly Hiram stormed into the parlor through the back door, breathless, his face ruddy, his hair tousled and wild, as though he had run all the way from the Petersens' farm, where he had gone for supper and visiting Mae. He hadn't even bothered to remove his coat, which was dusted in snow.

We looked at him in alarm.

"The Petersen farm will be foreclosed. The auctioneers are coming a week from Monday."

I covered my mouth, and next to me, Minnie stiffened. Mother gave a soft gasp.

"How come?" Luke blurted.

Dad frowned and shifted. "Couldn't make payments on the mortgage. I suspected this was coming. They churned through their savings already, and you can't make money off crops."

"Couldn't they have sold livestock or gotten credit?" Luke asked.

I wondered this, too, but the waves of cold that rippled down my spine and legs overrode my curiosity.

"There's only so long you can stave off the bank. They don't take kindly to requests for extending credit. I tried to loan Ole a little bit a month ago, but he wouldn't take it. And he's already sold off most of his animals."

"Where will they go?" I cried. I thought of Mae, her parents, her brothers and sisters and all their private, prized possessions, including Mrs. Petersen's antique walnut sideboard and dining table, strewn like trash in the front of their house for anyone to bid upon.

Dad looked past me, as though peering at a ghost. "Don't know, Reenie. Relatives in Idaho or Salt Lake, I reckon, until Ole finds work."

Beside me, Minnie blotted her eyes with both fists and managed to sit still, lips quivering.

"Can't we do something?" she asked.

"My word," Mother said. "All this winter they've kept to themselves. Haven't heard boo from Verda."

"Why don't we ask them to stay with us?" Hiram said.

"Aw, Hiram only wants them to stay here cause he's sweet on Mae," Luke said.

Hiram shot him a dark, glowering look, and Luke ducked his head and twiddled his thumbs.

"We can offer. But Ole's not the kind to accept charity. I suspect he'll want to move away and start over somewhere new," Dad said.

Hiram spun and stomped down the hallway. The door of the back bedroom slammed shut.

"Hiram," Mother called.

"Let him go," Dad said. "We can't fret over what's done and what can't be changed. He'll understand that. All we can do is trust in God's plan."

We bowed our heads while Dad prayed that the Petersens would be blessed by the spirit of the heavenly Father and find steady employment, peace and a bountiful table.

For many minutes later, we sat in silence until Minnie flicked on the kerosene lamp by the table. I rose and drew the curtains together. Dusk had fallen, and outside it snowed lightly.

◀ ♫♪ ▶

The next day, a Sunday, Hiram didn't say it, but I knew he was skipping church to go to the Petersen farm. I imagined he would skip school the next week, too, if he had to. Mother and Dad didn't mention his absence.

He arrived home in time for supper. I expected him to look somber, even mournful, but his face was locked grim determination, so that he almost passed for a man of Mr. Wallace's age.

During supper he said little, though it was clear he had plenty on his mind. As Minnie and I carried the dishes into the kitchen, Mr. Wallace excused himself and disappeared out back. Hiram remained at the table and cleared his throat.

"Mae and I are getting married, and there's not a thing anyone can do about it. We've made up our minds."

Mother, who had been finishing a bowl of soup, laid down her spoon and stared at him.

"We've already asked Mae's parents. They gave us their blessing."

"How do you plan to support yourselves? Where will you live?" Dad asked.

"I figured you could use an extra hand around the farm full-time. I thought we could live here for a little while at least."

"Here?" Dad repeated.

"We could turn the parlor into an extra bedroom. You said yourself we could do it. And Mae can help Mother and the girls with the chores around the house."

"You mean you'd drop out of school?"

Hiram stared at his hands. "For now. It wouldn't have to be permanent."

"If you drop out now, you might as well consider it's for good. The chances of finishing high school later, especially if you have a wife and children to support, would be darn low."

Hiram was silent. "Then all right, it would be for good."

"When you're so close to finishing!" Mother cried. But then she mused to herself, "Of course he doesn't want to let Mae go."

"You'd better be serious," Dad said. "Serious about that girl. Don't make a snap decision out of pity or guilt or something else. If you say you're going to marry her, you better understand what you're getting into."

Hiram raised his chin. "I love her, Dad. With everything I've got. Truth is, I was going to ask her to marry me after graduation. Only now it's come a little sooner. And she loves me, too. I can't think of anyone else I'd want for my wife."

"You're not even eighteen. For a lot of fellows, that's not old enough to settle down and raise a family."

Hiram met Dad's eyes without flinching. "I'll do it. I want to. And anyhow, I've made up my mind I won't lose her clear across the country where I might never see her again. I aim to stay and help you work the farm, and then after the economy turns around, get my own little bit of land someplace and raise a family with Mae."

Dad studied Hiram. "You do this. You sleep on it. Then see what you think in the morning. Things always seem clearer when it's daylight."

From the kitchen, I saw Hiram nod.

I turned to Minnie, who was drying the dishes I washed. "Seems we'll have a wedding here real soon."

CHAPTER TWELVE

July 2006.

When you're young, you're invincible, brimming with plans for the future. It doesn't seem remotely feasible that your body might one day betray you, that one by one, those things you love will slip away. The physical things, yes: dancing, running, hiking, but also the mental ones: remembering names, faces, dates, having the wherewithal to pay bills, reading books cover to cover, playing chess, piano. By the time you realize that it all goes incredibly quickly, a fleeting blip in the cosmic scale of time, it's too late.

A deep torpor has invaded my body, inviting me to steal away with it and curl up, surrender to sleep. Even walking around the Manor or bending down to pick a lost stocking from the floor sometimes produces a series of gasps, as though I can't catch my breath.

Deirdre has taken me to see Dr. Shah again, who warned in no uncertain terms that I must avoid sodium and alcohol at all costs. He seemed surprised, in fact, that I hadn't already known this, noting sternly that he must have told me on one of my previous visits. Tapping his fingers together, he advised that I must continue taking short walks, daily.

For me, the Courtyard is a perfect place for this. Before I left, his nurse gave me instructions for several simple exercises, such as stretching and marching in place to keep my symptoms at bay.

At least I am willing to listen to the doctors, though I am suspicious of the poison they prescribe; I'd prefer to take natural foods and vitamins. Harold, on the other hand, thumbed his nose at the entire medical profession, even when he was diagnosed with emphysema.

"What's the harm if I take a little smoke or a drink?" he said. "If I'm going to give up the ghost, anyway, I might as well have fun doing it."

Today I make several paces through the Courtyard, enough to get my heart pumping lightly, before settling on the bench and withdrawing my recorder and microphone from my pocketbook.

CHAPTER THIRTEEN

March 1933.

As I descended the stairs on Saturday morning, Mother hunched over the stove in her black mourning gown, which she had worn constantly in the first few months following Jeremiah's death. She stirred a pot of oatmeal mush.

"Hiram and Mae will be married next week," she said, "As soon as Dad and the boys build a door to close off the parlor. The Petersens signed the consent form we need to give the county clerk in Logan, on account of Mae's being just seventeen."

I drew in my breath. "A judge will marry them?"

"There's no time for anything else. But maybe, a year from now, they'll be sealed in the Temple."

"Will the Petersens be at the courthouse?"

Mother shook her head. "They'll leave before the auction. They're going to Idaho to stay with relatives."

As if anticipating my next question, she added, "Mae will stay in the attic with you and Minnie until the ceremony."

I thought about it. A wedding with the bride's family absent, under the most dire of affairs, no space or money for a reception afterwards, no piano for music.

"We can try to make it nice for them, can't we, Mother? Bake a cake at least?"

She continued stirring the oatmeal. "We'll make do with what we've got. Very least, we'll make Mae feel welcome."

Minnie entered the kitchen and caught my eye. I knew she was thinking the same thing. We would do more.

When we last saw the Petersens at the Paradise ward the following day, Mrs. Petersen wore a floppy cotton dress she must have sewn from an old flour sack. A man's oversized brown coat draped around her shoulders like a shawl. Although she was a tall woman, she looked stooped and diminished as she hobbled from church, clutching a soiled pocketbook against her sagging midsection. As we crowded around her, Mr. Petersen, and four of their children, she ducked her head and avoided our eyes. Calling out well wishes, we packed their Hoover wagon – the chassis of a dilapidated car hitched to a pair of mules – with pies, chicken sandwiches, potato salad, canned vegetables, rolls, tin plates and cups, and old blankets for their trip the next day.

The sun was out for the first time in a week, which seemed wrong. How could it preside over us like a bright and cheery party host when we had gathered under such depressing circumstances?

"We'll be family now," Mother told Mrs. Petersen, giving her a fierce hug. "Don't you forget that. We'll be forever united because of Hiram and Mae."

Mrs. Petersen turned her face away and hung in Mother's embrace, her arms limp and flaccid, her heavy breasts drooping. Her eyes brimmed with tears, which she attempted to chase away with an old handkerchief. After a moment, Mother stepped back and grabbed her friend's hands.

I couldn't help recall all the visits Mrs. Petersen had made to us over the years, especially in the weeks and months following Jeremiah's death, encouraging us and in particular Mother to be brave, forge ahead, have faith. Now she needed the same advice, but we didn't speak it, all of us floundering, unsure of the steps of this strange dance, uncertain how to bring comfort even as we awkwardly embraced. The Petersens' shame sat among us, unacknowledged, an unwelcome dinner guest, none of us having the heart to name it.

During the service, the Bishop had read a verse that resonated with the occasion, "Bear one another's burdens, that they may be light, ... mourn with those that mourn, yea, and comfort those that stand in need of comfort, and to stand as witnesses of God at all times and in all things, and in all places that ye may be in, even until death..."

Other members of our ward crowded forward to hug the Petersens, and a few men offered to keep the auction down as low as they could and buy back a few useful items for the family.

We waved as they rolled their wagon back home for the last time. Mr. Petersen sat next to his wife, shoulders slumped forward, eyes downcast, snapping the reins against the flanks of the old mules. When he raised his head to nod at us in parting, his wizened face, hollowed cheeks and dead eyes suggested that something essential and brave and hale within him had broken, as though he had lived his best years long ago, and was now resigned to a steady and sure decline. It was a look I grew to recognize in many other men and women during the Depression years.

Of all the Petersens, Mae alone had reason to hope; but she, too, looked solemn and scared as she climbed into the wagon and scooted next to one of her brothers, hugging her knees to her chest. She would spend one last evening with her family before they left for Idaho.

Minnie and I arranged a small bed of blankets and pillows in our room where Mae would sleep until the day of the civil ceremony. Knowing how cold it got in the attic, we gave one of our quilts to Mae, since at least we would have each other's body warmth.

Meanwhile, we helped Mother clear the parlor. The couch, together with the remaining mattress from the boys' room, would become a simple bed until we could find something more suitable for the newlyweds. We moved the pair of parlor chairs to the barn, where we would leave them until we could sell or trade them.

On Monday afternoon Hiram fetched Mae, who arrived with a small sack of belongings: one dress, in addition to the one she was wearing, one of her brothers' old coats, and a few simple toiletries.

"I don't need anything else," she assured us. "As long as I'm Hiram's wife and a sister and daughter, I have plenty." Her voice trembled.

"Don't you worry. You're family. We'll take care of you," Mother said.

That night, long after we had all gone to bed, I heard sniffles and strangled sobs from Mae's corner of the room. I held my breath, not wanting her to know I was awake. I glimpsed the white of her nightgown as she lay twisted, like a crumpled rag doll, on the bedding.

◄ ♫♪ ►

Dad, Hiram, Wylie and Mr. Wallace sawed, plastered, and painted a makeshift wall and door for the parlor. By Thursday they declared it ready, and Hiram, Mae and my parents prepared to catch the train from Hyrum to the courthouse in Logan.

In honor of the occasion, Mae wore her blue gingham dress and a dab of lipstick, and I plaited her hair into two French braids and twisted and pinned them together in a princess bun that crowned her head. For the first time since she had arrived at our house, she looked interested in what was about to happen, and her cheeks shone a healthy pink.

Because it was too expensive for all of us to go to Logan, Minnie and I stayed home from school to bake a two-tiered cake, prepare a special supper, and craft a few festive decorations: streamers made out of hair ribbons and crepe paper, and a foil-lined card we arranged in the dining room, where we would serve the cake. A handful of close friends from the ward whom Mother had invited would stop by later to join us. I longed for the piano, at least so I could play Mendelssohn's "Wedding March" to honor the occasion, or even a popular romantic tune like "Night and Day."

By late afternoon, after Wylie and Luke returned from school, we took turns peering out the window. I had swept the kitchen floor, rearranged the chairs around the dining room, frosted the cake as best I could with a handful of sugar and tablespoon of lard. Meanwhile, Minnie had assembled a bouquet of fir branches and holly berries. A frisson of anticipation surged through me, much like it had on Christmas Eves years ago.

"They're here! They're on their way!" Luke shouted from the front porch.

Minnie and I rushed out to join him, and Wylie sauntered after us. We waved at the small procession of the newlyweds and our parents as they promenaded slowly toward the house.

Mae had linked her hand in the crook of Hiram's elbow, and both smiled when they caught sight of us.

From the porch, Minnie, Wylie, Luke, and I cheered. I could wait no longer, and ran into the yard to greet them.

As I embraced Mae and kissed her cheek, she said, "Now we're sisters. I'm so glad."

I squeezed her. "Me too."

She looked lovely and elegant standing tall beside Hiram, her hair coiled in the French braid twist, a genteel smile on her lips. I noticed then she was not wearing the blue gingham dress but an ankle-length linen gown with a flared hem, puffy sleeves and lace collar in a green, blue, and pink floral pattern; and a pair of white gloves.

"You've got a new dress," I said, sucking in my breath. "It's beautiful."

"Your father bought it for me. Can you believe how kind that was? When we were in town, he said he wanted me to start my marriage with a few nice new clothes. So we stopped at the big department store on Main Street, and I tried on at least a dozen outfits. I've never felt so spoiled in my life. I'm over the moon."

She gestured to a small parcel wrapped in brown paper that Hiram held. "I still have the blue gingham, but Mr. Larsen, or should I say Dad, bought me two new dresses along with this one I'm wearing. And best of all, he bought matching wedding rings for Hiram and me." She pulled off her glove and displayed her hand to reveal a simple, thin silver band.

I tried hard to squelch the lick of envy that snaked up my belly and throat, warming my cheeks. I hadn't received a new dress in years. In fact, I had hand sewn the garments I owned. And now Dad, apparently on a whim, had bought Mae not one but three new dresses. We could ill afford such a luxury.

My face must have registered my surprise because Mae added hastily, "Of course you can borrow them whenever you want, Reenie."

Minnie pushed past me to embrace Mae, and still stunned by what Dad had done, I turned and forced myself to hug my brother, who was beaming like he hadn't in many days, his face suddenly young and hopeful and deliriously happy.

As we sat to a supper of roast chicken, potatoes and gravy and canned peas, we might have been celebrating Thanksgiving or Christmas as we hadn't in years. Around the table and the flickering candles, we smiled and dined while Hiram and Mae received our blessings.

Later, enjoying the iced wedding cake with a few friends from the ward, we made speeches in the newlyweds' honor while sipping hot cranberry apple cider spiced with cinnamon sticks. During one of the speeches, Mae's eyes welled. Hiram slung an arm around her neck, and she buried her face against his shoulder. I guessed what was wrong. Her family was not here to celebrate her wedding. She was marking what should have been the most joyous of occasions without them. While the Petersens started over from scratch, destitute, stripped of all they had acquired over the years, Mae was starting a new life in someone else's home, a well-meaning marriage that had nonetheless been assembled hastily under bleak circumstances on neither the bride's nor groom's terms.

Although I admitted to myself I still coveted the beautiful dresses that Dad had bought for Mae, my envy died as I watched her dab at her eyes, swallow, lift her head, and put on a brave smile.

For the remainder of the evening we sang songs, ate cake and sweets, told stories, and made merry. But we couldn't ignore the invisible member of our party. This silent guest sat among us like a miasma, a ghost of the missing. From time to time we paused, cocked our ears, scanning for traces. We should have heard the Petersens' laughter, touched their hands, seen their faces. Instead, the specter that usurped their places dredged up disappointment, regret, loss. Spilled each onto the table in front of us to see what we would make of it.

For every blazing candle round the table, it dared remind us of those who had no home and warmth or who might be huddled in a shantytown. For every bite of cake, we shared the knowledge that people were hungry, begging for handouts from soup kitchens. For every smile or laugh, we saw the shadow images of tearful children, downtrodden women and men in their Hoover wagons, plodding toward a frightful unknown. Even as we showered the newlyweds with well wishes at this beginning, we couldn't wipe from our minds the bitter endings, the crushed dreams of farming one's own land and supporting a family. The land and crops, homestead, livestock and fine accumulations of a lifetime all gone. The unspoken question hung in the air: Would it end well for my brother and his bride? The desperate truth is that no one is safe. Fortunes can fall as easily as they rise, lickety-split.

CHAPTER FOURTEEN

May 1933.

Mae, Minnie and I stood in a shady grove of box elders in Paradise Park, pouring cups of lemonade and arranging slices of pie, sandwiches and pickles on ceramic fruit platters for our ward's picnic luncheon. Hiram and a few other boys played baseball in the field below the clearing.

Wylie lingered nearby, showing no interest in the game. Hands stuffed in pockets, he strode back and forth between the long picnic table and a small cluster of children playing tag on the grass. Occasionally his gaze flitted to our table, resting on the three of us girls, and he continued pacing.

Mae smiled at him and called out a greeting, and he crossed over to us. Ever since the evening months ago, before the Petersens' departure, when Wylie had helped Mae with her homework, they exchanged friendly words when their paths crossed. Now that Mae and Hiram were married, though, and Mae had abandoned school, they had little time or occasion to chat.

"Want some lemonade?" Mae asked.

"Sure. That'd be swell. Why not fill up on good ole sugar water?"

"You're bad! Spoiling all the fun. Here." She handed him a paper cup, and he took a few sips, watching her.

"Why aren't you out there playing ball?" Mae said at last, sliding a plate of deviled eggs in front of him.

He reached for one, popped it in his mouth. "Got other things to think about."

"Yes?" She stood with hands on hips, saucily, her cheeks dimpling. "Like what?"

He finished swallowing the egg, continuing to gaze at Mae. "My future."

Minnie and I exchanged glances. Mae's smile faltered, and she dropped her hands to her sides.

"There goes Wylie getting all serious on us," I said. "Lighten up, for heaven sakes! We're at a picnic, not church. Don't pay him any mind, Mae. He can be a sourpuss." I made a face, and Minnie and I laughed.

Of course I was only teasing, but Wylie looked at me in annoyance.

Minnie put in, "We've all the time in the world to get serious later on. Today is supposed to be fun." And I knew Minnie and I were exactly in sync, that we both longed for a little sunshine and play after the terrible autumn and the past year.

Wylie bit his lip, as if considering saying something and thinking better of it. "Then I'll let you get back to your fun and games," he said scornfully. Casting a quick look at Mae, he sauntered away.

Mae gazed after him. When she turned to me, I shrugged. "Don't worry. He'll get over it, whatever it is."

Wylie slumped against the trunk of a tree, knees bunched, where he idly picked blades of grass and occasionally glanced in our direction or else at the boys playing baseball.

"He left his full cup of lemonade," Mae said. "I'll take it over to him at least."

She walked toward the tree, grasping the lemonade with both hands. Wylie rose quickly and took the cup from her. They moved together a few steps. He told her something, and she acknowledged it with the tilt of her head.

Twenty minutes later, the boys who had played baseball, including Hiram, idled in from the field, seeking food and drinks. I served them paper plates of sandwiches and dill pickles. When it was Hiram's turn, he asked me where Mae was.

"Over by that tree, talking with Wylie," I said, glancing behind me. But Wylie and Mae were no longer in sight.

"Talking with Wylie," Hiram repeated. "Why?" His mouth tightened.

I said nothing.

Hiram grabbed the plate from me, scanned the picnic grounds with a scowl, and headed toward the grassy field of picnic blankets. I watched as he marched to each spread, surveying its occupants with grim determination before proceeding to the next.

Sister Nygard, one of the ward ladies, urged me to fix myself something to eat. Minnie had just left with her own food and was saving a space for me at one of the cardboard tables on the lawn. As I spooned a lump of potato salad onto my paper plate, Mae appeared at my elbow, with Wylie close behind her.

"Reenie, I'm sorry for leaving you and Minnie to do all the work." She sounded out of breath.

"It wasn't work. Hiram's looking for you." I nodded toward my brother.

"Was he? We were standing near the grove of trees the whole time. I guess he couldn't see me."

I made no reply, but I worried what Hiram would say when he found her.

"Anyway, Wylie was telling me some wonderful news. You'll be so tickled when you hear it. Wylie, tell Irene. I can't understand why you haven't told anyone sooner."

Wylie gave me an uncertain smile. "I've been admitted to the BYU on scholarship."

My eyes widened. "Have you? Truly? Gee, that's marvelous!"

He grinned more broadly.

"When?"

"Just yesterday. I went to town and got the mail. The acceptance letter was in it."

I set down my plate and clapped. "This is cause to celebrate. We need to do something special. We can…"

"Not a word until I've told Mother and Dad. They need to hear it from me first."

Months ago, Wylie had confided in me that he intended to leave the farm, major in math or physics, and work for General Electric or Bell Labs, even if it meant moving away from Utah. Without the scholarship, supporting himself through school would be difficult, as there were little to no jobs for college students. He would break the news to Dad, he'd said, only if his plans aligned.

"Isn't it wonderful!" Mae cried. "And I had the privilege of being the first to know."

"You'll accept, won't you?" I said, recalling Wylie's serious mood.

"Seems like it. I'd be a fool not to."

I laughed out loud, uttered a cheer. A heaviness I hadn't known I still possessed lifted. The day swung open blue and wide, replete with possibilities. I could sprint like a colt until my legs tired, turn somersaults, or scramble up one of the tree branches and gaze, dangling, at the picnic goers.

Hiram strode toward Mae. Glowering at Wylie, he clasped Mae by the waist and drew her close. "Where'd you go?" he demanded.

"I was by the trees over there the whole time," she murmured. "Truly. Did you hear that Wylie…"

She stopped, realizing we were staring.

Hiram sneered and kicked a rock.

"Say, Hiram," Mae said, touching his arm, her voice unnaturally bright, "Your mother looks like she could use some help with that big box she just took out of the truck. It might be the ice cream."

Hiram followed her gaze, his eyes flat.

"You should give her a hand. You're the strongest man around here, after all." She giggled.

"Sure, if you can even call some of the dopes around here men," Hiram said. Snickering, he slung an arm around his bride and wandered with her toward a picnic blanket, Mother's box apparently forgotten.

Wylie watched them go, and his smile faded until he wore the pinched, serious look from earlier. He scuffed the grass with his big toe.

I touched his arm. "Don't let them bother you. They didn't mean anything by it. Come eat with Minnie and me."

Over the next few weeks, Mother brimmed with pride about Wylie's scholarship to the BYU. It was the first time in months she had grown animated, her cheeks glowing when she shared the news with the ladies of the Paradise ward and folks in town, declaring he was "one in a million," a true scholar, destined to do great things. Encouraging the spark they glimpsed of Mother's former self, the ladies offered congratulations whenever they happened to see her, remarking on Wylie's intelligence and great fortune.

Dad, however, didn't share her enthusiasm. As Wylie predicted, he was stunned that one of his sons had chosen to abandon farm life. He turned his hands slowly, shook his head as though to unscramble it.

"I can't see clear to it," he said to Hiram, who shrugged. But since Wylie had earned a full scholarship with his good grades and college admission test results, Dad didn't press his objection.

When Wylie left for Provo at the end of summer to study physics, I suspected he still carried a torch for Mae, though of course he didn't admit it. He refused to speak her name, referring gruffly to his sister-in-law as "she," "her," or as a last resort, "Hiram's wife." But his very departure, the fact he had gone through with his plans, gave me the shred of an idea that played at the back of my mind. Afterwards, whenever I pined for something to tether my hopes to, I withdrew that shard for inspection, long enough to sustain me.

CHAPTER FIFTEEN

August 1933.

"Right here. This is the perfect spot," Mae announced.

She set a black tub on one of the rocks outside the house and filled it with steaming hot water while, per her instructions, Minnie and I placed a "cold water" tub beside it. We scraped and dumped grease, pork rinds, and fat into the hot tub, dipped out the rinds, and added lye.

Although Mae no longer sold tickets at the movie theater in town, she had found another source of income by reclaiming her mother's old business. Now several of Mrs. Petersen's former customers took their laundry and mending to Mae in exchange for sugar or canned goods.

Losing no time, Mae organized us into an assembly line. After Minnie soaked each group of clothes first in the cold water, I wrung them out before plunging them into the hot water, where Mae scraped them with a board. Last we hung them onto a strung-up rope to dry overnight.

Although we wore gloves, our hands grew red, raw and swollen.

"How did you ever manage this on your own?" I asked at the end of the day, exhausted. It seemed incredible that Mae had helped with the laundry and tailoring jobs while she was at school, and I understood now why she had no choice but to drop out.

She shrugged. "You get used to it."

"You're a godsend. Truly." I wasn't kidding.

The laundry business was only one example of Mae's determination to work extra hard, perhaps to prove she was not a burden to our household. She rose earlier than anyone in the house to light the stove and make breakfast. While Minnie, Luke and I were at school from fall through early summer, she swept, scrubbed floors, washed dishes, canned the winter vegetables, mended clothes, baked bread and prepared meals – all the chores that had floundered in the months following Jeremiah's death.

The next afternoon, a few days before the summer school break ended, I crated a dozen eggs, bottled two pints of milk, gathered a bag of ripened peaches from the orchard, and set off for town, where I would trade them for sugar and a slab of pork. While there, I planned to post a few letters and collect the mail. Letters from Jacob, Wylie, and Mae's parents were prized treasures, to be read them aloud at the dinner table.

The soles of my shoes had started to wear out from these treks, and I felt the hot dirt road through the leather.

A small family in frayed clothes that hung from their bony frames also made their way toward town, likely in search of work or food. The man's face was withered, whether from sun or age it was difficult to know. He hoisted a gunnysack behind his back, and the woman and child followed. The trio turned to gaze listlessly at me as I overtook them.

Another group of transients camped along the roadside, huddling around a tent of raggedy sheets. Along the grass they had arranged a few old junky items they might have rescued from the ditch, which they tried to hock to passersby. I guessed they were what Mother and Dad would call bums, the folks who rummaged through trashcans when no one was watching in hopes of scraping together a little meal.

A man with a tangled beard, wearing a soiled work shirt, torn jeans and no shoes, parted from the group and called to me, "Hello there, Sister. Can you spare anything?"

I paused in my tracks, and his eyes roved over me and settled on my knapsack of fruit. He had sunken pockmarks in his cheeks and a wattled throat. It was difficult to gauge his age. His eyes were blue and his hair dull chestnut, uncombed and greasy, so that its natural color might have been lighter. Still I might have guessed he was somewhere in his twenties or early thirties, but his skeletal frame and the gray pallor of his skin made me decide he must have been Dad's age. Behind the blue eyes, his gaze was empty, like burned-out candles.

I hesitated and set down my knapsack. Mother had given explicit instructions to get three bags of sugar and one half pound of meat, but on the other hand, what could one peach hurt? I reached into the bag and pulled out a large peach, took a few steps toward him, and handed it over hesitantly.

He grabbed it and studied it with wonder, rotating it in the palm of his dirty hand, as though it were a pot of gold. "Bless you, Sister. May God bless you for your kindness!" A strong odor rose from his clothes, like urine mixed with feces and rotten garbage.

Smiling, I backed away. As I continued down the road, I glanced behind me. He was chomping hungrily into the peachy flesh, whose juice had squirted over his bearded lips and cheeks. I caught sight of a rotted black incisor. He didn't look up, and I hurried on to town, afraid other hoboes would approach and I would have nothing left to show Mother by the time I returned to the farm.

Later that night, the church held a potluck pie supper. Girls from the ward had baked goodies and arranged them inside sealed boxes, wrapped with ribbons, which the boys would bid upon while the auctioneer speculated about the wonderful food that might lie inside.

Although I wasn't going with anyone, three fellows I knew from church bid up the peach pie I had made. It sold for fifteen cents, and Dennis, the boy who won, shared a piece with me afterwards on a little bench outside the ward house. My cheeks grew hot while I tried in vain to come up with something to say, which instead became nervous chitchat. Dennis ate in silence, grinning at me occasionally and grunting "Huh" after I paused for breath.

I was certain that the evening had been a disaster, but before we parted ways, he asked me to go with him to town the next Thursday to watch one of the free pictures the Hyrum merchants showed twice a month to draw small crowds to the stores.

"Running out to see a picture in the middle of the week?" Mother said when I asked her. "We're up to our elbows with work. I don't see how I can spare you."

"I'll make sure to finish my chores ahead of time."

She crossed her arms and narrowed her eyes. "You seem awful intent on going with this boy clear into town, when you hardly know him from Adam."

I gazed at the floor. "He's from the ward."

"That's hardly enough to judge his character."

"He's a nice enough boy. You know his parents." Although I should have left it at that, I added, "Besides, I rarely get away from the farm. I only wanted to have a little fun the one evening."

Without warning, Mother raised a palm and walloped my face. "Fun? You want to have fun, when we're scrambling to make ends meet? When your brother and his wife have toiled without a break for weeks? My. I didn't realize I'd raised such a selfish girl who'd rather hold hands with a boy at the movies than help her family keep food on the table."

Stumbling backward, I touched my smarting cheek. My forehead felt damp, and a sickly heat washed over me. "I'm sorry, Mother. I didn't mean..."

"You'd have us treat you like a princess while your family works our fingers to the bone. What do you think, you're the only one who hasn't been away from the farm?"

"I'm sorry," I said again.

Mother shook her head.

"I never meant it like that. It came out all wrong."

"Then let that be a lesson to think before you speak."

"Yes, ma'am."

She continued to shake her head, puckering her lips.

"I'll start on dinner," I said.

Glowering, Mother untied her apron and tossed it across the table.

◀ ♫♪ ▶

At church the next day, when I explained to Dennis that Mother couldn't spare me, he shot me a skeptical look and shrugged. "Some other time, maybe."

"That would be nice," I said, but rather than returning my smile, he looked away.

Several weeks went by, and I had given up on going into town with Dennis, let alone seeing a picture. We had spent long days plucking vegetables from the garden and canning them, a hot, tiring process that left my face boiling red and sweaty, even after I knotted my hair behind my head and slipped on a thin cotton dress. Unexpectedly, one Thursday after supper Mother fished a coin out of her apron pocket and placed it in my palm.

"I know you've been wanting to see a picture. Take Minnie and go. This is for an ice cream soda afterwards."

I looked up at her. "I don't need to see a picture. I know we've got to save every last dime. Dad…"

"Never mind. It's free, after all. And an ice cream won't hurt. I expect it's been a long time since you've had a chance to enjoy yourself. You've been working hard. Go ahead. Both you and Minnie."

I closed my fingers cautiously around the coin. It glowed hot in my palm, like a tiny fleck of coal. I didn't even realize I was smiling until Mother said, "Go on now. With that grin of yours you'd think you'd found yourself in seventh heaven. You'd best fetch Minnie and start walking, or else you'll miss it altogether."

Minnie was beside herself with delight when I found her. "I don't have anything to wear! Tell me, Reenie, what should I do? I can't go looking like this!"

"Brush your hair and tie a ribbon in it, and you'll look nice," I assured her. But the rising hope that I might see Dennis made me think hard about what to wear myself. The trouble was, my only dress was worn and faded. I considered asking Mae whether I could borrow one of her dresses but thought better of it.

In the end, Minnie and I touched the backs of our ears with drops of vanilla extract and tied ribbons through our hair. By the time we had walked the two and a half miles into town, the picture was already half an hour underway.

A group of Hyrum merchants projected the film, *Forty-Second Street*, onto the back wall of the post office while people sat on spread blankets and backless plank benches and fold-out chairs. Since Minnie and I had arrived late, we squeezed together into the first available space on a bench in the back, next to portly Sister Lowery, a member of the Relief Society, and her husband.

I sat mesmerized by the tap dancing, singing and costumes: the fiery musical dance numbers, glamorous women, high kicks, trills. Minnie gripped my arm halfway through, and Sister Lowery let loose a shriek and rocked forward during a tense scene, causing the bench to tremble. Her thigh thudded against my leg.

"Wasn't Ruby Keeler marvelous?" Minnie sighed as the credits rolled. "And how that awful director forced her to perform and threatened she'd either be a live leading lady or a dead chorus girl! You know, I think I could watch it another dozen times and not grow bored."

I didn't reply, still turning the picture over in my mind. I tried to imagine myself on a stage, singing, tap dancing, pirouetting.

A local band struck up a tune from the little square across from the post office, and the older folks remained in their chairs to listen. I spotted friends from the ward, who had apparently arrived in a group. Several of the girls had paired off with boys and were holding hands, so I decided not to call out to them. Their laughter resonated from the hedges a few blocks ahead of us. I wondered how it would feel to be out with a boy, swinging hands under the moonlight and inhaling the scent of gardenias instead of chaperoning my little sister.

Minnie and I rounded the corner toward the drugstore, where Mr. Dawson served ice cream and sodas to a group of teenagers at the fountain in the back. One of the kids turned to smile and whisper something to his date, and I recognized the sharp drop of Dennis' jaw and his rust-colored hair. He stood close to a girl whom I had not seen before. She wore a blue floral dress, and her dark hair curled in a wavy bob below her chin.

I considered leaving the store before Dennis saw me, but on second thought I decided that would be cowardly and selfish, since Minnie had her heart set on sharing an ice cream soda.

Pretending I hadn't seen him, I straightened my shoulders. "So which will it be, Minnie? Chocolate, strawberry, or vanilla? You choose."

Minnie rubbed her hands together and stood on tiptoe to peer at the confections that Mr. Dawson dished out. "Ooh, strawberry, I think. Unless you want chocolate instead. Do you know it's the first time we've watched a picture *and* eaten an ice cream soda?"

"Hello, Irene," Dennis said. He had turned away from the counter, holding a silver dish of chocolate ice cream while his date walked to a table. He stopped next to us in line. His date glanced over her shoulder and dragged her eyes from Dennis to Minnie and me.

"Hi." I managed a smile.

"I'm glad your mother saw fit to spare you tonight."

I detected a hint of sarcasm in his voice and smug smile. Not knowing whether he was smirking at me, I continued smiling, though my cheeks felt hot.

"Did you like the picture?" Minnie said. "Wasn't it fantastic?"

"It was swell."

"Dennis, are you *coming*?" the girl in the blue dress called.

"See you around," Dennis said and followed the girl without a backward glance.

"I think he likes you," Minnie whispered, beaming. "He probably only wishes he could get rid of *her*."

"Sshh! Everyone will hear."

We slid into a tiny booth for two and drank the soda from a pair of straws. I peeked at Dennis, who sat across from his date, along with another couple – a boy from our ward and a girl from school. Dennis said something to the girl in the blue dress, and she leaned her head back and laughed. I took a long sip of soda.

"Do you think he's cute?" Minnie said in a stage whisper.

"Minnie! Keep your voice down."

"Sorry. I just thought…"

Minnie and I downed our sodas, or at least I did, and soon I convinced her we had better start back or else we would arrive home late.

On the way to the farm, Minnie maintained a rapid stream of conversation. "I kept thinking you'd go over to their table. Just to talk a little, you know."

When I said nothing, she changed the subject. "I had the best time! Watching a free picture starring Ruby Keeler and sharing an ice cream soda. Do you suppose Mother will let us do it again sometime? Every month or two?"

"It will be fall in another two months, and they'll have to stop showing the films outdoors."

"Then we'll have to ask her real nice if we can go again before then. In another two or three weeks? What do you think, Reenie?"

I glanced at my sister. Despite the worn soles of her shoes and the long walk back to the farm, she was practically hopping down the road, giddy with the intoxication of the evening's adventures.

"Sure. Maybe we can arrange to stay later next time."

But the way things turned out, it was the last picture either of us saw in years and the last soda we shared.

CHAPTER SIXTEEN

September 1933.

Kneeling beside Mae, I scrubbed the kitchen floor, my skirt tucked between my knees. Our conversation flitted from Marlene Dietrich and Clark Gable to the ice cream social at the ward, to my classes.

"Tell me all the latest at South Cache," Mae said, and she closed her eyes, as though sunk in a memory.

"Mr. Olsen just announced auditions for a musical revue. It's going to be songs from the 1920s shows: *Whoopee, Oh Kay, Treasure Girl,* and *Lady Be Good.*"

The parents' and school administrators' reaction to *Three Penny Opera* had made Mr. Olsen rethink the annual musical production, and he must have decided to play it safe and avoid sticky plots and wayward characters. Each song would accompany a dance number.

"You should audition for it, Reenie," Mae said without hesitation. "Try out for one of the vocal leads this time. I know you can do it."

Her suggestion surprised me. "I don't have your voice. I'm far better at accompaniment."

"You have a lovely voice. You don't give yourself credit."

"But I've never even had voice lessons."

She raised her head from the counter. "Neither have I, but I didn't let that stop me. Listen, I'll help coach you. We'll pick one or two songs and practice." Her face grew wistful, and I guessed she was remembering her roles in the school productions and missing the chance to perform.

A little frisson stirred in my chest, and I thought of all those times I had envied Mae her beauty, her encores in the spotlight. Even as I played piano from backstage, I had wondered what it might be like to perform before a crowd, hands clasped to my bosom, bedecked in a sparkling evening gown, trilling my voice in an aria.

Mae and I chose "Someone To Watch Over Me" from *Oh Kay* and "Love Me or Leave Me" from *Whoopee* as my audition songs. For the next three weeks, I practiced singing after school in the kitchen with Mae before the boys and Minnie, who was in a quilting bee at the ward, returned home. Since Mae was usually preparing supper, I stood at the edge of the kitchen near the dining room and rehearsed as she worked. She gave suggestions on the tempo, phrasing or dynamics, demonstrated how she believed a certain passage should sound, or asked me to repeat a stanza in a different way. Sometimes she suggested artistic touches – lifting my chin, keeping my elbows straight, raising my shoulders and upper spine to open my lungs.

More often than not, Mother stayed in her room in the afternoons during our practice sessions, increasingly dragged under one of her dark spells. When Dad was away on trips to work in the mill or trade cattle, as he was now, she retreated to her bedroom and shut herself in for hours, missing not only Jeremiah, I was sure, but Dad, Jacob and Wylie, all of them gone and our house filled instead with high-pitched female voices. Meanwhile, Mr. Wallace worked at the dam during daylight hours, and Hiram and Luke spent most of their spare time on outdoor chores.

A few days before the audition, Mother shuffled into the kitchen in her long dark dress and stood near my elbow in silence while I sang and Mae stirred soup on the stove.

When Mae turned from the stove, she nearly dropped the spoon into the pot. "Oh, Mrs. Larsen…Mother. I didn't see you there."

I broke off and whirled to face Mother.

"What in heaven's name are you doing?" she demanded.

"I'm practicing. Remember, I told you about auditions for the musical revue at school."

She stared at me with arms folded across her chest, eyes narrowed.

"Mae was giving me pointers."

"And you not raising a finger to help out when there's supper to make and plenty work around the house to do! What did you think, Irene? That Mae will do your chores for you? You get busy this minute. To think that while she cooked, you stood around lollygagging!" She threw me a look of disgust.

"It was my idea, Mrs. Larsen…Mother," Mae cut in. "I told Reenie I would help her practice for the auditions."

Mother frowned, as though she suspected that Mae was simply trying to save me from this bind. She shook her head at me.

"You've done enough crooning for one night, young lady. It's time to make yourself useful." She shoved a broom toward me, pointed at the floor. To Mae she said, "Go rest your feet and sit a spell. I'll make rolls to go with the stew."

Mae caught my eyes but obliged, as Mother had already elbowed her way over to the stove to stir the stew and had reached into the cupboard for the flour and bacon lard.

We worked in silence. Mother slapped and kneaded the dough into balls. "When's this try-out?" she said at last.

"Next Monday after school." I was careful not to betray any emotion.

"Well, see to it that if you get the part, you don't let it get in the way of your work around here. I won't have you running around while Mae works herself to the bone."

"Yes, ma'am. I promise I won't let it."

"And don't count your chickens before they've hatched, either," Mother added. Her voice was sour.

◀ 🎵♪ ▶

On the day of the auditions, I rose early to dress. Mae had let me borrow one of her dresses. It was a pale pink chiffon, trimmed with a satin ribbon. It was a little long, but Minnie helped me pin the hem and assured me it "fit like a dream."

I brushed my hair and twisted and pinned it into a bun, wishing Mother would let me cut it so I could wear it in a Marcel wave. My shoes were scuffed and dirty, but I had nothing else, and I hoped Mr. Olsen would focus on my voice and gestures, not my feet.

When the last class bell rang for dismissal, I hurried to the auditorium, where a group of kids had already gathered. Mr. Olsen and a helper named Bonnie, a girl in her senior year, organized us into sections: tenor, baritone and bass for the boys, soprano, mezzo-soprano and alto for the girls. After hearing my singing range, Bonnie grouped me with the mezzo-sopranos.

One by one Mr. Olsen called each boy or girl to the stage, and Bonnie played piano accompaniment. When it was my turn, Mr. Olsen pretended to do a double take.

"You, Miss Larsen? Singing? I thought you'd be tickling the ivories. See, I even had to find a replacement." He gestured at Bonnie.

I stood at stage left. The baby grand piano with its glossy keys sat behind me. On my cue, Bonnie played the opening chords of "Someone to Watch Over Me."

I sang slowly, sweetly, tilting my chin upward as Mae had advised, clasping my hands together, elbows and spine straight, shoulders back, letting the sound ring from my lungs.

To avoid being distracted by wild fears of how Mr. Olsen might judge me, I tried not to focus on his face. Instead I gazed at the imaginary audience in the empty rows and the scattered group of students in the back of the auditorium, and steadily lifted my arms at the song's finale.

When I finished, Mr. Olsen glanced at me, then scribbled intently in his notebook. At last he nodded for me to continue with my second song. "Love Me or Leave Me" was in a lower key, a bit outside my comfort range, but I threw back my shoulders and fancied myself bold and brash, a singer at a sultry jazz club.

"Love me or leave me and let me be lonely, you won't believe me, but I love you only, I'd rather be lonely than happy with somebody else."

As I left the stage and passed the other kids still waiting their turn, a few boys whistled, and Agnes and Julia pressed my hands. My palms were damp, and beads of sweat popped onto my forehead. The adrenaline whooshed from me, and I had a sinking feeling I hadn't made the cut. Mr. Olsen likely still thought of me as just the accompanist.

◀ 🎵♪ ▶

On Friday after school, Mr. Olsen posted the audition results. Minnie, whose last class was around the corner from the auditorium, broke into a run when she spied me in the hallway.

"Reenie, you won't believe it! Come see, come see!"

Clutching my books against my chest, I scrambled after her. Several kids crowded around the sheet tacked to the side of the auditorium door. Pushing through the crowd, I scanned the list of names.

"There! See!" Minnie, at my elbow, crowed in triumph. "Irene Larsen as lead singer for 'Love Me Or Leave Me,' 'Someone to Watch Over Me,' and 'Tea for Two.'"

Knees wobbling, I set down my books and clasped Minnie. Only four other girls were in the revue, and each of them had been assigned to sing one or two songs at most. That I had gotten the part for "Tea for Two" surprised me, as it was a duet, one of the centerpiece numbers from the musical *No, No, Nanette*. When I searched the list for the male vocal lead, I saw that Mr. Olsen had given the part to Thomas Jensen, a boy I knew as Tommy, also a junior at South Cache.

Minnie pulled me away from the crowd and hopped up and down. "You're going to be on stage in the spotlight, Reenie! I can't wait! I'll watch you from the front row."

When I told her my news, Mae clapped her hands. "I knew you'd get the part!"

"Thanks to you. I couldn't have done it without your help."

We were standing in the kitchen, and she turned away to gaze out the window, her face suddenly grown somber. Then she smiled and shook her head as if to rouse herself from a reverie. "You'll be marvelous. I'll help you anytime you need it."

Mother was not impressed. Without lifting her head from the peas she was shelling, she reminded me of my promise. "Don't leave your sister and Mae to do your bidding while you prance around on stage."

I hadn't expected her to be glad I got the part, but her words still stung.

CHAPTER SEVENTEEN

October 1933.

After school rehearsals began immediately. Most of the songs were not choreographed, but for "Tea for Two," Mr. Olsen directed Tommy and me to face each other on two stools on stage, step toward each other and grasp hands, and perform a little twist-apart dance as we sang.

Embarrassed, I stared into Tommy's eyes and gripped his hands, all the while smiling broadly, per Mr. Olsen's instructions.

Tommy must have sensed my discomfort because he winked and widened his eyes, trying to make a joke of it, until both of us were laughing and Mr. Olsen barked at us to start over. This only made us laugh harder.

After several attempts that ended in giggles, Mr. Olsen warned if we couldn't control ourselves, he would separate us and give the part to "kids who know how to be serious." This threat did the trick; we trained ourselves to stare into each other's eyes, smiling and singing, all the while knowing the other was secretly laughing at the silliness.

Backstage, out of earshot of Mr. Olsen, we collapsed into laughter. A wink from Tommy or a glint of mischief in his eyes sent me into giggles, which I desperately tried to smother. As we waited offstage for our next turn, he sang warped versions of the lyrics to me:

"I'm unrestricted now that I've been evicted. They even disconnected my phone. Without living spaces, I'm off to the races. This boxcar feels cold and alone."

On the evening before opening night, I tried on one of the costumes that had been donated to the school's drama department, a full length dark blue taffeta dress with a sequined bodice and long matching gloves. It was a gorgeous evening gown that hugged my hips and waist and tapered down my legs, and I had long since decided I would wear it for the revue. Since it was a little too long, I brought it home to hem and adjust the shoulder straps.

Minnie helped me pin the straps and hem, and I sewed tiny, careful stitches around the hem.

"All you need now is a necklace to wear with it," she declared.

Mother kept costume jewelry of pearls and rhinestones in her bedroom bureau. She had worn these pieces in the early days of her marriage when she and Dad attended dances in town.

"Maybe Mother will let me borrow one of her rhinestone chokers."

"She's gone to a meeting at the ward," Minnie reminded me.

Dad was still away on his trip trading cattle, and Mae and Hiram had retired early to their room for the evening.

"Why don't you get it, just to try on?" Minnie suggested.

I hesitated, then nodded. Shuffling down the stairs in the taffeta gown, I slipped into Mother's room and searched her bureau, feeling like a thief.

I found the necklace, a large blue stone dotted with rhinestones, tucked away in her top drawer. Even in the dim gas light, it sparkled in my palm.

I knew I should stop and leave it where I had found it, but instead I hurried out of the room and back upstairs to the attic with the chain dangling from my hand. Feeling apprehensive, I allowed Minnie to fasten it around my neck.

She stepped back to appraise the effect. "Ooh, Reenie! It goes perfectly with your gown! Here."

She thrust the mirror into my hands, and I admired the glittery jewels around my throat, which matched the color of my dress. Wearing the gown and necklace with my hair done up and a dab of lipstick on my mouth, I looked like someone older I had yet to become, a glamorous screen actress or a dancer a la Ginger Rogers.

The next morning, waking early, I wrapped both gown and necklace in brown grocery paper. We were required to meet backstage immediately after school, so I wouldn't have time to return home before the performance that evening. Mother was still closeted in her room when I left for school, so I reasoned that I would simply explain to her when I next saw her about why I had borrowed the necklace without asking her permission.

As the day wore on, I couldn't concentrate on my classes; I kept watching the clock, waiting for the minute hand to slither around until it was time for dismissal.

Mr. Friedrick, my geography teacher, noticed my distraction and scolded me before the class. "Daydreaming, Miss Larsen? That won't help the time go any faster, you know, and it will only put you behind in your lesson."

I blushed, but couldn't stop glancing at the clock.

When the last bell rang, I hurried past the auditorium to the girls' dressing room, where my outfit hung from a clothes rack. With care, I stepped into the gown, and Bonnie, who was backstage helping with last minute preparations, zipped it for me. I wore a slim pair of black heels, one size too big, that had also been donated to the drama department.

Bonnie clasped the necklace around my throat, scrutinized me, and declared I looked "like a fancy New York lady." She handed out dried fruits and nuts provided by the school and paper cups to fill with water from the fountain. It was best we not eat a big meal beforehand, Mr. Olsen had warned, as it might make our stomachs queasy.

Half an hour before the performance was to begin, we lined up backstage to wait our turns. Tommy spied me before I saw him. When he called my name and I turned, his eyes widened as he took in my gown, shoes, hair and necklace. He needn't have said anything; I guessed his thoughts as clearly as if he had told me I looked stunning. Nonetheless, he made a low whistle. My cheeks reddened, and my stomach dipped as my pulse quickened. Tommy wore a dark suit, hat and shoes.

I longed to peek behind the curtain to see who might be in the audience, since Bonnie had reported that people had begun to file in. "It's gonna be a full house," she predicted.

Minnie had promised to watch the first performance; and Mae had told me she might try to go, too, even if Hiram couldn't make it. Mother hadn't said she would attend, and I knew I shouldn't get my hopes up that she would.

As I waited my turn to sing "Someone to Watch Over Me," to be followed immediately by "Love Me or Leave Me," my heart flapped so loudly against my ribs, like a wild bird slamming against a cage, that I was sure that Bonnie, Tommy, and the other kids could hear it.

"Break a leg," Tommy whispered as Bonnie beckoned me on stage.

Lights flooded my face, preventing me from seeing the people in the auditorium. I could only make out rows of dark heads. A cough punctuated the hush. Now that I was standing before a live audience instead of concealed behind the baby grand piano, I felt strong and sure, like I could do anything.

As I began to sing, I pictured Minnie in the first row, and my voice grew louder. I didn't have to remind myself to smile. It was really happening; I was front and center, no longer the accompanist, but the focus of hundreds of eyes. A euphoria overcame me, an exhilaration about sharing something special and true from deep within me with dozens of people. When I sang the last note of the score and lifted my arms, the applause from the audience sent chills down my spine.

Tommy winked when I returned back stage. "You sounded swell."

"Tea for Two," the duet with Tommy, was my next scheduled act, and as I waited in the wings, my pulse and breathing gradually calmed. Tommy, however, had begun pacing back and forth backstage, until Bonnie instructed him to sit down and be still.

"When we go on stage, pretend we're rehearsing with no one else around," I whispered. "It'll be fine."

Grinning, he panned, "Picture you upon my knee, just you and me. Oh what glee. Say, call it a scam, and everyone will scram away, dear. Nobody near us to see us or hear us. Just me for you and you for me. That's the way I'd like for it to be."

Something about the way he looked at me made the heat rise to my cheeks even as I stifled a giggle, then Bonnie hissed at us to take our places.

As the curtain rose, we perched on the two stools on stage, smiling at each other, then gazing at the dark sea of faceless people.

As Tommy sang, "I'm discontented with homes that I've rented," I beamed at him, my face full of "adoration," per Mr. Olsen's directions, and tapped my knee. At the refrain "Picture you upon my knee," I rose and walked toward him, and at "Just for two and two for tea," my voice joined his as we simultaneously linked hands and looked into each other's eyes.

His forehead was dotted with perspiration, and his palms clammy, but he squeezed my hands and I gave his a short squeeze back.

At the next stanza, we dropped one hand each and swung ninety degrees so that we faced the audience, where we danced the simple routine that Mr. Olsen had choreographed. Tommy twirled me as I sang, "Day will break and I will wake and start to bake a sugar cake..."

While he sang, "We will raise a family," I clasped my hands and gazed at him.

At last we joined hands again and ended with the final stanza.

When the piano fell silent, we stood beaming, arms raised above our heads. The audience erupted into applause, and several people cheered while the curtain descended.

Now was our cue to scurry backstage so the next singers could take their places, but instead Tommy grabbed my shoulders and kissed me on the lips, shocking both of us. My stomach plunged, and I gaped at him.

"Off!" Bonnie hissed. "Now!"

As we disappeared behind stage, Tommy whispered, "I couldn't help myself. You looked so beautiful."

My face flushed, and I still felt the warmth of Tommy's lips against mine. Involuntarily, I tingled at the pleasure of it. Back in the girls' dressing room, I reapplied my lipstick, and adjusted Mother's choker so that it didn't hang lopsided.

Three more numbers followed, and Bonnie ushered Tommy on stage for the final number of the revue, "S'Wonderful."

When Mr. Olsen finally turned the house lights up, all of us took our places on stage for the final curtsy and bow.

I glimpsed Minnie in the front row, clapping and waving. The curtain fell, and Mr. Olsen roared, "Bravo!"

Backstage we embraced and congratulated each other.

When Tommy approached me, my stomach lurched, and butterflies quivered from my hips to my chest.

"I'll walk you home," he said.

"My sister's here. We're going home together. But thank you."

"Then tomorrow night?" Our show was to run three nights in a row.

I nodded, smiling, and his eyes lit up.

Minnie waited for me in the girls' dressing room as I shimmied out of the dress, hung it on the wardrobe rack, and pulled on my skirt and old shoes.

"Mae and Mother couldn't make it," Minnie said as we headed toward the farm. "Hiram couldn't get away, so Mae stayed with him. And Mother said she was too busy canning."

I nodded, not surprised.

"Reenie, you looked so glamorous up there! Like Ruby Keeler. Your voice sounded like a star's. And you and Tommy were perfect together singing Tea for Two."

I was glad it was dark, else Minnie would have seen me blush.

"He asked to walk me home."

"Gee, he has a crush on you. I knew it! Are you going to let him?"

"Maybe tomorrow night."

"Ooh, Reenie. You've got a beau!"

After a while we fell silent, both gazing at the floating sea of winking stars, and I let my mind turn over the evening: the kick of singing onstage in the shimmery gown, Tommy's kiss, the finale.

When we reached the house, I saw a light in the kitchen window, and realized that Mother was still awake.

Hushed, tense voices reverberated from Hiram's and Mae's room in the closed off parlor. Down the hallway came snores from the room that Mr. Wallace and Luke shared. Minnie and I crept to the edge of the kitchen.

Mother stood over the sink peeling, paring, slicing and dropping apples into the quart pot on the stove, which she had begun to boil into sauce. Unable to contain herself, Minnie rushed in to tell Mother about my performance.

I hung behind as Minnie described the musical numbers.

Mother nodded and smiled. I waited for her to say something congratulatory or to ask for details that might help her visualize what she hadn't been present to see. At last she turned to look at me. She took in my lipstick and the blush on my cheeks, then her gaze settled on my throat.

Her eyes narrowed. "Irene Larsen, what's that around your neck?"

My hands flew to my throat, and I realized with horror that I had forgotten to remove Mother's rhinestone choker.

"I needed a necklace for my costume, and you'd gone to a meeting last night at the ward house." My voice trembled.

"And you went into my room without permission and took it?" Mother broke in.

My mind went numb. I opened my mouth but couldn't form the words.

Mother stepped toward me, palm out.

"I'm sorry," I whispered. "I know it was wrong. I needed a necklace and I didn't know what else to do."

"You don't need a necklace anymore than you need chocolate cake," Mother said, her face wrinkled in fury. "You should have asked my permission. I won't let any child of mine turn into a sneaking thief. I should belt you for this."

"I meant to ask just as soon as I saw you. But you were in your room this morning, and I didn't want to disturb you. I'm sorry." I fumbled to unclasp the hook and handed it to her.

Her fingers closed on the choker, and she stuffed it into her apron pocket. "But you took it without my permission, anyway, knowing it was wrong." She reached for the broom.

"Mother, it was as much my fault as Reenie's. I asked her to try it on," Minnie interjected.

Mother waved her hand, shooing Minnie out of her way, and advanced toward me with the broom handle.

The first blow landed against my flanks. The next thwack thudded between my shoulders. Pain leaped like firecrackers up my spine. I sank to the floor on all fours and instinctively shielded my head with my hands. Mother smacked the handle squarely against my buttocks.

I let loose a moan. Minnie must have fled the room, because footsteps scrambled up the attic stairs. Mother cracked the broom handle repeatedly against my haunches, drumming it into my flesh, and a sharp, yelping sting spread across my backside. Like a dog crouching as it was beaten, I whimpered. Mucus gushed from my nose. The parlor door creaked open.

"Mother?" Mae's voice came questioningly. "Is everything..."

Mother slammed the broom back behind the stove. "Get up, Irene," she said, sounding resentful and weary.

I heaved to my feet, my face hot and streaked with tears, despite my resolve not to cry. Wishing desperately to be gone, anywhere else, I swiveled toward the stairs. Out of my peripheral vision, I spied Mae in her nightgown behind the crack of her door, but I dared not meet her eyes. Shielding my face with an arm, I stumbled to the attic like a banished pet fallen out of favor, a nobody.

Shaking, weeping silently, I crawled into bed. Minnie whispered something, but I hadn't the energy to carry on a conversation. She touched my head, gently. I might have cried longer, but sleep overtook me, mercifully.

When I awoke, my back throbbed. Like an elderly woman, I rose from bed, hoisting one foot heavily after the other onto the floor. Steering myself to the basin on the dresser, I doused my face with water. Minnie lifted my nightgown and inspected for bruises.

"You've got a reddish mark on the left side. Not a big one. Here. Let me." She reached for the damp washcloth, gingerly patted it against my back, then rubbed a little ointment we saved for cuts and insect bites.

For a replacement necklace, Minnie suggested we hook a round piece of lace doily onto a hair ribbon and tie it around my throat.

"The audience won't know the difference," she claimed.

But I shook my head. I would rather go without.

As I walked to school, I didn't allow myself to take pleasure in recalling last night's musical revue, singing under the hot stage lights, Tommy's surprise kiss, or even the possibility of his walking me home after the show.

Instead, what I couldn't shake loose from my mind was Mother's absence from any of my performances, the beating, and the severe look she gave me as I left the house. I understood the meaning behind that look, which was an accumulation of all the disappointments I had cost her over the years. The musicals were dalliances, the markings of a silly, selfish girl, when what she needed were strong, steady hands and sensible leanings, like Mae's.

CHAPTER EIGHTEEN

July 2006.

In the community area with the faux leather sofas and card tables where the staff assembles us to play games or watch movies, the ladies are abuzz with gossip.

"Have you heard about Loretta Lowe?" Marcie asks.

Candy and I shake our heads, but Midge and Bea nod, bursting with the knowledge of something bad, I suspect.

"What is it?" I ask with a quiver of impatience.

"They took her to the nursing wing," Midge stage whispers, "Kicking and screaming and swearing and lashing out, even slapping whoever's in her way."

"They had to restrain her," adds Marcie. "She doesn't know who she is anymore, the alzheimer's so bad. She doesn't even recognize her husband."

This doesn't surprise me, as Loretta has been on a rockier decline than any of us, ever since her husband placed her into assisted care, shortly after I arrived at the Golden Manor. It was a matter of time before she made the transition to the nursing wing.

"She hasn't got much longer," Bea remarks. "By the looks of it, she might only have weeks, if not days."

"It's a wonder she made it this far," I say. "How did they expect her to make a go of it in assisted living with her memory problems?"

We look at each other uneasily, just as Doris approaches our table with a broad grin.

"Hi, ladies. Who wants to play Bingo?"

And wouldn't you know, my friends follow her dutifully to the card table. I, on the other hand, turn on my heels and retreat to the courtyard.

CHAPTER NINETEEN

January 1934.

Not long after Christmas, his job on the dam ended, and Mr. Wallace secured a post in Milford, building a road with the Civilian Conservation Corps (CCC). In exchange, he'd receive food, shelter, clothing, and thirty dollars each month.

"FDR's getting this country back on the right track," he declared. His face shone like a boy's at a carnival.

Before his departure for the train, he trotted across the room to grip my brothers' hands and embrace Mother, Minnie, Mae, and me. "You can bet your bottom dollar FDR will lick this thing," he assured us.

After sending most of his earnings back home to his folks and paying Mother for his room and board with the remainder, Mr. Wallace had little money for his fare, so Mother loaned him a dollar, which he promised to pay back once he had gotten settled and begun working.

After he left, Mother hummed, smiling. "He might have left us shorthanded, but this is cause for optimism. Those boys have a chance to pull themselves up by their own bootstraps."

Because Dad was away so often during the winter at the wool mill north of Logan, Mother advertised in Hyrum for another boarder who would "help with farm chores and pay a small rent in exchange for room and meals."

"Sure you'll be able to help me tell the hardworking fellows from the drifters once they come calling," she told Hiram. "I don't want a lazy bones around here. Last thing we need."

Hiram and Mae exchanged glances.

When after a few weeks she received no responses to her ad, she decided to circulate wider, asking Hiram to go to Logan and tack up signs around the train station and post office and at the Logan ward.

One Saturday morning in early February, I stayed indoors with Mae and Minnie to do the weekly chores for Mother: wiping the kitchen counters, sweeping and mopping the kitchen and dining room floors, and beginning the week's load of laundry. Mae still conducted her tailoring business, but her customers had dwindled, and mainly she supervised our family's laundry and mended clothes that her customers brought to her to salvage. Mother knitted at the dining table.

I hoped to see Tommy that evening, as he had asked to take me to a dance at the Elite Dance hall in Hyrum. When I told Mother, her face darkened.

"By the grace of God, you won't step out that door with any boy until you've finished everything you need to do around here. And that doesn't mean rushing willy-nilly or letting Mae or Minnie take over. You take your time and do it real well. I'll be checking up, so don't think you can pull the wool over my eyes. I know your tricks, and I won't take any of your guff."

Her words bit into me with their usual speed, as though I were a child whose face had been roundly smacked. But the thought of going to the dance with Tommy eclipsed her reprimand, and I bent my head and scrubbed the floor. It was a small mercy I could let my mind wander, and I imagined my fingers racing across piano keys, playing a Brahms rhapsody.

After we had taken a break to eat a quick dinner of milk and bread with jam, several sharp raps rattled the front door.

Mother rose from the table, patting down her skirts, and opened the door a few inches. I followed her, wondering whether it could be Tommy.

A man in a slouch hat, dirty overalls, and frayed overcoat stood on the front porch. His face was craggy and rough, his hands like big swollen paws with dirty, broken nails. A bluish vein pulsed at his left temple. Greasy gray hackles speckled his hair, and I guessed he was older than Dad, possibly in his late forties or fifties. Whiskers grazed his cheeks, chin, and scruffy jowls. When he saw Mother, he removed his hat and held it in both hands. He towered over her.

"Ma'am. Mrs. Larsen, is it?"

Mother nodded.

"I seen your advertisement about the room and board for farm work. Fellow up at the post office said you was still looking for someone. Is that so?"

A pause. "Yes. For the right person."

"Then I hope that'll be me. Name's John Tanner. I'm a mighty hard worker. Can do jest about anything. Arms made of steel."

Tilting her head at me over her shoulder, Mother said, "Irene, go run fetch Hiram."

"I'll get him," Mae said. Shoving on her coat, she pushed out the back.

Mother held the door open to the man and nodded. "Come in."

He stopped in the doorframe and gazed unabashedly about him. I caught a whiff of dank sweat and a musty, cave-like odor. His boots were scuffed and muddy, and my first thought was that I would have to sweep and scrub the floor all over again.

Mother pointed to a chair at the dining table, and he scraped it back against the floor and heaved himself into it. The chair legs groaned.

"Are you from nearby, Mr. Tanner?" Mother asked, taking the chair across from him. She considered him with pursed lips, hands folded in front of her, an expression I had seen her use when inspecting potatoes for mold.

"Most recent Logan. Fellow there showed me your ad."

"Were you working in Logan?"

"I'm an honest man, Mrs. Larsen, and I ain't going to lie. It's tough out there. A fellow does what he has to. I'm looking to make myself useful. I'm a jack all trades. Done all kinds a jobs: herding cattle on ranches, threshing, painting barns and houses, and a little bit a carpentry."

"I see. Where were you before Logan?"

He gave a short grunt that may have been intended as a guffaw and propped his elbows onto the table. "Been all over. Grew up in Montana, worked on farms in Nebraska and as far east as Ohio, and did some ranching in Colorado and Wyoming. Even been down to New Mexico."

His eyes roved around the room, taking in the oilcloth and the candlesticks on the table, the potbellied stove, the radio, the painting of wildflowers hanging above the dining table, and snatching glances at Minnie and me.

Footsteps clattered through the back door, and Hiram appeared in his overcoat, with Mae behind him, bringing with them a blast of cold air.

Mother's face relaxed in relief. "This is my son Hiram. He'll speak with you, too."

Hiram nodded, his face still ruddy from the raw wind and cold.

Mr. Tanner lumbered to his feet and stretched out a paw. "Pleased to meet you."

Mother cut her eyes at me and gestured for me to come over. In a stage whisper, she rasped, "No need to stand around gawking. You and Minnie go on up to the attic till we're done here. Or else go outside and check on Luke and see if he needs a bite to eat."

Minnie and I scrambled to the attic, preferring to stay warm and chat unencumbered, as we hadn't had time to do recently.

Mr. Tanner may have stayed thirty or forty minutes, because within an hour Mother called us down to resume our chores and sweep and scrub the floor where he had left his muddy prints.

We learned from Mae that Mother and Hiram had decided to take him in. We needed someone, and it looked as though Mr. Tanner might be the only candidate. He wasn't a Mormon, but according to Mae,

Mother had made him give his solemn promise that he wouldn't bring liquor or smokes anywhere on the farm. And he had assured her he understood that there would be no coffee or tea at any meal. Mother had told him to return with his things on Monday. Apparently he had little more than the clothes on his back. Mae openly wondered where he had been living, and I guessed one of the shantytowns near the train station.

"He thought I was Hiram's sister," she confessed. "You should have seen his face when he learned I was his wife." She gave a little shudder of revulsion, but laughed and pretended to shrug it off.

Mother must have had her doubts about Mr. Tanner, too, because at supper, she said to Hiram, "Not a soul to recommend him. We're taking a leap of faith."

Hiram lifted his head from his plate and waved a hand. "If he doesn't work out, we'll send him on his way. Simple as that."

When Luke learned that he would soon share his room with another boarder, he wrinkled his nose. "Long as he doesn't snore or stink."

We all laughed.

That evening I escaped with Tommy to the dance in town, and I scarcely gave the farm work or Mr. Tanner another thought. I had nothing to wear but my old skirt and sweater, but Tommy whirled me around until I was hopelessly ablaze with the joy of being free and out with my beau. The band instruments glittered and winked in the dim lights. The hall hummed with swing music. Heels smacked against the scuffed wood floor as the room swayed in tempo with the wail of the saxophone and the pounding of feet. Tommy spun me out, taking care to avoid the crush of legs and shoulders. We danced for two hours until, flushed and damp, we limped off to the side. Squeezed together elbow to elbow, with Tommy's arm circling my waist, we sipped fruit punch from paper cups.

I had almost forgotten about the new boarder, until I returned home from school after a musical revue audition on Monday and saw Hiram walking

Mr. Tanner through the fields. Their heads were bent, Mr. Tanner trailing after Hiram, who pointed to the furrows at their feet.

Mr. Tanner joined us at supper that evening. He chewed noisily, slurping his food and not bothering to wipe the gravy from his whiskers. As he raised a glass of water to his lips and glugged it, I saw a sludge of dried dirt on the back of his hand. He had not changed his overalls, and a stale odor of sweat clung to him. I wondered whether he had anything else to wear. Hiram talked to him about the farm – haying, threshing, repairing portions of the fence.

"That's all right. I can do her myself," he said. "Won't take me but an hour to shore up that fence."

Hiram raised an eyebrow.

"I done the same thing on a ranch in Wyoming," Mr. Tanner persisted.

"Have at it, then," Hiram said. "Soon as it's done we can give the cows a little more space to roam."

Mr. Tanner must have forgotten about the fence, because a day or two went by and Hiram had to remind him that it still required the repairs he had promised. For the next several weeks, the fence become a sore spot between the two of them. Hiram brought up the subject, and Mr. Tanner dodged it with one excuse after another: the unexpected snowfall, the work he had to finish first on the barn, the tilling. Inevitably it ended with Hiram saying he would do it himself, and Mr. Tanner protesting no, it was his responsibility, he would take care of her, truly he would.

◄ ♫♪ ►

At school I was busy with rehearsals for our spring musical revue, where I was to sing "Smoke Gets In your Eyes." Mr. Olsen had selected Tommy to sing "A Hundred Years from Today" in the same show. Along with rehearsing, I was to help decorate the set's backdrops by stenciling in a sidewalk, flowers and trees and painstakingly painting the scene with pastel watercolors.

One afternoon when I returned home after rehearsal, I saw Mr. Tanner slumped against the side of the barn, in the lee of the eave. One hand was stuffed in the pocket of his old coat, and the heels of his boots had sunk so low they appeared rooted in the ground. His hat shaded his eyes. He didn't see me, and I paused on the back stoop, unused to seeing him so still, as though he were lost in thought.

I turned the knob and opened the door a crack, preparing to enter the house through the back, when I noticed he was drawing something from his pocket to his lips. I stood at the door, my hand on the knob, waiting to see what it was, what he would do next. Again the rapid movement – hand, mouth, down. A backward tilt of his head.

Mother's voice rang out, high and scolding, "Reenie, come in and close that door, for Pete's sake, before the whole house goes cold."

Mr. Tanner's head swiveled toward the back stoop, and I quickly entered the house and closed the door. His stillness out there and furtive movements, as though he were concealing something or shirking his duties, worried me. Did he have a flask of whiskey? Moonshine? I considered telling Mother but thought better of it. If any suspicion that he was drinking took hold in her mind, she might force a showdown, demand to know what he had been doing. And if he had simply been taking an innocent break and gathering his thoughts, as everyone was entitled to do, then it would come out that I had been his accuser. False accuser. Better to keep it to myself for now and see whether any other evidence presented itself.

At supper we passed around platters of baked chicken, peas and bread. Mr. Tanner was in a jovial mood, talking about the work he had completed on the barn rafters and the tilling out in the fields, but Hiram set his jaw and avoided his eyes. I suspected the fence remained unrepaired, and Hiram was sore that Mr. Tanner had brought up these other topics to distract from the original work he had promised.

Evidently tiring of Mr. Tanner's one-ended conversation, Mother turned to me. "I'm going into town tomorrow afternoon for a meeting at the ward. Mae's coming with me. I want you and Minnie to come home direct after school so you can start on supper. We might not be back till after seven, so you'll need to get things ready."

I nodded.

"And mind you come straight home instead of staying for any rehearsals. You spend enough time at school as it is when you're needed on the farm."

The next afternoon, remembering my promise to Mother, I stopped by the auditorium long enough to let Mr. Olsen know I couldn't stay for rehearsal that day. As Minnie and I trudged home, the light was already fading. The raw cold smacked against our faces as we walked, though we were wrapped in coats, hats and scarves.

At the back stoop, Minnie stopped to stamp her shoes and scrape the caked dirt from the soles. I pushed ahead through the door and made for the kitchen, planning to light the stove, when I heard a movement toward the back of the house. I peered down the hallway. A floorboard creaked, and I caught my breath.

A figure loomed in the doorway of the room that Luke and Mr. Tanner shared. I stood still, half expecting to see a specter, my heart thrumming madly. Then Mr. Tanner's face emerged from the shadows, and next his bulky frame and legs as he fumbled down the hall. He nodded when he saw me, as though we were two acquaintances in a park.

I rummaged through possible answers to the riddle of why he would be here when he was expected out in the fields. Using the privy? Taking a rest? Getting a drink of water? But no, he could have done all of those things outdoors.

I must have continued to stare at him, because he remarked, "Needed to find something. Looked all over like a son of a gun."

He didn't say what it was he was trying to find and I didn't ask, because the way he said "son of a gun" jarred me, as though he had spat out a dirty word. As he passed, I caught a whiff of something pungent, like a medicine tincture, or stronger. Much stronger.

I stared at him as he retreated into the fields. Minnie pushed through the door into the kitchen.

"Say, what was Mr. Tanner doing?" she asked, but I shook my head.

We had no time to speculate, anyway, as we had to make supper. Although we waited until half past six to begin eating, we remained a small group that evening around the table: Hiram, Mr. Tanner, Luke, Minnie, and I. The conversation stalled. First I, then Minnie, would take up a subject or pose a question, but Luke and the men made little or no responses. After several failed attempts, we let the topic fade and ate in silence. Just as he had on previous evenings of late, Hiram made a point of ignoring Mr. Tanner and avoiding eye contact with him, even when Mr. Tanner asked for us to pass more peas or bread. Hiram kept his head lowered, his mouth grim, eyes narrowed.

I scooped the leftover baked chicken, canned peas, and bread into a covered casserole dish and left it inside the oven for Mother and Mae to eat once they returned.

The following morning, I woke to Mother's shouts. As the haze from my mind cleared and I shook loose the fragments of a dream, I lay motionless beneath the covers, frozen with dread. From downstairs came commotion: pots banging; drawers opening; Mother hurling questions one atop another –her voice laced in fury; Luke answering in short phrases that I couldn't make out; and Hiram cutting in. Beside me, Minnie slept. Peering at the bureau, I could barely read the hands on the clock. It was a little before five, just before I normally awoke.

Mother roared "sneak," her voice echoing all the way upstairs, and I scrambled out of bed and dressed as fast as I could manage. I didn't bother running a brush through my hair or washing my face but instead navigated down the stairs. Lightheaded with alarm, I gripped the banister to avoid pitching forward.

Mother stood in the middle of the kitchen, hands on hips, glaring at Luke and Hiram, who sat at the table. Luke, still in pajamas, rubbed a fist against his eyes. Mae hovered at the stove, preparing oatmeal and toast.

They looked at me as I descended.

"What's happened?" I asked, alarmed.

For a moment no one spoke.

"That grifter has left with all my jewelry and the rest of the silver," Mother said, her voice hard and withering. "Took a couple loaves of bread and half a dozen cans of peas and peaches, too. Went in the middle of the night. Just up and left."

My shoulders trembled. The stairs creaked, and Minnie stumbled down in her nightgown and stopped on the bottom step, hugging her ribs.

"Mr. Tanner?" I said, the first thing that came out of my mouth.

"Who else?" Mother snapped. "Of course. Mr. Tanner. Assuming that's even his real name."

I chewed my lip, recalling the incident yesterday when he had emerged from his room. He must have been hiding Mother's jewelry among his things when I saw him. "Did he break into Dad's safe?"

"No, thank heaven. He may've tried, but your father nailed it to the floor beneath our bed, and of course he didn't have the key. I wear it around my neck always." Mother patted the chain that hung around her throat.

"And what a mercy," Mae said.

Minnie began to cry.

"Joke's on him," Hiram said. "Mother's pieces are costume jewelry."

Mother turned on him. "Not my sapphire ring. The one your father gave me when we were first married. That's gone. Absolutely gone."

The story came out in bits. Mother had entered the kitchen at a quarter till five to start breakfast and noticed immediately that the drawer of the cupboard was yanked open and its contents in disarray; and the loaves of bread we kept wrapped in clean dishcloths on the counter were missing. She peered into the room that Luke shared with Mr. Tanner and saw Mr. Tanner's empty bed.

At that point she roused Luke, Hiram and Mae and began searching for other missing items. Mr. Tanner must have taken advantage of Mother's and Mae's excursion into town the day before to raid their bedrooms of any small, valuable things and stow them in his knapsack. The only ones he found were in Mother's room, as Mae, Minnie and I had nothing of value. He then left in the middle of the night, taking care not to wake Luke, and likely nabbing anything he could stuff in his pockets and knapsack on his way out the door: bread, canned food, and our only remaining silver spoons and knives.

The thought of this con man sneaking through our bedrooms made the hair stand up on my arms. Hiram would notify the town sheriff at first light, though we didn't hold out hope that he would find Mr. Tanner. He must have been long gone, likely hopping the rails for another anonymous town in another state under another alias where he could employ the same trick.

"He wasn't worth two pennies rubbed together," Hiram said bitterly. "All talk and little work. Never did repair that fence, and he liked to spend a lot of time by the barn doing God knows what. I was going to send that knucklehead packing if he didn't up and leave first."

I stayed silent about my suspicion that Mr. Tanner had been drinking, not wanting to provoke Mother, who was already beside herself, questioning all of us about what we had seen or heard of the man and his shady activities.

Dad returned home from the wool mill immediately after Mother sent him word about what had happened. Arms crossed over his chest, he declared we wouldn't take in another boarder, no ifs, ands or buts. Jacob would help pick up the slack after he returned from his mission. Until then, Dad warned, we would have to make do and resign ourselves to the hard slog ahead.

CHAPTER TWENTY

March 1934.

Tommy carried my books as he walked me home from school, where we had spent a grueling rehearsal for the school musical *Flying High*, revised and directed by Mr. Olsen.

During one of our strolls to the farm, Tommy had the idea that we should learn a duet together, just for fun, "We'd Make a Peach of a Pair." I didn't think of the song as a romantic commentary about the two of us; I saw it as another joke that put us both in stitches.

Now as we wandered past town, where Main Street gave way to rolling fields and stands of Lombardy poplars, Tommy warbled, "From life's golf bag, when the goin's tough, I choose you to lift me from the rough, you're a fair maid I prize."

Smiling at him coquettishly, I trilled in my actress voice, "You stand out from other men I've seen, like a dandelion on the green, nice size, nice eyes, nice sighs."

Sneaking peeks at one another, on the verge of bursting into laughter, we belted out, "The breeze across the fairway, the blossoms over there are telling us in their way we'd make a peach of a pair. The whole world seems to pause now, no sound upon the air, just my heart calling yours now, we'd make a peach of a pair."

Joy dusted me from tip to toe. It wasn't any one thing, the gentle breeze or Tommy or the song. During the rehearsal, a powerful rush had sizzled through my body. Even more than singing, acting was an experiment with a new identity, becoming someone onstage whose circumstances were foreign from mine in time, place and personality.

As Pansy Potts, the female lead, I was a bold, sassy waitress who placed an ad for a husband with a five hundred dollar reward and parachuted from a plane. Playing the role was like exploring a parallel journey I might have taken had I not been born on a farm. Sometimes after slipping into Pansy's character, I considered what it would be like to continue to dwell there, long after the show's run. Certainly Pansy had a more exciting life than Irene Larsen.

"What on earth took you so long?" Mother demanded as I entered the farmhouse after Tommy had left me at the gate.

"I'm sorry. Mr. Olsen kept us later than usual. He wanted to go over the airplane scene again."

Mother scowled and shook her head. "Real life isn't all fun and games and prancing around. The sooner you wise up and see that, the better."

"I know it's not, ma'am."

"The way you run around with your head in the clouds, skipping out on chores, I'd have thought otherwise."

She peered out the window as Tommy retreated down the lane, dragging his books behind him in a looped leather belt.

"Tommy's no better. You spend far enough time with that boy as it is, clowning around. After this, you come home direct."

I slit my eyes as she turned her back, but for the next two weeks, I cut my rehearsals short, apologized to Mr. Olsen, and hurried back to the farm.

A few days before opening night, I asked Mother if she and Dad planned to come, already knowing the answer.

Her backside faced me as she boiled potatoes on the stove. "I know you've practiced real hard. But I've got to finish the quilt for Emma Addison's wedding, and we've got our hands full around here with the planting. We'll just have to see when the time comes."

I had expected this, but my stomach still clenched. Before she could say anything more, I trundled upstairs.

At rehearsal the next evening, I laughed extra hard at Tommy's banter. I wanted to lose myself in nonsense and jollity, forget the image of Mother at the kitchen with raw hands and potatoes.

"You make a swell waitress," he said, winking. "Say, after you give your line about going to the lumber camp to marry a chef, come back with a slice of apple pie and no husband. Then you and I'll eat it backstage. Mr. Olsen won't be the wiser." He elbowed me in the ribs.

◀ ♫♪ ▶

On opening night, as I stood in my pale blue waitress dress with the white frilly apron, reciting my lines in the heat of the spotlight, I already knew that Mother and Dad were not in the audience. Head held high, I told myself it didn't matter. I would sing my heart out, anyway, recite my lines as though I had always been Pansy Potts. When the cast sang and danced the last number before the curtains closed, I let Pansy rollick and cavort across stage. No more of Irene with her dour clothes and hemmed-in routines.

"I can't stand the thought of moving away after graduation next year," Tommy confessed as we set down Hyrum's Main Street later that evening, "when everything in the world that matters is right here in Cache County."

I knew he had no plans for college, as his family couldn't afford it. Although I felt him watching me, I quickened my pace and gazed at the darkened storefronts at the edge of town.

"We could work on my folks' farm until we've saved enough to get a place of our own and raise a little family."

His words stunned me. Heat swamping my cheeks, I turned, caught him staring at me beneath the glow of the street lamps, and tried to make a joke. "Tommy Jensen, what are you saying? That's the craziest scheme I ever heard."

"Not if I proposed to you it wouldn't be."

I stopped in the middle of the dirt road. "Really, now? And what makes you think I'd say yes?"

"I sure hope you would. But I'll do it proper when you're good and ready."

I put my hands on my hips. "And what if I'm never good and ready?"

He scuffed his toe in the dust. "That'll be up to you," he said quietly.

I preferred the funny Tommy, quick with quips and silly antics, to this new, serious version. On the way home, I refused to speak another word of it, until, to my relief, he returned to his banter.

All the same, his talk flattered me. Later that night, as I lay next to Minnie in the attic room, sifting over the day's events, I tried to picture being his wife and living with him in a little house, where we would eat our meals together and make each other laugh. These scenes coincided with the performance between the newlyweds in the song "Tea for Two," which, I knew, was likely an overly idyllic portrayal of marriage, and though unrealistic, approximately the extent of my understanding.

On Saturday afternoon, as Mae and I did our chores, I told her of Tommy's plans. I expected her to be pleased and encourage me, but she remained silent, her head tilted away from me as she dusted the dining table. Suddenly she trembled, as though from a spasm, and her right hand flew to her stomach.

At last she said, "Why not wait a while, Reenie? There's no hurry to start a family. Marriage may seem romantic and glamorous, like something out of the pictures. That's what I used to think. But it's not all a bed of roses."

I must have looked at her in surprise, because she added quickly, "Of course I love Hiram. But it's not always easy, especially when we hardly get to see each other alone. Your parents are generous, but we're living under their roof and rules. And we've got to think about saving money instead of going to dances or pictures. I guess every marriage has its ups and downs."

I realized the truth of her words. I would never want to trade places with Mae, not now. She worked harder than any of us. She was up at dawn cooking, canning, cleaning, sewing for Hiram, Luke, Dad and Jacob, back from his mission, and mending clothes for her customers at night. Her folks had made it into Idaho, where they were staying with relatives, but it had been over a year since any of us had seen them. It was hard to imagine she had any fun, except when she and Hiram stole outside or into town.

Besides, I had dreamed for years of traveling and singing, playing piano on stage. The high school musicals were just a taste; I yearned for bigger things. The more I thought about it, the less I understood how Tommy was so ready to relinquish performances for tilling, haying, threshing – all the mundane tasks that seemed to prematurely age my father and brothers and make them weary and glum as they forever bent into the soil, their eyes hard, their backs planted downward.

Mother must have guessed Tommy's intentions, too, because after church a few Sundays later, where we had chatted with Tommy and his parents, she remarked, "You know, I do believe Tommy's got potential. After he gets past all this silly business about the theater, he'll make a real good husband. You can see how steady he'll be."

I didn't reply.

On the way home from church, Hiram and Mae lagged behind the rest of us. She looked unwell, as she had recently, her face grown pale, and I wondered whether she was with child? Of course, it was a fleeting thought, because we could ill afford to feed another mouth, nor did we have room for a baby. Besides, Mae and Hiram had always said they would wait until they moved out and found their own place before beginning a family.

When I looked back at them, Hiram gripped Mae's shoulder, as if to steer her ahead, and she flinched at his touch. Later, as we approached the farmhouse, their voices clanged from behind me, twisted in a dispute about going into town.

After that, when Tommy talked again of remaining in Hyrum after graduation, a slow dread crawled up my stomach, and I began to dream of schemes that would take me away from town. College, for example. I had no earthly idea, however, how I would find the money to go or even whether I could gain admission.

CHAPTER TWENTY-ONE

June 1934.

Behind Mae's and Hiram's bedroom door, hissed murmurs strengthened into caustic words, like swelling winds before a squall.

"Get up," Hiram shouted. He hadn't bothered to lower his voice.

In the kitchen, I froze at the stove, where I was stirring oatmeal.

For the past few weeks we had overheard their vitriolic exchanges, whether it was early morning or late at night, and we had done our best to pretend we had not. But this time it was hard to ignore.

Mae's response was muffled and weak. I thought she said she was feeling poorly and couldn't rise.

"Dammit. You've got to. You can't lie around all day."

I sucked in my breath.

Now Mae said clearly, "Hiram, I'm telling you. I'm in such pain. You can't begin to understand.."

Next came the sound of a smack, like a hand against flesh, and I recoiled, a terror filling my throat. Had my brother just struck Mae?

A whimper or low sob, like that of an animal in pain, escaped from behind the door.

"We can have another. But you've got to get up and keep going. That's the only way. What will people think? They're talking at church already."

Another rustling, this time like a shallow breath or whisper.

"I'm going out there, and I want you up and dressed by the time I finish in the barn. Understand?"

Then their bedroom door opened and slammed, and Hiram entered the kitchen, red-faced.

Too appalled to speak, I gaped at him.

Not looking at me, he said, "Leave a glass of milk and a bowl of oatmeal on the table for me. I'm going to the barn for a spell."

I remained silent and fixed a steely gaze on him, but he was marching toward the screen door.

Not knowing what to make of his behavior and considering whether to challenge him on it when he returned, I continued stirring the oatmeal and set out bowls on the table. Half an hour later, Mae emerged from the bedroom, her face wan and sullen, her hair uncombed. She had drawn on a flimsy muslin dress she usually only wore on the days when she performed heavy-duty household chores, like scouring the floor.

I caught her gaze and held it. "Mae…"

"Don't think bad of us," she said, averting her eyes.

"Was Hiram…" I began hesitantly, but she had turned away to pour milk into a pitcher, and didn't acknowledge having heard.

I might have tried again more loudly, but Hiram returned from the barn and took his place at the table; then Dad, Luke, and Jacob assembled, and we ate in awkward silence.

Later I wondered how Mae could stand losing a baby, if that's what had happened, and on top of that, enduring my brother's cruelty. This is what happens, then, in a marriage, I thought. Even more when it begins with haste, arranged out of necessity for a teenaged bride and groom. My own parents rarely showed each other affection and sometimes went for days with scarcely a word exchanged.

"Minnie," I said, as we walked home on the following Friday, our last day of school before summer break, "If you had the chance, would you leave this town? I mean, leave Cache County, truly?"

As children, we had often talked about our plans to travel to Salt Lake or Los Angeles, ride the train for miles and dine out, attend operas, perform before a throng of people.

She arched her eyebrows. "I guess I would if I could. But I haven't any money, nor do Mother and Dad, so how would I leave?"

She continued staring at me with curiosity. "Would you?"

"Yes. And how. There's nothing here unless you want to be a farmer's wife."

"Or sell wares in town."

"That's not much, is it?" I said.

I meant that farming or working at a mercantile was not much of a life, not really. Hunching over a box of Indian jewelry or orange crates or toys and penny candy and waiting for poor people to stop and buy something on an impulse. Or worse, shaking out rugs, scouring floors and tables, feeding the chickens, mending, milking the cows, serving a grouchy husband who punished you for contradicting him, planting and haying until your bones ached and your skin was raw and calloused.

At last I changed the subject to the things we intended to do over the summer: returning to town to see a picture, swimming in the river bottom, picnicking by Paradise Lake. We avoided mentioning the threshing, haying and canning that awaited us.

Later, as the summer progressed and we hadn't gone into town, hadn't even found time to swim and had only cooled our feet once in the river, I began to fixate on the possibility of going off to college. At the start of August, I considered it from different angles. Could I major in music? Would that jumpstart a career as an entertainer, where I could play the piano, sing before an audience?

I pictured myself in a flowing evening gown, singing solos, bounding across a stage in high heels, or sweeping my arms across the keyboard as I played Chopin nocturnes and waltzes. Somewhere away, in a big city buzzing with interesting people, eager to indulge in music and art and culture. Then it seemed possible, all of it, even the chance that another life might await, something very different from this one on the farm.

The more I thought of it, the vision consumed me, until I was there, in that other role, so close to real that my skin tingled. At last I wrote Wylie that I'd like to apply for admission at BYU, and sought his advice. He had made it out, after all; his plans were in full motion. Regularly he sent us postcards with short descriptions of his math and physics classes and professors, his roommates and their failed attempts at cooking on the monkey stove in the one-room wash house where they boarded, the occasional dance he attended at the student union. Now he was staying on campus over the summer to earn additional credits.

He wrote back immediately, encouraging me to apply. *"You can do it, Reenie. It's not as difficult as you think."*

He added that BYU simply required proof of sixteen units of approved high school work over four years from an accredited school. Someone with grades as good as mine, plus a record of outstanding musical performances, would certainly gain admission.

Tuition for the first quarter and books, which I could buy used, would cost around thirty-five dollars, he explained. Several of his classmates were from Provo, and he could probably arrange for me to board with the family of one of these friends, in exchange for cooking, cleaning, and doing other household chores. This arrangement would save me ten or fifteen dollars a month.

I reread his letter until it was damp and crumpled around the edges. Still, I didn't know how I could possibly come up with thirty-five dollars for tuition and books, and I told Wylie as much in my response.

His reply arrived a few weeks later. *"I think I can help get your quarterly tuition down to $12 or $15 if you can give private piano lessons three or four times a week on behalf of the music department. But first things first. Send in your application."*

Deciding not to tell anyone, even Minnie until things were more certain, I stowed his letter in the bottom of my bureau beneath my underclothes. I didn't yet have a plan for how I would pay fifteen dollars, but it sounded more manageable, and I determined not to worry. I could take in more work for Mae with her laundry and tailoring customers or babysit for a quarter every Saturday night for the ladies in town. It would be a start; surely I would think of something. Within me, a glimmer of hope rose and soared like the bird from Snowchootaney that Jeremiah had imagined so many years ago.

CHAPTER TWENTY-TWO

October 1934.

As seniors, Tommy and I earned lead roles in the Gershwin musical *Funny Face*. I played Frankie, and Tommy was her legal guardian, Jimmy Reeve. During the weeks before the show, everything was exactly as it had been: our walks home after rehearsal, our playful crooning in the twilight, the school performances with Minnie and occasionally Mae in the audience, but never Mother or Dad. If Tommy talked of graduation, I steered our conversation to safer topics: the Homecoming Dance, church gatherings, new Hollywood pictures.

One evening as we prepared for bed, I confided in Minnie about my plans to go to BYU.

At first she laid down her brush and stared at me, open-mouthed. "It's so far away, Reenie."

"It's only a short train ride away, less than a day. Besides, I haven't been admitted yet."

"But you will." She peered at me. "I know you will."

I shrugged. "There's no telling. We'll have to wait and see."

"And Tommy..." she began.

"No point in telling him just yet. Nothing's set in stone, after all. I haven't even submitted my application."

She nodded.

"Don't mention it to Mother and Dad, either," I warned.

"I can keep a secret."

"I know you can. I wouldn't have told you otherwise."

She managed a thin smile.

After the show's run, I gathered my transcripts, filled in the BYU application, and mailed the bundle to Provo. Meanwhile, from the odd jobs I was able to find, I continued collecting coins and the occasional dollar, which I stashed inside a little cotton pouch at the bottom of my underclothes.

Dad had gone to work at the wool mill again, while Jacob and Hiram increasingly took over the farm's daily operations. We didn't see much of either of them except at supper, when Jacob sat in Dad's usual spot and Mother across from him. Mae and Hiram, opposite Minnie, Luke, and me at the table, said little to each other, either at supper or in their room. We no longer heard raised voices, nor, for that matter, did we hear much sound of any kind from behind their door, except floorboard creaks as they prepared for bed or dressed in the mornings. I preferred the quiet to the arguments, but it seemed to be an uneasy quiet, as though something unsettled and heavy lay between them.

One evening in February, as we finished eating a corn and potato soup that we had supplemented with stale bread, Hiram raised his head and addressed us all. "I've got to go into town tomorrow for supplies. You need anything?"

"Can you trade some eggs for a quarter cup of sugar?" Mother asked. "I thought I might bake a cake later next week, for Dad's birthday."

"I'll go with you," Mae said, turning toward Hiram. "I can get the sugar while you get the feed. And I'll buy a bolt of fabric, too, for making a tablecloth. This one's awful frayed."

"We surely don't need a new tablecloth." Mother puckered her lips. "There's nothing wrong with this one that a little patching can't take care of. No need to splurge on new fabric."

In unison Hiram interjected, "You stay home and help Mother. I'll get the sugar."

Mae looked crestfallen, and I realized she had hoped to use the trip as an opportunity to spend time alone with Hiram, or at least away from the farm. She looked at Mother, waiting for assurance that she could go, that her help at home wasn't needed. But Mother's pride had been injured about the tablecloth, because she remained silent, lips pinched, eyes snapping.

I started to volunteer to stay at home with Mother, but I would be at school the next day, and there was little I could do to help. I threw Mae a sympathetic glance, but she didn't notice. Her eyes had gone moist, and she blinked fiercely.

Later, as she dried the dishes, her hands shook.

When Minnie descended to the cellar, I touched Mae's shoulder. "If you want to go anywhere this weekend, into town or the ward, I can cover for you."

Mae turned toward me, and I realized with shock that she no longer looked like a high school girl. She was a proper woman, as somber as a matron in her thirties, the skin tight at the edge of her scalp where she had twisted her hair into a bun, her face angular, cheeks no longer plump but browned and freckled, the faintest of lines etched beneath her eyes, possibly from the many months she had worked outdoors in the orchard and garden or washed laundry without wearing a hat. How had I not noticed before?

"There's no need for that," she said promptly, "But thank you, Reenie, all the same."

To my surprise, she leaned against the sink and grasped her head with both hands.

Quickly I asked if she were feeling unwell, whether I could get her an aspirin?

"No, no, I'm fine," she choked out. Gradually the crease between her eyes softened, but her hands fluttered, as though a gale had swept across her, knocking her off balance. A blush rose in her cheeks, and at last I glimpsed the young girl beneath the shapeless frock and apron.

"God moves in mysterious ways, doesn't He?" she said. "He has a plan for us, even if it's not clear at first." Her voice quavered and went soft, while her hands flew to her chest like frantic beating wings. Her gaze darted around the room as quick as a hummingbird, not alighting anywhere, but at last searching out the window, as though she wanted to fly straight through and into the sky.

I recited from the hymn I often played on the organ at our ward, "His purposes will ripen fast, unfolding every hour. The bud may have a bitter taste, but sweet will be the flower. Ye fearful Saints, fresh courage take. The clouds ye so much dread are big with mercy and shall break in blessings on your head."

"Yes, yes," Mae said, and closed her eyes. As tears slid down her cheeks, I drew my arms around her, recalling a similar moment two years ago when she had comforted me.

Beneath my arms, she was all bones and sharp angles – the blades of her shoulders, her hips, even her lean arms. At last she heaved a sigh and gently pulled away.

Somehow, I realized, my sister-in-law and I had swapped positions: Mae bound to her duties on the farm under Mother's critical watch, and I singing the lead in school musicals, maybe later to something bigger. Her situation could easily have been mine, but the tables had turned in my favor. A twinge of guilt dashed me when I realized I had hoped for this long ago, before our troubles began.

"Things will get better," I whispered, though truthfully, I wasn't sure.

CHAPTER TWENTY-THREE

May 1935.

With trembling hands, I read the acceptance letter from BYU. Unable to stop myself, I broke into a broad grin and leaped, not caring who in the Paradise post office might see. Tucking the single sheet of paper into my skirt pocket, I ran the one and a half miles home, and breathlessly held it out to Minnie, who shrieked and squeezed me. Now that it was happening, the real possibility that I would go away to college, she had come around. I hoped she would let me pave a way out for her, too.

"Whatever am I going to do when you're gone?" she pretended to wail.

Over the past several months for nearly a year, I had scrupulously saved what I could: babysitting earnings, a few dimes from helping Mae with her laundry customers. However, since many people traded sugar, eggs, or bottled goods in exchange for these services, I had only managed to stash away four and a half dollars.

That evening, when I showed the letter to Dad, he offered to pay my tuition for the year. My knees went weak with relief. He couldn't afford to pay it all upfront, he said, but he could give me enough money for the first two quarters. Wylie's college experience had softened his opinion about getting an education. After all, he had witnessed the toll the Depression had taken on farmers.

"You've got a head on your shoulders, Irene. Might as well see what you can make of it."

Mother's lips tightened, and she shook her head as if I had declared I would participate in a long-running school musical, which of course she believed to be nothing more than tomfoolery and a waste of time.

"That's what you want? To make a go of it as a musician?"

I pursed my lips, forced myself to meet her eyes.

"It's not fit for a girl like you from a good family, and besides, it's a pipe dream. It's high time you settled down. You've got Tommy Jensen falling all over you, and goodness knows he'd make a decent husband. And yet you want to run away and play make believe?"

"I want to give it a try," I said, knowing she wouldn't understand, "To see where I can go with it."

Wiping her hands on her apron, she eyed me with scorn. "I never in my life heard of such a foolish thing. Throwing away something good and true for an empty promise that won't amount to a hill of beans."

"Let her see what happens," Dad said. "She might as well try it for a quarter."

"We'll see how quick she comes back, once she finally realizes how good she had it here."

Her mouth hardened, and I could see she expected me to return home in a few months, broke and eager to repent my mistake and resume farm life.

I waited to break the news to Tommy until the last possible moment, dreading his reaction. The following Saturday he walked me home from a spring dance, and we stood at the end of the lane leading to the farmhouse, cloaked in twilight.

In hopes of tamping down the shock of my words, I spoke rapidly, my voice hushed. But it didn't matter. He swayed on his feet and staggered backward, as if I had knocked the wind out of him.

"You applied without letting me know?" His voice came out barely above a whisper, rife with disbelief.

I turned away, biting my lip.

Sinking to his knees, he scooped up my hands. "Irene, I'm begging you not to go."

His protests spilled out one atop another. He loved me, he wanted to marry me, he couldn't bear it if I were to pick up and move miles away.

"It won't be forever."

"Might as well be. You might as well be sailing off to China."

He kneeled before me, his face grown contorted, his eyes wide and pleading. "You've got to believe me, Irene. I can't let you go. We're meant to be married. It's God's will."

My heart twisted, yet I forced myself to be firm. "I've already made up my mind. I've got to see this out."

"You can't be serious."

"I am. I've told you I've got to try."

"Why?" His lips curled into a sneer.

"It's the only chance I have to be a musician."

"You don't have to go away for that. Who says we can't make music together, here?"

"Not on a farm I can't."

He clasped my hands. "I thought what we had was more than any silly old musical."

"I've got to try," I repeated, blinking back tears of frustration.

Again we rehashed our positions until we may have been playacting roles in one of Mr. Olsen's performances.

"How can you," he groaned. "Just when things were going so good."

Realizing I wouldn't yield, he seized my wrists and yanked me toward him, forcing me to meet his eyes. In a harsh, bitter voice I had never heard before, he thundered, "Why're you doing this to me? You're making a terrible mistake. You'll regret it. We both will."

"Tommy," I said faintly, and shook my wrists loose.

He was no longer my passionate young suitor but someone else, harder and older.

"What I want to know is how if you truly love me you could keep this a secret from me for so long." He turned and spat on the ground.

"I promise to write to you every week."

"I don't care about letters. They're worthless if I can't see you."

I shook my head and turned away from him, casting about for the right words.

"What is it? Tell me, Irene. You can't throw a whammy like this then dodge me." Gripping my chin, he maneuvered my face toward his. "Tell me."

I didn't recognize what I saw: his eyes wary and slitted, a grimness around his mouth and chin, as though he might pounce on me. Shivering, I took a step back, though he swung me closer.

It dawned on me that I couldn't make him understand. We were at an impasse. He would forever wonder why I had to leave as much as I wondered why he had to stay. We may have talked for one minute more or fifty. In the end, it made no difference.

"I won't lose you to a jerk at BYU," he finally said, casting me an anguished look. Before I could respond, he pulled me against him and kissed me hard. As he trudged down the lane, he didn't throw a backward glance.

◀ 🎵♪ ▶

On the day of my departure, Dad drove me to the station. I had packed a small suitcase with my dress, skirt, blouse, sweater, and a few toiletries, including my silver brush. Mother gave me a bunch of raisins twisted in waxed paper for the train ride. Minnie threw her arms around me and begged me to write.

Tommy must have borrowed his father's car or hitched a ride, because he found me on the platform right before I was to board the train. Wordlessly he handed me an envelope, his eyes locking onto mine. Even as my mouth parted in surprise, he hustled to the back of the platform.

My pulse tapped out a sporadic rhythm. I tucked the letter into my dress pocket but dared not open it in Dad's presence. After I took my seat next to the window, on the station side, I found Dad, standing in his overalls and slouch hat, and waved. Tommy stood several yards behind him, alone and apart from the crowd. From where I sat, his face, lifted toward the train, was inscrutable. As the train lurched ahead, I broke the seal. Out slid a single sheet of paper.

"Come back to me," he had written. "I'll wait for you."

I folded the letter back into the envelope, stuffed it into my dress pocket, and pressed my forehead to the window, seeing nothing, my mind emptied and numb. Only over an hour later, after the train huffed clear of Cache County, did I feel a spark of anticipation and interest in what awaited me.

CHAPTER TWENTY-FOUR

August 2006.

Although it's outside the scope of the job that Deirdre has paid her to do, Cindy takes me to the Golden Manor hair stylist today to have my hair done.

"It's going to be fun," she says, when I protest I don't care how I look. Who's here to see me, after all, save my daughter and my friends, who prefer my jokes to my physical appearance any day. Nonetheless, to humor her, I agree.

When the stylist asks me what I'd like, I wave my hands and suggest she does whatever she thinks will look best, fully expecting I'll end up with one of the stiff dos that so many of the ladies around here wear. Resting her hands on her hips, she studies me, as if noticing me for the first time. "All right. Let me come up with something cute. You've got a heart-shaped face that works well with a lot of styles."

While Cindy waits in one of the lounge chairs, the stylist washes my hair, then snips and snips, keeping my head turned away from the mirror, until I'm fearful I'll come out with an army-style buzz cut. At last she swivels my chair around so I'm facing the mirror.

She beams at me. "What do you think?"

A woman framed in white feathery layers, angled in a bob beneath her chin, stares back at me, and my eyes widen. The reflection in the mirror could be a slightly older version of Deirdre.

The stylist hands me a mirror and slowly turns my chair, letting me examine the sides and back. "Is it okay? Do you like?"

To my surprise, I nod and smile. "Yes, I believe I do."

CHAPTER TWENTY-FIVE

September 1935.

When I arrived in Provo, I considered it nothing short of a minor miracle. Here I was, a farm girl, plopped onto a sprawling campus over one hundred twenty miles away from home. Whatever might happen, I was certain my future would look nothing like what I had known. It might have been sheer naivete that let me hope I could guide the direction that future might take.

As he had promised, Wylie arranged for me to stay with a family in town, a twenty minute walk to the BYU campus. In exchange for room and board, I did most of the family's cooking and cleaning. He also helped strike a deal in which I provided private piano lessons for the music department and played accompaniment during dancing classes in exchange for a reduced tuition of only six dollars per quarter.

At the Samuelsons', the family with whom I boarded, I busied myself with a steady schedule of morning chores, classes on campus, then private lessons or dance class accompaniment, depending on the day of the week. It was the voice lessons with Mrs. Packard I eagerly awaited. In the early evenings I returned to the Samuelsons to help with supper preparations.

After I had cleared and washed the dishes, I retreated to the small room I shared with the Samuelsons' twelve-year old daughter, Edith, to study. Because Edith had to go to bed at nine sharp, I had at most one to two hours to finish homework or prepare for exams, and I often fell to bed exhausted.

Wylie, whose friend Byron was the Samuelsons' son, joined us for supper three or four times during the first school quarter. Otherwise I didn't see him on campus, as his classes were in the math and physics buildings, and he was busy with his studies.

Every week or two, I wrote dutifully to Mother, Minnie, and Tommy. Mother returned my letters sporadically, so I had to gather most of my news about the farm from Minnie. She reported that Tommy had come by the house once to pay his respects to Mother and Dad and inquire about me, and he seemed "quiet, not himself."

Tommy didn't enjoy writing, and he often scrawled his letters on a single folded sheet of paper. Without fail, he ended them with the question of when he would see me again.

"Who's your young man?" Mrs. Samuelson inquired playfully, when she handed me an envelope with Tommy's name scrawled on the return address.

I felt myself turn scarlet. "He's just a friend from home. We keep in touch every now and again."

Mrs. Samuelson shrugged her shoulders and made to turn away. "It's none of my business, of course. But a pretty girl like you – I thought sure she's bound to have a fellow somewhere."

My classes at the BYU mostly met in the same building in the quad, so I spent my spare time before piano lessons or dance class accompaniment holed up in one of the empty classrooms or outside on a stone bench with my satchel of books. My head ached from staring at my books and taking notes, and when I couldn't stand another minute of sitting still, I circled the quad. The swarm of students, marching past with purpose and energy, bewildered me.

By Christmastime, I was weary of Provo, and longed to return to Paradise for the winter break. Wylie had planned to remain on campus and share Christmas dinner with a friend's family, but when he learned how desperate I was to go home, he agreed to concoct a plan. Returning by train the entire way was out of the question, as we couldn't afford tickets. Eventually Wylie found us a ride with two of his friends who were driving home to Salt Lake City. From there we would catch a train to Logan, where Dad would meet us in his truck.

The trip took an entire day, and it was after eight o'clock on Christmas Eve when we finally arrived at the Paradise farmhouse. Upon learning of our plans, Mother had sent a discouraging letter, questioning whether returning home was worth the money or time. But when we entered the house, her hands fluttered to her mouth, and her eyes became moons.

Wylie bounded over, and she let him embrace her so hard that her feet lifted from the floor.

At last she stepped back, tears in her eyes, muttering, "I need to get a good look at you. Can't believe my eyes! My tall, handsome, smart boy."

She pinched his waist. "But you need to eat more. I'm going to fix that if it's the last thing I do."

He joined her in a chuckle. "Reenie's here, too, Ma."

She broke away from him long enough to give me a cursory hug. "You've lost a little weight, also. What in heaven's name are they feeding you kids down at the BYU?"

After church the next morning, Mae, Minnie, Mother and I hurried home to help prepare the Christmas dinner. We feasted on a stuffed goose, potatoes, sweet peas, cranberry sauce, bread and sweet potato pie. For presents, Mother and Dad gave us a box of tangerines to share, believed to bring good luck. I had knitted a scarf for Dad, mittens for the boys, a shawl for Mother, and hats for Minnie and Mae.

Wylie entertained us with carols on his pocket harmonica as we sat around the kitchen table, singing, laughing, and telling tales near the fire that Dad had kindled in the great stove. Although we had no space for a Christmas tree, Mae and Minnie had made the house festive by stringing green paper garlands, chains of holly berries, and popped corn on the banisters of the stairs and around the wainscoting. For the table centerpiece, Minnie had arranged fir boughs and holly berries.

As Mae and I washed dishes and Minnie cleared the table, Mae confessed in a whisper that she and Hiram were expecting in late June.

Until then I hadn't noticed the faint bulge in her waist. I gripped her hands.

"I'm so tickled for you! We need a new generation in this family. Children playing and laughing."

My mind strayed to Jeremiah. He would have been ten, in fourth or fifth grade. I bit my lip but continued smiling as Mae discussed the bonnets she was knitting for the baby, the layette and quilt for its cradle, the rattle and changing table that Hiram had promised to make. It must have been a comfort to her, knowing she would soon have a blood relative with her, since her family was still far away, in Idaho.

Later that evening, we gathered again around the dining table, enjoying more of the sweet potato pie, when a rap on the door interrupted the conversation.

Dad strode across the room to the door. "Must be someone from the ward," he announced, to no one in particular.

"Won't you come in," he said. "Please, it's no trouble. You're right in time for pie."

Tommy stood in the doorway, bundled in a coat and overshoes. He looked bigger than I remembered. The strenuous work on his folks' farm had added bulk to his frame. His hair was thick and a little longer, his cheeks hollowed and ruddy from the cold.

"Tommy, how nice," Mother called, shooting me a glance. "Come sit down."

Tommy removed his hat. "Thank you, Mrs. Larsen. I didn't mean to disturb anything." He gazed steadily at me.

"Go on, Reenie," Mae, seated to my left, whispered.

As a heat crawled up my cheeks, I rose and walked toward him. His eyes glittered, and I sensed he had to restrain himself from springing to me and seizing me by the waist.

"Irene." His voice wobbled on the last syllable. He touched my hands. Conscious of my family's eyes upon us, my face froze into a smile as I led him to the table.

As I served him pie and apple cider, we chatted about nothing important – the decorations in town, the ice in the fields, the boy from Hyrum who, scandalously drunk as a skunk, had crashed his father's car into a neighbor's fence. I could almost forget he was my beau, but instead a polite young man from the ward, struggling to make conversation. It occurred to me that it would be better if he were a friendly stranger, no one to whom I had ties or obligations.

When Tommy buttoned his overcoat and prepared to leave, he whispered, "When can I see you?"

It was obvious from his face that he meant alone. Wylie and I wouldn't be returning to Provo for another week, on New Year's Day.

I hesitated, then named a day shortly before our departure. A shadow fell across his face, but he nodded.

"I'll pick you up at noon in Dad's car. We can go for a drive." He pressed into my hand a small brown parcel, tied in string. When I unwrapped it, an emerald-colored stone slid out, into my palm.

"It's not much," he said apologetically, "But I wanted to give you a Christmas gift. I found this by the creek and thought of you, cause it's near the color of your eyes."

I turned it over in my palm. He was right. Although it had cost him nothing, it was gorgeous, but the light in his eyes as he gave it to me, and the meaning of what he wanted, heaved a weight of one hundred stones down my chest.

For the next few days, I knitted with Minnie and Mae, baked bread with Mother, and visited with school friends and members of the ward. Two or three times, I played accompaniment for the church choir. Folks inquired about BYU and asked how I was getting along. Most of them listened to my replies with slack-mouthed surprise; they didn't see how I could stand being away for so long.

On December 30th, Tommy arrived at noon, as promised, his face scrubbed shiny, and his hair slicked back. Reading the hope and unspoken expectations on his face, I worried we would once again face the same impasse we had come to before, when I had first broken the news of my plans to go to BYU.

Instead of objecting to my leaving, Mother told me privately, in the kitchen, that she hoped I would give a long, hard thought to a future with Tommy.

"Think of the money you'd save if you'd put behind those foolish ideas of yours and move back to Paradise and settle down with him. He'd be a good husband."

When I didn't respond, she hissed, "Think it over, Irene Larsen. Don't pass up an opportunity like this."

At the door, when she asked when I planned to return home that day, I told her an hour, two at most.

If Tommy had hoped for longer, he didn't say. He helped me into the passenger side of his father's truck, making sure my dress and coat were neatly tucked inside, then closed the door and climbed into the driver's seat.

"Thought we'd drive to Logan," he said. "Maybe get a soda in town. We don't have time for much longer than that, I reckon." His unspoken reproach sat between us. He started to say something else, but seemed to change his mind.

We drove in silence for a few minutes. The tires crunched over the hard-packed snow, and Tommy shifted gears. Outside the window, snow-blanketed farms flew by.

"You're liking the BYU?" he said at last. "Minnie said you were homesick. I could tell from your letters, too."

"It's big. So much bigger than I thought. But I'm getting used to it, by and by."

"I miss you, Reenie. Something awful."

I swallowed. My palms, clasped together in my lap, were damp. I hoped he wouldn't prepare a speech, make a grand confession.

He cleared his throat. "And I wondered whether you feel the same."

"I miss home. All of it, everyone, including you."

"Then come back. You don't need to stay in Provo any longer."

He watched me slantwise, and I wished we weren't trapped in the truck, where my reticence was all the more apparent.

He pulled up in front of the soda counter in downtown Logan, parked next to the only other vehicle in the lot, and helped me out.

Although I had brought a nickel, he insisted on paying for my ice cream soda. We slid into a booth next to the window. I gazed at the sidewalk that followed Main Street all the way up and down both traffic lights. The sky glinted a steely-white sheen, the color of blunted snow.

Across the booth, he reached for my hand and threaded his fingers through mine. My throat was hollow. Sipping my soda, I concentrated my gaze at the sky with its promise of snow.

"Will you consider coming home for good?" he was saying.

His words fluttered like the snowflakes that circled through the parking lot, fleetingly dusting the car windows and sidewalk, then gathering in a frenzy, until anything in its path would be trapped and smothered before long.

I turned to him and shook my head. "No. I can't. I won't. Not until I've gotten my degree or else found a way to become a musician."

"You're already a musician. You play the piano; you sing!" His voice rose impatiently.

"Tommy, I'm sorry. I don't want to be stuck in this town. Even in Cache County."

He blinked, and pain surfaced in his eyes. I would have to squash any hope he had left; otherwise, he would only cling to it until we saw each other again, forcing me to repeat myself in so many words.

I hesitated, then made myself look him squarely in the eyes. "I think it best that we stop seeing each other. It wouldn't be fair when we're not in the same town."

I waited for an outburst from him, but possibly he had expected this, deep down. "Being in the same town doesn't matter so much. I can wait."

"I don't want you to wait."

"Is there some…"

"There's no one else. I promise you that. But you're bound to stay here, and I'm bound to leave."

Bowing his head, he sank back against the booth. I was unsure whether to say something comforting.

He put his hands to his forehead. "I saw this coming."

We sat in silence for several minutes.

At last he shot me a piercing look, narrowed his eyes. "Are you sure? Is this truly what you want?"

I swallowed. "Yes."

"Things used to be so good. They could have been even better."

When I didn't reply, he grunted. His voice was low and defeated. I said nothing, but relief swept through me, as though I had been freed of a heavy knapsack that had all the while sent a splintering pain against my spine.

We finished our sodas, but all conversation ground to a halt. After that, Tommy refused to look at me.

Like an elderly, infirm couple who have run out of things to say, we returned to the truck, stiffly. He took my arm to help me in, but then dropped it. It might have taken us thirty minutes to drive down Logan's Main Street, back through Hyrum, and onto the gravelly back roads outside Paradise. I dared not break the silence. When we drove up the lane to my farm, he leaned across the seat and kissed me on the cheek.

"Bye, Tommy," I said, sliding out of the truck.

He lifted a hand in parting, waited as I walked up the lane. His tires squealed as he maneuvered the truck around and drove away.

Two days later, Wylie and I journeyed back to Provo. Little did I know it, but the next time I returned home, a year later, my life would take an unexpected twist, causing me to banish plans of finishing my degree.

CHAPTER TWENTY-SIX

August 2006.

They've gathered us in the community area for a showing of *Swing Time*. Rarely do I go to the film nights, because, although the Golden Manor staff tends to show the old classics instead of the Hollywood shoot-em-ups, it's usually nothing I want to see. But this time they tacked up flyers and even mimeographed copies of the original movie posters, and when I saw that the next movie night featured one of my all-time favorites, I couldn't resist. In the movie poster, Ginger Rogers as Penny dances beside her love interest, Lucky, played by Fred Astaire. Their eyes are radiant, chins tilted skyward. Seeing their faces cupped together, captured permanently as the glamorous dancing couple of the nineteen thirties, I catch a glimmer of the same anticipation I felt in 1936, the year Harold and I met.

It was one of the first films we saw together. As we held hands in the theater and watched, spellbound, Lucky and Penny sashayed together in a budding romance of surprising twists and turns. When Penny learned of Lucky's engagement to another girl, the couple threatened to separate for good, and I gripped Harold's hand and leaned against him.

Despite the poverty that had fallen on the country, Lucky and Penny dressed in elegant suits and gowns and waltzed around lavish clubs and sumptuously appointed hotels. Watching them on the big screen, I had imagined how it might be to live as one of the wealthy socialites in New York or San Francisco, who didn't feel so much as a pinch from the Depression. Admittedly, I also fancied myself as the graceful Penny, bedecked in hat and fur, except dancing with Harold.

"That could be us up there, honey," he had whispered, squeezing my shoulders.

The staff has moved a pair of sofas into a long row in front of the big projection screen. Behind the sofas they've lined up two rows of chairs, padded with pillows, and on little side tables, they have arranged bowls of buttered popcorn.

Candy, Marcie, and I have claimed one of the sofas, and Midge, Donna, and Bea have staked out the other. Anna Fox enters the community area on Nelson Rowd's arm. They advance toward the sofas and stop short as they realize that both are occupied.

Anna sweeps an accusing gaze across us and says stiffly, "Come on, Nelson. We'll find something more quiet."

Smiling daftly, Nelson allows Anna to tug him away, and they totter toward a pair of seats in the back.

"That's the second woman I've seen with Nelson today," Candy says. "The first was Lavinia what's-her-name."

"Morrison," Marcie says.

"They were sitting like two lovebirds in the dining room, long after lunch had been served. Exchanging meaningful glances."

"How do you know? Were you standing inches away from them, taking proper notes?" I say.

"I was putting together a little snack to take to my room for later, and their table was right next to the buffet. Anyway, I wonder whether Lavinia knows that Nelson's two-timing her?"

"Or maybe Anna's the one who's being two-timed," Marcie suggests.

"It doesn't hurt a thing if everyone's having fun," I say. "What harm can it do? Course, Nelson seems to be the one who's getting the biggest kick out of it all. Two women, no strings attached, no chance of being forced into a shotgun wedding. And he seems to have most of his marbles in place, to boot."

Candy glances in Nelson's direction. "He looks like the cat who swallowed a canary."

"Not much of a treat, if you ask me," I say. "The Golden Manor and a gaggle of old ladies?"

My friends laugh weakly.

When the staff starts rolling the film, I sense Harold sitting next to me, just as he was when I first met him: restless, vibrating with energy, bouncing his knees, cutting his eyes at me in that sly way, as though he's about to crack a private joke, whisking me under his arm, squeezing my shoulders.

He whispers, "I'm crazy about you, sweetheart. Just crazy. But what the hell are you doing with these old bags?" His whiskers brush against my cheek.

His scent wafts through my nostrils: a mixture of tobacco, Old Spice cologne he sometimes dabbed behind his ears, and whiskey.

I whisper back, "I'm lonesome for you."

I might have stayed there, nestled against the sofa cushion, eyes shut, for thirty or more minutes. When I open my eyes, the picture is nearing its climax. Lucky's fiancée, Margaret, calls off her wedding to Lucky, and Lucky stops Penny's wedding to another fellow. At last, in a happy reversal of fortune, Lucky and Penny are together.

The shot pans over the couple as they sing and gaze from a skyscraper window at a New York snowfall. When they embrace to a combination of "A Fine Romance" and Harold's and my song, "The Way You Look Tonight," the credits start to roll and the room applauds. Midge, Candy, and I rise and move to the doors.

A few feet ahead, Lavinia Morrison pushes a walker and mutters to herself. A few times she stops to catch her breath and throws a haughty stare back at Anna, who grasps Nelson's elbow, pretending not to notice.

When at last I enter my apartment and close the door behind me, I give a start. For a moment I'm sure Harold has been there, and I just missed him. I see the deck of cards spread on the table. A game of solitaire, as he waited for me? Next to it sits a tumbler with an inch of whiskey, or it might only be apple juice or water. I can even smell his signature scent.

"Harold?" I call softly. I peer down the short hallway that leads to my bedroom, half expecting to see him reclining on the duvet, listening to the radio.

"Harold?" I repeat, advancing down the hallway, sure I will find him there, grinning, arms outstretched to embrace me.

A knock on the door makes me whirl around. My heart gives an erratic kick, and my hands instinctively flutter to my chest.

"Irene? Mrs. Stallings? It's Cindy, here for your nighttime meds."

The door opens, and Cindy's round face with her wide-set brown eyes appears.

"Are you all right, sweetie?" she asks me, sounding concerned. "You look like you've seen a ghost. I hope I didn't startle you."

I wave my hand to dismiss that notion, but I can't seem to find my voice.

Cindy hurries to me, and I croak, "I'm all right. Just about to turn in."

She gently places a hand on my arm and guides me over to the bed, then plumps it, like you might do for a child, inviting me to sit.

"Let's get you under the covers, and then we'll take our medicine."

I open my mouth to protest, but think better of it, and clamp my lips together. Cindy is simply doing her job. What good would it do to cause her trouble?

"Your daughter said the doctors are pleased that your blood pressure's evening out a bit." This she announces with a ring of praise, as though I had earned a perfect score on a math test.

I say nothing. As far as I'm concerned, I have nothing to do with my blood pressure. Whether it goes up or down seems irrelevant, and I certainly won't claim credit for it one way or the other.

"Ready for your medicine?"

She doesn't wait for me to respond, but prepares the colorful array of red, yellow, and purplish-black pills that look deceptively like Easter jelly beans. I've stopped keeping track of what each one is for: blood pressure, blood thinner, cholesterol reducer.

I've hinted to her of my disagreement with Deirdre about the mood leveler and Dr. Shah's inclination to prescribe it. So far he has not, as far as I know. He wanted to see how the new blood pressure medication worked first, I recall. But then, and this is where I am fuzzy, I'm not sure how long it has been since I've been taking the new medication, and whether Deirdre has already or very soon will persuade him to prescribe the antidepressant.

"I saw you out in the courtyard again today," Cindy says, and her voice reverberates across the room, jolting me out of my thoughts. "You seemed busy out there."

"I've been working on a little project."

"Oh?" She hands me a pill, which I swallow with a sip of water. "What kind of project, if you don't mind my asking?"

I debate whether to say more. But she is watching me with genuine interest, and I know her well enough to understand she is mainly a person of good intentions.

"You could call it my memoir. I've been recording my life story on a little cassette tape."

"Really?" She pauses to clasp her hands together and regards me thoughtfully. "That's a wonderful idea! What a treasure that'll be for your children and grandchildren."

"They'll be surprised, I expect."

"They don't know about it?

"Not yet. And I'm not sure I'm going to tell them."

"I love secrets."

"So don't go spilling the beans to Deirdre or anyone else, for that matter," I say, and playfully wag my finger at Cindy.

She pretends to zip her lips with her fingers. "Mum's the word."

"Sweet dreams," she calls, closing the door behind her.

Sleep comes fast, slipping me into its folds like quicksand. In my dreams, I am sure I see Harold, just as he was as a young man in the late nineteen thirties.

CHAPTER TWENTY-SEVEN

January 1936.

Often you don't realize the significance of something until you examine it in hindsight. Then you might recognize it was one of those rare moments that helped define the course of your life. It might have begun innocently, like running late for a train, or deciding to go to the pictures on a particular day. In my case, it was a summer job. I didn't know it, but my life was about to take a completely different turn that would change everything, irrevocably.

As I walked out of the classroom in the School of Music, where I gave piano lessons, I paused to read a bright blue poster on the bulletin board: "College students wanted for summer employment at Zion." The fine print read that Mr. Hugh Visick, Manager of Zion National Park, and employed by Utah Parks Company, was seeking high school and college aged girls and boys who could serve as cabin maids, waitresses, bellhops, groundskeepers, and curio shop clerks from June through September. He also intended to conduct auditions for musicians and dancers, who would entertain the tourists by putting on skits and shows during the summer evenings at Zion Lodge.

For the first time since returning to the BYU for the winter quarter, my chest leaped, like a guitar fret vibrating at the strum of a finger. Employment at Zion would allow me to earn a little money for next year's tuition. If all went well, I might also have the opportunity to launch a music career. My other options included working at Woolworth's part-time while continuing to lodge at the Samuelsons' or dropping out and returning home, which I refused to do, as it would be akin to defeat.

Rapidly I copied down the Springdale address and submitted a letter per the instructions, including a list of my coursework at the BYU and my musical talents, both vocal and piano. I wrote that I would love the opportunity to work at Zion and, if possible, perform on Mr. Visick's summer show. To prove my competency, I enclosed a recommendation from my voice instructor, Mrs. Hannah Packard.

◄ ♫♪ ►

Two weeks later, I received a return post, indicating I had been accepted for the assignment. Upon arriving at Zion, I would serve as a cabin maid, and I could audition for a singing role in the evening variety show. Without intending to, I threw my arms in the air and shrieked. Mrs. Samuelson came running into the room.

She stopped short when she saw the smile on my face. "Gracious, I thought you were in trouble."

I read the letter to her, and she clapped her hands. "That's wonderful news. And such a gorgeous park. I hear the CCC boys have cut out new trails over the canyon. What fun you'll have."

Two other girls in the music department had also received summer assignments at Zion. When school ended in June, we pooled what little money we had to buy train tickets from Provo to Cedar City. From there we could catch a ride to the park with other Zion employees. It was the first summer I wouldn't spend in Paradise. Rose, one of the other girls, called it her greatest adventure ever, and announced she intended to record every day in her diary.

On the train ride down, we sang a chorus of show tunes and gazed, transfixed, as the scenery transformed into the rugged desert canyons of Southern Utah and broad fields peppered with creosote, rabbitbrush, Indian paintbrush, and sage. Fiery reds and golds streaked across the sandstone cliffs, tops flattened like crowns with spiky stone ridges. Cacti grew by the side of the road, and the bus huffed dust as it coasted through the little desert towns: Paragonah, Parowan and Summit.

We reached Cedar City in late afternoon. Because we hadn't eaten for nearly eight hours since leaving Provo that morning, the three of us, Rose, Annie, and I, bought a small loaf of bread and oranges from a peddler near the train station. Not having realized how parched I was, I sat slumped on the bench at the depot, savoring the juice from the orange slices. Our dresses were filthy from the dust, and even the scarves we had tied around our heads hadn't prevented grit and sand from settling into our hair.

Eventually, a boy about our age drove up in a sputtering car and clambered out at the train station. He wore a brown derby and suspenders, and introduced himself as Perc.

"You the gals from the BYU who're going to Zion? Got to warn you, be prepared for a lot more dust and muck."

Perc tied our three small suitcases onto the top of the car, and secured them with rope. He said he would drive us straight up to the Zion Lodge, where the Utah Parks manager would show us to our cabin. Annie rode in front with Perc, and Rose and I climbed into the rumble seat in back.

As we motored out of Cedar City, the ridges of the canyon towered into the clouds like ancient pyramids spiked in rust colored reds and oranges, salty grays, and sandy beiges, which Perc explained was a result of iron and other minerals in the rock. I gazed at them in awe, humbled by the enormous alien formations that, instead of civilization, had colonized the otherwise desolate landscape. After an hour, we passed through the town of Springdale into the entrance to Zion, marked by the National Parks sign. A pair of rangers at the guard gate smiled at Perc and waved us through.

Perc maneuvered up a dusty unpaved road of hairpin turns, passing a bubbling river. Banks of scrubby trees dotted the peaks of the craggy rocks, grazing the sky. The majestic giants of rock surrounded us, centuries-old witnesses to all that had come before, destined to outlive us, I considered. Overcome by the breathtaking beauty of the place, I was momentarily speechless. I couldn't take my eyes from the canyon's gold and vermilion spires. Sprung from Nature, it was a temple that commanded silence, meditation. We were guests come to worship, mere dots upon its craggy surface. While the others chatted, I gripped my hands together and drank in the fresh air, letting my chest swell.

My brain emptied of thought. It was somewhere on the canyon floor, scurrying around like an animal driven only by sight, scent, and sound. I had a primeval urge to flee the car, dash barefoot along the riverbank into the canyon bowel, skim rocks, as I had done as a child. From the open window, I gulped the stinging fragrance of fir and pine. As we ascended higher into the canyon, and Perc shifted gears to manage the switchbacks, the car's thumping engine interrupted the peace surrounding us, an unwelcome intruder breaking in upon something sacred, timeless.

The Lodge lay nestled against the base of the canyon. It was a sprawling, dark-stained timber structure. Two stone chimneys flanked either end, joined by a low sloping hipped roof. The second level featured a portico angled in front of a panel of windows and a walk-out terrace, supported by four or five evenly spaced stone piers. A circular drive in front allowed guests to pull up their cars, so bellboys could hop out to greet them and shuttle their luggage into the lobby. An American flag fluttered in the breeze on the grassy bank across from the pebbly, dusty drive. To the right of the lodge, separated by several hundred yards, sat a dozen or more cabins, which Perc explained were for the park employees.

When Perc stopped the car, Rose, Annie, and I scrambled out, nearly collapsing against each other onto the drive. As Perc untethered our luggage, we bounced on our toes, hugging our arms to our chests, elbowing each other and whispering excitedly about where we would stay, when we would meet our employer, and when we might get to audition for parts in the nightly shows.

Perc and a bellboy grabbed our luggage, and we followed them onto the rough pine floor of the lobby. Long, exposed beams straddled the ceiling. Antlers' heads and Indian blankets decorated the plank walls. In the back sat a deep brick and stone fireplace with a few chairs drawn around it, occupied by a young couple and an older gentleman.

A tall man in gray trousers and matching vest, accompanied by a bespectacled young woman in a straight brown dress, around my age or a few years older, rose from a bench and moved toward us, smiling.

It was Mr. Hugh Visick himself, our employer. The woman beside him introduced herself as Violet, Vi for short. She squinted at us through her glasses, then explained she would review the employee rules with us, and take us directly to our cabin in the girls' dormitory.

Bed check was at 11:30 at night. No exceptions. We must be there on time, or else we would risk losing our jobs. We would rise at seven, and go to the employee cafeteria, a slightly larger cabin, for breakfast. Although the Park had employed two chefs to cook meals and supervise the ordering of supplies, each cabin of girls would take turns washing dishes. The washroom was also centrally located between the cabins. After making our beds, dressing, and eating breakfast, we would head to our assigned jobs at the curio shop, lodge, guest cabins, swimming pool and bathhouse, or restaurant. We would receive one and a half days off per week on a rotating schedule. Supper was at six, in the employee cafeteria. All supplies and food would be stocked weekly. But nothing fancy, Vi hastened to say. They stocked canned foods as staples.

The variety show in the Lodge for the guests began in a week, starting at eight o'clock, Vi continued, and auditions would take place tomorrow evening. She assured us that anyone who had exceptional talent in singing, dancing, or playing an instrument was hired. However, she warned, Zion employees who made it into the show would not be paid extra.

Rose, Annie, and I exchanged glances. I knew they hoped the same thing. While the extra money for the day jobs would be nice, what we really wanted was the privilege to perform in the show.

Finally Vi led us to the girls' dormitory, a row of six cabins. We entered an empty cabin with a plank floor, lined with five bunk beds. The seven other girls who occupied it were at supper, Vi said. Opening the windows at night would provide cool air for sleeping, she explained, as the temperatures in the desert dropped by at least ten to fifteen degrees after the sun plummeted. We learned later that the boys lodged in cabins about a quarter mile away.

Vi advised that although we had missed supper, if we went to the employee cafeteria in the next half hour, while it was still light, we might find flour, oil, potatoes, and a few cans of beans that we could use to prepare a quick meal for ourselves, providing we washed up and left everything exactly as we had found it for the breakfast crew the next morning. She pointed us to a few flashlights stowed behind the bunk beds, but warned us not to use them unless absolutely necessary, to conserve the batteries.

After she had left, we unpacked and hurried toward the dining cabin.

My stomach growled. "I could eat just about anything right now," I told Annie and Rose, "Providing it isn't still moving."

We met a group of the other girls on their way out of the dining cabin. Several had been working at the Parks for at least two or three summers. They told us that Vi was strict, but Mr. Visick was even stricter. He would not tolerate any deviation of the rules, and was true to his word about firing anyone who was late to bed check or her job.

"He sounds like an old scarecrow," Annie confessed to Rose and me, when the other girls were out of earshot.

"I don't care if he's the meanest man in the park as long as I get a singing part. He can be as strict as he pleases so long as I'm on his show," I said.

In the morning, Vi arrived to accompany Rose, Annie, and me to our jobs. She had brought us uniforms, based on her rough approximation of our sizes. My dress was too big, so I hemmed it with my spare needle and thread.

All three of us were to be maids, though Annie and I would clean guest cabins, while Rose was assigned to guest rooms in the Lodge. Our routine included scrubbing down each of our assigned cabins with soap and water, sweeping the floors, straightening the beds, wiping the table, stocking wood in the stoves of the standard cabins, washing the soot from the corner stone fireplaces in the deluxe cabins, and throwing out the garbage.

Annie and I met at lunchtime break to share apples, bread, and a canteen of water. We both discovered that neither of us could concentrate on our tasks. We were too excited about the audition. When our duty ended at five o'clock, we changed into our skirts and blouses, ate supper with the other girls, and hurried to the Lodge.

Vi directed us into a large recreation room off the lobby where the guest shows were held. A dozen or more girls had queued in front of an accompanist at an upright piano. Several girls performed short dances, while others sang.

When my turn came, I handed Mr. Visick a carbon copy of my letter of recommendation from Mrs. Packard. He asked if I could sing "Ain't Misbehavin."

As it happened, I knew this song well, as I had performed it in one of Mr. Olsen's high school shows. When I finished singing, and gave a deep curtsy, Mr. Visick motioned me over.

"Congratulations! You're on the show. I'm going to pair you with Benny Quinn. The two of you will sing duets."

My cheeks grew warm, and I stared at him before remembering my manners and gasping out a quick thanks.

"Everyone on this show is here to entertain the tourists. You've got to remember that. They don't want dreary or dull or commonplace. They want spectacular. Cheer. Fun. Even hope. They came here to forget their troubles. Escape all that out there." He swept his hand toward an invisible town.

"Yes, sir. I won't let them down."

Unable to contain my excitement, I ran the entire way back to the cabin. Neither Annie nor Rose had made it onto the show, but another girl in our cabin earned a dancing part. It was difficult to conceal my elation, though it would have been impolite to gush in front of the other girls, so I tried to downplay it.

"Visick's plain impulsive," I told them. "He doesn't really know what he wants or what he's doing. He picked me before he'd even heard all the others. What kind of sense does that make?"

"It's because you're beautiful, and your voice is heavenly," Rose retorted. "He knew exactly what he was doing."

CHAPTER TWENTY-EIGHT

June 1936.

We had a week to rehearse before the show opened. Between my maid duties, cooking and cleaning rotation for the girls' cabins, and rehearsals after supper, I fell into a corpse-like sleep each night, my arms, back, and legs aching from bending over buckets.

Benny Quinn, my duet partner, had worked at the park for three summers and had performed in the show each time. Like Tommy, he had a strong voice that complemented mine. Tall and thin, with a lanky frame and solemn demeanor, he took his role on stage seriously. Although he must have only been a few years my senior, he acted far older.

"Wrong way," he frowned, when I turned right instead of left during our routine, and sharply propelled me in the opposite direction.

We sang three songs together: "Smoke Gets in Your Eyes," "Indian Love Call," and "Ho Hum." By opening night, we had settled into a comfortable rhythm. He stepped back slightly as I sang a solo measure, and I did the same for him, until our voices joined and we gazed upon the crowd, faces radiant, arms rising in triumph during the finale.

I couldn't wait for the guests to file into the Lodge, ready to be entertained after a long day of hiking and fishing. They seemed to hunger for beauty and Nature, where the harsh realities of the world could temporarily be forgotten, and they could slip into a bubble of music, art and dance, things of the soul. Always when the lights dimmed, their conversation halted, and they gazed in anticipation at the stage.

The other entertainers on the show included several soloists, musicians, magicians, and four dancing couples, one of whom was a college-aged boy from Salt Lake City and his sister. I enjoyed watching their snappy tap routine, "Sunday Afternoon," apparently inspired by a picture starring Buddy Ebsen. The pair tapped toward each other from opposite ends of the stage and joined in the center, where, beaming at the audience, they moved in perfect sync, feet clicking in rhythm, arms pinwheeling until they struck the same pose.

Halfway through the routine, the boy flew into a series of handsprings, then bounded back into his toe-heel tap-tap-tap amidst cheers. His sister, dressed in a black and white checked chiffon dress and beribboned bonnet, took her turn in the spotlight with a short tap solo. Sashaying in a semicircle, she flashed her deep dimples and winked at the audience. Near the end of the set, still tapping steadily, the boy swooped his sister above his head, sailed her around the stage, then dipped her down like a rag doll to shouts and applause. The pair shared a striking resemblance with their large, brown eyes, full lips, and dark hair.

During the day, I occasionally saw the boy, whose name, I learned, was Spike, strolling jauntily up and down the path from the bathhouse and swimming pool, where he was a lifeguard in the afternoons. I noted that he also bell hopped at the Lodge in the mornings before the pool opened.

Late one afternoon, when Annie and I left a cabin we had just tidied, we met him on the main path as he wound his way toward the Lodge.

He tipped an imaginary hat at us, and we stopped to greet each other.

"Say, I've just made a marvelous speech at the swimming pool," he announced, winking.

"Have you, now?" I said, noting his sly smile and figuring he had a punch line to follow.

"Sure. There's a shortage of towels up there, and they've limited us to a hundred a day. But wouldn't you know, these dames are using one towel to stand on, one to dry with, one to put around their shoulders, and one to take back to their rooms. So I gave them a little speech. Told them this is an unnecessary extravagant use of towels and a shameful waste, given the country's economic situation, so on and so forth. You should've heard it! It was a fine speech. Put all my oratory skills to use. But sad to say, they didn't take me seriously. Fact, they just howled with laughter and called for an encore."

"You poor thing," I teased. "I for one would have listened to you."

He grinned and took a step closer. "I do believe you would have." He turned a scrutinizing gaze upon me, and a blush crept up my cheeks. "Do you go to the BYU?" he said finally.

"Yes, I just finished my freshman year there."

"You look mighty familiar. I must've seen you around the campus."

"I'm a music student in the fine arts department."

"That's probably why. I teach dance over there sometimes."

I blushed again. "You and your sister dance like champs."

"Thanks. Jimmie's my younger sister. She's a good kid. Works awful hard at it. You've got a damn swell voice, like an angel's."

◀ ♫♪ ▶

The next day, we saw him again on the same path.

"So did they take you more seriously today?" I asked.

"Who? Those old bags at the pool? Nah. They think I'm a joker or else their personal entertainer. They're still using four or five towels apiece. Sipping lemonade and having a ball."

I suppressed a giggle.

"Say, you won't believe what happened to me today, though. Hell of a day. Turns out I thought it would happen, and now it has."

"What's that?"

"I fell in the pool with my clothes on. See, first I bell hopped, and that made me late starting at the pool. Then when I got there, I found a big branch that had blown in the pool. Entire bottom was covered with dirt. So I hooked up the vacuum, and just as I was leaning over the water, the damn thing slipped, and there I was in the pool, cussing. Finally finished vacuuming in my trunks."

Now I laughed outright. Never had I heard a boy say such things. Spike was a maverick. Annie rolled her eyes and continued up the path.

Later that day in the washroom, as Annie and I ironed our uniforms, I declared I was smitten with Spike.

"He's such a kick," I mused. "Full of practical jokes."

"He's a character all right," Annie said, shaking her head. "Got a mouth on him."

"And you know something else? I'll be dating him in a week. I just know it."

Out of the corner of my eye, I saw Jimmie, Spike's sister, on the opposite side of the washroom, scrubbing a stain out of her waitress uniform.

"I'll bet you a nickel you won't," Annie replied.

Jimmie raised her head and smirked. "My brother? He's been at the Parks for ten summers. Seen hundreds of girls around here. There's always some dame or other who falls for him. Happens so often he doesn't give it a second thought anymore. They're all the same to him."

She must have seen my crestfallen look, for she quickly added, "But maybe you're different. Maybe you'll catch his eye."

"You watch," I said to them both, and flounced out of the washroom.

I didn't see Spike for another two days, but recalling my bet with Annie, I tried to time my breaks with the occasions when I knew he would be walking to the pool in the early afternoons or returning to his cabin at closing time.

On Friday afternoon, as I was shutting a guest cabin I had finished cleaning, I glimpsed him rounding a bend in the path that led to the Lodge. I straightened, and put my mop and pail aside. Pretending I hadn't yet seen him, I pinched my cheeks to make them rosy and took a few steps in his direction.

He was humming a tune, moving rapidly, his body wiry, lithe, tanned.

"Why hello, Spike," I called, transfiguring my face into a look of pleasant surprise.

"Irene." He halted in his path, and broke into a grin. "Something about this trail by that grove of trees. We keep meeting here, eh?"

A lick of heat seeped into my cheeks, and I wondered whether he suspected I had planned to catch him on the path.

"Also on the show," I said weakly. But we barely had time to exchange more than a nod, at best, in the evenings. The girls and boys stayed in separate dressing areas backstage, and when the show was over, we went our separate ways, the boys to their lodging and the girls to our cabins.

"That old show. They've got it pretty well tied up, haven't they?"

"Who?"

"Visick. Rogers. All of the Utah Parks managers. Putting on swell shows for nothing."

"I can't see how they can charge for it. The guests are already paying to stay here as it is."

"Sure, but Visick and the others can line their pockets by hiring cheap labor like us. Think about it. Where else can you find employees who'll work around the canyon during the day for a little over a dollar, then entertain at night for free?"

I hadn't given it much thought, admittedly. "I don't mind. It's lucky enough to have a job, isn't it? Besides, so long as I can perform on stage, I don't care a fig about getting paid."

He said nothing for a while, looking at me. "All right if it's only yourself you got to support. But some kids have to send their paychecks back home. It's a lot of hours to work. Ten hours a day including the show, six days a week, for three four bucks?"

I wondered whether he was one of those who sent his paycheck home.

As if reading my thoughts, he said, "I'm not broke like some of these saps. I've been working in the parks long enough that I've saved up a little nest egg. See, I can send a little money home to Mother and still have enough to get along here just fine."

"I'll bet." I turned away from him sassily. "You strike me as the big man around Zion."

"You're new here, so you don't see how things work. Believe me, I could tell you a few stories."

"Is that right?" I put my hands on my hips, "Try me."

A crinkle of amusement played upon his lips. "There's a dance tonight after the show. Meet me there, and I'll tell you some things that will raise the hair on your head."

I pretended to consider. "All right, Spike Stallings. I will." Before he could reply, I turned on my heel and retreated down the path, my heart cantering like a runaway horse.

CHAPTER TWENTY-NINE

September 2006.

In the languid hours of twilight, when the Golden Manor staff expect their charges to be indoors, winding down, I come out to the Courtyard to fill my lungs. The air is invigorating and fresh. From two blocks away, kids in the park shout and laugh. Soon their voices will die away as they're called home to supper.

After we opened our dance studio in Ashland, Harold and I took walks with the kids in the evening, down to the local playground, where they ran around, exhausting their last vestiges of energy before bedtime. Deirdre loved swinging, insisting that Harold or I push her higher and higher, so she could "touch the stars." That was her favorite thing to try, and she believed if she spread herself as long as she could make her limbs stretch, and we bounced her into the sky, she might actually make contact with one of those gleaming orbs of light. She must have been five or six at the time. Because the kids didn't have the benefit of doting grandparents, aunts and uncles, we tried to do our part to make them think of childhood as a magical place and time.

Harold used to say Deirdre was a living doll, supple and lithe, with a natural dancer's body. We both had high hopes that she or one of the boys would teach dance lessons at the studio, or else make a go of it in the entertainment business. In hindsight, it was a silly thing to expect. Deirdre was her own person, with her own plans, and she had a head for reading and learning. Harold later admitted she took after his mother and older sisters, the bookworms of the family. She made up her mind to earn a college degree and get involved with local politics and community affairs, where she could make an impact. And she did. She saw it all the way through.

CHAPTER THIRTY

June 1936.

Had I lingered a little longer on those evenings after the performance ended, rather than hurrying back to the dormitory with Evelyn, the girl from my cabin who also had a part on the show, I would have discovered that the Lodge held dances four or five nights a week. Although these events were intended for the guests, the park managers unofficially allowed employees to attend, as well.

Several bellboys cleared the recreation hall of the fold-up chairs that guests had claimed to watch the show, and a band assembled at the foot of the stage: a trumpet player, saxophonist, trombonist, cellist, and drummer. The pianist who accompanied the kids on the show slid back into his place on the bench and danced his fingers across the keys.

Within fifteen minutes the band was playing full swing, and couples took the floor. I had left my blue rhinestone-adorned gown in its usual place in the ladies' dressing room backstage, and now I stood awkwardly in my frayed, hemmed-over skirt and blouse, the only set I had brought to Zion. Discreetly, I scanned the faces around the perimeter of the dance hall for Spike, but didn't see him. To avoid appearing anxious and to kill time, I resorted to small talk with another girl I recognized from the show.

Someone tapped me on the shoulder, and I spun around. When I saw Benny Quinn looming over me, I had a difficult time concealing my disappointment.

"Care to dance, Miss Larsen?" His face was grave.

Out of the corner of my eye, I saw Spike enter the dance hall, spiffed up in dark trousers and starched shirt. My heart gave a little quiver, and my hands went cold.

While Benny led me onto the floor, I hoped Spike would take notice and feel sorry he hadn't arrived sooner.

As we danced a simple box step, with Benny stiffly lifting his arm as his cue for me to turn, I forced myself to smile at him and strike up a conversation. Predictably, his replies were terse.

Halfway through the number, as I strained to hold my smile, Benny unexpectedly let go of me, and Spike stepped forward. Grinning, he swallowed me into his arms and swiftly glided us across the floor.

"Had to break in before that knucklehead bored you to death," he said with a wink.

"Just in time." I giggled, feeling wicked.

Spike swept me into a fast foxtrot. This, I realized, is how it felt to be in the arms of an expert dancer. He was in perfect control, guiding our movements, but he made it look as though I was the natural – spinning me away from him, folding me back into his arms, swinging us out into the center of the dance floor, maneuvering around the perimeter, past the clumsy, clinging couples.

We blended into a colorful whirl of feet and arms, dipping into the orchestra's pounding drumbeat, galloping past the other couples, hearts thrashing, perspiration streaming down our cheeks. A breeze fluttered against my legs and cheeks as we traveled around the floor. Pressing against Spike, I inhaled his scent of Ivory Soap and something else, woody and burned, as he twirled me in a movement so intense and fast I imagined we might lift into flight and soar above them all.

"Gee, I never felt more like an acrobat in my life," I said, as Spike pivoted me under his arm and snatched me back. "You dance like the cat's meow."

"You're not bad yourself."

"Is that all?" I teased. "Not bad?"

"Fishing for compliments, missy? Okay, here's the truth. You're not a pro, but you could be good with a little training. You're light on your feet, not like some girls." He paused. "See, I tell it like it is. How you holding out?"

"I could use a break," I admitted.

We jitterbugged off the floor, and a couple and a few kids on the sidelines gazed at us with what I imagined was envy. Spying no available chairs, we wandered outside the Lodge. It was after ten o'clock. Moonlight splattered into the canyon, and the air had turned cool. Lights from the Lodge cast long shadows onto the grounds. A couple of bellboys standing on the drive stopped talking and turned as we approached. Almost unconsciously, we meandered up the same trail where we had met all those times before, and followed it around the girls' dormitory of cabins and toward the pool and the boys' lodging.

As we walked, not caring much where we were going, Spike asked how I had found the gig at Zion. I told him about leaving the farm, going to the BYU, seeing the summer employment notice.

He nodded. "That's how they get most of the kids."

When I asked him the same question, he made a wry smile. "That'll take some explaining. I'm not like the others here."

In a low voice, he told me about his hardscrabble upbringing. His father had died in a mine accident in Nevada, leaving Spike's mother at home in Saint George with an older son, eight daughters, and three-year-old Spike. Knowing she needed to make a living, Mrs. Stallings left her oldest daughter in charge of Spike and five of his siblings, while she took her youngest daughter to Provo and attended classes at the BYU. After finishing school and finding a teaching job in Salt Lake City, she brought Spike and a few of his sisters to live with her.

By age seven, Spike hit the streets to help earn money for his family. He sold newspapers after school, and made up headlines like, "Read all about it! Big shipwreck in Murray!" Murray, a little town south of Salt Lake, was nowhere near the ocean, but people smiled and bid him over to buy a paper.

Something rustled in the brush off the path, and I gripped Spike's hand.

"Probably a rock squirrel," he said. "Coyotes and mountain lions won't get this close to people."

"I hope you're right." I laughed to show him I wasn't afraid.

"I ran around like a hooligan," Spike admitted. "My best friend was a kid named Stinky who showed me where to buy a dozen doughnuts for a nickel and buttermilk, and a policemen's pool where we swam for nothing. We stole chocolates and skipped school to play pool and go to the pictures."

I smiled, considering what Mother would think if she knew I was promenading with a bad boy. Off to our left, the Virgin River burbled as it cascaded down the canyon rocks.

Spike skipped a stone into the river. He told me that later, he shined shoes at a little parlor run by a Negro named George, who taught him old Negro clog dancing routines called "Suzy Q," "Trucking," and "Booting up Sandy." Eventually, his sister Miriam, herself a dancer, talked the owner of a local dance studio into giving him a few free lessons. Miriam was the reason he came to the parks.

"See, one summer she worked as a waitress and dancer at the Grand Canyon, and she convinced W.P. Rogers, that's the manager of the Grand Canyon Parks service, to give me a job if I could get there."

It was Rogers who had nicknamed him Spike, and the name had stuck for the past ten summers. He and Miriam had performed at Rogers' variety shows at Zion, Bryce, and the Grand Canyon.

"It didn't matter what the hell I did on stage." Spike turned to me with a grin. "Everyone was always staring at Miriam."

Before long, they danced like professionals, borrowing snippets from Fred Astaire and Ginger Rogers movies and incorporating rigorous dance steps and ballet spins and leaps into their tap routines. Spike found bookings for them in Salt Lake and up and down the West Coast.

"A couple years ago, Miriam and I almost signed a contract to go to Hollywood with a producer who was making a picture at the Grand Canyon with Wallace Beery."

I looked at him with new awe. "Truly?"

"Miriam decided to go to college instead. She wanted me to get an education, too. She's always working on improving me."

But, he explained, Miriam dropped out of college to marry her boyfriend and was now pregnant with her first child, which was why Spike was dancing with Jimmie this summer.

"Besides," he told me, "This is my last summer in the parks. At the end of August, I'm getting the hell out of here. I'm heading to New York and going into show biz."

By now we had made a loop of the trail. He stopped in the path and leaned toward me conspiratorially.

"Fact is, I planned on leaving for New York sooner, but Rogers talked me into waiting. He said he'd give me a decent salary to help Visick run the variety show here over the summer and hire some of the talent. He thinks the world of Visick, though I can't see why. That guy's a damn shark. He'll do anything to get ahead."

I laughed. "No kidding?"

Neither of us wanted to say goodnight and return to our cabins, so we slid onto the wide shelf of a boulder against the side of the trail and continued talking.

A shiver of adrenaline bolted up my spine. Spike was the most unusual boy I had met: the way he casually inserted swear words into his conversation, the tales of his adventures on the streets of Salt Lake City, his wicked laughter, how he put me at ease. Opening up to him felt perfectly natural.

"I'd like to give a try of making a career out of singing. Someday," I said, twisting my fingers together in my lap. I told him more about growing up on the farm, playing piano and singing, the high school musicals, my dream of making it on stage.

"Your singing's first-rate, but it'll be tough to make a go of it in Utah. You've gotta go where the producers are. New York, Hollywood. Say, you could join me and head to New York when this gig's done."

We shared a chuckle, but there was something to what he said. We both wanted something bigger and brighter than the towns we knew, more than a life of farming or shining shoes or sweeping stores or selling papers.

Sitting next to him in the dark, in the shimmer of moonlight, I felt his hand graze mine, and my stomach dipped, as though I had skipped a step going downstairs. Our murmurs blended with the winds that swept through the canyon. We might have been the only two alive in the park. Just us and the desert grasses, juniper, pines, and rocks.

Suddenly Spike raised his head with a start. "Oh hell. It's gotta be after 11:30. You'll have missed bed check. Come on. I've gotta get you back to your cabin."

He grabbed my hand and helped me up from the rock. We scrambled down the trail back to the girls' cabins, laughing breathlessly. The consequences hadn't yet occurred to me.

Outside my cabin, he pressed my hands in his, and leaned down and grazed his lips against mine. Not a kiss, but the promise of one.

My heart fluttered. Gripping his hands, I whispered I was worried about getting fired for missing bed check.

"No one's going to fire you," he assured me. "That's just talk to scare the girls."

We bid goodnight, and I slipped into the cabin and into the bunk beneath Annie, where I wordlessly peeled off my clothes and slid my nightdress over my head.

"That you, Irene?" Annie whispered, amidst the snores of a few of the girls. "You're in a world of trouble. Vi was here for bed check, and she said she's reporting you to Visick."

I took this in, feeling sick to my stomach, but had no answer.

After a long time of tossing in my threadbare bedding, I fell asleep. In the morning, I rose with the other girls, and dressed hastily.

"Where were you last night, anyhow?" Rose asked. "Were you with a boy?"

My cheeks must have reddened, because she cried in glee, "I knew it!"

Several of the other girls repeated Annie's warning that Vi had threatened to report me to Visick.

I didn't reply, not daring to let them know what Spike had told me.

After a quick breakfast in the dining cabin, Annie and I walked to the Lodge with the other cabin maids, where Vi would assign us our duties for the day. My palms were sweaty, and I wiped a drop of sweat from my brow. I braced myself for the worst.

When we entered the room in the back of the Lodge, Vi raised her head and frowned. She ran through the list of girls and announced their assigned locations, but didn't call my name. While the others departed for their jobs, she motioned me over. My chest tightened, and I felt my face go pale.

"Where were you last night at bed check?"

"I'm so sorry. I went to the dance after the show, but I'm afraid I lost track of time."

"You know the rules, Miss Larsen. All girls must be back by 11:30. No exceptions."

"I'm awful sorry," I repeated. "It won't happen again."

"I had no choice but to report you to Mr. Visick. And you can be sure of his reply. He says you're fired."

To my horror, I burst into tears. As Vi stood watching me, I clamped my hands over my eyes. Tears leaked down my cheeks, onto my uniform, wetting my apron.

"I know this is difficult," Vi said, "But we've no choice. Rules are rules. If we bend them for one girl, we have to bend them for all."

Clamping my hands against my eyes to staunch the tears, I thought of the disgrace of packing my belongings in front of the other girls and spending my meager earnings on a train ride to Logan. Then surely I'd have to contend with Mother's disapproval.

Vi handed me a folded handkerchief, and said crisply, "You'd best get your things ready. We'll make arrangements for you to go home straight away."

She looked away, and I blotted my face and ducked out of the room.

Bowing my head to avoid curious stares, I stumbled out of the Lodge. As I staggered to the dormitory, I clenched the handkerchief and wondered if this is what I deserved: a terrible, bleaching rawness as penance for the joy I had drunk last night.

Once I was alone again in the cabin with the empty bunk beds, its inhabitants off performing the tasks I should have been doing, too, I cried anew. All of it, my summer earnings, performance in the variety show, shot at a singing career, destroyed in an instant, and I inevitably on a journey back to the farm in Paradise, as though none of it had ever happened.

Numbly, I threw my things into the battered suitcase that I had dragged out from beneath my bunk. I had brought so little that it took me no time at all. For several minutes, I stood staring at it, eyes brimming.

Then I thought of Spike. He had said no one would fire me. Surely he would want to know what had happened, if I boarded a train this evening and vanished from the park without saying goodbye.

He wouldn't be at the pool yet, but maybe he was at the Lodge, bell hopping. Wrapping a kerchief around my head, I picked my way up the path to the circular drive. A panicky feeling funneled up my chest. Things were moving too fast, beyond my control. I scanned the small cluster of bellboys who stood in front of the Lodge, but didn't see Spike among them. At last, uncertain where to look, I took a few steps toward a bellboy who slouched against one of the stone pillars.

Evidently mistaking me for a hotel guest, he straightened and approached. "Help you, miss?"

"I'm looking for Spike Stallings. Do you know where to find him?"

A grin curled around the boy's lips. "Sure. He's in the Lodge. You want me to fetch him?"

I hesitated, then told him no, I would go myself, and he continued watching me in amusement, as though on the verge of elbowing the bellboy to his left and cracking a joke at my expense. With as much dignity as I could muster, I turned and entered the Lodge.

I gazed around the lobby, but didn't see Spike. Deciding not to embarrass myself further, I settled on the bench near the fireplace, prepared to remain there until he appeared.

Fortunately, I didn't have to wait long. As I glanced at the guest check-in counter, Spike bounded down the stairs two at a time. He wore the Zion bellboy uniform of trousers, button-down shirt with double-breasted pockets, and sturdy leather shoes. He didn't look much different from the CCC boys, whom I often saw working in the canyon building dams to contain the Virgin River, constructing fences, and cleaning campgrounds. He was humming, jiggling something in his pocket that sounded like loose change.

"Oh ho, Irene." He stopped short upon seeing me. I was gratified to see him break into a broad smile. However, he must have discerned something troubled in my countenance, because he blinked and said, "What's wrong?"

I rose and went to him, explaining what had happened.

Spike listened in silence. Finally he said, "Chrissake. How can they do that?"

I shook my head, ready to burst into fresh tears.

He put his hands on my shoulders. "They can't go through with it. Visick will take a big hit if you leave the show."

"But they can. Vi is already making arrangements for me to leave."

Despite my struggle to contain them, tears streamed down my cheeks. I put my hands to my eyes and lowered my head.

"Listen. I'll take care of it. I'll go to Visick and get it all straightened out. It was my fault you missed bed check."

"They say rules are rules. It won't matter whose fault it was." I broke off when an elderly couple hobbled past and peered at us in disapproval, she on his arm.

Spike didn't seem to notice. "Damn rules are meant to be broken. I'll tell him if he fires you, I'm walking, too. He'll come around. Your act is one of the highlights of the show."

I found my face pressed against his shoulder. "You really think so?"

"Course. The whole thing's nuts. Visick won't go through with it. Hell with him and his prissy secretary."

I tried to straighten and extract myself from Spike, dabbing at my eyes. "We're making a scene," I whispered, as other guests passed us, staring openly.

"Who cares what these stiffs think? Bet your bottom dollar we're doing them a favor. Giving them a little excitement for nothing." He glanced at his watch. "I'll catch him now. Don't worry about a thing."

He winked, to reassure me. Then he was gone.

Not knowing what else to do, I returned to my cabin, where I paced back and forth, alternately staring out the window and whispering a prayer. At last I grabbed a broom and swept, though the floor was clean.

In the early afternoon, Vi appeared in the doorway. Wordlessly, I showed her into the cabin and waited for her to speak.

"Mr. Visick has changed his mind," she announced. "He's giving you one more chance just this once."

Relief flooded me, and I sank onto my bunk, silently giving a prayer of thanks. Spike had influence; he got things done.

Chapter Thirty-One

October 2006.

It's after eight thirty in the morning when I stir. Once again, as has happened to me lately, I feel sure I'm back in the attic room in Paradise, a young girl with her future still shiny and wide ahead of her. When my mind clears and I open my eyes to gaze about the room, I experience the sharp disappointment at my surroundings: a mare at the end of her line, sent out to pasture. But there it is again, the sensation that I've just missed Harold, that he's slipped out of bed to avoid waking me, and has strolled onto the patio to watch the hummingbirds flit to the sugar water feeder. I lie still with the thought that he's around the corner, and we'll surely meet in another half hour when he enters the room with my morning coffee.

When someone knocks and the door opens, it's Doris who peeks in on me. Angular face, sharp chin, glasses and lipstick, blondish-brown hair that is going gray.

"Well, well, well!" she coos, "What have we here?"

"An old lady in bed," I retort, but she knows I am joking, and shoots me a look.

"A birthday girl, that's what we have. Did you remember that today is your birthday, Irene?"

"Good grief. I'd just as soon it weren't," I say, bewildered. "Are you pulling my leg?

"No, ma'am. I wouldn't do that, would I? Maybe some of the younger ones around here would pull a prank, but never Doris. I tell it like it is. Yes, October 16th. That would be your birthday, wouldn't it?

For a frightening reason, I'm not sure. Undoubtedly the medication is affecting my memory, but the date sounds familiar.

"If you say so," I allow. "Does that mean I'll be treated like a queen for the day?"

"Mrs. Stallings. Aren't you treated like a queen every day?" She winks.

"Queen of the Golden Manor? Now that hardly counts."

"This is an especially important birthday. A little birdie tells me you're turning ninety."

I absorb this in silence. "Yes, that must be right. I was born in 1916." I give a short laugh. "I lose track. Old people shouldn't have to observe their birthdays. Birthdays are for the young."

"They're for everyone. And as far as I'm concerned, the older you are, the more of a right you have to celebrate."

"I don't want to be reminded of how old I am. It only means I'm that much closer to the end."

"Nonsense." Doris waves her hands as though to clear the air. "We're having a little party for you out in the courtyard today, if the weather holds. You'd like that, wouldn't you?"

The Golden Manor staff holds parties for every resident's birthday and special occasion. Equanimity is their motto, and to their credit, they don't neglect residents whose families may have forgotten them completely. That is to say, whose relatives have abandoned them here, signed away checks, and, like the three monkeys, closed their eyes and ears to any bad news from inside these walls.

The party committee trots out a cake, candles, ice cream, birthday hats, paper plates and napkins, streamers, balloons, even a few presents, and favors for the guests. Many of the residents seem to enjoy it. I've seen a few shed tears, just as though they'd been transported back to childhood.

And truly, engineering a transcendence to happier times is part of the staff's plan. In fact, it might be the measure of their success. Isn't it society's general belief that the older you are, the more you naturally revert to your early years? You require more care, hand-holding, gentle admonishments, even spoon feedings and diaper changings. As your time here progresses and your body continues its decline, you're pushed around the garden in wheelchairs that might as well be adult-strollers and a nurse holds a cloth against your lips to wipe away the drool.

If you return full circle to your childhood, then why not relive the carefree experiences of a boy or girl with none of the hardships many of us may have endured in reality. Or at any rate, this seems to be the staff's philosophy. They don't dare publicly acknowledge the other possibility, that we are entering a horror - far from a joyful time but instead a steady downward spiral where our bodies and minds, rather than strengthening, sharpening and growing, are weakening, faltering, shrinking.

Half an hour after lunch, the staff sets up for my party: a pretty pink-flowered paper tablecloth, matching napkins, pink and white balloons tied behind a dozen chairs. As Doris predicted, the weather cooperates, and we gather on the patio. My friends Candy, Marcie, Donna, Midge, and Bea arrive, as well as the other residents. They push me into the chair at the head of the table, and Candy plops a party hat onto my head.

Cindy rounds the corner with a big white frosted birthday cake, nine giant candles glowing on top. Deirdre and Tom follow her. Deirdre clutches a silver cake knife, and Tom balances a jug of pink lemonade and another of iced tea.

Cindy sets the cake in front of me and breaks into song. The others join in caroling Happy Birthday, and afterwards someone whoops, "Three cheers for Irene!" They urge me to make a wish and blow out the candles. I start to protest, but their faces turn eagerly toward me, eyes shining, like kids at a long-ago neighborhood party.

Deirdre carves child-sized slices of the cake, and she and Tom hand them to the residents gathered around the table. We eat noisily, wiping our lips, slurping pink lemonade. The cake is sugary sweet, so much that my stomach hurts and my lips pucker after a few small bites. I try to push it aside, but Cindy cries, "Oh, go on, Irene, a few more bites won't hurt you! Go ahead and indulge."

But she has it all wrong. I'm not watching my weight. In fact, I've never had to worry about gaining too many pounds, one odd benefit of having to go hungry as a teenager. I slide a small piece into my mouth, which seems to appease her.

Deirdre approaches me, smiling, and grabs my hands, "Oh Mom, I'm so happy we're celebrating your ninetieth! I only wish the boys could join us, too."

"The boys?" I repeat, because the way she says it reminds me exactly of how my mother used to refer to my brothers – Jacob, Wylie, Hiram, Luke, and little Jeremiah.

"Rod and Jack. Your sons. Though they're not boys anymore." She laughs, and I laugh, too.

Deirdre whispers something to Tom, then leans toward me. "I've got a surprise for you. I'll be right back."

Tom pretends to look confused, and shrugs his shoulders at me, smiling. I recognize the conspiratorial smirk on his face, and know he and Deirdre are up to something.

My friends urge me to open a few cards they have placed on the table, but I shake my head. "I'll wait for Deirdre."

I can't imagine what surprise she has in mind. Dr. Shah has advised me to avoid too much excitement, on account of my heart. "What kind of excitement can a woman of my age expect, anyway, in the Golden Manor?" I had playfully retorted.

A few minutes later, a familiar jaunty voice booms across the courtyard. "Where's my girl? I hear we have a birthday girl!"

My hands flutter to my chest; the voice sounds so much like Harold's. Then, in disbelief, I see Rod striding across the courtyard. He is beaming, his broad shoulders and frame vibrating with impatient energy as he hustles to me. I grip my hands together, unable to speak. He is upon me, so close I can smell his aftershave and observe the beginnings of a mustache.

I rise, and he sweeps me into his bear grip, squeezing me fiercely, until Deirdre calls in alarm that he needs to be careful.

He steps back, and I take a good hard look at him. He has his father's strong jawline, dark eyes, weathered cheeks, a few creases below his eyes and around his mouth. His hair is graying at the temples, but he still has his shock of wavy brown chestnut. Thick, luscious hair, my Rod always had, even as a toddler.

I gaze at him in astonishment, and tears spring to my eyes. "You're here. I can't believe it."

"You doubted me, Ma?" he jokes. "Don't think I'd miss this for a second! Your ninetieth birthday? Now that's one helluva party!"

We stand locked in each other's embrace, until Doris slides a chair next to mine, and Rod helps me back into my chair before easing into his. He has flown in for a few days, he explains, and is staying with Deirdre and Tom. As a real estate agent, he has flexibility with his schedule. His wife, Ruthie, sends her love, but she had to stay home to keep an eye on my youngest grandkids, Boyce and Adam, who are still in high school and knee-deep in exams and after-school sports.

Evidently Deirdre is not finished with her surprises. Four young women in short black dresses arrive with instruments that they assemble at the edge of the courtyard: a flute, violin, viola, and cello. Doris and Cindy arrange stands and chairs for them, and within minutes, they are playing a beautiful rendition of Pachelbel's Canon in D.

Closing my eyes, I sink into my chair, utterly transported. Rod rests a hand on my arm, and I squeeze his fingers. When I listen to music this melodic, it doesn't matter that I'm not easily mobile; my legs and heart can't pump the way they once did; my mind is often foggy; and I have stage C heart disease. The music carries me back to my girlhood. Just as I used to invent stories to match the piano pieces I once played, I immerse myself in Pachelbel's canon, letting my mind spin up images of gardens, waterfalls, forested glades.

The party, guests, and family gradually float away until I am a girl again in Paradise, racing Minnie across the fields on our farm, hair streaming behind us, laughing. Mae and I chat in the kitchen while washing dishes, and she helps me rehearse for an upcoming musical. Jeremiah sits on my lap as we whisper stories to each other about Snowchootaney. Another moment: I sing a duet at Zion Lodge, the first summer I arrived. Yet another: Spike twirls me on stage, our steps perfectly matched, our eyes glued to each other. I am pulsating with life, leaping, dancing, singing, running, and the people I loved so deeply as a child and young woman are there beside me, alive, also in their primes.

When the musicians finish Canon in D, we applaud loudly, and they launch into a Haydn quartet.

I don't know how much longer they play. It seems like minutes, but it might have been an hour or more, because many of the guests have moved away from the table, and the staff has begun clearing and cleaning.

Deirdre breaks into my thoughts. "Mom, do you want to go back inside? It's getting cold."

"No, I'd love to stay out here all afternoon, listening to the musicians. They were marvelous."

"I paid them for only an hour. They've got to pack up their instruments and leave."

She bends her face to mine, and I kiss her cheek.

"But this is only the beginning. We'll continue the celebration back at home. Probably tomorrow, since you've had enough excitement for one day."

Before I can protest, she adds, "You'd better open your friends' cards so as not to disappoint them."

Candy, Midge, Bea, Marcie, and Donna have drawn their chairs into a chatty circle, and I join them, taking the birthday cards with me. They have been sweet. Marcie's card reads, "You're never too old to have fun." Midge and Candy have written long notes, expressing their gratitude for our friendship. Donna has enclosed a photo of the six of us, including Bea. We are in the cafeteria, clowning around, making silly faces at the camera and wearing goofy hats and scarves, as though we were teenaged girls.

I hug them one by one. They are not Minnie and Mae, but they are here, and they are friends. Alive. Now.

CHAPTER THIRTY-TWO

July 1936.

Spike squeezed my hand as we circled the Lodge on our evening stroll. In the moon's buttery glow, he pointed out cougar tracks, a bird's nest hovering on a pinyon pine, a rabbit hole. If need be, he confessed, he could camp on his own and survive solely on the land. He swept his hand toward the canyon.

He had acquired his cunning survival skills by necessity. Now he confided that at age thirteen, he had become the youngest boy in Utah to make Eagle Scout by swimming a mile without stopping, camping out fifty nights in Parley Canyon, and bicycling seventy-two miles roundtrip to his uncle's ranch in Morgan, where they trapped for a month, and lived on canned milk and beans, oatmeal, dried apples, deer meat, sage hens, and rabbits.

"But in Salt Lake, I'm bad," he admitted. "If I'm not dancing, I drink beer, shoot pool, smoke, get chased by the authorities."

"You're a terrible influence." I pretended to tsk. "My parents would disown me if they knew I was going with you."

"Honey, what they don't know won't hurt them."

"I don't plan to tell them."

When he pulled me against him, a smoldering heat channeled up my chest.

We sauntered back to the Lodge, where the dance was underway, and Spike escorted me onto the floor. Lately he had begun teaching me advanced steps to add to my repertoire of foxtrot, waltz, swing, and jitterbug in the style of Cab Calloway and the big bands.

"Like this, see." He steered me, then swirled me in dips and circles until I swooned, my skirt tenting around me. Both of us exploded into laughter. Always he seemed to be elevating me, winging me over the crowd, like a bush pilot maneuvering his aircraft from a dizzying height.

"Tap will take more practice, though," he said, squeezing my waist, when I failed to imitate a few basic steps he demonstrated. His taps clicked in syncopated cadence like percussions.

"You know what else is great?" he asked as he walked me back to my cabin. "Jazz. Count Basie, Chick Webb, Tommy Dorsey, Duke Ellington, Louie Armstrong, and Benny Goodman. I'll play a record for you sometime. You'll see."

I looked at him. I had always heard that jazz was unscrupulous, born of rebellion.

He must have seen my expression, because he winked. "There's something about it that's so pure and spontaneous. Like painting a picture, but with music. When a crowd starts dancing to it, they're like a single pulsing animal that just woke to life. You'll see."

"Say, Irene," Annie said, as we dressed for bed, "We never see you anymore. You're always out with Spike."

"I won that bet," I reminded her.

She conceded with a giggle. "Didn't think you'd do it, but you've gone and done it."

She reached into her purse to give me a nickel, but I waved her away with a smile. "I'm not taking your money. Not for something where I came out ahead."

◀ ♫♪ ▶

On the rare day off or on Sunday mornings, while the others were at worship, Spike and I packed a picnic lunch of cheese, bread, and raisins and walked the canyon trails to Emerald Pools, the Watchman, Weeping Rock, even the West Rim. Often we encountered CCC crews with their picks, shovels, and mules, cutting new trails through the canyon or digging out foundations for campgrounds and park buildings.

I laughed as he described the pranks he had pulled on the other bellboys.

"I put a twisted rope, like a snake, at the foot of Ziegler's bed in the middle of the night. You should have heard him scream when he saw it at first light. He got me back by pouring ice water down my bed clothes."

At Weeping Rock, we found a secluded clearing beneath a mossy overhang, where we spread a blanket and ate our lunch, gazing at the Great White Throne, the shimmering mountain of white Navajo sandstone. Spike pointed out the birds that fluttered near our hide-away, which he identified by name: golden eagles, red-tailed hawks, peregrine falcons and pinyon jays, as well as mule deer, rock squirrels, and rabbits that scurried several hundred feet beneath us on the rocky switchbacks.

He lay on his back, arms propped beneath his head. I sat next to him, cross-legged, my skirt tucked between my legs, shoes kicked off.

"This is the life," he said, "Lazing here like a fat cat."

"Mmmm. Yes."

I had never before had so much fun. Visick had graduated me from cabin maid to working in the curio shop, where I stood behind the counter and rang orders or else greeted customers and chatted with park visitors, an immense pleasure. Performing duets in the variety show gave me the chance to hone my voice before an audience who never failed to applaud loudly and shout "Encore," their faces beaming as they journeyed from the grim realities of the country's economic nosedive into an enclave of song and dance, with gorgeous views of the park as the backdrop.

Visick had even hired a publicity photographer to take several shots of Annie and me, perched at the edge of a cliff on the Watchman Trail, arms drawn around our knees, peering into the canyon. Across from us, the Great White Throne climbed into the sky. This same photo was to be used as a billboard, advertising Zion as a tourist destination. And of course, dating Spike, a boy who was so brash and different from anyone I had ever known, was icing on the cake, all things considered.

"Come here," Spike commanded, "Let me kiss you proper."

We had kissed many times before, deep smooches that sent shudders down my body and put my heart into a full-tilt gallop and made me uncertain whether I was doing something immoral.

I leaned against his chest, and he encircled me in his arms. "You're the cutest little jitterbug I've ever known."

As we kissed, I felt the world spinning away from us – the cliffs of the canyon, the ferns in the clearing, the Great White Throne that towered into the sky, even the twitter of the birds and the thin smear of sunlight that streaked our blanket.

When we came up for air, he reached into his pocket and handed me a thick wad of bills.

I looked at him in surprise. "What's this?"

"That's over six hundred dollars. Nearly all my savings for New York. I want you to keep it safe for me."

I was astonished. "You want me to hold onto this much money?"

"You're more responsible than I am, honey. I can scarcely keep track of my own shoelaces. I've damn near lost everything more than once in my life. I trust you to keep it safe."

"I don't know. I've never had this kind of money. No one I know has. If I lose it, then all your plans will be up in smoke."

"I trust you," Spike repeated. "You keep it safe for us. Who knows? You might see through to come with me to New York and make a career of it. We can dance our way onto Broadway. Wouldn't that be a kick?"

"Gee, I don't know. LA, maybe. New York's awful far."

"I'm just a bum without you. Pure and simple."

I ignored the implications of what he was saying. "I don't know where I'm going to stow all this cash."

"You'll think of something. Probably safer in that girls' dormitory than where I live. The fellows had a rock fight last night and nearly wrecked the cabin."

"You're too much. A rock fight? Truly?"

He chuckled. "No one got hurt. Not much, anyhow."

"They'll kick you out if you're not careful."

"They won't. Visick knows he can't lose me."

I sighed in mock exasperation, and he pulled me back toward him. "I do all these things cause I'm crazy about you."

"Crazy as a loon is what you are," I said, smiling.

"A sharp looking one, though. Not like some saps around here who don't bother to run a comb through their hair and can't stand straight."

I giggled. "And ever so conceited."

"Only because I don't want you talking to other fellows at the dances. That puts me in a blue mood."

He was pouting, or pretending to pout.

"Then I promise I won't talk to other fellows. There. Better?"

"Because honey, it drives me to distraction, and I might do something really crazy. You know, I'm like the foolish man who made the mistake of falling in love with a sweet girl who wasn't true to him."

"My poor, poor baby needs a little sympathy," I murmured, curling against him, and kissing him again.

◀ 🎵♪ ▶

Several weeks later, near the end of summer, I received a troubling letter from Minnie. She wrote that Mae's baby, who had been born a little over a month ago, was fussy, colicky, and losing weight. Mae was beside herself, trying to care for the baby, and Mother and Minnie were too busy with summer canning and the wheat harvesting season to be of much help. Dad and Jacob were scheduled to leave again in a few more weeks to sell more cattle, presumably to meet expenses on the farm, while Hiram and Luke struggled to hold down the fort. There was even talk of finding another boarder, though after the unpleasant experience with Mr. Tanner, they were loath to do so.

Wylie had stayed in Provo over the summer to finish a project for his physics professor, whom he would assist in the fall, as a meagerly paid student researcher, before applying to graduate schools. Although we were all terribly proud of him, his absence compounded the lack of help back home. The atmosphere at the farm sounded tense, on the brink of a collapse. I sensed that money was tighter than ever.

For a long while after reading the letter, I considered my options. I had planned on returning to the BYU in the fall to resume my music degree, but given my family's dire affairs as I frolicked at Zion, that plan suddenly seemed frivolous. Spike intended to travel to New York when summer ended, to try to break into Broadway shows. As much as I hoped to continue our relationship, there was no way I would follow him there, certainly not without a marriage proposal and given the uncertainty at home.

Shivering, I flopped onto my bed. I understood what I had to do. I would take my summer earnings and return home to Paradise in a few weeks, when the Zion summer programs ended. I would help Mae, Mother, and Minnie until we could see a way clear out of the crisis.

When I broke the news to Spike, he took my hands. "I know you have to go back to your family. But I'll be terrible lonesome without you."

"You won't miss me once you're in New York, dancing on Broadway and meeting all kinds of interesting ladies." As soon as I spoke, I realized how peevish I sounded, but I wasn't sorry.

"I've changed my mind. I'm not going to New York. Not yet, anyway."

I peered at him, wondering if this was true. "Why not? I thought that was your biggest aspiration, as soon as you finished this gig."

He shrugged and avoided my eyes. "It was. But it can wait."

"Why?" I pressed.

"Could be cause I found Utah a lot more interesting all a sudden."

"And why would that be?"

"Irene, are you being coy, or just pretending to be daft?"

I turned away from him, biting my lip. "Spike Stallings, you make me mad."

He grabbed me around the waist and tried to kiss me as I struggled away from him. "Cause I met a cute little bearcat named Irene that I happen to be crazy about."

I blushed with pleasure.

"I figure I can return to Provo and take a few more classes at the BYU while working a job or two. And on at least a couple of the weekends each month I can get away to see you."

I squeezed his hands, and my body lightened.

◀ ♫♪ ▶

On the last evening before I was scheduled to return to the farm, Spike borrowed a car, and we rode into the canyon to the Temple of Sinawava, the highest point at Zion. Spike told me it was named for the Paiute Indians' Coyote God or Spirit. Moonlight shone into the canyon, so we could glimpse the outline of the towering, stone amphitheater with its complex network of spires. Above us, the aperture of the canyon bluff opened into a big top of thousands of brilliant stars.

Spike had brought a flashlight, so we left the car and walked slowly along the North Fork Virgin River of the Temple. Because it was dark, and I stumbled several times on little rocks on the trail, we didn't go far.

Mostly I clung to Spike's arm, as he shone the flashlight onto the trail a few feet ahead of us, and we talked.

"You know Desmond?" Spike said. "The kid I bell hop with? Well, we've discussed everything from opening a beer stand to taking over the Bank of England."

I fixed his profile with a disappointed stare he couldn't see.

"Anyway, we may go into business together as soon as we leave this million dollar job at the park. We might go to Flagstaff and open a dance studio. Then maybe get into a club."

"And what happened to your plans to stay in Utah?" I cut in.

"Oh, honey, we'll be married by then, and you'll come with me."

"What makes you so sure of that?" I demanded.

"Cause you're as crazy about me as I am about you. We're bound to be together."

I didn't like his tone. "Don't you think you're being a little presumptuous, mister?"

He laughed. "Hear me out. If I practice with him each day, we'd be ready by fall, and under my superior management, we'd save about a thousand dollars a month and sink it into oil stock. Desmond and I would do a lot of comedy numbers, and I would dance with you, and you'd sing and play piano, and we'd wow 'em. Desmond's a fine trumpet player, and he could do the contracting for the dance school."

"Spike Stallings, you're something else. First you tell me you'll get a job in Provo and take classes there, and next thing I know you're talking about taking up with Desmond and moving to Arizona. I can't keep up with all your ... schemes." I had to catch myself before inserting the word harebrained.

"I'm only thinking of how I can save a little extra money for us. I'll be damn near broke by the time I finish driving back and forth to see you in Paradise."

"Then you needn't do all that on my account," I said, haughtily.

"Nothing's too good for my baby. I'd drive to the moon and back to see you if I had to." He swung me around, switched off the flashlight, and kissed me, hard. "All I know is I want to squeeze you, kiss you, and love you to death."

While we embraced, he stepped on my feet by mistake, and we tumbled sideways onto the bank of the river, gasping with laughter.

"This your idea of loving me to death?" I cried between giggles, "Because if it is, you're doing a mighty good job of it."

I brushed bits of twig and soil from my skirt and tried to arrange my hair, while worrying out loud. "What on earth will I tell the girls back in the cabin? I look like I've rolled around in a haystack."

"Let them think what they want. Give them a little excitement."

"Spike Stallings, I'm warning you."

"Just remember," he said, as we returned to the car and stood in the moonlight, "I'm still crazy for you, even though you're full of backhanded compliments for me and won't give me any sympathy."

This, of course, caused me to whisper the line he had come to expect, "My poor, poor baby needs a little sympathy."

◀ ♫♪ ▶

In the morning, Spike used the same car to drive me to the train station in Cedar City. I returned the bundle of money he had asked me to keep, which I had hidden in the suitcase beneath my bunk bed, all the while terrified of what might happen if someone had discovered it. He had urged me to take ten or twenty dollars back home with me, but I refused. In the end, against my better judgment, I accepted money for the train fare.

We made promises to write.

"I'll visit you every chance I get," he said, "So you better be true to me and not take up with any turkey farmers in the meantime."

As the train pulled away, I waved and waved as Spike hopped back and forth on the station platform in a mime of a slapstick tap dancer, trying to get me to laugh, I was sure.

The startling vermilions and golds of the canyons of Southern Utah swept past me as the train chugged out of the station. I had expected to feel melancholic leaving this place, but somehow Spike's spunky dance on the platform, the promise of seeing him again, and the possibility of returning here another summer to perform at the variety show and hike through this gorgeous park with its natural beauty and peace, filled me with hope. It was likely the same heady emotion the National Park visitors experienced as they rode the open top buses that now circulated between Zion, Bryce, and the Grand Canyon. Progress, opportunity, a way forward.

CHAPTER THIRTY-THREE

October 2006.

Sylvie, a new staff member at the Golden Manor who takes turns with Cindy and Doris in administering my pills, peeks in on me as I'm preparing for breakfast.

"Miz Stallings, you bout ready for your meds?"

"In a minute. I'm just straightening up a few things."

"That's okay. I'll wait for you right here." She lowers herself into my easy chair.

I assume she will sit quietly until I finish getting ready, but she must not be the type to stay still and shut up.

A few minutes later, she says, "Lord, I'm not used to working on Sundays when I should be at church. This is some crazy schedule."

I'm not sure how to reply, or even whether I should. At last I say, "Don't let me stop you. Go on to church, if you'd like. I can take care of myself."

"Naw. I didn't mean that. It's just that my church is down the street. Hope Valley Baptist. So it's like I'm playing hooky or something." She laughs. "Do you go to church, Mrs. Stallings?"

"Not anymore. I did, though. For many years."

"Where?"

When I tell her the Church of Latter Day Saints, her eyes widen. "Are you Mormon?"

"I was raised in a Mormon household."

She starts to say something, then apparently reconsiders and clamps her mouth shut.

"What is it?" I prompt, curious about her reaction.

She shakes her head. "I just wondered… Did your father have more than one wife?

I let loose a chuckle. "What on earth gave you that idea? My father was married to one woman, my mother."

Of course, I'm not being completely forthcoming. I know many folks still believe that Mormons practice polygamy.

After Sylvie explains she has heard that Mormon men keep multiple wives, I correct her. "That happened well over a century and a half ago, when Joseph Smith first founded the religion, but the Church condemns it now, and no one practices it anymore."

She absorbs this information in surprise, and I dare say it gives her pause to realize the rumors she heard over the years have turned out to be false. When it comes down to it, people often find myths more interesting than the truth.

◀ 🎵♪ ▶

Rod arrives after brunch to drive me back to Deirdre's place. I close my eyes as he talks, partly because he sounds so much like Harold, but also because his voice is a comfort – musical, ringing with the familiarity of home and unexpected outbursts of humor I so miss.

"You're looking beautiful, Ma," he crows from the driver's side.

"Stop. How can I possibly, at my age?"

"Because you're a peach, like Dad always said. Through and through. You've still got the dancer's figure and your singing voice, even if you're now a nonagenarian."

I laugh. "Oh, Rod. You've always been a lady's man with your compliments."

"Can't I praise my own mother without raising her suspicions?"

I twine my fingers through his hair.

We circle into the driveway, past a long line of cars parked along the street.

"I thought Deirdre said this would be a small celebration," I say. "From the looks of these cars, it's much bigger."

"You know Deirdre. She can't do small. She's an organizer and a planner, and once she gets going, there's no stopping her. She goes all out."

I lift my hands in resignation, and Rod helps me out of the car and through the front door. A throng of people moves through the open family room with drinks in hand, chatting, leaning against the banisters of the sweeping staircase, reclining on the sofas, heads bent together conspiratorially.

I wish they would continue as they are, oblivious of my presence and immersed in their private conversations. I could observe them from a perch, not thrust myself against them. But someone catches sight of Rod and me, and a murmur ripples through the crowd until they turn to gaze at us. Someone in the back whom I can't see, maybe Deirdre, begins to clap, and the others join in. Thunderous waves of applause, and for a moment, I'm in a ballroom with Harold, after one of our performances, looking upon the audience.

I put on a big smile and step forward, waving my hands. "Hello, hello, hello!"

Rod helps me to the center of the living room and into a chair. Pushing through the crowd, Deirdre brushes her lips against my forehead and places a glass of iced tea into my hands.

A petite middle-aged woman plays songs from the thirties and forties on the piano. I sink against the chair. All at once I see them clearly, as if I were back in the Razzle Dazzle nightclub: dancing couples, singers with rouged cheeks, hands clasped to bosoms.

Deirdre is beside me. She murmurs into my ear, "Jack didn't want to miss your birthday for the world. He's flying in later tonight, first chance he has. And Amy wanted to be here, badly, but she's hardly in a position to pick up and leave, given her situation." She sighs. "Tom Junior can barely afford a plane ticket, let alone a flat in New York. He just started clerking somewhere in the city. But we'll fly one or both of them out here over Christmas. You'll see them then."

"If I'm around then."

"Mom!"

"It was only a joke."

The pianist segues into the opening notes of "Happy Birthday."

Deirdre guides me to the piano, and the guests congregate in a semicircle, facing us. I recognize many of them, neighbors and friends of Deirdre and Tom, most of whom I have met before.

They stare at me politely, singing. Someone yells, "Speech, speech!"

Heads turn to me.

Automatically I smile at them. "Thanks for coming. I'm so honored and pleased. I - I can't believe I'm ninety. It doesn't seem right." I pause and rack my brains for something to say to make them smile back. Harold would have had a quip on his lips; he was always quick-witted.

"When you're my age, your joints are more accurate than the Weather Service. Your secrets are safe with your friends, because they can't remember most of them. And the candles at your birthday cost more than the cake." Polite laughter.

"Anyway, I want to say thank you, especially to my daughter Deirdre and her husband, Tom, my sons Rod and Jack, and my grandkids. I'm so very blessed." I pause, absorbing this truth. "Now go ahead and eat cake."

They do. They indulge. I remember how I used to have the appetite and energy for parties, too, the ravenous desire, like a puppy, to experience it all – paw the trappings, trot around the room from person to person, fill myself with sweets and biscuits until my tummy ached. And why not? This is how you should live life, given the chance.

CHAPTER THIRTY-FOUR

August 1936.

Minnie had been right. Mae was weary from lack of sleep and tending to the fussy baby. Her normally shining hair lay dull and lackluster, shorn to her chin in an uneven bob. Dark circles surrounded her eyes, and she had lost so much weight that her dresses hung on her loosely, like the Hoover aprons I had grown accustomed to seeing in recent years.

The baby, whom Mae and Hiram had named Mary, wailed a constant high, thin keen during the day, and woke every half hour during the night. She, too, looked underfed and scrawny, even for a newborn, and seemed inconsolable, even while rocking or suckling at Mae's breast. Dr. Thomas had paid his rounds and advised making a warm, weak tea of mint, ginger, and basil to feed Mary in a bottle, which Mae had tried, to no avail. He had also recommended burping the infant and playing gentle music for her. Without a piano, Mae sang an endless stream of lullabies, until, she confessed, her voice was as hoarse as a bear's and her throat positively raw.

In a whisper, she told me that several times, she had been so exhausted she had simply laid Mary in her cradle amid shrieks and gone to lie down on her own bed, where she had surrendered to sobs nearly as shrill and desperate as those of her baby's. However much she struggled to silence her tears, they had wracked her body.

Mother, it seemed, wanted nothing to do with the crying child, and had more than once criticized Mae for her inability to console her.

"Surely a mother should know how to calm her own child," she muttered as Mae, in the other room behind closed door, begged the baby not to cry.

Minnie, who had tried to help by doubling up on chores and picking up Mary when Mae had reached her wit's end, confided, "I'm so glad you're back. So are Mae and Mother."

With Dad and the boys out in the fields all day cutting and binding the grain, it was up to us, the women, to tend the garden, can as many fruits and vegetables as we could pick, make the meals, gather eggs, pitch hay, milk the cows, and sew and mend clothes.

I busied myself with these chores, but also gave Mae a break several times a day by attempting to rock Mary. Her tiny pink face seemed permanently wrinkled in a crying fit, and I understood how, given the unfortunate circumstances of her colic, she could try the patience of even the most saintly of mothers. Other times I urged Mae to eat, both for her sake and the baby's. I prepared her favorite dish, chicken dumplings with corn on the cob on the side, and a pudding. This seemed to cheer her, but still she ate little, or what she did consume she burned just as fast, because she remained unnaturally skinny.

"Remember what Dr. Thomas said," I reminded her. "By the time Mary's six months old, her crying should ease."

She nodded somberly, looking unconvinced.

Less than a week had passed since I returned home, and I had been so busy with canning and pitching in at the farm, that I was genuinely shocked and pleased to receive a letter from Spike, which Luke had collected at the post office in town.

"Dearest Irene," he had written. *"One day's gone since you left, and I'm still here at the park for two more weeks. Last nite I had such a queer*

feeling when I went to bed I would have said a prayer, but I guess it's because I'm used to having you around. It's not the same without you, and to prove it, I've got a toothache. If it's true that nothing can live in saltwater, by now my mouth should be a place of uninhabited creatures, since I've used about fourteen pounds of salt and taken eleven hundred aspirin tablets. Did you have a good trip home? It's strange how much I miss you, you little devil.

I made a dollar and a half tip today bell hopping, which isn't bad. Tonite I thought about going to the dance, but I decided I couldn't go unless I had a cute little jitterbug, and I only know one person who is cute and sweet enough to dance with and she isn't here. So all I've got left is this toothache and lonesomeness something awful.

Goodnite, honey. I'm lonesome for you to say, 'My poor, poor little baby needs sympathy,' and hold me tight and kiss me.

When you go to bed tonite, think of me standing on a chair, grabbing one of the pipes near the ceiling, and swinging into bed like a monkey, then trying to fall asleep amidst all the snores. (I'm in an upper bunk).

Love,

Spike"

I read his letter over several times, laughing when I read the passage about the fourteen pounds of salt and eleven hundred aspirin tablets he had supposedly taken, plus his maneuvers to get into his top bunk.

That night, as Minnie and I prepared for bed in our attic room, I shared the letter with her and told her a little about Spike.

"Do you have a photo of him?" she asked eagerly.

"Not yet. I'll write and ask him for one."

"You got to tell me more. What's he like?"

"Wicked sense of humor. Impulsive and hotheaded. And ever so good looking. He's got dark hair and eyes and a chiseled face. Plus he's a swell dancer. He and his sister almost signed a contract to make a Hollywood picture."

Minnie's eyes went wide.

We sat cross-legged on the bed, whispering, until she convinced me to light the kerosene lamp and write him a proper letter.

Dutifully I described our travails on the farm and Mae's troubles with her baby. Next morning, I promised Luke half a dozen wheat rolls plus a nickel for candy if he would run into town and mail it for me.

A little over a week later, Luke returned from town with another letter from Spike, which I hurriedly stashed into my apron pocket until I could steal away to read it in privacy.

"Dearest Irene,

Your letter made my day. I'm glad you got home safe, but I'm sorry to hear about all the trouble you're having. Listen, it seems almost every woman gets irritable after they have babies, and probably that's the matter with Mae.

They're making a picture here, taken mostly in the air. Planes fly over the canyon all day long.

I have a confession: I've cut off my hair. It's now about one eighth of an inch long and stands like the bristles on a ladies' brush. But even minus my hair, I've still got the same charm.

I thought again about dressing up tonite and going to listen to the dance music, but I don't want to be around knuckleheads and without my choicest girl. At least my toothache's easing, and believe me that's something. I'll bet you're going to church today. You really are the sweetest, most precious girl I've known.

By the way, I forbid you to talk to former boyfriends. Gee, I wish you wouldn't look at anyone, but if you do, remember that you can't find a guy who really cares for you like I do, and gee, you wouldn't want to break a poor fellow's heart. Enclosed is a picture you asked for. It didn't turn out so good, but here you go. Send me one of you, please.

Love,

Spike"

Once again I showed the letter to Minnie, and we chuckled, wondering how he could have concluded that the trouble had originated with Mae, not with her baby.

"Just like a man," Minnie declared, and we laughed even harder, knowing firsthand how little Dad, Jacob, Wylie, Hiram, and Luke got involved with babies and small children.

"When are we going to get to meet him?" Minnie demanded, examining Spike's photo. "He *is* handsome."

"Soon. As soon as he gets settled in Provo, he'll come up to see me."

"Reenie, do you suppose you'll ever return to Provo? To the BYU, I mean?"

I hesitated. The question troubled me, since it seemed my music plans had gone wildly astray. "I don't know. I think I might have a better chance at a singing career if I were to find an engagement with a club or two." This last part was inspired by what Spike had told me about his own dance progression.

Minnie made a face. "A club? Where they drink alcohol and smoke, and the patrons are seedy?"

"Not everything's like the variety show at Zion. Most singing opportunities are in dance and jazz clubs. It's a start, you know. It wouldn't be the end. But it's what you have to do before you get noticed by any Hollywood producers or..." I groped for the right words, but stopped at Minnie's shocked expression.

"Never mind." I turned away, disappointed and annoyed that she didn't understand.

"Oh, Reenie, I didn't mean..." she began, but I had turned my face to the wall and remained silent, pretending to go to sleep.

A week or more later, Spike wrote to let me know he was settled back in Provo, where he had become the manager of a dance band he had previously hired at Zion. He had rented a studio apartment over a bowling alley, where he slept and taught dancing lessons to a few students from the BYU. He was also able to find a permanent job for the dance band, playing in a town near Provo, and they played for most of the school dances at the BYU, too. On top of that, he had done something hard to believe. He had gone into town and bought a new Ford, paying over five hundred dollars for it. He confessed he made this purchase so he could drive the one hundred forty plus miles to visit me in Paradise every chance he got. But the best news, which left me slightly dazed and giddy-headed and turned my cheeks pink, was that he planned to drive up to see me, weekend after next.

Hurriedly I consulted with Minnie on how to break this news to Mother and Dad. They knew I had met a boy at Zion, but they didn't know how serious we had become. I also worried that his decidedly un-Mormon habits – the drinking, smoking, and swearing – would turn them against him, and they might forbid me to see him. I hadn't even disclosed these habits to Minnie.

"Write to him," Minnie urged. "Let him know he has to be on his best behavior."

In my letter, after expressing my excitement about his upcoming visit, I asked Spike to watch his mouth, leave his chewing tobacco and smokes at home, and understand that I came from a family of strict church-going Mormons. Sure, they heard about the occasional boy in town who went out drinking, and to this news they looked the other way, but they were not willing to forgive this behavior in their own kin. I also informed him that we would address him by his Christian name Harold. My family needn't wonder how he got the nickname Spike.

Meanwhile, I told Mother that my friend Harold Stallings from the BYU was driving up for a visit the following weekend.

"Is he courting you?" she demanded.

Despite myself, I blushed.

"Tommy Jensen's still in town and would love to take up with you again, now that you're back home."

"We aren't going together anymore, Mother. You know that."

"First loves have a way of rekindling. And Tommy still carries a torch for you."

"Mother, I don't feel the same about him anymore. Anyway, I want you to meet Harold."

She frowned and pursed her lips. "How long is he staying?"

"He's driving a long way, clear up from Provo. I expect he'll stay at least the afternoon before he has to go back."

"Make sure to let him know that he can't stay here overnight. We simply don't have the space." With that, she turned away.

◀ 🎵♪ ▶

On the Saturday that we expected Spike, I rose before dawn and swept the house, starting with the kitchen then working my way through the dining room. The parlor, which was now Mae's and Hiram's and the baby's bedroom, would remain shut off. When I had finished sweeping, I opened the windows to air out the two main rooms, and scoured the floors. After soaping down the dining table and kitchen counter, I prepared an apple pie, which I planned to set in the oven an hour before Spike's expected arrival, to fill the kitchen with aromatic scents of cinnamon and allspice.

Feeling ambitious, I cooked a chicken with carrots and peas and put it in the icebox, then tried to find other ways to occupy myself around the house, as difficult as it was to put my mind to a task. The men had gone to the fields, but Minnie, Mae, Mother, and the baby had arranged themselves in the two front rooms. Mae knit a layette for Mary, who wailed intermittently from her cradle; Minnie stood over the kitchen stove, canning more vegetables; and Mother made a quilt.

At last I grabbed my own needle and thread and darned a pair of Dad's socks. Admittedly, I was nervous about reuniting with Spike in public, and equally worried about how he and my family would get along.

At quarter till two we heard the distinct rumble of an engine puttering up the rutted dirt lane. Throwing down my sewing, I ran to the window and spied a light yellow roadster chugging toward the house. Mother and Mae raised their heads from their work, as well.

"I'm going outside," I announced, and before anyone could respond, I flung open the door and hurried onto the porch, where I skipped back and forth, shielding my face with my hands as the roadster approached.

At last the engine cranked down, the car screeched to an abrupt halt, and Spike hopped gracefully out of the driver's side, grinning from ear to ear. His face was shiny and clean-shaven, and he wore a dark fedora, trousers, and a long-sleeved, button-down khaki shirt, not unlike the kind the CCC boys wore in the canyon. As he had warned, his hair was bristly and short, army-style.

"Spike!" I cried, forgetting my promise to call him Harold, and ran to him.

He caught me into his arms and lifted me off the ground, laughing. "How's my favorite girl in the whole wide world?" He smelled of aftershave and mint, not tobacco, thankfully.

We kissed, and I pulled away, fearing eyes at the window.

He stepped back to give me a good look. "Honey, you're sure a sight for sore eyes. So lovely and cute I could eat you all up. I tried getting here as quick as I could, but the roads this way are something awful."

Behind me, the door opened, and Mother, Minnie, and Mae, the baby in her arms, walked onto the porch, squinting in the sunlight. They stood side by side, looking bashful, and glancing with envy at Spike and his sporty new car.

"Mother, meet Harold Stallings."

To my delight, Spike took her hand and brought it to his lips. "Very pleased to meet you, Mrs. Larsen." He produced a nosegay from the passenger's seat of his car, which he presented to her.

"My stars, how nice." Mother looked genuinely pleased.

Spike winked at me.

When I introduced him to Minnie and Mae, they openly admired his car, and Minnie gave me a look to indicate, "You know how to choose your boyfriends."

"Irene, don't keep Harold standing outside, for Pete's sake. Invite him in, so he can rest a spell after that long road trip," Mother said, and I knew that Spike had made a favorable impression on her.

Inside, sitting at the dining room table and sampling my apple pie, he patiently answered Mother's questions about his mother and sisters and the BYU. His manner and words were so charming and polite that I could have jumped up and squeezed his neck.

Mother turned her questions to his employment. "You're manager of a dance band, Irene tells me?"

"Yes, ma'am, that's right. We play at American Fork, which is a little north of Provo, and we play at the BYU, too." He also explained that he taught dance lessons, and all in all, he was making good money.

Mother nodded, and her gaze strayed to the window in front of the house, where Spike's car sat gleaming in the sunlight.

At half past four, Dad and the boys returned from the fields, and I made a new round of introductions.

The boys peppered Spike with questions about the car: how did it run, what make and model was it, where did he buy it, how much did he pay for it.

Luke even begged to go for a ride, which Mother quickly dissuaded. "Not on your life, young man." She leaned over to apologize to Spike for Luke's impudence.

I reheated the chicken and vegetables in the iron stove, and we ate generous helpings with wheat rolls, water, milk, and pie.

All the while, Spike complimented my cooking, declaring it was the tastiest meal he had eaten in months.

"How do you get your meals?" Mother inquired.

"I admit I don't eat well. I've got a little kitchenette in my studio. Most times I open a can of beans, or else I grab a sandwich at the hall where the band plays."

"Oh my." Mother considered this information, shaking her head sadly, as though it were a pity. She glanced my way.

For their part, my brothers and father, except to ask about Spike's car, remained taciturn and shy in his presence. Next to Spike, with his lithe dancer's body and clean hands, they looked like the farmers they were: clad in overalls, faces and arms leathery and brown from the sun, dirt caked around their rough, jagged nails.

Nonetheless, after dinner, the men retired to the porch while Mother, Minnie, Mae, and I cleaned the kitchen. From outside floated laughter and an enthusiastic stream of conversation. I suspected that Spike, with his gift for storytelling and his boyhood adventures in the wilderness, had charmed them, and they had found common ground.

An hour before evening fell, the men returned inside, and Spike asked me to show him around the orchard, garden, fields and barn.

I looked over at Mother, who simply nodded her assent.

"Only chance I could steal you away," Spike said as we walked out the screen door and headed toward the orchard. He squeezed my hand.

"They like you. I can tell."

"Even compared to your old boyfriends?" he said in a teasing voice.

"Stop. Yes."

"I wasn't so sure about your dad. I'll bet he thinks it's a little queer I'm a dancer."

"I explained to him that you manage a dance band."

"Yeah, but I also let it slip that I dance, too. Don't think he knew what to make of that."

I shrugged. "He can tell you have money. That's a big deal these days. I'm sure that made a good impression on him."

"That's what I wanted him to think, anyway," Spike said slyly. "Guess I pulled the wool over his eyes."

"You behaved yourself real well."

"I promised you I would. I tried to be a good boy. See?" He held out his hands. "No smokes or liquor or swearing. Clean as a whistle."

I smiled. "Good. Cause any slip up there, and they'd send you packing in a second."

We arrived at the peach and apple orchard, and strolled through the rows. I reached up to pluck an apple from a low-hanging bough, and handed it to Spike.

He polished it on his shirt, and took a bite. "This fruit's as sweet as you. I'd eat you up, too, if I could. Just looking at you makes me crazy."

Tucking the apple into his pocket, he put his arms around my shoulders, and kissed me. "Been wanting to do that for ages."

We kissed again, and he stirred and hardened against me. An ache spread from my groin into my stomach, and my heart twittered like a wild warbler.

"If you marry me, we can dance the clubs, and you can sing. We'll have a swell time."

I leaned my head against his chest. "Soon."

"I can support us both. I've got a snug little studio. You wouldn't have to work much if you didn't want to."

"I want to work and pull my own weight."

"That's what I love about you. You're like a queen who has to have her own way. Won't let anyone tell her what to do."

I wasn't sure this was the most flattering compliment he could pay me, and told him so.

He laughed. "That's exactly what I mean. You're headstrong."

"If you think this is headstrong, just you watch."

He swung me into the air and sailed me over his head. "You're so light, you'd do a perfect routine with me. Fact, we'll be the most glamorous dancing couple folks have seen. In Utah, anyway."

"Put me down this instant." Despite myself, I broke into laughter. That was the thing about Spike; he always had me in stitches.

Evening was starting to fall, so I guided him into the garden, the barn and chicken coop, and pointed out the wheat fields, and the small herd of cattle in the distance.

He studied all of it with an appraising stare, as if trying to decide what it would be like to live here as a farmer.

Back at the house, he explained he had to return to Provo for an engagement with the band the following day.

We gathered outside to see him off. Even Mother smiled as he bid his farewells.

Right before he climbed into the driver's seat, he whispered, "I'll try to get up here again first chance I get." To my ears, he was promising to rescue me from drab and dull and sashay me into color, glamor, dancing, and singing.

I waved as he puttered down the dirt lane in his smart roadster, a cloud of dust trailing him. When he turned the corner of the lane, he tooted the horn and disappeared from view.

"You've found yourself a mighty nice boyfriend," Mother said as we returned to the house.

A smile spread across my face. I knew full well I couldn't have asked for a higher recommendation.

That night, while we prepared for bed, Minnie told me that Spike was swell.

"He's sure good looking," she added, "And you never told me he's rich, to boot."

I didn't bother to correct her, but simply teased, "Keep your hands to yourself, Minnie Larsen."

CHAPTER THIRTY-FIVE

October 2006.

Deirdre takes me to lunch today to the corner coffee shop, a few blocks away from the Manor. It's a chance to get away for a little while, she says, and I agree.

I order a chicken salad sandwich, but when it arrives, I find I have no appetite for it. I start to apologize to Deirdre, but she reaches across the table and pats my hand.

"It's okay, Mom. What do you think you have the appetite for instead? Is there anything that appeals?"

I agree to chicken soup, and she arranges for the waitress to remove my plate and replace it with this steaming bowl.

"You know, honey," I tell her, as I spoon the broth into my mouth and find it tastes delicious, after all, "Your dad and I were always awful proud of you."

This remark apparently takes her by so much surprise that she puts down her sandwich mid bite and hastily wipes her lips. "Oh, Mom."

"No, it's true. We didn't tell you enough. Should have, though. Neither your dad nor I ever managed to get a college degree. Course, those were the Depression years, and you know how Dad would get one idea after another, popping up and taking over what he was doing. These days they'd say he had adult ADHD. He couldn't settle down long enough to crack open a book and take a test. But you, honey. You put your head to it, and you studied and studied and got a degree. You're the first one in our family to graduate from college. And..." Suddenly overcome with emotion, I stop to wipe my eyes.

"I'm so proud of you," I finish. "You've always had the ability to learn, to really go places. And you have. You've gotten involved in the community, and made a name for yourself." I reach across the table and grasp her hand, and when I look up, her eyes are shining, too.

CHAPTER THIRTY-SIX

October 1936.

Beaming, I clutched the card that Spike sent for my twentieth birthday. In it, he proposed I take the train to the BYU for the long Armistice Day weekend in November, which happened to fall on his birthday. He promised to make arrangements for me to stay with a female student at the BYU, a good friend of his sister Miriam. I could accompany him and his dance band to American Fork, where they had an engagement on Saturday evenings.

To my surprise, Mother and Dad agreed to Spike's plan. Evidently he had made such a good impression on his previous visits to the farm that they didn't question the arrangement, and assumed I would be safe and in good hands.

On the Saturday morning of Armistice Day weekend, I packed a small overnight bag with toiletries, my nightgown, and a spare dress Mae had loaned me, and boarded the train in Logan. I wanted to run up and down the Pullman cars, thrilling with the novelty of escaping the dreariness of the farm and bursting with the anticipation of seeing Spike and dancing with him in American Fork.

At the station in Provo that afternoon, Spike swept me into his arms in a bear hug, lifting me off my feet. "Oh my little darling, you made it."

He gave me a long kiss, until I squirmed, uncomfortable about the passersby who were undoubtedly staring at us.

"Say," he retorted, "When do I have the chance to do this in Paradise? Who cares what these sods think, anyhow? Let's give them a free show."

"Oh, Spike." I bit my tongue and giggled.

As we climbed into his roadster, he handed me a fresh bouquet of flowers.

"Truly for me this time and not Mother? Gee, you're full of surprises."

He chuckled. "You haven't seen anything yet."

"Where are we headed?" I asked, as we motored away from the station. "Are you taking me to the place where I'm to stay tonight so I can meet Miriam's friend and leave my things there?"

"All in due time. I was thinking we could grab a bite first. We've got a little over three hours before we have to drive up to American Fork. There's a café in Provo around the corner here. We can have a light supper."

He pulled onto a side street several blocks away from the BYU campus and helped me out of the passenger's seat. Inside the diner, where apparently he was a regular, he guided us to a booth by the window.

"Afternoon, Mr. Stallings," the waitress on duty greeted him. "And what can I bring you and your...friend?"

"Lila, this is Miss Larsen. She'll accompany me and my band to American Fork. We're playing there tonight."

"Why, what fun." Lila gave me an appraising look.

"Bring us two of the blue plate specials, and coffee for me." He looked at me. "Okay with you, honey? It's roast beef sandwiches with mashed potatoes on the side."

I nodded.

"Coffee for you, too, miss?" Lila asked.

I shook my head, declaring that water was fine.

When the food arrived, we tucked into it with relish. Spike told me about the band – the drummer, saxophonist, trombonist, trumpet player, and pianist.

"You could take over the piano for him, I'm sure," he said. "He can't hold a candle next to your playing."

"You've hardly ever heard me play."

"I know you'd do swell. Hell, you'd run circles around the singer they've got in American Fork, too."

I smiled. "Are you trying to talk me into a gig with your band?"

He reached for my hands across the table, then glanced at the counter, where Lila was chatting to a customer and pouring water into glasses. "More than that. You know, honey, I'm driving over two hundred fifty miles round trip to see you in Paradise every chance I get. Truth be known, I'm getting tired of all that driving. It's awful expensive, and we hardly ever have any time together at your folks' place, anyway."

I stared at him, stricken, and withdrew my hands. "So you're telling me I'm not worth the trip, and you don't want to bother yourself with seeing me anymore?" Even to my own ears, I sounded hurt, defensive. I turned to look out the window, biting my lip.

"Not so fast. You're not getting away from me that easy. Here's what I'm trying to say. All you have to do to keep seeing me is to marry me. Today. Besides, tomorrow's my twenty-third birthday, so it would be a real nice birthday gift."

I turned back to face him, slack-jawed. "Are you proposing to me, or is this some kind of joke?"

He plucked my hands and squeezed them. "Never been more serious in my life. Irene, will you marry me?"

I continued staring at him, stunned. "You mean today?" I said at last.

"If we're going to do it, today's our best chance. There's a little town between here and American Fork where we can stop and get a license and get married, all in the same day."

I caught my breath and gazed at my plate. This wasn't at all what I had expected, which was to say a formal engagement, followed by a proper, albeit small temple wedding with our folks in attendance.

When I looked up, Spike was watching me. As if he had read my mind, he said, "There'll be time later for a regular ceremony if we want it. The important thing is that we get married while we can, so we can be together always. No more driving back and forth or taking the train or any of this other nonsense." He waved his hand at the window. "And when we're married, you can teach lessons with me, and we can dance together at the halls and in the clubs. We'll be the new Fred and Ginger."

I wanted to ask him what the hurry was, but I already knew. Spike was impulsive, bursting with impatience and nervous energy, hatching plans, then bustling to make new ones. Once an idea seized hold of him, he couldn't let it go.

"Also," he went on, "I don't want those turkey farmers you know to get on the inside track while I'm away. Then I might lose you for good."

The implications of his proposal whirled through my head. It seemed he had offered me a life of glamor and color, away from the farm: the promise of dancing engagements, singing performances, trips up and down the coast to LA and Hollywood, Oregon and Washington State. Life with Spike would never be dull. I wouldn't have to milk another cow, tend to vegetables in the garden on hands and knees, feed chickens, or scrub farmhouse floors under Mother's supervision. In essence, I would be free to pursue my dream of a singing career.

He leaned forward and peered into my eyes. "What do you say, darling?"

He might have been a magician, intent on hypnotizing me. One wrong answer, and the spell would be broken, and all fantasies of a romantic life together vanquished in a puff of smoke.

I took a breath. "Yes. Yes, I'll marry you today."

His eyes glinted with surprise, followed by a blaze of supreme joy, made more sure, I suspected, in the knowledge that he had succeeded in persuading me.

We stared at each other across the table. My heart was aflutter, and I was awash with nervous excitement.

He leaned over and whispered, "Let's get out of here and do this."

◀ ♫♪ ▶

The judge at the County Courthouse was an older gentleman with spectacles and a shock of white hair. He didn't look surprised when Spike told him we wanted to be married that day, in the courthouse. I had expected him to appraise us sharply, in frank disapproval, but he didn't seem particularly interested in either us as a couple or Spike's request. We were undoubtedly one of many whom he had married over the last month or more. At least we were dressed nicely, Spike in a white collared shirt and dark trousers for the dance later tonight, and I in a navy blue dress with an intricate pattern of tiny yellow and red flowers that Mae had loaned me for my weekend in Provo.

When it became clear we had arrived by ourselves, the Judge summoned one of his clerks to serve as witness, then ushered us into a tiny chamber. Each of us wrote our full name, birthdate, current address, and parents' names and addresses on the license. Beside his father's name, Spike wrote "deceased."

I turned to him in half disbelief, wanting to ask, "Is it truly this easy? Can we really waltz in and do this without a second thought?" It appeared that getting married would be as fast as checking out a book from the library.

Spike grinned as he signed his name in the groom's space on the license, and when he finished, he returned the pen to the judge with a conspiratorial wink, or so it seemed.

For a fleeting moment I wondered at how shocked Mother would be, had she known what I was doing at this very minute, but I banished the thought from my head. We could arrange it, of course, to look as though we had just gotten engaged, with a proper Temple ceremony to plan in the months to come, and she needn't be the wiser.

When we emerged from the Courthouse as man and wife, I could scarcely believe it. Spike kissed me and spun me around on the courthouse steps in a spontaneous dance, looking as slyly mischievous as the Cheshire Cat.

"How's Mrs. Stallings, my lovely bride?" he said, beaming. As we returned to the roadster, he thrust the bouquet he had presented me earlier back into my arms. "Wasn't this a lark? And wasn't it perfect you've got these flowers? Every bride has to have flowers."

"Harold Stallings, if I didn't know better, I'd say you planned this from the start."

"You never know. Don't put it past me."

"Except for a beautiful engagement ring and wedding band. Every bride needs that," I teased.

"Nothing's too good for my baby. Oh, I'm going to buy you a beautiful ring. Just give me time."

And with that, he squealed away in the roadster, only to blast his horn at the car in front of him, who, in his words, was "poking along like a tortoise," until I begged him to go slower.

◀ ♫ ♪ ▶

When we arrived at the dance hall in American Fork, Spike's band was already setting up their equipment on the dark mahogany platform. Taking my hand, Spike led me to his crew. Dressed in dark suits and ties, they bent over their instruments, alternately experimenting with notes and kidding around with each other. Cigarette smoke drifted through the hall.

Overhead hung a big sparkling ball, winking with bits of mirrored glass.

"Lee, Hank, Curtis, Jim, Al, meet the new Mrs. Stallings."

The drummer put down his sticks and swiveled in my direction. "No kidding? You're not pulling our legs, are you?" he demanded, raising his eyebrows.

"Not on your life. We just got married, didn't we, honey?"

I affirmed this with a smile and nod and extended a hand, which the drummer accepted and pumped enthusiastically.

"Congratulations! I'll be damned! Didn't think this old dog had it in him to settle down. Mighty nice to meet you, Mrs. Stallings."

"You can call me Irene."

The saxophonist, trombonist, trumpet player, and pianist crowded around me, congratulating us both and slapping Spike on the back.

"Spike, you lucky devil!" the trombonist whooped, and to me, "How did such a pretty doll like you agree to marry this bum?

"Yeah, this guy's a tramp. But it looks like he hit the jackpot," the sax player said.

"Knock it off, fellas," Spike interrupted, grinning.

"Here, here!" the sax player cried, setting down his instrument and rising, arms outspread. "Three cheers for Spike Stallings and his beautiful new bride!"

The band broke into applause, and I blushed as they encircled us. The drummer dipped onto one knee to salute me, and the trombonist followed suit.

"Don't you dopes get ideas," Spike joked, slinging an arm around my neck. "Go find your own girls."

"All the stunners have been taken already. No thanks to you, Spike," the trumpet player said.

"And let me tell you," Spike continued, "This girl can sing and play the piano, too. You fellows might be out of a job if you're not careful."

In an hour, the hall filled with customers, who clustered around the tables on the perimeter of the floor or waltzed in time with the band's snappy swing tunes.

Spike and I glided onto the floor, where he twirled me tightly against him until we were practically eye to eye, then spun me away. After a few minutes, he signaled to the band, who played a smooth rag tune in 4/4 time. As the music crescendoed, Spike swept me into a foxtrot. While at Zion, he had taught me the steps, including several advanced moves, and now we danced the length of the ballroom, moving lithely, our arms and legs in perfect sync. Several couples stood back to watch us.

"Well, well, Mrs. Stallings," Spike whispered, "We sure know how to wow 'em."

As the tune finished, the sax player took the microphone and announced, "And now, ladies and gentlemen, in honor of our manager,

Spike Stallings, and his lovely bride, Irene, who were just married this afternoon, we'll play 'The Way You Look Tonight.'"

The song was from the picture *Swing Time*, which released a couple months earlier, and starred Fred Astaire and Ginger Rogers. Spike and I had driven to Logan to see it during one of his visits.

We sashayed around the floor in a foxtrot. "Honey, this song is perfect. It might as well have been written for us," he murmured into my hair.

"Let's make it our song," I said with a powerful joy, like I could float to the ceiling and touch the mirrored ball, then slowly descend and do it over and over again.

Spike sang the lyrics to me, while I hummed to the tune.

"Someday, when I'm awfully low, when the world is cold, I will feel a glow just thinking of you, and the way you look tonight."

When the song ended, Spike donned his black and white tap shoes and performed an intricate number for the remaining guests, who whistled and cheered. I admired the way he sailed across the floor, arms outstretched, toes clicking smartly like drums.

The band announced another number from *Swing Time*, "Waltz in Swing Time," a lively, syncopated waltz with tap overlays. Spike swept me into his arms and whirled me across the ballroom, imitating Fred's and Ginger's dance steps, tapping with gusto and precision. Closing my eyes, I felt awash in the blissful fullness I used to feel while playing piano. I had attained the near impossible. I, a poor farmer's daughter, now pirouetted across a stage before an audience, and it struck me that my new life might be like the song: a colorful, whirling fusion of classical music, jazz, and dance.

After midnight, as the hall was ready to close, Spike urged me to stand by the mic and sing "Smoke Gets In Your Eyes" to the accompaniment of Hank, the pianist.

"Bravo!" he catcalled when I finished, and the smattering of guests clapped politely.

Outside the hall, in the crisp cold air, we bid our farewells to the band members, who again offered their congratulations and wished us well.

Spike lost no time helping me into the car, then swerving and speeding into the empty streets.

"You drive like a madman," I told him as he ran a red light.

He chuckled. "Can't wait to get you back to my studio."

◀ 🎵♪ ▶

Spike's apartment, as he had warned, sat above a bowling alley in downtown Provo, not far from the university. As we climbed the stairs, I heard shouts, cheers and the thunder of the balls as they careened down wooden lanes and crashed into the pins.

I hadn't fully understood what Spike had meant by studio until we entered. It was a single large room with an old green couch pushed against the wall, where apparently Spike slept, and a small kitchenette with a stove and sink. A washbasin and toilet stood in a corner, opposite the kitchenette.

Spike deposited my overnight suitcase by the sofa. "Welcome to my bachelor pad," he announced.

I said nothing, hugging my shoulders and inspecting the place: the worn-out carpet, dented, whitewashed walls without pictures, tiny window over the sofa with the rust-brown curtains. Several dirty dishes lay in the sink, which reeked of days-old food. I also detected the stale scent of cigarettes. Beneath us droned the raucous cries of the bowling alley patrons, coupled with the tumbling balls.

"Don't worry. I'll find a nicer place with a regular kitchen, living room, bedroom, and privy," Spike hastened to say. "The works. This is temporary."

I nodded, feeling shy and awkward and a trifle terrified. It was the first time I had been alone in a man's bedroom. For a fleeting moment I wished I were anywhere else, bunking at the BYU with Miriam's friend or riding the train back to Logan.

Sensing my discomfort, Spike put his arms around me and led me to the couch, where he encouraged me to sit. He strolled into the kitchenette and poured a smattering of whiskey into two glasses from a half-empty bottle.

My discomfort intensified. Never before had I drunk alcohol, which of course was against the Mormon Word of Wisdom and all the warnings, teachings, and rules I had grown up with my entire life.

"It's just to help you relax a little," Spike explained. "It'll calm you down. You don't have to drink anymore of it if you decide you don't like it."

He handed me a glass, and I wrapped my fingers around it, staring at it.

"Besides," he added, "It's our wedding night. I thought we could drink a few sips to celebrate. What do you say?"

"I married a bad boy, didn't I?" I smiled at him coyly, and he leaned over and kissed me.

"Those rules about not doing this and that, no alcohol, tobacco, caffeine, you name it, they're just to keep people in line. To keep them scared with their tails tucked between their legs. That's all they are. Anyone who can't think for themselves follows rules. But if you've got half a brain, you understand that rules like that are meant to be broken," he said.

"In this case, those rules are meant to keep people healthy."

"Chrissake. The people who are so uptight all the time are the ones who'll die young of a heart attack cause they can't slow down and unwind."

"Spike Stallings, you're a terrible influence." I twirled the glass in my fingers and looked at him from beneath lowered eyelashes.

"And you're stuck with me now. You married me, honey. No turning back."

"Right. So here goes." I held the glass out to him, and he clinked his with mine.

"To our wedding!"

Taking a sip, I immediately wrinkled my nose at the stinging, bitter taste.

Spike laughed. "It takes some getting used to. Try a little more. It grows on you."

I felt a charge of adrenaline. I was just married this afternoon, had played the dance with Spike and his band, and was now sitting with this same rogue in his studio, drinking whiskey.

I drank a few more sips and giggled, listening to Spike and resting my head against his chest, my feet tucked beneath me.

"I see it didn't take much to corrupt you, darling. But I haven't done my job if I haven't known you in the most biblical sense. And what better time to start than now."

Most of the cries from the bowling alley had quieted down, and shouts and muffled laughter rose from the street as the patrons departed and tumbled into cars.

Before I could protest, Spike unbuttoned my long dress and helped me out of it, until I lay in just my brassiere, chemise, and knickers. I reached behind my head and unfastened the hairpins, and my hair fell heavily onto my breasts.

"I see your scheme. You've plied me with drinks to take advantage of me."

"I'm a scoundrel. You should know that by now, Reenie."

He undressed and began kissing me all over, starting with my lips and working his way down my body. As he went, he unhooked my brassiere, and unfastened and removed my undergarments.

"Ah, you've got a beautiful body," he breathed, astride me, stroking my skin. "What a swell birthday present."

◄ ♫♪ ►

The following afternoon, a kerchief wrapped around my head to keep my hair from flying, I squeezed against Spike in the front seat of the roadster. He slung his arm around me as he drove to the train station.

"I won't let my folks know we're married," I said. "I'll tell them we're engaged. That way we can get married again in the Temple."

He frowned. "The hell... We're already married. I'm not getting married again in the Temple."

"Mother has her heart set on a Temple wedding."

"Wait a second... Who did I just marry? You or your mother?"

"She'll faint straight away if she learns we eloped and didn't invite a soul."

"So let her throw a little party for us later."

I looked at him imploringly and squeezed his arm. "This is the only way to start our married lives on the right foot. If I don't get married in the temple, she'll never forgive either one of us."

"Are you that scared of your own mother?"

"I'm not scared," I said sharply, knowing full well this is exactly how I sounded.

He shrugged in resignation. "If that's what you want to do. So long as we get it over quickly. I'm not going to wait around for months on end to marry you all over again."

"They'll expect you to pay regular tithing to the Church," I went on, "And I imagine you'll have to get a recommendation from the elders."

"Now how the hell," he started to say, then stopped as I turned on him warningly.

"Spike."

"I tell you, darling, if you ever doubt my love for you, then here's surefire proof. Going through all this baloney to get married in the church should show you how I feel about you. Cause you're the only one I'd do this for."

"I know that," I said sweetly.

CHAPTER THIRTY-SEVEN

November 2006.

It's morning, I know it, and Harold and I are in our cute bungalow in Ashland, around the corner from our dance studio. Harold must be out on the patio with a cup of coffee and his binoculars, watching a hummingbird dart around the sugar feeder he's hung at the eaves. The flitting red dazzle of plumage has become a private show.

"Harold!" I call from bed, my voice still hoarse with sleep.

He doesn't answer, so I suspect he's either dozed off or has decided to ignore me.

"Don't pretend you're going deaf on me," I tease.

He chuckles. "Whaddya want, ya old bag?"

"Don't dare call me an old bag. I want a cup of coffee."

"Okay, you helpless little sweetheart. I'm coming."

"Have to keep her happy," he mumbles, as the patio door slides open and he moves around the kitchen.

Clutching a steaming mug, he enters the bedroom, where I lie propped against pillows.

"Thank you, honey. You're a good little mama's helper."

"Aw, you're nothing but a lazy bag." He winks and starts to leave.

"Hey, wait a minute. Why, you haven't even combed your hair! Come here and let me do it."

"Reenie, I wouldn't go near you to have my hair combed if I was in the army and a lieutenant told me to." He stops in the doorway.

"What're you talking about? Come here, you naughty thing!" I pick up a comb from the bedside table.

Grumbling, he perches on the edge of the bed, while I smooth his hair with deft strokes. "Can't have you going around town with your hair uncombed and that old hat and baggy pants again, looking like a tramp."

"The hell..."

I laugh as I swipe the comb from his head. "There, that wasn't so bad, was it?"

"You think you know everything, but you're nothing but a floozy."

I swat at him.

"A real cute floozy," he amends.

"Now go bring me the paper. I hope you didn't throw it out. I didn't have a chance to read it last night because of my bridge tournament. Did I tell you we won?"

He scratches his forehead and looks down at me, blinking in mock disbelief. "Hey, you're awful bossy. 'Get the paper! Get my coffee!' Lying there like a queen and giving me crap."

"Don't be a big baby. Go get it."

In a minute, he hands me the paper. "See the kind of things I do for you that no other husband would put up with? That must make me perfect."

"You're the most imperfect man I've ever met. I've been trying to make something out of you for fifty years, and you haven't changed a bit. In fact, I'm almost to the point of giving up ever changing you."

He catches my hands in his. "Irene, you fit me to a T. You're what the doctor ordered."

"Had I known you smoked cigarettes and drank and hung around seedy people and played poker and shot pool, I would never have taken up with you."

"You're crazy about me."

"I'm crazy all right, but not about you. Just crazy. I should have run away the minute I saw you."

"I never get any damn sympathy. It doesn't take Sherlock Holmes to figure out who made out in this marriage." He strokes my hair. "You're cute and as sweet as a preacher's wife at a prayer meeting. No wrinkles, not a gray hair in your head. Hell, you were a barefoot country gal when I married you, and now I've made you into a dancer and bridge player. It's a regular Pygmalion story, for sure."

I snort with laughter.

"And look at the other side of the coin. I'm stiff and sore, hair's white, lungs are black with emphysema. Been climbing uphill my whole life.'"

"My poor, poor baby needs a little sympathy."

I wrap my hands around him and pull his head against my chest while singing an old-time lullaby.

Then I must have fallen back asleep, cause I jolt upright as a girl enters the room, yelling, "Top of the morning, Irene!"

Harold is gone, save for an impression he made against my right shoulder and chest. My arms are empty.

CHAPTER THIRTY-EIGHT

November 1936.

Mother threw her arms around me when I broke the news of my engagement.

"We'll throw you a little shower," she crowed. "Minnie, Mae, and I. And then we'll make preparations for your ceremony in the Logan temple."

Dad took me aside. "He's a nice fellow, Irene. Probably a good thing he's not counting his chickens on farm work. You'll make out fine."

The only person who knew the whole truth was Minnie, whom I had sworn to secrecy.

"Not a word," I warned, as we prepared for bed that night in the attic room. "No one else need ever know."

"You can count on me," she said, and I could tell she was delighted to be my accomplice.

In addition to my usual chores on the farm, I began secretly practicing and rehearsing the dance moves Spike had taught me in the attic room at night. Minnie sat on the bed, mesmerized.

"Is this what you'll do when you're married? Dance?"

"A little, maybe. Sing some and play piano, too, if I can."

"Gee, Reenie, you're awful lucky."

I reached over and hugged her. "You will be, too, someday. I know you will."

When I tired of practicing by myself, I grabbed Minnie and taught her a few of the basic steps. On these occasions, we awkwardly turned around the tiny circumference of our room, clutching each other's shoulders and giggling, especially when Mother hollered up the stairs, "What in heaven's name is going on up there? Sounds like someone's stomping on the bed, for pity's sake."

A letter from Spike arrived two weeks before the shower. I had convinced Minnie to help me steal his letters away if they contained any reference to our marital status.

Fortunately, he must have anticipated this problem, because he made no mention of our marriage.

"Dearest Irene," he had written,

"Honey, I miss you something terrible. Last nite I was looking back on last summer and what a swell time we had. We did more fun things than the average person in a lifetime.

I want you to know I've reduced living to the bare essentials. I rise each morning, but unlike the saps I know, I don't brush my hair because it never needs brushing. Then I eat oatmeal for breakfast and teach a few lessons. At night I go with the band to American Fork and so on day after day. So in a way I'm content living a simple, useless life. I say useless because without you, life is useless and sad.

Tell the folks hello, and don't work too hard. Well, I must go catch a streetcar and make a little money. But what's the use of money without a girl to spend it on. Goodnite, dream of me, and soon I'll have you in my arms again.

Your sweetheart,
Spike"

◀ ♫♪ ▶

To my surprise, I saw a folded note at the bottom of the envelope, addressed to Minnie. She snatched it from me, laughing, and read aloud.

"Dear Minnie,

I'm writing to see if you could do me a favor. I want you to report all signs of unfaithfulness in your sister, including looking too long at a picture of Clark Gable, smiling too much at the streetcar conductor in Logan, you get the idea. Never let her go downtown alone. In bed by eight o'clock and anything else you think of to keep her from flirting with other men. Also, record all the times she's muttering about me or wearing makeup in public without her fiance' along. Any infraction of these rules will be cause for breaking our engagement, and I know you as a lady who loves justice, and one who would be shocked at anything less. Let me know at a moment's notice. I remain your best friend.

Darling, see that you obey these rules and everything will be ok. I miss you, Goodnite.

Spike"

Minnie and I erupted into giggles so explosive we grabbed our sides. "Isn't he a kick," I gasped between howls of laughter.

◀ ♫ ♪ ▶

Mother and Mae had arranged my shower to be held at the Paradise ward house on a Wednesday afternoon in early December, with all the ladies of the ward in attendance. Mae, Minnie, and several of my old school friends had decorated the little room off the main chapel with pink crepe paper and streamers, and fashioned a big sign out of construction paper and ribbons that read, "Best Wishes, Irene and Harold."

We gathered in a circle of folding chairs while Mother, Mae, and Minnie served lemon pound cake and apple cider. Minnie played a few celebratory tunes on the piano for entertainment. In between numbers, I unwrapped gifts to oohs and aahs: a set of linen dinner napkins from Sister Nygard, a knitted sweater for Spike from Sister Parker, a pair of candlesticks from Sister Jacobsen, a porcelain angel from Sister Thomas, a crocheted set of baby socks from Sister Ingalls. Mother, Mae, and Minnie gave me a lovely soft quilt, adorned with yellow and pink ribbons, that they had secretly taken turns crafting over the last few weeks.

When the ladies inquired about the wedding date, I replied that it would be sometime in the spring. "Harold's going to talk with a family friend of his who's an elder at the church in Salt Lake. They're trying to see how soon it can be arranged," I hastened to explain.

To this they nodded approvingly and squeezed my hands.

Later that day, I wrote to Spike about the shower and gifts, and mentioned plans to go ice skating with friends that weekend. I hoped I would see him before Christmas, but it looked like he wouldn't be able to get away until January, sometime after the New Year. This made me feel particularly low. More than that, thinking of all the dances he attended with the band, I asked whether he missed me, or whether he had found other girls to occupy his time. This last bit, I realized, sounded petulant and fretful, so I confessed that the waiting was too much, and I was terrible lonesome for him.

December 15, 1936
Dearest Irene,

I read your letters about a thousand times. Know that I only have eyes for you. The thought of anyone else makes me cold.

It sounds like you made out at the shower. I don't know about ice skating, though. There's a lot of room for meeting the wrong kind of people, and the way I see it, everyone but me is the wrong kind.

I'm being good. Just a few beers to be sociable and a couple games of pool. I've arranged to meet with Dr. Nickles in late February, after he returns from his mission. Then we should know how soon we can have this temple wedding.

Promise me you'll be more regular about writing. It seems like I waited about a year to get your last letter. I miss your kisses and companionship and all the little ways you have of making me understand you won't share me at any price. I feel the same about you.

After looking in my dilapidated wallet and surveying all possible resources, I found I'm slightly short of the million dollars I need to buy you the Christmas present you deserve.

Still, I'm sending you a little gift along with my next letter. Now I'm going to bed to dream about the sweetest little sweetheart in the world.

Goodnite.

Spike

February 8, 1937

Dearest Irene,

Right when I was so mad at you for not sending a letter in nearly a week, I received the Valentine's candy and there went all my doubts. Your card was so sweet and original. But if you ever forget to write more than two days in a row again, I won't be held responsible for my actions because I imagine all sorts of things and am liable to do anything.

Sweetheart, I'm in a blue mood tonite from missing you. It's only been a couple of weeks since we saw each other. I wonder how I'll feel in a month.

About going to the show in Logan, you can go as long as they ride in a bucket seat. Too many things could happen otherwise. Some cocky fellow might slide next to you and flirt with you, and I'll have to drive straight up there and tell him off. You can see how I get when I start imagining these things, and then I have about as much spirit as a sunflower in the Sahara Desert.

Besides, I can't help feeling you'd like me to move to Logan. So forget about it, and furthermore, I'm allergic to cold weather.

Until I see you again, my love.

Spike

February 20, 1937

Dearest Irene,

I received your letter and sympathize, as I've felt the same while waiting to hear from you. Without you I get to feeling as unbalanced as the Federal budget. Last nite I lay awake thinking about you and when we'll be together for good, so today I'm so sleepy I can't keep my head straight.

I'll bet you're the cutest girl in Cache County, and as far as Minnie is concerned, you could take all her boyfriends. But just cause I say it, doesn't mean you're supposed to do anything about it. Think of your poor sweetheart down here.

I'm scheduled to meet with Dr. Nickles later this week. I'll let you know what happens. Say, tell me how much tithing to send to the Temple. Ten percent is high for me. I know what you're thinking. You're probably saying, 'that Scotchman, such a conceited so-and-so, learn to spell.' But I love you more all the same. And how!

I've got good news. I've rented a basement apartment in Provo with the works: kitchen, privy, living room, and bedroom. It's a swell little bird's nest. I arranged to rent it for thirty-five dollars for two months by paying in advance. Sweetheart, you'll love it.

Enclosed you will find not a million dollars but the nearest I could come to the mark, about five decimal points short. Please keep it for us for a rainy day. I owe you the balance and will try to make it up to you by loving you the rest of my life.

Yours,

Spike

Reading this latest letter, I grew giddy, and cornered Minnie in our room the first chance I got.

"So the end's in sight?"

"Sure seems."

We drew out our cross-stitching from the bureau and sat beside each other, heads bent over the fine needlework.

"It won't be the same when you're gone," Minnie said.

"I was gone near all last year at the BYU and Zion."

"I know. But this'll be different. You won't stay in this room after you're married. Married for good, I mean."

"We'll still talk, as always."

"You don't know that."

"Minnie, I'll always be your sister no matter what. We can share everything with each other."

She hesitated. "I've got an awful queer feeling we won't see each other much, if at all."

"Don't be silly, of course we will," I said quickly, trying to laugh it off, though her words made me uneasy.

She lifted her head and looked ready to say something, but in the end bent over her stitching again, her eyes troubled.

Later that night, I dashed off a quick letter to Spike, which I persuaded Luke to run into town and post first thing the next morning by promising him the first and largest piece of a custard pie I was baking.

Each day over the next week, I waited for a letter, becoming increasingly alarmed when none arrived. I considered the possibilities. The conversation with Dr. Nickles had gone badly or hadn't yet occurred. Worse, a calamity had befallen Spike: an illness, accident or something dreadful I couldn't even begin to imagine.

I posted another letter, then took to pacing through the garden and orchard, bundled in my heavy overcoat, mittens and gloves, when I wasn't doing chores. The baby had quieted down, as Dr. Thomas had predicted, her colic apparently under control, but now I found myself wishing for her anguished wails and shrieks, if only to give my mind a distraction and find an outlet for my own disquiet. At night I tossed and turned, unable to shake off nightmares: visions of Spike deserting me, leaving me at the altar or vanishing with a band of gypsies, or his frozen body lowering into the earth. Each time I woke in a cold sweat, then turned my face to the ceiling to mutter a prayer.

CHAPTER THIRTY-NINE

March 1937.

In the late afternoon on a Saturday, I was on hands and knees, scrubbing the dining room floor, when I heard the growl of an engine as a car puttered up the lane. My heart ricocheted, and I scrambled to my feet and ran to the window. Sure enough, the familiar light yellow roadster careened around the corner into view, a cloud of dust billowing behind it.

Wiping my hands on my apron, I untied the strings, tossed it, and flung open the front door. Mother, Minnie, Mae and the baby followed me onto the porch.

Unable to help myself, I ran to the roadster before Spike had shut off the motor, and bounced up and down. "Oh my darling, I can't believe it's really truly you! Gee, this is a surprise!"

Spike climbed out of the driver's seat a bit warily, it seemed to me. He embraced me, then greeted Mother, Mae and Minnie.

"Aren't you going to give us flowers this time?" I joked.

Something in Spike's expression, a furrow of his brow or a shadow that fell across his face, gave me pause.

"Is something wrong?"

In a low voice, he asked, "Is your father around? I need to speak with you, him, and your mother, alone."

I didn't like the sound of this, and my hands went cold. "Dad's out in the fields or else in the barn with the boys. Why…why?"

"Can someone get him? I can't talk about it now."

"I'll go find him," Minnie said. She returned inside to grab her coat, then disappeared behind the house.

Spike put his hands on my shoulders and whispered, "Don't worry, honey. It'll all work out."

"But I can't imagine what it is you have to tell us. I don't like this one bit," I said, feeling an unspeakable doom. Twisting away from him, I gripped my hands.

Mae excused herself to return to the house with the baby.

"Let's go inside with your mother," Spike said, and I flinched at his tone, so gruff and curt, as though he were angry with me.

Mother stood awkwardly apart from us, perhaps to grant us privacy, and I touched her arm. "Mother, let's go sit at the table. Harold has something he wants to tell you, me, and Dad."

She raised her eyebrows and looked from me to Spike. "About the wedding, I expect? Harold, has Irene told you we're all ready to go with the ceremony, just as soon's we get word on the date?"

Spike ducked his head and nodded. "Yes, Mrs. Larsen, do you mind if we sit down at your table?"

"Well of course we can. Irene, where are your manners? Why don't you invite Harold inside?"

I wanted to scream, but I led the way into the house and to the dining room table. The door to Mae's and Hiram's room was shut, and I heard Mae crooning a lullaby to the baby.

"Would you like something to drink?" I asked Spike, sounding cross, even to my own ears. I had an urge to smack him, if it weren't for Mother's presence, or else turn on him in fury, demanding he tell me everything at once, lest I break down in tears.

"Some water would be nice," he said, and I turned on my heel and busied myself in the kitchen, pulling down a glass and filling it from the pitcher.

Before returning to the dining table, I braced myself against the kitchen counter, then pinched both cheeks to coax back a little color. I already knew I looked awful – face sullen, hair in disarray.

Smoothing the folds of my dress, I returned to the table and plunked the glass in front of Spike without a word.

"Thanks, honey." He tried to catch my eye, but I averted my gaze and went to sit opposite him, next to Mother.

The room felt funereal – somber, gray, cold. I clenched my fingers in my lap and bit down on my lip.

When it became clear that neither Spike nor I was about to say anything, Mother cleared her throat and inquired about Spike's trip from Provo.

Fortunately, the screen door banged open, and Minnie entered, with Dad behind her.

Spike rose from his chair. "Mr. Larsen. It's good to see you, sir."

They shook hands.

"I'm sorry for pulling you away from your work. I wanted to have a word with you, Mrs. Larsen, and Irene. In private. It won't take long."

Dad looked baffled. Sliding off his coat, he removed his hat and sat in the chair next to Spike. He nodded at Minnie, who remained frozen at the doorway. "Minnie, can you go to your room, please?"

Casting me a worried look, she said, "Yes, of course," and fled up the stairs. The door to the attic room slammed shut.

Mother, Dad, and I turned toward Spike. My fingernails pierced the flesh of my palms, and a lump settled in my throat, making it difficult to swallow.

"I went to see Dr. Nickles last week," Spike began. For my parents' benefit, he added, "He's a Bishop and a family friend in Salt Lake City who said he thought he could arrange for me to get recommendations from the presiding elders to marry in the temple."

Mother nodded encouragingly.

"My meeting with Dr. Nickles included some of the presiding elders, and they asked me a lot of questions. Did I smoke or use tobacco in any form? Do I drink alcohol?"

I opened my mouth, horrified.

Spike looked at me. "I said I did not. Then they asked whether I pay my tithing regularly. I had to admit I haven't paid tithing, ever. Times are awful hard, you know."

Dad broke in, "It's never too late to begin paying tithing. The Church understands that times are tough. They understand folks can only pay what they can afford. Doesn't have to be much." I wondered whether he was thinking of Spike's flashy new car and his swanky gig as a band manager.

Recalling Spike's latest letter, in which he had asked for my recommendation about how much tithing to pay, I added, "You've started to pay tithing now, haven't you?"

Spike ignored me and said to Dad, "You're right, sir. I don't think that would have been an end to my recommendation, except for his next question."

The lump in my throat hardened, and my breath went shallow.

Mother looked up in alarm. "And what was that?"

"Dr. Nickles asked whether I was already married. And I said yes."

Dad shot a look at Mother and me and said sharply to Spike, "Now look here. Are you telling us you've got a wife somewhere else?"

Spike swallowed. "No, sir. What I'm saying is that I've already married your daughter. Irene."

In the shocked silence that followed, Spike explained, "The Church's rule is that if a member marries outside the church, he must wait a year before he's eligible to go through the temple."

I sucked in my breath. Next to me, Mother covered her mouth with both hands.

Dad leaped out of his chair and turned on me. "Irene, is this true?"

I bent my head, unable to stop the tears that rushed down my cheeks.

"You," Dad roared. "You married this man? You eloped with him, then lied to us? When did you do this and disgrace our family?"

I was sobbing so hard I couldn't get the words out.

"She married me over Armistice Day weekend when she came down to Provo," Spike said.

"Oh dear Lord in heaven, what kind of daughter have I raised?" Mother gasped, also collapsing into tears. "Deceiving her own family. What a black heart."

"Why did you marry him, when you knew how upset your mother and I would be?" Dad bellowed.

"It was…" I choked on the words, sputtering with tears, until Spike came to my rescue.

"I talked her into it. I convinced her to go with me to the county courthouse."

"Get out of my house this instant!" Dad yelled at Spike. "You're not welcome here. We don't ever want to see your face again."

I slumped over in my chair, my body wracked in sobs as intense as when Jeremiah had died. I wrapped my hands around my face, unable to look at Spike. I heard his chair scrape back.

"Go on!" Dad yelled again.

Footsteps pounded at the door, followed by a tug and bang as it slammed shut. Outside, the engine cranked, and we heard him swerve down the lane as fast, I was sure, as he was able.

Mother turned on me. "To think of the shame you've cast on our good name with your lies. And the ingratitude after everything your father and I have done for you your whole life. You wicked girl! Get out of my sight!"

Beneath the table, she kicked my shin. "Get! Now!"

I expected to receive a stinging slap against the side of my head, too, but when it didn't come, I picked myself out of the chair and tripped up the stairs, still weeping.

From downstairs the baby fussed, undoubtedly triggered by the mayhem, and Mae attempted to soothe her in hushed, desperate murmurs.

As I entered the attic room, Minnie caught me by the arms and helped me to the bed.

"You don't need to tell me what happened," she said, sitting beside me and supporting my back with her hand. "I heard it all."

For a long while, we sat that way, my head sagging against her shoulder, her palm pressed firmly between my shoulder blades. My tears continued to flow, though I muffled the sobs that threatened to escape from the well inside my chest.

Eventually Minnie rose to find a clean handkerchief, which she discreetly pressed into my palm.

I raised my head to blow my nose and wiped my cheeks. "It's all of it in ruins now."

I couldn't imagine how I could ever hope to see Spike again, now that Dad had ordered him out of the house. My parents, I suspected, believing him to be a good-for-nothing rogue who had corrupted their daughter, would likely arrange to have our marriage annulled. Then Mother could comfortably announce to her friends and the ladies of the ward that we had broken off our engagement.

"You don't know that," Minnie countered when I described my fears, but she looked uncertain. "You could write to him," she suggested.

I thought of Spike, undoubtedly jaunting back to Provo in his sleek roadster as Minnie and I huddled together on our bed, and I felt a rising fury. I had no desire to write to him. Couldn't he for once have kept his hot head in check? Why did he have to drive up here to break the news to my folks, when he could have told me in a letter, or else taken me aside and let me know in private?

He had miscalculated, I supposed, hoping my parents would accept the news reasonably, give us their blessings, and calmly proceed about their business. I could have told him otherwise, had he bothered to consult with me first, and we could have crafted a different plan. It was no skin off his nose, though. With a soon-to-be annulled marriage, he would be free to pursue any number of other girls, and I imagined he wouldn't lose any time.

That was the trouble with him. He was impetuous, impatient, and if any one if his plans were foiled, he simply developed a different scheme more suited to his liking. Even now, he was probably considering his options before meeting the band at the dance hall in American Fork, and deciding which girl to ensnare next in his trap. Another thought made me go cold. How many other girls before me had already fallen prey to his charms, only to be cruelly abandoned once something or someone better had come along? His own sister Jimmie had alluded to this, after all, when Annie and I first talked with her in the washroom at Zion.

"He makes me so angry!" I cried.

Minnie rubbed my shoulders. "Oh, Reenie."

"I'd like to smack him, truly I would. He doesn't care a fig about me. Why else would he do this? He must have guessed how it would end."

Deciding this was his way of breaking things off with me, I burst into a fresh stream of tears.

As Minnie attempted to console me, Mother hollered up the stairs, "Minnie! Get down here and help with supper!"

From the kitchen echoed my brothers' voices, rattling plates, and the heavy movements of boots and creaking chairs. Apparently Mother wouldn't require me to join them, for which I was thankful. I couldn't bear facing her, Dad, Mae, any of them. Mae would have heard everything, too, and would tell Hiram. The idea that they all knew about this shameful episode mortified me.

After Minnie left, promising to bring me a slice of bread, I climbed dizzily into my nightgown and crept under the covers. Exhausted, I must have cried myself to sleep, for I didn't hear her return to the room later that night.

When I woke before first light, the memory of what had happened flooded me, and I sat up heavily. Beside me, in the glimmer of remaining moonlight, I made out Minnie's slumbering form, her left hand flung over her face. If I dwelled upon my new reality, I would surely be reduced to tears all over again.

In the chill of the attic, I hastily dressed and went downstairs to start breakfast. To my relief, I was the only one in the kitchen, though I heard Mae and Hiram murmuring in their room and the sounds of suckling, as Mae nursed Mary.

Lighting the stove, I made oatmeal, sizzled bacon on the griddle. Today was Sunday, so the men wouldn't go to the fields. Instead, we would drive to town to attend church. This thought made me nauseous, but I was grateful to have something to occupy me.

In another hour, at daylight, Mother, Dad, Hiram, Jacob, and Luke began to file into the kitchen. They didn't look surprised to see me. Jacob cast me a pitying look, but he and the others accepted the bowls of oatmeal and the plates of bacon and biscuits I handed them without comment.

I had just sat down to eat my own breakfast, when I heard the beginnings of a faint rumble half a mile or more away, growing increasingly louder.

Across the table, Mother fixed me with an icy stare.

As the engine's roar grew near enough to assault our ears, I threw down my napkin.

"Irene," Mother warned.

Without heeding her, I ran to the window as the yellow roadster swung up our lane. Not caring what she or any of the others said, I tripped out the door to meet Spike.

"Honey," he said, stepping out and swirling me into his arms, "I rented a cheap room in Logan last night and thought about it long and hard. And here's what we're going to do. You'll pack your things in your hope chest, and we'll take it and get the hell out of here. For good."

I kissed him, sorry I had ever doubted him. My heart swelled, and the tips of my fingers quivered with pins and needles from this sudden, glorious reversal of fortune.

Spike remained outside as I sped back into the house and up the stairs to the attic room.

"Irene," Mother called after me sharply. Angry voices rose from below as she and Dad discussed the situation. At any moment I expected they would burst into the room and bar me from going.

"Minnie, help me," I gasped.

My sister was dressed and sitting at the mirror, brushing her hair. She jerked her head toward me in alarm. "I heard lots of noise downstairs. What's wrong?"

As I explained, she leaped up to help me drag my cedar chest out from beneath the bed. Together we frantically stuffed it with my clothes, the shower gifts, a few books, Spike's letters, photos, and my modest set of toiletries.

When we had finished, we debated how we would bring it down the stairs. At last she seized one end and I the other, and we made our way down clumsily, step by step.

Mother, Dad, the boys, and even Mae and the baby stood at the foot of the stairs, watching us in shock, I suspect.

"Don't you dare leave with that ne'er do well," Mother spat, causing me to lose my footing and nearly trip down the rest of the stairs, which would surely have caused Minnie to plummet backward onto her head and spine or break her neck.

Jacob came to our rescue. Bounding up the risers to where we hovered with the chest swaying between us, he grabbed it in the center, hoisted it over his head, descended, and made straight for the front porch.

I opened the door, and he stepped outside and hauled the chest to Spike, who thanked him.

Mother pressed a worn handkerchief to her eyes.

"Mother." I hugged her thin frame. She remained standing rigidly, though her eyes went misty, and her lower lip quivered.

I hugged Mae, who whispered well wishes into my ear. Minnie and I clung to each other until she drew a long, raggedy breath of air and dabbed at her eyes.

The boys stood back, except for Luke, who grabbed my wrist. I encircled him with my arms, and at last he broke away.

"You make your bed, you lie in it, Irene," Dad said from across the room, studying me with a stern face.

At his words, my eyes smarted. Dimly I was aware of Minnie's silent weeping. On top of that, the baby began howling, upset by the latest racket.

"Never in my life," Mother began, shaking her head. "If you're leaving, then get out of here now, and don't come back."

I understood her meaning. If I left, I wouldn't be welcome at home, ever again. Shivering, I let the weight of this sink in. They watched me – Mother with stony chin, Minnie and Mae tearful, my brothers somber, Dad with a glimmer of hope.

I hesitated. If I chose, I could call it off with Spike, return to my family's fold, where we would pretend none of this had happened. Next summer, I might return to Zion or eventually even college.

But when would I ever get another opportunity like this? I bit my lip. I had already made up my mind. This was the only possible choice. Fighting not to cry, I flung open the door and dashed to the roadster, where Spike sat waiting, engine cranked. He had secured my hope chest onto the trunk with a couple of ropes.

As soon as I slid into the seat beside him, he shifted into gear and chugged down the lane. I swiveled in my seat toward our farmhouse, but it was obscured in the cloud of dust the tires had kicked up.

"Honey, we're finally free," Spike said. "Getting the hell out of Paradise. Say, that's some joke, huh?"

Sliding close to him, I managed a smile. He placed his right hand on my thigh, steering with his left.

"Now that I've got my little woman with me, things are looking better by the minute," Spike said, whistling.

Past the farm, we rolled and bumped onto the rutted highway and headed south. The snowy peaks of the magnificent Wasatch Range of Mountains towered behind us. I gazed back once, to mark in my mind, like a postcard, the summit of those majestic crests, but then I faced the road ahead.

Squealing the tires, Spike catapulted us forward like a race car driver, his eyes hot and glittering. Veering the car back and forth across the road, he broke into a long, crazed cackle. My stomach dropped, and I gripped the seat, petrified. For a terrible moment, I wondered what I'd gotten myself into, even if he didn't crash the car and kill us both. Was I linking my future with a madman's? After all, I'd known him for little more than six months, and most of our relationship had been through correspondence. But it was too late for second thoughts, so I dismissed them as nerves and shoved them aside.

Determined to be brave, I assured myself that this is what I'd chosen. I'd slipped free of the farm and Cache County, a narrow escape from a fate like Mae's. We had a fighting chance, Spike and I, of making our plans come true. I wanted everything possible and more — playing piano and singing before audiences, dancing with Spike in ritzy ballrooms. It was just ahead of us, so close my heart crashed against my ribcage, and my body thrummed. Maybe this desperate longing made me loony, too. If so, I didn't mind. I was a parched traveler charging toward an oasis.

CHAPTER FORTY

November 2006.

Cindy turns on the TV for me as she prepares my pills, and it's a fashion show. Skinny girls slink down the runway in tight-fitting dresses and high boots.

Suddenly Harold is beside me. "Those girls don't have any love handles for a fellow to squeeze."

A sullen girl sashays past the camera, her hands on her bony hips.

"Not one of those dames is smiling, and they've got blue rings under their eyes."

"Those aren't rings, honey. That's makeup," I say.

"Like hell it is. That's the look I've seen in pictures of starving people in concentration camps."

We continue watching the girls strut across the stage.

"I think I've figured out why they walk with their hips forward," Harold says. "It's to keep their balance so they can get back to their dressing rooms; they're so weak with hunger."

I shake my head. "You're something else. And what's more, you don't know the first thing about fashion, the way you run around town with your hair uncombed and your buttons undone."

He turns to me and snags my waist, hard. "Say, me and Moe from down the hill, we were picking mushrooms earlier today."

"Moe and I."

"And some kid comes up and orders us off the property, can't we read? Then he made a few other remarks about trespassing. So I said, tell your dad or whoever posted this, if he wants to fence this no-good damn land and put a sign every fifty feet or so, I'll respect it. Otherwise, get the hell out of my way."

"Honey, you didn't."

"Sure I did."

"Weren't you a little hard on that boy?"

"He had it coming."

A familiar looking girl brings in a plate with a donut. I half expect Harold to gobble it down, as he's a mad fiend for pastries.

He teases, "That's what I married you for, those swell donuts you used to bake, now that I think about it. And you don't even make them anymore."

Then he's gone, and the girl – it's Cindy, I realize – is standing in his place, urging me to sit up on my pillows and eat.

I want to ask her where Harold went, but an instinct warns me not to say anything, with the realization I would cause her more alarm if I did. She looks concerned enough as it is, her face peering into mine, as though I'm a sick child with a fever, staying home from school.

"Irene, are you feeling all right?" she asks.

"Just fine. Nothing to fuss about."

"Won't you eat the donut? You're not supposed to take this new pill on an empty stomach."

I look at the glazed sugar confection, and shake my head. "I'm not particularly hungry right now."

Upon my request, she helps me into the bathroom, and halfway there, I have to lean against her heavily, my pulse racing. To my dismay, I find it difficult to catch my breath.

Cindy tuts and frets. "I'll ask your daughter if we can get a doctor from the nursing wing to come over and take a look at you."

"That's not necessary," I say. "I'm just…" I search my mind for an explanation to appease her, but come up blank. The inability to find an appropriate excuse or even a satisfactory word bewilders me, and I struggle to contain my frustration, lest she use it as additional evidence that I need a doctor.

She pats my hand. "It's all right. No one's going to probe you. Here, you rest a bit, and then we'll go to the bathroom."

Somehow we make it to the privy, and she helps me to the toilet and fortunately closes the door to give me privacy. Later I even brush my teeth and change out of my dressing gown into slacks and a sweater.

Dr. Pirelli, one of the doctors whom the Golden Manor employs in the nursing wing, is a tall, gaunt man with a horsey face: long angular nose and chin, big teeth, flappy ears, gray eyes. Dragging a chair next to the bed, he lowers himself creakily into it, and I expect the legs to give and the entire chair to collapse and splinter onto the floor from the shock of his bulk.

"Mrs. Stallings, how do," he says, and wastes no time placing the probe of his stethoscope against my chest, while instructing me to take several deep breaths.

Cindy snaps a blood pressure cuff onto my arm and takes a reading, which she reveals to the doctor in a low voice.

As though I'm a young child unable to answer for myself, the doctor asks Cindy a series of questions about my symptoms. I can't hear her answers.

I must have dozed, because when I wake, I see Mother at the door, talking in hushed voices with a girl who looks a bit like my friend Annie. Upon seeing me stir and stretch my arms, Mother takes a few steps toward me.

"Mom," she says. "Oh Mom, you're awake."

I squint at her in confused silence.

"They've been telling me all about Dr. Pirelli's visit," she continues, and Cindy materializes at her elbow. I realize, then, she is not Mother at all. This is my daughter Deirdre, so I raise my head and put on my listening expression to show her I know who she is, that I am alert, and wholly myself.

Deirdre takes my hand. "They've recommended a transfer to the nursing wing. That way you'll be even more comfortable, and the doctors can watch you more closely. It's just for your own safety."

"What's wrong with me?" I ask in a small voice.

Deirdre responds with a stream of medical jargon: Stage C heart failure, high blood pressure, shortness of breath, angina, arrhythmia, edema, memory loss. She says some other things, but I don't want to hear her any longer, and close my eyes.

◀ 🎵♪ ▶

The strong odor of urine and something foul, like un-flushed bowel movements, assaults my nose. Cindy – or is it Doris – is wheeling me through a dim hallway with walls the color of puce yellow. Nurses chat at a way station and glance up as we pass. Further down the hall, a young man in jeans and a tee shirt mops the floor.

Deirdre trots beside me. Heels clicking down the hallway, she makes sanguine comments about the nice pictures on the wall, the cleanliness of the place, the attentiveness of the staff.

She explains that we're in the nursing wing of the Golden Manor.

"Why?" I ask, unable to hide my annoyance. I don't want to be in this smelly wing; I want to be back in my own room.

"It's for your own good. Remember, we talked through this. The doctors just want to be able to monitor you a bit more closely."

"Dr. Thomas, you mean?"

"Who? No, Dr. Pirelli and the others they've got on call here. I've already placed a call to Dr. Shah. He agrees it's best to transfer your care over to these doctors, since they can be with you every day."

To this I make no reply, though a surly comment is on the tip of my tongue.

Deirdre reaches over and touches my head, the way a mother might placate her fussy toddler. The realization that she thinks of me as her young child causes me to flinch and jerk my head away, and she withdraws her hand.

At last we enter what looks like a hospital room with whitewashed walls, an adjustable hospital bed with privacy curtain, a chair, bathroom door, and tiny window.

Doris wheels me to the edge of the bed. "Here we are, my dear. Let's get you under the covers."

I glance at Deirdre, to see whether she will raise an objection on my behalf, but she simply nods and pulls back the top sheet.

"No," I say, "I'm not staying here."

Deirdre and Doris exchange glances.

"It's a very comfortable bed," Doris begins.

"Of course it's not," I cut in. "This is an invalid room in a hospital, and I refuse to stay here. Take me back to my apartment in the Manor."

"Mom, this isn't a hospital," Deirdre says. "This is still part of the Manor. We're just in a different wing. You'll still be able to go to the cafeteria and see your friends and attend those card games and movie nights."

I shake my head. "You can't fool me. This is a hospital."

A woman in blue scrubs wheels an old, scrawny man in pajamas past the room. His arm is hooked to an IV machine, which drips unpleasantly down a yellowish tube into a vein in his arm.

"If that doesn't prove it, I don't know what does," I say in triumph, though this is hardly a victory I wish to celebrate.

Deirdre sighs.

"Irene," Doris says briskly, "Your daughter's right. You're still in the Golden Manor. Now let's get you into bed and under these covers so you can rest."

She has locked the wheelchair in place, and has lowered the bed with a touch of a button so it's level with the chair. She grips one of my arms, while Deirdre takes the other.

I struggle. If I'm to be stowed away in a hospital, I won't do it without putting up a fight. "No," I groan, "I won't go. I won't do it. No!"

My body is lifted and positioned – no, heaved – into the cold white tomb of the bed. Someone draws the sheet to my chin, even as I continue to thrash and cry out, sure they are sending me to certain doom. A needle sinks into the flesh of my arm, causing me to whimper, before everything goes dark and silent.

CHAPTER FORTY-ONE

November 2006.

How many days has it been since they banished me to this hospital room? Ten, fifteen, or even more than thirty? I've lost track. Could be, in part, because my brain is foggy, as though I'm in a perpetual sleep. They come around with pills for me every hour, a candy-colored assortment of greens, yellows, pinks, and blues. I've no idea what they're intended to do, except keep me in this haze.

Yesterday morning, one of the rotating nurses announced that Thanksgiving is around the corner. "Next week," she said, smiling.

She must be looking forward to time off, away from this place, celebrating with her family around a cozy dinner table where ailing, elderly patients with their loose bowel movements, wrinkled faces, and dying gasps are a distant memory.

This morning the nurse on call pulls back the privacy curtain from my bed and says brightly, "Mrs. Stallings? Irene? I've got good news for you today."

I raise myself onto my elbows and accept the pink tablet she gives me, along with a Dixie cup of water.

"Do you want to know what it is?" she persists, as I swallow my pill.

I wonder whether this is a trick to test my cognitive abilities, but I play along. "What?"

"You'll get to see your friends today! They're coming for a visit this afternoon. Isn't that marvelous?"

I smile, thinking of Mae, Annie, Rose, even Minnie. "Yes, how nice. I wonder how Mae's baby is getting on. Minnie will be around to help, of course. And Annie is returning to Zion this summer. She's going to..." I break off, because the nurse is looking at me strangely.

"No, sweetie. I'm talking about your friends at the Manor. A few ladies named Candy, Midge, and Marcie are coming to see you. Do those names ring a bell?"

I stay silent for a moment, then nod. "Yes. Of course."

She nods back at me and smiles. "Good. You rest up, and we'll freshen you before they arrive."

I close my eyes, and when I open them again, a different nurse is peering at me. This one, whose name tag reads "Amanda," urges me to eat a sliced grapefruit and yogurt she has brought on a tray. She tells me my friends will be here any minute.

To my surprise, I devour all of the food, even the yogurt. Afterwards, she helps me to the bathroom and closes the door partway. I'm disappointed to spy her bulky white pants waiting just beyond it; I'd prefer complete privacy.

Amanda knows about the imminent visit, because she brushes my hair and helps me into a sweater and slacks. Because the slacks are loose at the waist, she cinches them with a long scarf, and remarks that they look lovely. I'm sure they do not, but I am long beyond caring about fashion.

Someone has dragged two extra chairs into my room, and Amanda arranges them, together with the third, into a semicircle. She guides my wheelchair toward the chairs.

"Yoo-hoo! Anybody home?" a voice calls from outside the room.

Marcie, adorned in a long flowery dress and clutching a potted plant, pokes her head inside the door.

"Hello," Amanda crows, rising and gesturing toward the chairs. "You ladies come right in, and make yourselves comfortable, and then I'll make myself scarce so you can catch up."

Marcie enters, smiling, followed by Candy and Midge. She starts to hand me the plant, then reconsiders and places it on the bureau. "It'll catch a little sunshine here," she explains. "How are you, Irene? We've missed you."

The trio arrange themselves into the creaky chairs, which have no business holding school children, let alone grown women. They look around my room, taking in the sparse surroundings and the patchy sunlight filtering through the prisoner porthole of a window. Marcie's eyes dart to me, as she assesses my thin frame and hollowed cheeks. Candy stares at me, her mouth hanging open slightly, while Midge folds her hands onto her lap, looking for all the world like she'd rather be anywhere but here. By now I am used to the pale walls and pungent odors, but I'm sure they are an unpleasant assault to my friends' senses.

"I've missed you, too," I say. Leaning toward them conspiratorially, I add, "Think you can find a way to squirrel me out of this place? Wheel me to safety when the nurses are turned the other way? Like now?"

They laugh.

"Irene, you're such a hoot," Midge says. "You and your jokes."

"Only I'm not joking this time. I'm dead serious."

Midge and Candy glance at each other, but Marcie chortles.

"Tell me the news from the Golden Manacles. I've lost track. Fact, I don't even know how long I've been here."

"Going on three weeks, I think," Candy says, and looks to the other two for confirmation.

Marcie nods. "They sent you here in early November. It wasn't long after your birthday." She rocks forward in her chair, biting her lip.

"And next week's Turkey Day," says Midge. "You haven't missed much. It's the usual stuff going on: movie nights, bingo and bridge, trips over to the South Square Mall. Same bad food. Holiday parties. Budding romances between old folks. And..." Here she hesitates, as though she had just thought of something.

"What is it?" I say.

"You remember Anna Fox?" Midge goes on. "One of Nelson's girlfriends?"

Candy shoots her a warning look.

I nod.

"Well, she's passed on. It happened right after you came here, in fact."

I absorb this news in silence. Although I wasn't close to Anna, I feel a bit of a shock. I hadn't known she was ill or that there was even anything substantially wrong with her. Of course, it shouldn't come as a surprise. These things happen monthly, even weekly around here. It's the nature of the beast, as Rod would say.

"What happened?" I say.

"No one seems to know," Marcie says. "It was sudden. Some think it was a stroke or heart attack. Others say she just died peacefully in her sleep. Of old age."

"Nelson doesn't know the difference," Midge says, waving a hand. "He's got a few screws loose, anyway, and now Lavinia Morrison has claimed him all to herself."

"As much as she can chase after him in that walker of hers," Candy says.

We laugh, halfheartedly.

In an obvious effort to change the subject, Midge says, "You haven't told us what *you've* been up to, Irene. What's it like here?"

Marcie peers at me. "They're not feeding you well, that much is sure."

I shrug. "Food's no different here from there. They give you mushy things to eat. Jello, yogurt, soup."

"When will they release you?" Midge wants to know.

Another warning look from Candy that anyone could intercept from a mile away.

"If, you mean. That's the million dollar question. And I think the answer is they're not."

My friends hurry to correct me.

"Of course they will." (Candy).

"You don't know that." (Marcie).

"They just want to monitor you." (Midge).

Now that we have named the elephant in the room, they one by one cross their legs, fold their hands into their laps, purse their mouths, shoot worried looks in my direction, then inch ever so slightly away, and gaze out the open door into the hallway.

They are being polite; they know as well as I that once people arrive in the nursing wing, they don't come out alive. Ever. I could tell them my body is like an old car that has used up its mileage, fallen behind on repairs now too numerous to name. Clutch shot, paint peeling, body rusted, engine sputtering, fenders smashed, every spring, shock, and strut groaning from the abuse of wear and tear. Fact is, I've gone on an inevitable, ever rapidly increasing decline from which recovery and restoration are impossible.

And despite the conventional wisdom, there's nothing decent or respectable about the process. You've no choice but to acknowledge the physical limitations that come by and by: the inability to go upstairs, skip, dance the shag or run, the gasps after taking a few steps, your once youthful bursts of energy hobbled by necessity. When your mind begins to go, too, you don't even have the dignity of arranging your thoughts. Your ideas and creativity slip away, until you're unrecognizable, irreconcilable with the person of your youth.

I start to say these things, because it's the truth, but in the end, for their sake, I stop myself. They don't want to hear it, and would rush to contradict me. Besides, it's not my habit to be the party pooper who puts a damper on gatherings. My friends know it, anyhow. The room goes still, and I can sense their shock as they acknowledge my circumstances and the forgone conclusion of it all.

But some things, however dire, call for humor. Thinking of Harold, who was always quick with a quip, I say, "So, ladies, work out an escape plan for me, and we'll talk again. And to spice things up, why doesn't one of you vie for Nelson's affections? Lavinia needs a little competition. It will be good for her."

This, of course, elicits a chuckle, and soon we're sharing our familiar jokes about the food, the Golden Manor staff, and the other residents.

Our conversation comes to a halt when Amanda returns.

"Time for your next round of pills, hon," she says, handing me a paper cup. Despite her protests that my friends can stay, they rise from their chairs, offering a litany of excuses, and hug me.

When they've gone, and Amanda settles me back into bed, I lie still, letting the bleached sheets cover me from head to toe like a shroud. I have the sensation that I've just seen someone very dear off at the train station. I don't exactly feel desperate enough to shout after the train as it chugs down the tracks, or dissolve into tears on the platform. Like a doomed movie character cast in shadows, who has experienced an epiphany about the thing that's approaching, I fill with the quiet, inescapable knowledge that the person who has left will not return.

CHAPTER FORTY-TWO

December 2006.

Outside my room, in the corridor, the nurses have hung streams of garland and holly. Propping myself onto my elbows, I try to peek, as eager as a child watching a parade. I'm sure it's not the first time I've seen these decorations. It's the female voices in the hallway that have drawn my attention. I strain to hear them; they sound so familiar.

The voices grow louder, and I spy Minnie – her long, flowing blond hair, the profile of her upturned nose – and Mother, her hand on Minnie's shoulder. My chest stirs with excitement, and I struggle into an upright position against the headboard.

"Now remember," Mother says, "She might confuse you for dead relatives, or people she knew years ago. If she does, just play along. Don't try to correct her, she'll only get upset."

Minnie murmurs something in response.

"But sometimes she'll surprise us by being completely lucid, where she knows exactly who we are and where she is. And like I told you, music helps her. Sometimes it triggers memories. Are you sure…"

"It's okay," Minnie says. "I can handle it. Should I go in now?"

I give up trying to follow their conversation, but I no longer need to, because Mother enters my room, with Minnie right behind her.

"My word," I say in astonishment as Mother guides Minnie toward me.

"Mom," Mother says, "Here's your granddaughter Amy come to visit you all the way from Florida. Isn't that splendid?"

"Hi, Grandma." Minnie walks to my bed and takes my hand. Her beautiful blond hair is arranged in a ponytail, in much the way the younger girls these days wear theirs. Her face is fresh and clean and free of makeup, a natural rosy complexion.

I stare at her for several minutes, transfixed.

"Grandma, it's me, Amy." Minnie looks at me imploringly, then glances back at Mother.

Amy. It's my granddaughter Amy. I know this, with sudden clarity. And that's my daughter Deirdre, standing just behind her.

"Oh, honey. Amy, I'm so happy to see you."

Amy breaks into a broad grin, her teeth gleaming, and behind her, Deirdre smiles, too, and squeezes Amy's shoulder.

"I'll leave you two alone for a little while so you can catch up," Deirdre says, and disappears down the corridor.

Amy sits in the wooden chair and scoots it next to my bed, and it's then I notice her bulging belly. I can't tell how far along she is. Seven or eight months? She's wearing a maternity dress and leggings. Her eyes are a startling blue like a clean, freshwater lake, so like her mother's.

"I've missed you," she says. "I so much wanted to make it here for your ninetieth birthday party. But Mom probably told you, I'm low on cash. I'm trying to save up, because I'm about to have the baby. So I decided to wait until Christmas to fly home. This way I can see you, and since I'm due right after the holidays, I'll stay around a little longer, until after the baby's born."

She sounds breathless, and her cheeks go pink.

"A baby. Isn't that something? My first great-grandchild. I'm so tickled. And your grandfather would have been, too. He would have hoped for a girl, cause they're far less trouble until they get caught with the boys."

Amy smiles. "That sounds like Grandpa. He was always kidding around. He'd say, 'Half past kissing time, time to kiss again.' And he had that big VW bus he used when he took Tom and me on camping trips. He'd drive about eighty miles an hour down the canyon and scare us half to death."

"Your grandpa was a real character. One in a million." And I miss him fiercely, all over again.

Amy produces a tiny blue metal-looking rectangle from her oversized purse. "I brought you something I want you to hear. It's a song that Louie Armstrong recorded in the thirties."

I gaze, perplexed, at the shiny rectangle in her hands.

"This is an iPod," Amy explains. "I brought headphones, too, so you can listen." She reaches into her purse and drags out a pair of miniature white bulbs fastened to a long white string. She attaches the end of the string to the little rectangle, and carefully places the white bulbs into each of my ears.

She presses a few more buttons on the rectangle, and to my amazement, the big band instruments crank up, followed by Louie Armstrong's gravelly warble as he sings, "I Surrender, Dear."

I close my eyes, and suddenly, the present buckles and gives way to the past, and I'm dancing with Spike, swishing along the ballroom floor of the new Sun Valley Lodge in my sequined emerald green evening gown with the glittering rhinestones and matching pumps, levitating over his head. In the first time in many months, I feel mobile, even young, as if the promise of the future is just ahead.

When the clarinet wails and crescendoes to its fever pitch, then dies into spent submission, I raise my head.

Amy is smiling at me. "Did you like it?"

"Oh honey. And how. It was lovely."

She presses the little rectangle, and the music that had begun abruptly stops, and she leans over to pluck the bulbs from my ears.

"Your grandfather adored Louie Armstrong. He had almost the entire collection the jazz greats ever recorded. "

"That's what Mom said. You and Grandpa danced to that music, too, didn't you, when you played in the clubs?"

"Before we bought the studio, we danced all the way up the coast, and I'd sing, wherever Grandpa could get us bookings, from San Diego to Seattle."

Amy nods and rests her hands on her belly.

"Every so often, when things were going a little too well for his liking, he got itchy feet, and we'd have to pick up and move. He liked that I was the steady one. I'd make the new place into a home by painting the walls and hanging curtains. And I paid the bills, kept the books, figured out how much we had to spend. The best thing was that I played accompaniment for the studio classes, and even performed in a few big public recitals. So long as I could play piano, I didn't mind where we were."

She squeezes my hand. "You're so resourceful and talented."

"You take after us," I say with a wink, "Of all the kids and grandkids."

Amy stands and rocks back on her heels, hands supporting her belly. "That's cause you and Grandpa inspired me. You were such a glamorous couple. I remember the way Grandpa lifted you and swung you high, and you moved together in perfect sync. I wanted to be out there, too, leaping and entertaining people to beautiful music. One time when I was around seven or eight, Mom asked me what I wanted to be when I grew up, and I told her a dancer. She said it was fine for a hobby, but not for a living. She and Dad wanted me to be a lawyer or doctor or a wheeling and dealing executive." She grimaces.

"Let me tell you a little story about your mother," I say.

Amy settles back into her chair.

"When she was a senior in high school, we lived in Ashland. Grandpa wanted her to stay home after she graduated and teach lessons at the studio. She has that natural dancer's body, the long legs and graceful carriage. But she was never interested in dancing. She wanted to go to college. She had her nose in a book from the time she was six; she loved to read. Grandpa said she took after his mother and a couple of his older sisters."

Amy listens intently, cradling her belly.

"Anyway, they went back and forth about the studio, Grandpa telling her that college was a waste of time, and your mother replying that she had no interest in teaching dance lessons. She went ahead and applied to a few colleges. California Long Beach accepted her, and she decided to go.

The night before she was supposed to leave, she and Grandpa got into a big argument. He told her she could read anywhere she liked; she didn't need to go to college for that. She said she had made up her mind and wanted a college degree. Grandpa didn't think you need a college degree for most jobs, and told her she was being stubborn and wasting time and money. Your mother shouted that she didn't want to be trapped in a studio in a dead end town, and she was heading to Long Beach to get her degree, come what may."

Amy's eyes are wide.

"They argued for so long that I thought one or both of them would say something they'd regret. In the end, your mother marched into her room and slammed the door. The next morning, she was up at first light. She had her little red suitcase packed and ready to go, and she had everything planned. Rod would drive her to the bus station, and she would buy a ticket to LA. Grandpa was so hurt that he refused to see her off, but I gave her a kiss before she and Rod drove to the station. And you know, she went to Long Beach and got a history degree, and became a city planner, which she loved and was so good at. She would have been miserable teaching dance lessons. I know that now. It's a terrible waste to live someone else's life."

Amy walks to the window, peers out. "I didn't know that about Mom."

I wink. "Just like Grandpa, who rebelled against traditions."

Amy swivels around. "Not just Grandpa. You never gave a damn about conventions, either."

"Grandpa was the one who did his own thing and broke all the rules." I chuckle, expecting her to join me.

"Especially you," Amy insists. "More than Grandpa. Consider your Mormon upbringing, and how you went after a career that few other girls back then had the guts to try. Mom told me the stories."

I shake my head. True, I didn't follow the conventional paths expected of a girl in the thirties, but I wasn't a hotheaded maverick, either, not like Spike. And yet, Amy might have a point. I'm quiet, thinking this over, and a surprising realization grips me. For better or worse, I've inspired her. That should count for something.

I lean closer. "Truth is, some of the things I did cost me dearly. If I'd been a girl today, I might not have married so young. Fact, I might not have married at all. I might have struck out on my own."

Amy returns to the chair. "As a dancer and single mom, I can easily flop and not amount to shit. Excuse my language."

I touch her hand. "That's just it, honey. It doesn't matter how things end up. But if you don't take the risk, you'll never know, and when you're my age, you'll always wonder."

A shadow of a smile plays around Amy's lips.

I think of something I haven't considered in days, possibly weeks and months. "Amy, I have something I want to give you. It's in my old cedar hope chest."

I scan the room. "For Pete's sake. Where did they put it when they moved me over here?"

My granddaughter is on her feet. "I don't see a chest."

"I know I had it in the other part of the Manor. Try looking over there by the bureau."

She walks slowly around the room, and I feel a growing anger. Where did they put my keepsakes? Did they lock them in storage, or worse, throw them out with the trash? Wouldn't that be like the Manor?

"There's nothing here but the bureau."

"The bed - try looking under there."

Amy struggles to her knees and cries, "You were right! There's a chest underneath."

In a minute, she has pushed the chair back and dragged the chest into the space near the doorway.

"Open it," I tell her. "There's no lock, don't worry."

"It's beautiful," she breathes. "Hand carved, looks like." I smell an aroma of cedar and pine, reminiscent of the mountain range outside Paradise.

"My father made it years ago. You'll see a tape recorder in there. It should be near the top."

"Yes." She removes it carefully.

"It's a tape I made about growing up during the Depression until your grandpa and I eloped, and I finally left home for good."

"Oh my God! That story's like a family legend. See? This is what I mean about you breaking rules."

I meet her eyes. "But I paid a steep price. After I left with Grandpa, I didn't see my home or parents again. They couldn't forgive me and wouldn't allow me to visit."

"What?" Amy gapes at me. "Mom didn't tell me that. How could they be so hard?"

I feel a dollop of ancient grief, that familiar wedge inside my chest, and go still. It's a loss I've navigated for decades, always present, beneath the surface, layered upon the first. But I swallow and set it aside. "Sometimes people can't let go of their ideas of who their children should be."

Amy furrows her brow. "That's so sad, Grandma." She moves toward me, catches my hands in hers. Like a mother attending an injured child, she watches me with concern.

It's the first time in many years I've spoken of it to anyone, and I feel my body loosening, unburdening itself of this old pain. At last I lift my head. "Your grandfather and I finally let go of our ideas about your mother. And she will, too. With you."

As I speak, I know I'm right. Despite her disapproval, Deirdre won't cast off her daughter and grandchild. She may have inherited her headstrong nature from Harold and me, but I think she may yet master the ability to step aside gracefully and respect her children's choices.

After several minutes, Amy gently releases my hands, kneels beside the chest, and pops open the recorder. "Is this the tape?"

"I imagine so. I want you to have it."

"I can't wait to listen to it. I'll try to figure out a way to transfer it to my iPod and upload it so we don't lose it."

"There are some other things. You should see a poster inside the chest. You might have to dig a bit. It's rolled up in red ribbon."

She searches through the chest and produces the long cylinder of paper. "Found it!"

"Go ahead and open it."

She spreads it out on the bureau and unties the ribbon. Before long, she utters a cry. "Is this you at Zion?"

"Yes, that was the summer I met your grandfather, '36. The manager of the park wanted a photo of me and another girl, my friend Annie, for advertising on billboards."

"You are so totally beautiful!" She brings the poster over for me to see, and I come face to face with that younger version of myself, along with Annie, in blouses and long flowing slacks, perched on a rock near the Great White Throne, our faces serene and hopeful, gazing into the canyon. Our lives are just beyond it, about to begin.

I take a breath. "And there are letters from Grandpa I'd like you to have and keep safe. They're bundled up in ribbons, too. You should see a little packet."

Amy stoops and searches through the remaining contents of my chest. "This must be it."

I nod. "Your grandfather wrote good letters. Funny and witty. Don't read them, though, until..." I hesitate.

"No, I won't open them until you want me to."

She shuts the chest and pushes it back under my bed. Her handbag is so large that she is able to fit both the tape recorder and packet of letters inside it. She studies the poster again, then slowly winds it back with the ribbon.

"Grandma, I'm honored you've shared this with me." Amy lowers herself beside me. Her eyes shine, and she seizes my hand.

We sit together, and I feel her warmth and essential vitality spreading from her hand through my core. It seems right that Amy should be the one to look after these things, mementoes of my old self.

"Is everything all right?" a voice calls from the door.

Amy pivots around.

Deirdre stands in the threshold. "I just came to check on you."

"We're fine," I say. "We've enjoyed catching up."

Deirdre smiles, steps toward Amy. "I'm so glad."

"Yes, Mom, it's been nice," Amy says.

Deirdre notices the rolled-up poster on Amy's lap and raises her eyebrows. "Is that..."

My daughter is close enough that I lean over and touch her hand. "Yes, it's the Zion poster. I gave it to Amy, along with a few other things."

An understanding flashes across Deirdre's face, and our eyes lock.

Then Deirdre is helping Amy to her feet, explaining I need my medicine, and they must let me rest. Each kisses my cheek.

After they have gone, I close my eyes. It's as though I'm there again, whispering with Minnie in our room, pitching in on the farm, performing at school. Funny how that world, though it happened nearly a century ago, seems more true than the stucco walls and fake potted plants of the Golden Manor.

The thought occurs to me: what if Deirdre, Jack, Rod, or Amy and my other grandchildren were to experience the Depression? What if the system came crashing down again, and they found themselves in dire straits, barely scraping by?

Why, at first they'd be thrown for a loop, because the experience would be so foreign and difficult compared to anything they know. But then, because it's human nature, they would adapt. They would learn to make do with less, relinquish the trifles that don't matter – the laptops, cell phones, video games. In the end, stripped bare of all but the most basic necessities and forced to face each other, they would find courage, come together, and get through it. We are resilient, a family of survivors.

Sleep must steal upon me, because I'm back in Paradise, together with Minnie, Mother, Dad, Jacob, Wylie, Hiram, Luke, Jeremiah, Mae and the

Petersens. At first I hear snatches of a childhood melody, a waltz Minnie plays on the piano. As I listen, joy unfurls within me like a rose in accelerated bloom. The song is real and true, a brush with that girl from across the decades.

Suddenly the mountains, trees and creeks of Cache County come sharply into focus, like the negative image of a photo in its finishing wash, crystallizing into familiar lines and shapes. Before me stands our farm. Rows of wheat, gentle and golden, billow in the wind.

Acknowledgements

WALTZ IN SWING TIME has been a labor of love: a project I began well over a decade ago. Basing the novel loosely on my maternal grandmother's life and taking extensive creative liberties, I used old letters, stories, photos, and online research as my guides.

I am grateful to friends and family for their encouragement, and in particular to the following people for reading early drafts or excerpts and providing feedback: Dragana Pavlovic, Cathy Downs, Laura Frombach, Sandra and Neal Hurley, Elisabeth W., Members of the NC Writers' Network Spring 2017 Fiction Master Class, Jon S., Mary Ellen Bramwell, Reagan Rothe and the Black Rose Writing team.

Last but not least, I am especially thankful to my husband, Dan, and our daughter, Lara, for their love, optimism, and undying support. Since you entered my life, each year has been happier and more meaningful than the one before. Thank you!

Discussion Questions

1. Describe Irene's relationship with her mother. How does this relationship compare and contrast with Irene's relationship with Deirdre, and with Deirdre's relationship with Amy? Which similarities do Irene, Deirdre, and Amy share?

2. In 2006, Irene lives in an assisted living home. What are her views about her situation? Why does she decide to record the story of her life as a girl during the Depression?

3. Music is an important motif throughout the novel. How does Irene's relationship with music impact the choices she makes?

4. At the end of chapter one, Irene in 2006 remarks, "It wasn't a decision that charted my course, not at first, but a ripple of unforeseen events, which swept my family and our neighbors to the brink of ruin." Which

events in Irene's life during the Depression are unforeseen, and which are decisions? How do Irene's circumstances influence her decisions?

5. Compare and contrast Irene's life in 2006 with her coming-of-age during the thirties. In 2006, why does she say, "When I consider it for a little while, I know if I could exchange my life now for the hardest period I ever experienced, I would surely do it?"

6. How does Jeremiah's death change Irene's mother and her attitude toward Irene's musical pursuits?

7. Mae is a major character in the novel. In which ways does Mae influence Irene's musical career? Compare and contrast Irene's life with Mae's. Do you believe that Irene learns from Mae's circumstances? If so, how?

8. Irene's brother Wylie inspires her to leave home. Do you believe she would have attended college without his help?

9. Describe Irene's first meeting with Spike. How is he different from anyone she knows? How does Irene's upbringing compare with Spike's?

10. Do you agree with Irene's choices regarding her relationship with Spike? Why or why not?

11. Do you believe that Zion National Park serves as a symbol in the novel? If so, what does it represent?

12. Describe the significance of the title, *WALTZ IN SWING TIME*. Why does Irene compare this name with her new life?

13. Describe Irene's views about aging. Do you agree with her? Why or why not?

14. Do you agree with Irene's granddaughter, Amy, when she says that Irene, even more so than Spike, disregarded conventions and broke rules? Why or why not?

15. What do you believe is the novel's central theme?

16. How does Irene change from the beginning of the nineteen thirties story to its conclusion? In 2006, which of Irene's views about herself and her family change by the story's conclusion?

17. Consider the novel's conclusion. Do you believe it ends on a hopeful note? Why or why not?

NOTE FROM THE AUTHOR

Word-of-mouth is crucial for any author to succeed. If you enjoyed *Waltz in Swing Time*, please leave a review online—anywhere you are able, even if it's just a sentence or two. It would make all the difference and would be very much appreciated.

Thanks!
Jill

ABOUT THE AUTHOR

A Stanford graduate and award-winning marketing manager with over twenty-five years of experience in the high tech industry, Jill Caugherty lives in Raleigh, North Carolina with her husband and daughter. Her short stories have been published in *805Lit* and *Oyster River Pages*, and her debut short story was nominated for the 2019 PEN/Robert J. Dau Short Story Prize for Emerging Writers. *Waltz In Swing Time* is her first novel. Learn more at www.jillcaugherty.com.

Thank you so much for reading one of our **Women's Fiction** novels.

If you enjoyed the experience, please check out our recommendation for your next great read!

The Apple of My Eye by Mary Ellen Bramwell

"A mature love story with an intense plot. This book has something important to say." –William O. Shakespeare, Professor of English, Brigham Young University

View other Black Rose Writing titles at www.blackrosewriting.com/books and use promo code **PRINT** to receive a **20% discount** when purchasing.